Rick Hankin
BACKTIME

First published in Great Britain as a softback original in 2023

Copyright © Rick Hankin

The moral right of this author has been asserted.

Editing, design, typesetting and publishing by UK Book Publishing

www.ukbookpublishing.com

ISBN: 978-1-915338-91-4

BACKTIME

I t began soon after the shortest day of 2788. There was little to see from my window other than the lights from the residence tower opposite. I saw them for the first time when they appeared in the middle of my room bathed in a rainbow light. It was difficult for me to communicate with them; they could speak but their language was almost unknown to me, an odd word I could guess at, but they didn't understand much I said at all. I am not an author by the way, this tale was dictated to me by what I believe are two people from our past.

I was desperate to ask questions, impart information and receive it as well. One was slightly smaller than the other and obviously female. They both had long hair: the female's reached halfway down her back, the male's almost to his shoulders. The female crossed her legs and sat beside my chair. She slowly began to show and teach me how to speak and draw their language. I used the tools and knowledge they gave me to make this tale.

They have given me a strange small device like the viewscreen that covers the short wall in my room; it has limited voice controls and some characters have to be inserted singularly. On the back is the name of this ancient machine – it is called an iPad; the letters are etched into a cold hard surface that looks like a rare material called aluminium; we don't see it anymore – a small piece of it is extremely expensive. It contains a lot of pictures and some video; it's to help me write the tale.

They came to visit me several times. I can record this now I have enough words of their Old English. My education is not complete, however; I know that if I can write down all they have told me about their lives when they were here it will be a unique record of some of *our history. Unique because there's nothing left in the world now from their days. For myself I know my time is almost upon me. I will soon be thirty-three cycles – they call them years – there are few who live longer than this.*

They have asked questions about my life. I cannot remember when I was last outside in what they call the fresh air. The city sits in bright manufactured light, the sun is a sickly red and the moon is hard to see, if indeed it is the moon. Some of my friends think the moon has vanished, blown to pieces many years ago in the final war. Some of my friends think I'm crazy.

The tale is not too long, I have told it as it was told to me, if the story is true – and there is no reason why it should not be so, there are many terrible things from the past which have not furthered mankind's development in the slightest. Any spelling errors and extremely suspect punctuation are all my fault. Their language is full of holes.

Lastly I do not profess to understand everything that is written or why they have asked me to record it this way. They said the tale was how they lived their lives, they tried to live good lives when they were here; it came naturally apparently, the sense of right and wrong. There are things that make no sense at all and some that seem oddly familiar. They told me their lives were full of love and enjoyment, but they had to endure sad times as well.

It was partly to satisfy my curiosity as to how things were that I undertook the task. They said I could show it to anyone I wanted, it might make them and me laugh, or think. I read it a few times and as I understood more of the old language I did laugh and think, for the first time in a long while. Then came the day I imagined myself as the male human from the past, I began to see things a little clearer, then I began to imagine I was the female and matters became clearer still. I think that finally as I approach my thirty-third cycle, I think I know what love, trust and friendship must have felt like. Also, I would have liked to have experienced anger, humour and some of the other feelings and emotions my visitors did. I didn't know that very soon I would.

To help me understand where some of the things that happened in the tale could be found they have left me a strange artefact which I have placed next to the iPad. The male said it was called an atlas; it looked very well worn. The pages are made out of paper, some with curling edges or a small tear. This was something I had heard about but never seen. The pages are joined together along one edge with large plastic rings, they fan out to show what are called maps. Each page is a drawing of a place on Earth as seen from above. This atlas has maps of a place called Europe – it doesn't exist today, it shows the world as it was in their time. Before things went wrong it seems.

I was told to try and understand as much of the tale as I could. Their next visit would be the last one. If I had managed to understand some of the tale and studied the atlas, they would answer any questions I had. Just before the rainbow took them I was told to summon up my courage and go outside into the world and look around.

The tale is therefore told from the point of view of a human who was alive almost 800 years ago. There is much for today's scholar to unravel if they choose. Good luck.

In order to continue with this story it is important that you, the reader, are happy with a few things that are unprovable at the moment and are based solely on the increasingly growing amount of circumstantial evidence and scientific speculation. For this tale involves knowledge without proof – you could call it belief if you want. The first item of unprovability is the suggestion that the human race is not alone in the universe. Look up into the sky on a clear night where thousands of stars are visible to the naked eye. Telescopes from our recent past through to the Hubble and the James Webb have increased the number of stars, planets and galaxies we can see well enough to photograph. Is it reasonable to suggest that it is next to impossible for advanced life not to exist, on at least one other of these trillions of possible locations?

Orbiting the planet we call Earth was a large irregular shaped structure that appeared to be scarred and travel-worn. Inside were beings from a distant galaxy who looked down at the land and seas below. A few billion years had passed since the planet came into being, during which time the core and outer crust went through severe dramatic changes. On this particular day primitive life had begun in the ocean. It would take many more years for anything more complex to evolve. The structure departed, time passed, by human standards measured in thousands if not millions of lifetimes. During this period the Earth was revisited more than once. The visitors looked and observed the changes, assumedly making notes for comparisons with their previous studies. Subsequent visits followed a similar patten until on one visit an unspoken urgency was expressed between the visitors; they seemed to communicate in a low hum. It suggested a particular point in their observations had been reached.

Soon afterwards their vehicle altered position to place itself in a closer orbit. Slowly the structure underwent a metamorphosis, folding and stretching like a huge ball of potter's clay shaped by inexperienced hands, before finally emerging as a smaller but less detailed version of the planet below. After the manoeuvre was complete, the new satellite spent some time making adjustments. The orbital distance from the Earth was varied until it seemed the correct position had been achieved. Slowly at first then with increasing acceleration it began to spin upon its axis, finally holding a steady speed. In a relatively short period of time the Earth took on some new characteristics. Now the seas had tides and the planet moved with a considerably greater degree of stability. To keep an accurate watch on any activity below, the visitors ensured the satellite always kept the observation ports facing the Earth, achieved by trimming their set rotational speed if the need arose. Smaller ships often left the new satellite, heading into deep space from the dark unobservable side of what we will now have to call a space station.

At some point the note-takers decided the surface of Earth was sufficiently safe to stand on. A small craft left the station, entering the atmosphere, heading for a large land mass. In a clearing where several hundred large rocks had slid from a now silent nearby volcano, a river had been forced to change course, creating a shallow clear lake in the process. Stood on its hind legs was a furry life form that would one day become a brown bear or Ursus Actos. The visitors watched and hummed softly between themselves. This creature was docile and spent most of its time in the river, attempting, with a reasonable degree of success, to catch fish, which it ate. One of the visitors took a device from a soft sided container, pointing it at the bear as a rainbow beam of light erupted from the front section. The illumination of the creature lasted for a minute before the colours began fading to a single red beam which lost itself in the furry head. The bear seemed to be unaware of the beam or the visitors, the fishing for food occupied all of its thought processes, which also failed to realise that the last trout-like looking fish it had scooped from the warm waters was now being probed by another visitor's red beam. They also shone their red rays briefly onto the trees, into nearby vegetation and several flowering plants before leaving.

New life-forms began, lived and often became extinct. More creatures came from the seas and populated the land; these too lived and sometimes died, others evolved and became something different. One day man arrived, or to be more accurate man and woman arrived. The visitors' humming intensified. Here is the next unprovable issue. There are many theories on human evolution. We have the problem of the 'Missing Link' a cross between humans and apes, along similar lines we have the problem of 'Missing Technology' where ancient human races acquired technology far in advance of the times, only for it to vanish without trace relatively soon afterwards, often taking the advanced humans with it.

We must consider the civilisations that had knowledge of the near universe and mastered the accurate measurement of time. From the pyramids of Egypt and the Mayan, to the discovery of tribes so remote they had not progressed much further than the six original engineering devices; one of which is the wheel, who knew accurate information about the Dog Star, or Sirius as we named it.

It has been mooted that during those early days the visitors helped mankind grow. Carefully they suggested and taught skills to ensure survival in those wild and unpredictable days. It has been further posited they even changed the genetics of humankind, by either artificial insemination or through having sexual intercourse with human women, who would then give birth to what might be termed a hybrid. For in order to ensure that life continues there is the biological fact that almost every species on the planet we have discovered so far has a male and a counterpart female. The hybrid females' subsequent pregnancies would now carry the alien gene forward. If these two ideas are true it could be the reasoning behind why humans embraced these new technologies and flourished. Learning to reason and think elevated them above the other animals. Intelligence and instinct had now markedly separated, with an ever-widening gap which outstripped any other process underway anywhere on the planet. Why they lost these technologies and in certain cases disappeared themselves is unknown.

One of the most notable advances in human life was in the number of children born in a single pregnancy. Quadruplets and even higher numbers of offspring were more common in the ancient days when many were subject to an early death by predator, disease or famine. Over the ages women began to give birth to twins or triplets as the norm; further down the timeline a single baby was the usual birth.

Along with a sadly unprovable small number of other animals, men and woman would also begin to indulge in sexual intercourse purely for pleasure, although procreation often happened at the same time. As we know, the sexual side of human life is an essential in our makeup, ensuring a continued existence, just as it does for every other species on Earth. This importance can be seen first-hand when considering how intense and strong sexual attraction is and the lengths humans will go to in order to indulge in this instinct.

From this improved intelligence agriculture developed, some docile animals could be used to provide food, the seas and rivers were explored yielding more food and a medium for another mode of transport. Boats allowed humans to cross rivers, then seas and finally oceans. Humans learned how to build structures and left the windy ledges, cliff dwellings and natural caves they had always called home. Many other skills and arts were developed during this age of mankind. From those early days we learned how to help the other humans close to us, more than any herd or family instincts could teach. This help took the shape of providing food for all members of the tribe, keeping everyone safe from dangers, both inside and outside the collective home. Caring for the sick and old, raising children to live as you lived, the passing on of knowledge, then perhaps in respecting others' views and beliefs the first steps to civilisation were taken as time albeit very slowly passed. Even today we seem to be a long way from having a global family, there still appears to be powerful and vicious forces within the human credo. Violence is also present in animals forming part of everyday life.

The days of Earth can now be related to in centuries. The might of Egypt came and went, the same for Rome, the Greeks and many others. Drawings and petroglyphs were made on cave walls and the faces of cliffs, clay tablets recorded the thoughts of scholars. Papyrus scrolls and finally paper stitched in journals were used later by people recording everything from the trivial to the world shattering.

Almost all of these mediums have stood the test of time and can be seen both in the field and displayed in museums across the world. Explanations of these drawings, carvings, sculptures and writings seemed to agree that several of the depicted figures were called Gods. Gods who came from the sky. Mankind called the visitors Gods. During this period the visitors noticed the birth of what would become known as religion. It seemed to start in various places across the globe, at differing times and had the common factor of placing a God at the head. What they did to encourage it, if indeed they did, will perhaps never be known. As religion expanded across the known world it was discovered different races worshipped different Gods. Humans do not readily accept others who are not in tune with their beliefs, friction occurs and before long a power struggle emerges and violence breaks out. The terrible levels of violence and accompanying hatred which mankind inflicted on itself in the name of their various Gods can be found throughout recorded history. Despite their differences, religious or otherwise, violence was often the first action instead of words. Soon mankind had a word for all the violence – they called it war – and several Gods of War were called on by the conflicting sides. We know of them today, from Agurzil the Berber in Africa through the Aztec Mixcoatl, Celtic Anann, Chinese Chi-You, Menhit the Egyptian Goddess to Zorya Utrennyaya who shows up in Slavic mythology. Other words soon joined war, words like bigotry, racism, control, murder, power and money, humans were becoming articulate if nothing else. The visitors looked down from their space station – mankind had named it the Moon – and hummed to each other intensely.

In another thousand or so Earth years mankind had still failed to eradicate war; in reality, as time passed each conflict became bloodier, longer and increasingly pointless. One day the concept of war changed forever. Until this one day, war had been fought hand to hand, maybe on horseback, later with weapons which developed in sophistication and accuracy. A new weapon, born out of the study of physics had now come to fruition on this one day. This weapon was so deadly it would change the face of the planet, perhaps even destroy it, and kill indiscriminately on an unimaginable scale. With this knowledge firmly proven in tests conducted on remote islands, out at sea and in underground bunkers mankind still used it against itself. It was less than a quarter of a century after the world had fought 'The War to End all Wars'. The visitors hummed in horror. They began to watch at close quarters every time a nuclear explosion occurred. Their observation ships were spotted and reported many times, first called flying saucers after their apparent shape by the newspapers; a little later when the military became involved, UFOs, or unidentified flying objects became the official title.

After the so called 'ultimate weapon' was witnessed by the whole planet it served as a warning and a strangely effective way of keeping the peace: in an oddball sort of perspective. Mankind continued with smaller wars and skirmishes, but all nations lived under the shadow of the Atomic Bomb.

There have been several methods of keeping track of time, the version that works worldwide today has only been around for a short while, relatively speaking, and on a windy day in March 1922, John Marstone was born in Otley, England. A year later in April 1923 Avril Summers arrived in the same manner in Bristol, England. If anyone had been looking at the building where Avril was born, they may have spotted an unusual weather condition in the early morning sky. As she made her debut appearance a rainbow appeared, as rainbows do seemingly out of nowhere, with one end piercing the hospital roof, the other just hanging in the air, pointing roughly at the faint outline of the moon. It was not raining, nor had it been for some time. The rainbow was not the normal arch shape either; this one was as straight as a ruler's edge, and hummed softly just within the range of human hearing. It would have been similar to the sound heard when holding certain seashells to your ear.

In 1940 John joined the RAF in the war against Nazi Germany as a navigator. By early 1942 his squadron had flown thirty missions and he was unharmed, physically at least. A two-week leave had been given to the entire flight and their planes were being fitted with a radar; a recent invention, now manufacturable in a more compact unit which fitted easily in a Lancaster or Wellington bomber. After spending some time with his parents in Otley and attempting without success to find any of his old friends, John made his way south to the radar training school on the last day of his leave. The course was supposed to be delivered over two days; as it turned out, the new equipment in the classroom was not working all that well so the course overran. This turned out to be a lucky break for John as it was here on the morning of the first day he met Avril, 'a stunning beauty from Bristol' according to his friend who had spotted her first, a trainee WAAF radar operator and as such was in the next room on her specialist course.

The pair managed dates at the Roxy cinema, a quiet night in the local pub and finally a hurried picnic in the park on the last day. They parted after exchanging addresses and went back to work, or war, depending on how you see it. In the following years John managed to avoid the fate of many aircrew, and Avril worked long hard hours peering into and also repairing radar screens. They had written a lot of letters and managed to spend their leaves together in Lincolnshire where John was stationed. On their last meeting they could contain themselves no longer. The uncertainty of wartime and the ever-present knowledge that death could be waiting in the wings everyday accelerated desires in friends who could easily become lovers. In a rural Lincolnshire village inn overlooking the duck pond passions rose and two bodies became one. Cupid had managed to do to both of them what the Germans had thankfully failed to achieve, two hearts were fatally pierced that night and for all the right reasons.

The war ended and the pair moved into a small flat near Lincoln. John found a good job with an automobile sales and repair company in Bradford, Avril managed to fall in love with the Yorkshire Dales as well as John and happily set up home in Leeds. In late 1951 she announced she was pregnant, the following summer she gave birth to a boy. He was named Eric after two of his grandfathers, one from each side of the family. An arrow-straight rainbow could be seen for a few minutes above Leeds maternity hospital, if anyone was looking of course.

In September and October 1922 Robert Bowden and Helen Clifford were born in Stevenage and Letchworth, England respectively. This cottage hospital had an odd rainbow to contend with as well later in the year, and as expected nobody noticed.

Robert and Helen met at school in 1933 and found they were attracted to each other in much the same way as magnets. Biological magnets work the opposite way to normal ones inasmuch as the like poles attract. Friends and family joked how they seemed to be 'joined at the hip' but as the teen years passed the tension of what was rapidly becoming an intelligent, mature relationship was becoming increasingly difficult to manage. One Sunday afternoon in the autumn of 1938 they went on their usual walk by the river, undressed in a copse of beech trees and released an incredible amount of love and lust until the sun began to set. Helen often recalled it was the best birthday present she ever had.

The pair graduated and also joined the war effort. Robert became an aircraft technical engineer building Mosquitoes, an aircraft the RAF so desperately needed, in nearby Hatfield and undertaking risky specialist repairs to damaged aircraft further afield. Helen joined the first all-female Air Transport Auxiliary, also based in Hatfield, having obtained her pilot's licence by virtue of her father being a member of the London Aeroplane Club who taught her to fly from her sixteenth birthday. The ATA had the dangerous task of delivering new aircraft to squadrons on the front line. As their relationship grew so did an understanding of what could happen to couples who met and became besotted early in life. The thing to do, they agreed, was wait. Let time be the test; if they continued to feel strongly for each other then they could consider an honest commitment for the future. Time passed, the bonds grew stronger, the war ended, they decided to marry. In 1952 Deborah Felicity Bowden arrived on a sunny autumn day without a cloud in sight. There was another straight rainbow over the nursing home in Letchworth though.

Rain beat on the roof tiles of the Bowdens' house, wind stirred the leaves into a whirlpool of rustles. In a small bedroom overlooking the rear garden a four-year-old Deborah lay asleep untroubled by the noises of the night. A small straight rainbow pierced the window, making a circle on the carpet next to the bed. A shape began to materialise in the centre, it quickly grew and became what could only be described as a large turtle-like creature with reptilian skin. The surface reflected the rainbow at first then began changing to a dark sandy shade with a mottled diamond pattern often associated with rattlesnakes. The turtle lookalike had much longer legs than usual and the head joined what would have been the carapace but was in fact its torso. The proportions of the being were also at odds with an earthly turtle, the body width being greater than its length but not to the extent of imitating a member of the crab family. It looked round the bedroom taking in the furniture and the girl herself. Its attention fell on a low bookshelf; with deep set eyes it scanned through the books, page by page. About halfway through the fifth picture book whatever it had been looking for was discovered. A second shelf sat above a wooden box full of games and playthings and held Deborah's collection of soft toys and dolls. Down on the carpet a slight humming accompanied the slow metamorphosis of the reptilian being. A few more seconds passed as the skin erupted with a million microscopic holes each shooting forth a single strand of hair so close to the next it could only be described as fur. A slot opened and closed from just below what was now distinctly an oval hairy head down to a point in the torso where the two legs joined, seemingly by the operation of a zipper mechanism. As the minute hand on the wall clock reached twelve, the circle of light on the carpet, now just a bright green, faded to nothing as it retracted through the window. A walnut brown teddy bear with bright eyes, a black nose and a permanent smile sat on the shelf, having spent a minute moving the other occupants closer together to make enough space. In the zipped compartment was a small nightdress with pictures of pink rabbits printed on it. In the morning Deborah found it and decided to call him Eddy.

Eric was going to be tall and as such became a 'spindly lad', as his grandfather called him, until at the age of fourteen the muscles and poundage arrived turning him into a suitable candidate for any Yorkshire rugby club looking for a prop forward. The interest in all things mechanical began early. The plastic tool set soon gave way to Meccano and Betta Bilda. John once gave him an old spinning reel to repair, knowing the gear mechanism had over twenty parts to it and several items were well worn. At the end of the week Eric had returned the fishing reel to his father, commenting that it had not been too difficult to fix, someone had tried before and put a spacer in the wrong way round. John decided the next item was going to be a lot more difficult. Over the years father and son pulled apart and repaired just about every model of car and van on the road, several species of washing machine and poked about inside more than one lawnmower. There were times when Eric hit a wall. John waited until he asked for help. He began learning the basics of engineering, without being forced, pushed or cajoled, never with any terms or conditions that might be construed as biased and certainly with lots of tea breaks.

His school days were peppered with incidents that often ended with John or Avril being asked to see the headmaster. Two of the interviews concerned Eric's method of doing things. On the first occasion he'd found three boys tormenting a cat by dragging it by its tail fastened to a length of rope fixed to a bicycle. Eric had, according to the two witnesses, simply reached out and pushed the cyclist over, knocking him to the ground. After releasing the cat he used the same rope to tie the boy to the bike then rode off at speed with the cat inside his coat, only stopping when his anger had abated, roughly a mile up the road. His parting words were, 'Now you know how the cat felt.' He then pedalled to the local veterinary surgery.

A year later aged sixteen he stopped a girl being attacked in the local shopping centre by three skinheads. Despite the odds being against him the first attacker found his uppercut more than enough to put the lights out, it also broke his jaw and removed two teeth at the same time. The second assailant came at him with a fishing knife but had no idea how to use it in a fight. This is why the hefty kick in the groin with a hiking boot swung the balance in Eric's favour. As the unfortunate thug doubled over in pain a swiftly delivered knee to the descending head finished the job. Thug number three fled having seen his two friends dispatched in under ten seconds. The police had commended his heroic action whilst recommending he tried at least once to talk to the people causing the trouble before wading in 'all guns blazing' as the Sergeant had told his father. Eric said he had asked them to stop but they just laughed at him and continued trying to grab the girl and her handbag. He reasoned his actions were the only way to make them leave her alone. Thankfully the rest of the interviews concerned the massive effort he was putting into his studies.

Two hundred miles south Deborah also proved to be heading for the clouds standing at almost five foot tall by her twelfth birthday. Her long legs and red hair were inherited from her mother, as was the elfin face. The tomboyish stage had passed but her preference for male friends and company prevailed; girls were 'OK but'. It became her stock answer when she needed help to get something done she could not manage on her own. A leaning towards animals followed to the extent that Helen thought she was heading for a career as a veterinary. From horses and dogs through to slugs and stick insects, Deborah expressed a close intense interest. When she was legally allowed to work a few hours a week at the age of thirteen instead of getting a newspaper round or sweeping up in a hairdresser's salon, she promptly took her new certificate into the local vets and asked for work. Robert wasn't surprised when he discovered a sectional plastic model with interlocking parts showing the four stomachs of the cow in vivid colours on the sideboard. Mavis, Helen's older sister, hadn't been surprised either; shocked and stunned were two better words. She voiced her opinion that a young child ought not to see such horrors when Deborah gave her the guided tour of the bovine digestive system. Probably Mavis would have been over the worst sooner if she hadn't proceeded to then tell her mother rather graphically using the text books the surgery had loaned her about how the artificial insemination programme was going and that she would be helping with the semen doses.

Over the next two years the transition from girl to woman progressed; by the late autumn she could easily pass for eighteen, a situation that gave her father a few sleepless nights until his wife assured him she had every confidence Deborah was not going to do anything stupid. Fathers are insanely protective of their daughters and Robert had the double dilemma of having a daughter who was rapidly becoming as stunning as his wife.

Eric and Deborah met for the first time in September 1966, at The Science Museum in South Kensington, London, a favourite venue for schools who used it as a field trip for pupils leaning towards the subjects on display. This is why both Eric and Deborah, or Flick as her friends called her, met outside on the lawn whilst eating their packed lunches. Flick took hers out of a rucksack. This appeared to be a largish teddy bear with strategically placed straps giving the impression it was riding backwards across her shoulders.

"Oh you stupid girl," she said to the world in general. "Father's cheese and bloody beetroot butties, I've picked up the wrong packet."

Eric looked round at the red-haired girl and said, "A problem in the sandwich department, I take it. Tell you what, if you can manage ham and tomato, I don't mind sharing. My dear mother thinks I'll starve to death if I'm out of her sight for more than four hours, so she makes plenty."

Their eyes met and the gaze was held for perhaps a second or two longer than normal as the large sandwich box was raided. Whilst the meal break ticked away they talked about the things people who have just met tend to cover, adjusted for the situation in hand. These topics were: I hate beetroot, do you think the museum's OK, what's your name, where're you from and other assorted trivia. Flick shared her coke and Eric offered his orange juice. By the end of the break they were laughing and joking like they had known each other for years. This was all happening under the light of a small rainbow that nobody seemed to see, perhaps because it has reduced itself to just the yellow band. The girl sat next to Flick told her they had to be back at their coach in five minutes. Flick thanked Eric and told the girl she was going to visit the toilets first. He said it was great meeting her and the mane of red hair was amazing. This got him a cheeky smile and a blown kiss. It was ten minutes later when his party were issued similar instructions that he noticed the smiling bear rucksack on the grass close by. At the coach stand the bus for Leeds was the only one left, he got on and proceeded to go through the backpack looking for an address, or the name of a school without success. The only thing that might have helped was the school blazer she was wearing – he recalled it had a Hertfordshire school badge on the top pocket. Unfortunately, Eric remembered the mischievous, twinkling brown eyes, the shock of really red hair and had been concentrating quite unabashed on the rather larger than average bosom hidden underneath a white blouse. No wonder the bear's smiling all the time, he thought.

Meanwhile in Hertfordshire Deborah also drew a blank as to where Eric hailed from – other than Leeds she had nothing to go on. Having only noticed a pair of large warm hands, an ear-to-ear grin, steel blue eyes and a nice bottom in detail which did nothing to help recover her lost rucksack, if indeed it was him who had it. After a month had passed, she gave up on finding it; the sorrow over the loss diminished as time went by.

In Leeds Eric had found a use for it in the garage. Kensington, the bear's new name, was loaded with his more sensitive precision tools; his father's old micrometer, callipers and suchlike along with the technical drawing equipment he used on the various engineering projects his education was steering him towards. He hung it on a nail above his bicycle. One night about a month after he acquired it, a rainbow pierced the roof and lit up the rucksack in a narrow beam of green light. Five minutes later it was dark again, Kensington hummed slightly for about an hour then silence fell in the garage.

On July 20th, 1969, the Apollo space craft launched from the Florida coast landed on the moon. The visitors had been waiting for this to happen for some time; the Mariner and Venera programs were also running, expecting that mankind would apply the technology it had discovered and invented to visit space. Humming between themselves it appeared humans had now reached a certain level. They watched with interest when the three astronauts returned safely to Earth, without destroying themselves or their vehicle. In November of the same year a second Apollo craft landed. The visitors added to their observations, but other visitors were humming a different tune as it were. They were watching the ongoing nuclear tests, the continuing wars and the violence surrounding racial tensions.

n 1970 with their final examinations behind them, it was a year for decisions. Both Eric and Deborah had choices to make regarding university. Before that, however, was a second chance meeting that was so beyond the rules of probability that it should never have happened, or should it? What are the odds of meeting someone you know, even slightly, in a crowd of over 600,000? It's been pointed out that the chances are better with a larger group than a small one due to the sheer numbers involved. This is fine; however, when the amount of time needed to filter through the crowds is factored in does the argument stack up? Whatever the odds are and the laws of probability say, everything worked out just great for them. On Friday 28th August 1970 Eric met Deborah, a.k.a. Flick, for the second time, by one of the concession stands at the Isle of Wight music festival whilst Chicago were on stage.

Flick spotted Eric first, mentioning to her friend that the tall guy with a really nice bottom further down the queue looked vaguely familiar. As the line shuffled forward the conviction inside her head grew as the memory banks yielded to her probing thoughts. He was maybe with two others and about to move off when he turned from the counter, looked up and saw her. The same sense of half recognition ran through his mind until he realised he was staring at her. Memories began stampeding into his head. The fog lifted for both of them at roughly the same time, Eric walked over and asked very politely and seriously; to avoid it sounding like a crass pick-up line, if she happened to be the girl he had shared lunch with at the Science Museum in 1966. Flick's face lit up and pleaded guilty as charged.

"In that case I may have something belonging to you in my van," he said.

"Is it by any chance a bear-shaped rucksack that once held cheese and beetroot butties?" she inquired.

"The very same; I did, however, have to dispose of the beetroot sandwiches."

For the rest of the afternoon they sat together, enjoying the music and the sunshine whilst making idle conversation. Acts came and went on the stage, the sun went down and finally someone announced the show would start again the next morning.

Making their way back to the camping area guided by moonlight was one of those little milestone moments, the sort people seem to recall many years afterwards. A recall so crystal clear and fresh in the here and now as it was on the day. Flick had thin sandals on which almost led to a twisted ankle several times. Eric solved the problem by scooping her up in his arms and effortlessly carried her the remaining half mile back to the field full of tents and camper vans.

"Where's your tent?" he asked, setting her down in the short grass.

"Do you know I'm not sure now, it all looks so different in the dark and the site seems to have grown and filled up somewhat," she replied, whilst looking round for a landmark or anything to get her bearings from.

"My van's over by the hedge, let's grab a torch and see if we can spot it."

Despite searching for half an hour Flick's friend's tent remained elusive.

"I think we'd be better off in the van, come on, I've plenty of room and a spare doss bag."

She nodded and they made their way through the canvas jungle to the hedge, easily finding the van again by looking out for the large white rose flag of Yorkshire Eric had fastened to the roof rack. She would tell her friends a week later she never hesitated about spending that night, and then the rest of the weekend with him. It was more than just a feeling of being safe, she knew there was absolutely nothing to fear. Flick always went with her gut feelings and intuition.

Eric busied himself in the cab whilst she partially undressed and slid into the spare sleeping bag, then he followed suit and turned the overhead lamp off. They spent a while recalling the events of the day in the half-light with the low burble of voices outside just audible. Slowly they dropped off to sleep. A rainbow, seven colours, straight not bent, arrived about 3 am. The van slowly turned light blue inside, except the bear rucksack; Kensington went violet. Fifteen minutes later everything appeared normal.

A drop of rain with the normally bent rainbow afterwards appeared during the early hours. Thankfully the sun soon dispelled the dew. The clock glued on the dashboard said 0820, Eric was sat cross-legged by a camping stove heating baked beans. The small grill underneath the burners held a plate of bacon and two eggs sizzled in a tiny frying pan on the remaining ring. Flick stirred, popped her head out and with half open eyes visible through a shock of red hair, scanned round the van before asking what the fantastic smell was.

"It's your Majesty's breakfast, eggs, bacon and beans, with toast to follow, coffee is in the pot on the shelf behind you, as are the mugs."

"Ah, I'm going to have to be careful round here, one afternoon of musical enjoyment and an evening spent wandering round a field searching for the rare, lesser-spotted-four-berth-tent and suddenly I find myself elevated to royal status."

With this she disappeared into the sleeping bag only to emerge just as rumpled and announced, "Is my bra or shirt down there by any chance?"

"Jeans yes, sandals yes, bra no, shirt yes."

Eric reached out to pass the linen blouse up to her then turned round so she could put it on. After the coffee pot had been emptied, pans cleaned and bra eventually located in its hiding place between the elevated bed-frame and the van's wall, they dumped the trash and made their way over to the tent area. Locating Flick's friends in daylight was easier even though as she had surmised the camp had grown. They found three tents the right colour, shape and size but still not the right one. When the correct one turned up the occupants were still snoring well. They left a note pinned with a tent peg to the water carrier and wandered off towards the stage. The second day of the festival turned out to be much better than the first, due in part to the acts being more appealing to Eric and Flick's tastes; also, the sun was shining brighter.

Evening fell on the second day; Flick's friends had not shown up, giving credence to the belief that if you became separated in a crowd of 600,000 you stay separated. Walking back to the van he asked her if she wanted to stop a second night or go to the tent.

"There's no contest," she replied, then tilted her head and offered a lopsided smile, "they only bought cereals and by now, stale sandwiches, whereas you have bacon and eggs."

"Ah, you only want me for the toast and coffee, you naughty girl," he said in his best imitation of Peter Sellers doing Bluebottle.

Minnie Bannister appeared to answer, "Not quite, Henry, not quite, little do you know but inside my bag is a whole fresh packet of–" here she paused for dramatic effect– "chocolate digestives, you hear me, Henry, chocolate digestives."

The last few words came out a little muffled as it's hard to do an imitation when you're doubling up with laughter. After picking up her bag, her friends were still elsewhere, a grassy newly beaten track led them to the edge of the camp where the moon appeared to be held captive in the leafless branches of a dead tree. Sitting on a low rock they looked out over the island's green fields and began to tell each other about their lives. The conversation lasted till well after midnight, concluding in the van with a mug of tea and a chocolate digestive. Curiosity got the better of him eventually, so he asked how her nickname had come about.

"Most people think it's short for Felicity, my second name, but actually it started at school, I had the habit of flicking my hair out of my eyes. I guess I did it a lot as it grew longer, and the name just stuck."

He nodded.

"Somebody pointed out later in art class that you had to be careful how the letters were spaced – or it looks a bit rude." She grinned.

Eric lowered the bed and told her to get in whilst he washed the mugs. What appeared to be a disembodied head covered in red hair peered out of the sleeping bag.

"It's been a great day, Eric, thanks for this – ooh, and the food. A packet of biscuits isn't much to offer in return."

"My pleasure, I'm glad you're having a good time, I sure am, and don't forget we've got Hendrix tomorrow."

He reached up and clicked the lamp off.

"Breakfast today, your Highness, is exactly the same as yesterday, with sausages instead of bacon."

"I suppose it will have to do," she said, nose pointing at the roof, in her lady of the manor voice. "I've done it again! Where has that bloody bra gone this time. I'm forever losing it, I need to nail it to the wall or something."

Eric looked in the pile of clothes under the suspended bed. "It appears to have vanished good and proper this time, I'll pass your shirt up."

"It's a pain but I have to wear it: – I'm bigger than the average girl, Boo-Boo," came the muffled reply imitating Yogi Bear from the depths of the sleeping bag.

After breakfast and a tidy round of the van, the runaway bra was located, this time between the mattress and the base-board, discovered when Eric wound the bed back up to the roof.

"Oh dear that's going to be tricky to get out in one piece, the straps have wound themselves into the strut hinges."

After ten minutes of fruitlessly persuading the material to untwist itself Flick decided, "It can sodding well stay there," and shut the side door.

The final day of the festival was another music-packed extravaganza which would prove to be the last time Jimi Hendrix performed live. The added bonus of spending the day together was the icing on the cake. For Eric watching Flick dancing to the music, some parts of her dancing more than others, was something he would remember for the rest of his life. She seemed to be dancing only for him. From somewhere in the back of his mind the word 'Enchantress' popped up. The final night was spent back on the low rock talking about the festival and what a fantastic time they'd had. Back in the van, sat up in their sleeping bags with a last cup of tea, the conversation turned to talking about the ongoing Vietnam War, which still had another few years to run, the festival, now being compared to Woodstock, held the year before in New York state and finally what they were doing about finding a university. Eric reached up, wished her goodnight and turned the lamp out before turning on his side.

"Goodnight, pleasant dreams," she replied pulling her shirt off.

Monday saw breakfast reduced to a couple of slices of bacon, half a sausage each, toast, jam and the remains of the chocolate digestives. The van was tidied up and put into Canned Heat or 'I'm-on-the-road-again-mode' as Eric called it. As he grabbed Flick's bag and Kensington the bear to take over to the tent area, she stopped him and said he could keep the bear, he'd made better use of it than she had, and it would be a reminder of her for him. After exchanging names and addresses and jotting down phone numbers, both silently wondering if there was any possibility of seeing each other again, they made their way through the sea of half-down tents to discover a patch of flattened grass where the one they were looking for should have been.

"It appears they have all buggered off," Bluebottle commented.

"I don't think they would do that, perhaps they're loading it onto the car."

As it turned out Flick's friends had gone; on a stick in the corner was a note pinned to the grass. It explained that one of the friends' parents had suffered a heart attack and knowing they'd never find her in the crowd they broke camp and left. Seeing as they'd all come in one vehicle this was the only option. Flick told him this news was not unexpected, it was nothing short of a miracle the victim had lasted this long.

"They panicked a little I guess, logic says you were OK, thankfully we left them that note, it sounds like they worked out the best solution available. I'm guessing they found out through one of the stage announcements. Anyway, you only live in Hertfordshire, I can easily make a detour, it's less than forty miles adrift to get you home."

This statement earned him his first kiss and an unforgettable braless hug. Once clear of the festival site they found a phone box and rang Flick's parents to put them in the picture.

The island's ferries were running at maximum capacity, the efficiency of which was amazing, considering the amount of foot passengers and vehicles they had to contend with. It came as a small surprise when the van was signalled to drive up the ramp exactly on time. On the Portsmouth side of the Solent the traffic soon thinned out and the A3 took them closer to London. Over a coffee at Guildford, Flick looked a little sad and despondent. Slowly she revealed the story of her previous boyfriend who turned out to be, as she put it, all boy and no friend. This only masked the real reason she felt low, the actual reason being she'd enjoyed the weekend so much, one of the best times she could remember and was somewhat sad it was all over. Eric looked at her and said she'd made the weekend for him too and he would like to continue the friendship if it were at all possible. With a thousand thoughts running through their heads at the speed of light the van nosed closer to Hertfordshire. Eric told her about his ex-girlfriend, who wanted a steady relationship, a large house and three babies...

"In no particular order," he laughingly told her.

A giggle turned into a laugh then abruptly stopped as Flick spotted something in the door pocket.

"Have you read this," she exclaimed, pointing to a half page advert in the New Musical Express. "Glastonbury Festival, 19th September, and just look at the line-up. I'd love to go to that."

"Me too, when did you say it was?" The same thought hit them together. With the blues evaporating faster than a puddle in the desert they sketched out a plan that would give them another weekend together.

6

F lick issued instructions about meeting her family as they drew closer to home. It consisted of just one thing to remember.

"At home call me Deborah," she said.

Eric nodded.

"The reason is Aunt Mavis. Up until five years ago my family had little to do with her and Sydney her husband, they lived in Eastbourne and the journey from Letchworth was not one of the easiest. All that changed when Sydney lost his job and they sold their 'crumbling pile' on the south coast. They bought a brand-new house in Stevenage, just up the road from us. They visited often, too often for my parents' liking, then Sydney announced he would have to work away during the week. Mavis went ape but it seemed it was either work away in Kent, or join the ranks of the unemployed. Top and bottom of it, she started calling in on Mondays; she'd be there when I got home from school, inviting herself for tea."

"I think you're going to say Aunt Mavis used Sydney's absence from Stevenage to inveigle herself into your home."

"In a nutshell; these days Sydney is still working away but only three days a week, so the chances are one or both of them will be at my gaff when we arrive."

"So what's with the 'Deborah' bit then?"

"Hard to describe, but I'll try. Mavis is the most pompous, overbearing, dictatorial, bossy, racist prig – and quite the most conceited high-and-bloody-mighty Victorian prude it has been my misfortune to meet – and it's completely totally embarrassing to admit that the sodding bitch is a member of my family."

"OK, but apart from that she's fine then?"

She continued once her internal temperature has dropped a few degrees. "My father thought 'Flick' was witty, so did Mother; Mavis disliked it immediately and intensely. My second name's Felicity as you know; it's her second name too, although I'm actually named after my great-grandmother on my father's side. She, that's Mavis, is a sly fox, she never lets her unwelcome comments develop into an argument, oh no, she's far too much to lose for that, her tactics are to have her say in the hopes you'll agree with her because of what she likes to call her 'breeding'; 'breeding awful' more like. She would like me to be Felicity, so I deliberately use Deborah at home. Did I mention she's so sodding snobby la-de-bloody-dah doesn't get a look in."

"Caution, Deborah, you're coming to the boil again."

"Sydney's a man of few words, not surprising with her around, Mother tolerates her older sister but Father goads and baits her at every opportunity, bless him. Blood might be thicker than water but in our family there'd be a steward's enquiry."

The traffic was light and the miles rolled by until a pleasant house on a quiet avenue appeared through the windshield. After the introductions, where Eric met Flick's parents, Robert and Helen, and her Aunt Mavis and Uncle Sydney, the six of them sat in the garden, chatting. Eric managed to remember to address Flick as Deborah on every occasion. The talk turned to the festival and eventually Mavis just had to ask very indirectly about the sleeping arrangements. She seemed reasonably happy with Flick's version of events which were told with a wink in her father's direction. Robert started to recall how he and Helen would grab every opportunity to indulge in a lusty romp wherever they were and the festival sounded an ideal spot. Mavis, just as Flick had predicted, obviously held the unfailing belief that sexual intercourse only took place between married couples, in a bed, at night, with the minimum of clothing removed, probably just once a month and solely for the purposes of procreation and said so. She continued the diatribe, expanding into the permissive society, the amount of excessive sexual content on television and how wonderful Mary Whitehouse was with her tireless campaigns. Helen joined in the fun by passing an aside to Sidney saying she had done an awful lot of procreating with Robert but she wasn't very good at it, they only had Deborah to show for all their efforts. Sidney looked a little flustered when Robert added that it was a lot of fun practising. Mavis remained quiet afterwards.

Later on, Eric talked to Robert, who wanted to see the van, Helen and Deborah chatted about the death of her friend's father. Mavis commented that if proper medical healthcare had been in place the man would probably still be alive. She blamed the failings on the National Health Service and all the immigrants pouring into the county in their thousands looking for handouts from the Welfare State. Helen and Flick turned their eyes towards the ceiling and let out a long sigh. On the lighter side, Helen, remembering the affair of the beetroot sandwiches and lost rucksack at the Science Museum when Flick reminded her, laughed even harder when she heard about the chance meeting at the festival and the missing bra saga.

"H'I see you did not manage to locate your undergarment," Mavis sneered whilst glaring at Flick's tiny t-shirt.

"No, Auntie, it's still knotted up in one of Eric's complicated mechanisms that make the bed go up and down," she replied, relishing the detail about the bed.

Around seven Eric said his goodbyes, got into the van and wound down the window. Mavis glared again as Flick reached up saying 'roll on Glastonbury', and gave him a huge hug and a kiss almost losing both breasts out of the bottom of the cropped t-shirt in the process.

"Don't be so shocked, Mavis,' said Helen, 'I sometimes went braless when I was her age."

Back in Leeds, Eric put the van behind the garage workshops; a family business, started a few years after John and Avril settled in Yorkshire. He unpacked, noting the bra trapped in its hiding place. It would have to stay there until he could remove the side rails of the bed mechanism.

The next day John and Avril returned from their holiday in the south of France, John was excited and couldn't wait to tell his son what he'd found. Whilst travelling through Belgium they had come across a Mercedes 407D van which had belonged to a local bakery. It was a 1967 model and had unfortunately been involved in a rear end shunt. Both the rear doors were bent and buckled but the more serious damage was the fire caused by the shorts in the wiring in the rear light clusters and the battery compartment.

"To cut a long story short," John said, "the insurance company wouldn't pay out for one reason or another, the baker started legal proceedings, then the van was passed to a salvage company who weren't allowed to repair it because of the legal entanglements. The court decided the insurance company had to pay the baker, they put the van up at auction. I bought it after reading about the sale in the local Bruges free-sheet and got it for a song – there wasn't even a low reserve on it."

With wide open eyes Eric said it would be absolutely fantastic for his main engineering project at university.

John continued, "We need to take a new battery, a couple of rolls of wire, terminal blocks and tools, we'll take the wrecker in case we have to tow it back, but I would like to drive it if possible, just to see if there's anything else we need to fix."

That afternoon the preparations were made and a ferry booked. Over dinner Eric told them about the festival, meeting Flick and the bear rucksack connection. Next morning after one of Avril's gigantic breakfasts, the pair set off for Belgium. Three days later father and son returned with their prize. It stood in the rear of the smaller workshop. During their absence a letter had arrived for Eric from one of the universities he'd applied to. Avril placed it on the mantelpiece.

In Hertfordshire Flick attended the funeral of her friend's father and spent some time trying to improve her understanding of death and the way it left people devastated and sad. Her friend bordered on inconsolable, to lose your father at eighteen is bad enough but when the father was only forty-five it's especially hard to bear. For three days she tried to comfort her friend, becoming more depressed herself as the days passed. She phoned Eric, cheap rate after six, most days and spent an hour talking things through. She found it easy to talk to him, he was an excellent listener, a quality few men seemed to have. He lifted her up out of the sink hole she'd slid into just by being there, if only on the end of a phone. He made her laugh by telling her in his Bluebottle voice how his father had helped retrieve the tangled bra, his mother had also found her linen blouse in the bottom of the sleeping bag.

"She's washed them both for you and I've been instructed to take them with me when we go to Glastonbury."

By the end of each call the sun was shining in her life again. That week she also began receiving replies from the universities she'd applied to.

John began using his skills as a motor engineer on the sheet metal doors of the van. 'Wolfgang', as they had named the Mercedes after its German pedigree, was not actually as bad as was first thought. Avril's wartime work on radar wiring came in useful – she repaired the burnt-out wires so well it was hard to see the join.

"And a lot cheaper than replacing the whole wiring loom," Eric told Flick later.

The new battery was permanently installed once the box had been cleaned up. As far as the rear doors were concerned it was as John remarked, a whole different kettle of fish. In the end Eric said it would be easier and better if they could remove the hinges and door handles along with the seals, latching rods and locks before welding the doors back into place. John agreed; this way the alignment problems would be avoided and a better interior design layout could be used, but access would only be available through the side door. By the end of the first week the hard work had been done. Flick had started relaying progress on Wolfie, as she called it, to her parents as the phone calls continued between Letchworth and Leeds. Robert was becoming quite excited about the whole thing and spoke to John on a regular basis to keep abreast of the project as it unfolded.

The phone rang as usual on the Friday evening of that first week. Flick announced she had a load of curtains, odd remnants of thick fabric and the disassembled carcasses of the Bowden's old kitchen.

"They might make good cabinets for Wolfie," she added.

Around midnight her father's Volvo estate arrived in Leeds loaded to the roof.

"There's just enough room for me," she announced whilst pushing an unruly bundle off the gear stick. The lights in the Marstone household stayed on for an hour whilst the Volvo lost its load and three worktops of different lengths came off the roof rack. A late supper followed. Flick dumped her bag in the spare room, brushed her hair and dropped into bed. Within ten minutes she was dead to the world.

In the morning they began sorting the wood into usable piles, the girls examining the fabric and old curtains in the hope of finding enough of the same patten to make new cushions and curtains for the Mercedes. Most of the weekend was spent on the ongoing transformation of the baker's van into a camper. Flick left Leeds at seven on Sunday night; Robert would need his car the next morning. The goodbye kiss lingered a lot longer this time.

"See you soon," they said together.

"Not frightened of getting her hands dirty that one," John commented after the Volvo disappeared into the night.

"Takes after her mother from what I'm hearing on the phone," Avril added, "a very nice girl, Eric."

"I think so too, I like her a lot," he agreed with a smile.

The next week saw them both getting down to selecting a university. They drew up a short-list of three each and asked their respective parents for comments. Eric set off on Thursday morning, driving down the M1 before switching to the A1 near Sheffield. Arriving in Letchworth around noon he was received by a jubilant Flick who was nothing short of ecstatic. She was ready to go, her bag packed and a cool box prepared to receive the food and freezer blocks.

"If you don't keep opening the lid all the time it might last till Sunday," Helen called out from the kitchen.

Robert was keen to see the pictures of the van's insides – the recycled kitchen cabinets had been worked into the design almost everywhere. The evening was spent discussing universities, the Black September hijackings at Dawson's Field and the state of the world in general, made a lot better without Mavis butting in. Eric spent the night in Flick's childhood bedroom, now used as a combined storage space and guest room. He lay in bed looking at the shelf full of books and toys. He spotted Eddy looking down at him smiling his permanent smile. He yawned, sleep overtook him as Eddy glowed violet for a few seconds.

They set off shortly after ten on Friday morning, hoping the traffic nearer the London section of the trip had thinned out. Near Slough they managed to avoid the roadworks, which supposedly would improve Heathrow Airport access, and forged ahead, making their way towards the A3 and the west country. By late afternoon they arrived at Glastonbury and made camp.

"The Mercedes should be a lot easier than this to set up and a fair bit more comfortable," he said, opening the huge bag of sandwiches Avril had slipped in the van, 'to ward off starvation'.

Flick made a pot of coffee and bought two steaming mugs to the rear seat before picking up the newspaper they'd bought at the filling station.

"Oh no, listen to this – yesterday morning the American guitarist Jimi Hendrix was found dead at his London flat."

"We only saw him what, less than a month ago; that makes three now: Brian Jones in '69 then 'Blind Owl' of Canned Heat went just after the Isle of Wight," Eric replied. Looking up from the paper she continued, "It says here they were only 27, both of them."

"So was Brian Jones. It's sad about Hendrix, I learned a lot about guitar playing through watching him; my standard certainly improved."

"Me too, I learned a lot from the Experience, Mitch is one of my mentors, him and Charlie Watts."

Later, they walked down the road to a pub in the nearby village. They ambled towards four lighted windows and a creaking wooden sign hand in hand, something that had automatically happened on a few occasions, whilst chatting about the journey and the festival tomorrow. The pub was busy, a few people were eating in the lounge, the locals looked deeply involved in a darts and dominoes match playing out in the bar with a silent juke box sat in the corner. They took their drinks into a small room with 'snug' written on the frosted glass panel of the door and found it empty. Two drinks later Eric had picked up enough courage to ask Flick the question which had been on his mind for a while.

"Lately I seem to be thinking about you rather a lot. I'm talking about you all the time to friends, finding a way of mentioning you even when you're not connected to the subject in hand. When I'm with you I feel so happy, elated and full of life I tingle. Every night in bed I work through my memories of the festival before I nod off and you're the first thing that pops into my head in the morning as well." He paused, looked into her eyes and with hope in his heart said, "I was wondering what your feelings were and if they were perhaps similar."

Flick, with her head tilted slightly to one side, smiled and reached out for his hand. "You have, and not for the first time, taken the words out of my mouth. I know exactly what you mean, I feel it too, the sensation and pleasure of being together, the way our minds seem to run in parallel."

"I have a sneaky suspicion I'm falling in love with you, Minnie Bannister," he said mimicking Henry Crun.

"Oh Henry, you romantic, mad, passionate fool, it's probably nothing more than a bad case of the Lurgi, but if it is I appear to have caught it too."

Looking into each other's eyes they leaned forward and kissed gently in the room's low light. Several more sensual kisses were exchanged before Flick commented that it seemed to be getting rather hot in the pub and some fresh air might not be a bad idea. As their glasses were empty, they left and walked slowly back to the campsite where the inevitable question was silently asked and the answer found. Soon two puddles of clothes sat on the van floor whilst three feet higher up the ceiling-mounted bed was being tested rather more thoroughly than its design expectations warranted. About two hours later Eric discovered that if he wasn't kissing her at the time, Flick had incredibly noisy orgasms.

"Would His Majesty be desirous of tea this morning?" Flick asked, returning the royal status he had conferred on her three weeks ago.

Getting out of the suspended bed was not as easy this time – she had to mention that her bosom went wherever she went. He stopped lying on her hair and reluctantly returned her left breast so the kettle could go on. After a quick wash they dressed and begin exploring the cool box for items that could be called breakfast. Helen had thought things out, layering the contents in the box so it resembled a large dish of lasagne with ice blocks instead of pasta. Everything was still very cold and usable so Eric did the honours, presenting 'Her Majesty' with a full English breakfast his mother would have been proud of twenty minutes later.

The festival began, the weather held up and for them everything was perfect. All too soon the sun fell over the horizon, the stage lights shone a while longer then the final notes of the last song died away in the night air.

"What a brilliant day," Eric said as he picked up their blanket.

She turned to face him, put her arms round his neck and said with a saucy smile, "It isn't over yet."

On the Sunday morning the absence of any tension between them was noticeable. They always were at ease with one another, now the step from friends to lovers had been taken the togetherness factor had reached a new level. While the tea infused they made a plan for the day. Exeter wasn't too far away; it was one of the universities Flick had a choice of. After packing up they made their way towards the city but as they reached the outskirts her expression told Eric everything he needed to know. Pulling into a retail park he turned off the engine, looked her way and asked if something was wrong.

"I don't like this place, Eric, I'm getting bad vibes, let's forget this one and head up to the next."

He consulted the atlas and scribbled a few notes.

"Birmingham it is then, 'let's hit the road, Jack, ain't comin' back no more, no more'," he sang, giving her a smile.

As they joined the A38 northbound she thanked him for understanding how she felt.

"You really do seem to be in tune with my side of things."

"My mother taught me to value a woman's thoughts and opinions, Father added that to dismiss 'female intuition' is at one's own peril."

Birmingham would have been good for both of them as they each had offers, albeit on two different campuses. In the late afternoon they arrived in the university quarter; thankfully most of the traffic had died down. Flick's 'vibe-o-meter' wasn't going crazy so they started looking the place over. It turned out to have some good points and some not so good. After taking a look at both colleges they filed them and the city away as a 'maybe'. Manchester was to be the next stop so the van was taken to an all-night transport cafe on the A5 Holyhead Road where it slid into a gap between the wire link boundary fence and a large truck. As the cool box was no longer cool and the sandwiches were worse than anything only British Rail would attempt to sell, they decided to walk over the gravel parking area and see what delights the cafe offered.

Over sausage, egg, chips and peas, Flick whispered, "You certainly take a girl to all the best places."

"No expense spared, your Majesty, this is a greasy spoon cafe of the highest order, they even offer a choice of desserts, OK, OK, puddings. You may indulge in the plum duff or a portion of raspberry fool for sweet."

Breaking into her impersonation of Aunt Mavis, complete with the extra 'h' prefix, she answered, "H'it's you who's the fool h'if you think you're getting me h'up the duff."

Picking up the menu again, Eric giggled and suggested the apple tart or spotted dick as alternatives.

"H'I hope you're not h'inferring h'i h'am a tart, young man, h'and I'll have you know h'ime not h'interested h'in any dick, spotted or h'outher-wise."

Eric, and two other truckers on the next table, erupted into laughter.

"I'm sorry," he said, "I can't take her anywhere, not even to apologise for the first time."

Back in the van they listened to the distant rumble of traffic making its way along the road towards Wales. Flick felt safe in Eric's arms, they wrapped around her like a cocoon, keeping her shielded from the terrors of the night and warm as well. He looked down at her sleeping face, lit by a half moonbeam that had fought its way through a clink in the curtains into the van. Gently moving a strand of red hair from her forehead he smiled, stroked her cheek and kissed her softly. Not for the first time did he imagine he was lying next to the elf-queen Galadriel from The Lord of the Rings. The night progressed as they slept. It might have been the neon light of the transport café, but the inside of the van suddenly lit up blue. It seemed to be reflected off Kensington; now known as Kenny, the tool bag bear who if you looked closely was actually glowing violet. The light went out ten minutes later and the darkness slid back into place.

Manchester University was a choice for both of them, so after another quick wash and breakfast they pulled out and headed north. This time everything seemed to fall into place and by the late afternoon they'd made up their minds to enrol. On the way to Leeds they realised they could save money if the old saying that two could live as cheap as one was true. After bringing John and Avril up to date about their choice of university, the van headed south for Letchworth but not before both 'humming urchins' as John had described them had showered.

"Do you know why we're humming?" questioned Flick in her Minnie Bannister voice.

Avril grinned and shook her head as she offered them towels and shampoo.

"Because we don't know the words," they shouted together.

"Enough already, oh Avril, Avril, my life, the worst most parents have to cope with is black paint on the bedroom walls and a huge bill for acne cream. What do we get? We get Goons in the bathroom," John joined in with his best Jewish accent.

9

arly in October Janis Joplin became a member of the 27 club and their parents joined together to bankroll them for a cheap one bedroom flat in Manchester. Flick started her Biology degree whilst Eric read Engineering. Four evenings a week they both worked in a busy Manchester pub that had live music. On the weekends they didn't work they went to Leeds or Letchworth. Slowly 'Wolfie' came together, culminating in December when after a complete respray in electric blue – John had a lot of it left over – they took it for a MOT test which it passed with flying colours. Robert and Helen came to Leeds for Christmas and Aunt Mavis had to be content with spending the holiday with Sydney instead of indulging in her usual freeloading in Hertfordshire.

The Bowdens were introduced to the Yorkshire Dales, a totally different experience for somebody who lived in the south of England. Avril recalled the first time she'd looked down on Swaledale from the top of the Buttertubs Pass. On the last day of their break John took them over the Pennines into the Lake District. All good things come to an end, however, so on December 29th John and Avril found themselves with an empty house whilst down in Hertfordshire Helen was trying to make light of the impending visit of Mavis and Sydney.

Making herself comfortable in the armchair nearest the television, Mavis began her long-winded, time-worn tirade against the permissive society, the pornography one was forced to watch on television and the amount of black people who were sending the country deeper into the fiery furnaces of hell. Whilst the main part of the gospel according to Mavis rumbled on, it soon spluttered out when nobody rallied to her flag. Sensing defeat once again she assembled her last attack, the permissive society, and struck knowing she had two members present, both of whom ignored her completely and utterly.

Helen said to Flick afterwards that she wondered what actually went on in Mavis's head. She seemed to revel in pontificating and passing judgement on several matters she'd obviously never experienced, or knew anything about if Helen's memories of her sister were accurate. She had an idea that would get a laugh and take the wind out of her sails. She leaned forward and whispered confidentially in her daughter's ear.

"Don't let on to Eric or your father, we'll do it on New Year's Eve." The two plotters gave a sly wink and went back into the lounge.

Mavis had now ceased another sermon and was half watching the television whilst noticing that Flick had sat on her father's knee to give him a big thank-you hug and kiss just for being the best dad on the planet. She bristled and commented that Flick was far too old to be acting in such a childish manner. She missed Sydney stealing a longing look down Helen's low cut dress as she bent over his chair to reach the wine glasses from a side table. Helen, being responsible for Flick's figure and still bearing a close likeness to it, was a splendid example of womanhood, something that had passed her sister by completely. It would take some believing the two were even related, Helen's many charms were permanently absent in Mavis and thus from Sydney's world.

Eric came in from working on Wolfie's plumbing.

"The shower's sorted, so there's no more humming for days and my father pushing us into the bathroom with a forked vermin stick, and also to complete the job we now have a proper cassette toilet, your Highness; squatting in fields behind bushes is now a thing of the past," he announced with a sweeping bow in Flick's direction.

"Ooh, luxury, I do hope you've remembered the super-soft toilet tissue as well?" she squeaked.

"This was your Christmas present to each other I take it?" Robert enquired.

Eric nodded. "It was the two things the old van didn't have, there just wasn't enough room for them and they're a bit expensive."

"I don't believe you bought a portable toilet for Christmas – Sydney would never, ever, do anything like that would you, Sydney?"

"No, dear," ventured Sydney, uttering his first words since their arrival.

"Sydney always buys me the most beautiful presents for Christmas, don't you, Sydney?"

"Yes, dear."

"I always make him a list of the things I want so he doesn't have to worry about buying the wrong thing, like a porta-potty for instance, isn't that right, Sydney?"

"Yes, dear," came the expected reply.

Robert shot Helen a sideways look.

"You working him with your foot or something?"

She smirked.

"I think it's Pavlovian response – or sheer naked terror."

After dinner Eric and Robert, who grabbed two six packs of beer, ushered Sydney out to the van on the pretence of showing it to him. Sat in the back on the couch arrangement they reclined with a can apiece.

"It's a damn good job this van, Eric, damn good," Robert said after examining the new shower and toilet.

As the beer went down Sydney loosened up a little and began telling them about Mavis's involvement with the Women's Institute, the local church organ fund committee, her support of the campaign to clean up television, and last but by no means least the constant battle she waged with the younger generation. Robert slid back into the kitchen for beer reinforcements, overhearing Mavis telling a story about how disgusted she was when she discovered a breastfeeding mother in the local park. Flick was stating in a loud voice there was nothing indecent or immoral about a mother feeding her baby in a public place. Helen then passed a languid comment that 'breasts were like a model railway set; supposed to be for children but in the end played with by the adults'. He left them to it and snook back with the beers.

A little later the ladies joined them in the van, Helen bringing a large tray of nibbles and Flick armed with more alcohol. The van party gathered pace, well for five people at least, Mavis sat on the swivelling passenger Captain's seat armed with a sweet sherry and a low mood. Sydney was at the other end where the kitchen unit wall shielded him from the dragon's gaze and enabled him to steadily make his way through a six pack all on his own. Around midnight the conversation arrived at that point where there's nothing else left to be said and contagious yawns were slipping into it. Sydney was left on the long couch in Wolfie, Flick threw a blanket over him and Helen poked a pillow under his head.

"Oh boy is he in for it tomorrow," Eric commented whilst examining a small teddy bear he'd seen before: it had fallen off the shelf behind the bed onto his head.

"Let's hope then that 'tomorrow never comes' – that's Eddy by the way, he's a nightdress holder, there's a zipper in his belly." Flick finished brushing her hair and put Eddy back on the shelf before sliding into bed.

"Remember Mavis is in my room next door," she whispered, purposefully throwing one leg over him then placing both hands on his chest. She lowered her grinning face close to his. "Put your hand over my mouth at the end."

Outside the house, on the roof near the chimney, a vertical straight white beam appeared. It quickly split into the usual seven colours, hummed, refracted as if viewed in water, then dispersed as singletons. The red segment went through the van roof and bathed the snoring, sozzled Sydney. The orange section swept through the house, coming to rest at the bottom of Mavis's bed. Here the hum muted and began to sweep up her body until it reached the head. Both the yellow and green bands stayed together but without any trace of merging. This pair found the master bedroom, the yellow band focused on Helen's head before slowly sweeping down to her toes and then returned to the head coming to a point roughly five millimetres in diameter in the middle of her forehead. The green band mimicked the yellow one using Robert as its target. Finally the blue and indigo portions found where Eric and Flick where sleeping. These beams widened out into a fan shape before slowly moving up the two sleeping bodies starting at the feet. The indigo beam concentrated on Flick, the blue traversed Eric. Inside twenty minutes all the earlier beams returned to the splitting point, leaving the indigo and blue portions humming in Flick's former bedroom. The hum dropped in register, the two beams widened until both bodies were covered by both lights. Up on the shelf Eddy went an eerie deep violet, out in the van Kenny the tool bag bear followed suit. Less than ten seconds later it was completely dark again.

The morning of New Year's Eve arrived bringing a frost but not snow. Eric left Flick in bed and went off to the kitchen where he found Helen doing things with sausages. Robert had gone to check on Sydney, Mavis could be heard walking around upstairs. Robert opened the back door as Flick shuffled in from the dining room.

"Yea Gods, Lazarus has risen," he commented as the red mane wandered wraithlike towards the fridge.

"She's not a morning person, dear," Helen opined.

Mavis entered, took one look and scowled.

Eric took his cue, slid over to Flick by the open fridge, took her in his arms as actors did in 1920s black and white movies before looking intently into her eyes and saying with a cod French accent, "Good morning, Deborah, my darling, do you know you're the most ravishing creature in the whole wide world," as he leaned her gently backwards over his arm and kissed her.

"That has to be love or insanity, no doubt about it," giggled Robert with a wink at Helen.

The day passed in the usual manner; around lunchtime it seemed Sydney the Sot's condition was forgiven but in Mavis's eyes not forgotten. Lunch was late, it began around three, then Helen announced the go-as-you-please after the washing up was done. Sydney wanted to know what a go-as you-please-was. Helen explained it was something done at family gatherings, hers used to have one at Christmas or New Year. In the 1930s television sets were rare so families made their own entertainment and she would like to revive the custom. The idea was each person would take it in turn to do something to entertain the others. Singing songs, playing the piano, telling tales or jokes, dancing or anything else that might raise a laugh.

The lounge furniture was pushed back, Robert gave everyone a drink including Sydney despite Mavis looking daggers at him. Standing with his back to the window he raised his glass and said:

"The toast is Absent Friends."

Traditionally guests went first so Eric being the youngest was given the dubious privilege of opening the proceedings. He asked for a pack of cards and for the next twenty minutes treated them to a magic show ending with him pulling the four of hearts Mavis had selected out of a face-down pack from behind Helen's ear. Applause rolled round the room then Robert went next.

Sitting in a large wing back chair he recalled a ghost story centred on the aircraft factory in wartime Hatfield. Carefully and slowly he mesmerised his small audience until they were hanging on his every word. Just as the story was about to climax, he turned off the standard light he was sat under leaving them surprised and in the dark before delivering the punchline to what was actually a complex shaggy-dog story.

Helen got up and asked Eric to move over to the record player.

"When I call out, put the record on please."

With that she disappeared with Flick and ran upstairs. A few minutes later a voice called out from the kitchen:

"OK, Eric, now."

The record turned out to be an old recording that sounded like the music a snake charmer might use. The sound was distinctly Arabic, Indian pipes or a pungi with a drum beating rapidly in the background which offset the unusual rhythm. Two detached arms appeared from either side of the kitchen door, finger cymbals clicked and rang, suddenly two figures dressed as belly dancers swung through the doorway into the room. Perfectly in time Helen and her daughter gyrated to the music, hips moving with lightning speed, bellies vibrating as muscles were alternately clenched and relaxed, bosoms in tiny silky sequinned tops shook and shimmied, bare feet with brightly painted nails flitted and slid across the carpet. Both wore bells on the waistbands and hems of silky full skirts and very wide smiles. Robert and Eric began a hand clap that accelerated with the music until the drummer brought the piece to a close. The dancers gave one final twirl then slid theatrically to the carpet entwined round the two men's legs, their arms above their heads, the finger cymbals poised but silent.

"Fantastic, utterly fantastic and incredibly beautiful, I'm blown away," gasped Eric, clapping his hands furiously whilst still hardly believing what he had just witnessed.

He looked back and forth at the two dancers and smiled the widest smile at Flick she'd ever seen. Robert had walked over to his wife and held her tight.

"Do you know how long it's been since I last saw you do that?" he asked before supplying the answer, "about twenty-three years ago I guess, one Christmas bash at Hatfield. I recall it had the same effect on me then as Flick has just wrought on Eric."

In Eric's head the word 'Enchantress' made a second appearance.

The two women slipped off their cymbals before sitting on the sofa and waited to see if Mavis or Sydney would go next. Mavis appeared to be getting a bit hot under the collar so Robert asked Sydney to perform. The belly dancing routine, a flagrant display of lust, they reckoned Mavis would view it as, purely designed to provoke her had definitely worked – she was getting up a good head of steam to match a face like thunder and lips stretched so thin and tight they were almost invisible. What happened next almost burst the old boiler and brought on a coronary.

Sydney stood up and reached for a can of beer, pouring it carefully. With one arm resting on the mantelpiece and glass in hand he proceeded to deliver a stream of the bluest side-splitting jokes, the sort that definitely didn't get aired on the BBC, for fifteen minutes non-stop. Most of them involved a 'mother-in-law' type figure not a million miles away from a certain person, who was by now beetroot red and incredibly angry. It was only the uncontrollable laughter that stopped her going into meltdown; she realised no-one would have noticed her. The final straw came when the hastily stitched seam of Helen's thin belly dancer's top yielded under the pressure of laughter as she slid involuntarily off the sofa and some of her fell out. Mavis didn't see this at first, but Sydney did.

Mavis announced she was tired and departed for her bedroom.

"She's bloody livid," Robert whispered to Eric who nodded his agreement with a smile. Sydney asked if he might sleep in the van again, Eric nodded again. Robert suggested supper, eaten in front of the television whilst they watched Big Ben strike midnight. A toast to the new year followed then the usual good wishes, kisses and hugs were exchanged. Suddenly it was 1971.

10

ife continued, as it does. For Eric and Flick the university became the central hub of their world until the term ended at Easter. Robert and Helen had accepted John and Avril's invitation to spend the holiday with them in Yorkshire, Helen had been smitten by the Dales and was keen to investigate deeper into the countryside known as the Broad Acres. Flick and Eric had been saving what they could from the bar work – in reality the tips were better than the wages – and decided to take Wolfie on his longest trip so far by venturing up into the Cairngorms National Park in Scotland.

The roads out of Manchester were busy. Good Friday traffic had been building on the M6, by Carlisle it was down to a snail's pace and now, only five miles into the A74, they had ground to a halt. The engine was turned off after being stationary for five minutes as they could see the traffic queue ahead for at least half a mile. Flick was driving and took the opportunity to use the toilet. Eric made them a coffee, keeping one eye on the line for any sign of movement. Thirty minutes later a set of blue lights announced the arrival of a police car with an ambulance hot on its heels. Shortly afterwards the traffic began to move as it was diverted onto a minor road near Ecclefechan.

As they drove slowly north it became apparent that the A74 was almost gridlocked the closer to Glasgow it went.

"This is awful, if we stay on this road it'll add a load of time to the journey," Eric said, looking up from the atlas.

"Plan B?" Flick enquired, swinging the wheel hard right over a narrow bridge.

"Go left here and pull into that clearing by the trees."

They were a few miles north of Moffat at the junction of a reasonably fast road heading in the general direction of Edinburgh.

"I suggest we wild camp here tonight, we're about three, four hours adrift, it's half dark already and hopefully the main road will be better in the morning. From here we can go two miles further on then look down on the Glasgow road and know for sure if it's running well."

"I think that's a good idea, two bites of the cherry," she replied looking up from the atlas he'd passed over.

The plantation hid Wolfie from the road, not that there was anyone about to disturb them. As they lay in bed listening to the sounds of the forest and the owl which had landed on the metal roof, they talked about their friends Alan and Dan who wanted to form a college band to earn some extra money. Dan was a good bass player and Alan could sing, play piano, organ or basically anything with black and white keys on it. The plan was to add Flick on drums and Eric on lead guitar. They agreed a fair bit of practice would be needed to get up to speed; Eric's guitar was in the attic at Leeds and Flick's drum kit had lain idle for well over a year in Letchworth. Concentrating on getting good results at school, good enough for a university place, had led to hobbies being put on the back burner.

"When we get back let's round up our kit, drop it in Dan's dad's garage and give it a go – after all, what have we got to lose?"

"Sounds good to me," she agreed. The light went off, Flick turned on her side facing the wall. Eric slid up behind her and wrapped his arms around her shoulders; as she sighed he felt her relax against his chest. One of the problems, if you in fact see it as a problem, is that sometimes it was very hard to just go to sleep when lying next to Flick. The hardest part was down at waist level where things appeared to have developed a mind of their own. A sleepy hand reached out and gently steered him between slightly open legs before her body slid down the bed a few inches causing him to catch his breath.

"Long and slow please, your Highness, long and slow."

Around 3am a small silver-coloured craft with no wings dropped soundlessly and gently into the same clearing as Wolfie. Two tall beings glided across the leaf-lined forest floor and looked in the direction of the parked van. A low hum rose to a level just detectable by a human ear but caused several rabbits and a variety of other forest animals to scatter into the undergrowth. A short, narrow white beam left each being's hand, joined together, then became a seven coloured rainbow. The pitch of the hum rose slightly, paused and rose again as the violet band shone on the back doors of the Mercedes. The sheet steel proved to be no barrier, the beam found Eric and Flick still lying together deep in sleep. After bathing them in violet light for a few minutes the beam broke into two smaller violet beams which found their way onto Eddy and Kenny. The two bears stayed lit by the rays for almost twenty minutes before the inside of the van returned to darkness. As the beam retracted into the two beings it vanished; seconds later the small craft left the clearing as silently and swiftly as it had arrived. The only witness was a small red squirrel which sat on a fallen branch wearing a slightly bemused expression for a few seconds before going about its usual nocturnal business. The sun still had three hours to go before it rose; the moon, however, was shining exceedingly bright.

The A74 turned out to be almost empty at 6am, the time they looked down from the hill towards Evan Water. Wolfie ate up the miles, they changed drivers somewhere to the east of Glasgow and pressed on till mid-morning, stopping for lunch near Dunblane. Eddy's belly was raided for diesel money; his new job being that of a disguised purse and holder of important documents. In the afternoon Inverey came into view through the windscreen wipers; the small camp site was just outside the village on the road to Muir.

Eric unpacked his father's Pentax SLR camera and loaded a fresh roll of film. Part of the reason for coming to the Cairngorms National Park was for Flick to add more information to her course work portfolio for the current term. The park had many sites of special interest including golden eagles and the mountain hare, both relative to her studies. Of the nineteen Special Areas of Conservation, they calculated it was possible to visit three or four on this trip. Flick had made a light meal and coffee. Eric pulled out the OS map and found the village and the five sites they hoped to visit if everything went according to plan. Once located and marked they were put in the itinerary for the week. Saturday, now moved forward to Sunday or Day One as the journal recorded it, was a walk to the nearby Mar Lodge estate. The object of the exercise was to identify one of the remnants of the Caledonian Forest and try to find rare black grouse, parrot crossbills and Scottish crossbills. Monday was a drive east to Glen Tanar and Muir of Dinnet where it was the insects' turn to be discovered. Eric laughed at the names of the noteworthy specimens.

"Is this for real, we're looking for, and I quote, the bumblebee robber fly, the false blister beetle and the green hairstreak butterfly?"

"Makes you wonder what the brain-boxes who named this little lot were on," Flick muttered.

"No idea. Do you fancy finding out if the fridge has kept the beer cold?"

Bright brown eyes twinkled, a pink tongue lolled out, two hands drooped at the wrists of held out arms bent at the elbows. An imitation of a panting dog begging finished her reply. He opened two cans.

"I'll take that as a yes then," he said, patting her on the head and passing a glass over.

Darkness fell, and with the failing of the light came the sounds of the forest. The river Dee whispered its way towards Aberdeen and the North Sea. The night dropped cold; despite two extra blankets and the heavier-rated sleeping bag they woke around 4 am with chilly arms.

"They said to expect four seasons in one day up here," Eric told her, whilst using their clothing to plug any gaps between them and the bag.

He kissed a shoulder and wrapped his arms round her. Fifteen minutes later they were back in dreamland.

The morning revealed frost on the grass and a weak sun poking through light grey clouds. They made the preparations for the walk into the forest, set off and managed to stay dry all day. The biology journal had started to thicken out, nineteen photographs waited in the camera and now the major decision of the day had to be made: what shall we have for dinner? Sausages, onions and instant mashed potato won. The second evening, in contrast to the first, was warm enough to sit by the river until the sun dropped and the midges and mosquitoes came out.

"Time for bed said Zebedee," mimicked Flick, picking up the rug, the Magic Roundabout being one of her childhood favourites.

Eric grabbed the glasses and plates then followed her back to Wolfie. Later, she finished writing up the day's finds from the insect world, then glanced back through the pages to check she'd not missed anything out. Eric had been reading the New Musical Express whilst she was writing. Folding the paper up, he looked thoughtful.

"How long do you think it lasts, this wonderful, somewhat inadequately named feeling called love?"

"I think besotted is a good word for us at the moment: who knows, a month, a year, a decade, a lifetime, perhaps forever? Our parents have managed to stay the course; it changes over time, we know that, it mellows and deepens so I'm told, but as to the intensity, that's a very personal thing I'm guessing," she opined.

"I suppose we'll just have to wait and see." He nodded, kissing her on the cheek. "We move in the morning, Nethybridge I think, so we'd better have an early night."

"Correct, day three, Abernethy Forest." She consulted her notes. "And we're hoping to spot, you're going to love this one, a rare plant called 'creeping ladies' tresses' and the crested tit." She giggled as the notes slid to the floor.

"OK, we've plenty of film, if there's nobody about, whip your top off and I'll grab a few shots. It might be a bit awkward when we get the prints processed though, I don't reckon Boots are keen on tits, crested or not."

The giggle turned into a laugh; she picked up her cushion and hit him over the head. A small fight ensued, ending in a draw. After tidying the van they lay in bed facing each other, propped up on one elbow. The conversation returned to the subject of love then expanded into how remarkable it was that such intense feelings for someone could run alongside the gentle and caring aspect of a relationship. How respect for a partner grew and how the whole thing gently bubbled, simmered and meandered along one minute then burned and raged with fiery lust the next. They fell asleep talking; it wasn't as cold that night.

Wolfie just fitted down some of the park's narrow tracks, the secondary or 'B' class roads were only a little wider. Around eleven they found the next camp ground and parked in their allocated space, leaving the setting up until an investigation of the tea shop near a stone bridge in the village had been made. A small general store next door would also do to restock the fridge.

The rest of the day was spent in the forest attempting to find specimens to photograph without much luck. Thankfully the rain kept off and the centigrade thermometer tried hard to make double figures. The restocked fridge and food cupboard returned to a respectable level thanks to Eddy coughing up some more cash, enabled dinner to be Chicken a la Flick followed by chocolate Instant Whip. Although Eric possessed sufficient culinary skills to prevent stage one starvation, Flick was Cordon Bleu in the necessary art of 'eat the fridge', an exercise designed to create something edible and hopefully appealing before the ingredients went off or walked to the bin unaided.

The last place on the list was Glenmore. It was almost midnight by the time the day's exploration had been written up and the roll of film exchanged. The next day they intended using the Glenmore Forest car park as a base to see the reindeer herd first before trekking into the stretch of forest to the north of Loch Morlich. Eric turned the overhead light off and lay on his back, staring at the roof. Flick wiggled into the crook of his arm then rested her head on his chest. They listened to the soft drumbeat of the rain's rhythmic tapping on the roof mingled with the louder irregular thud of larger drops falling from the tree the van was parked under.

Morning arrived wet and windy. The radio weather forecast predicted it would die down about mid-day with the afternoon and early evening staying dry if not bright. Eric drove to the forest whilst Flick got their rucksacks and hiking gear together. Breakfast was eaten in the car park after trying to find more than the three reindeer lounging against the wooden fence. The forest ran from the edge of the loch north to Abernethy, where they were the day before. Today's hike was going to explore more of the Caledonian Forest and try to find some of the rare species that had evaded the camera so far.

Three hours into the trees they halted by a fallen trunk. The rain had stopped soon after they left the reindeer and now weak spring sunshine was above the treetops.

"Time to lose a layer, I reckon the waterproofs can come off as well," Eric said.

"We should be crossing two logging tracks at a crossroads if my navigation's right," Flick commented, "we can have lunch there and take a breather."

"Sounds good, I'm ready for something."

They carried on, the map said about four miles had been covered, picking their way slowly through the old trees. The morning had yielded some interesting finds and the camera was now on the last roll of film. The crossroads appeared as predicted, complete with a stack of rocks that made two impromptu seats.

Flick looked up from the map, had a bite of sandwich then took a compass reading before drawing a chinagraph pencil line on the plastic map case.

"OK, north-east, for about two and a half miles, then east for roughly two more, the last leg south is back to the car park."

"Got it, ready when you are, your Majesty."

As they moved east the weather shifted again. A mile from the expected turning point rain began to fall and the grey sky moved steadily towards black. A sharp wind began to stir the debris on the forest floor, a mist began rising out of the undergrowth. Waterproofs and another layer went back on. The camera was bagged next before they continued along the narrow trail.

"No more than three to do, let's go." Flick let the map fall on its straps and strode off.

Progress was slow, the track had been deteriorating for some time, the mossy soil was waterlogged and half hidden stones made the risk of a sprained ankle greater. A mile later the rain began in earnest and the wind blew harder and colder. Soon the trees echoed to voices singing.

"Hi ho, hi ho, it's through the woods we go, we tramp, tramp, tramp, bugger, who put that rock there, tramp, tramp, tramp, we tramp the whole day through."

Eric called for Flick to stop.

"Can you hear a cat of something or is it the wind playing tricks? You said there may be Jaguars round here."

"I can't be sure, it's hard to tell but there seems to be a faint crying sound underneath the whistling. Jaguars in Scotland are about the same size as a domestic cat and only found in the Highlands, so yes – it could be."

"That'd be one for your album, girl, listen hard we might get lucky."

A few minutes later the wind dropped sufficiently, leaving the quieter drizzling rain in the background. Both of them heard it, a cat-like cry coming from the trees to the north of them. They looked at each other. Eric retrieved the camera as they made their way through the thinning undergrowth.

"We're getting closer, it can't be moving, that cry was definitely louder," he said. She pulled his arm to stop him walking further.

"Wait for the next cry, try and get a fix on it."

When it came they both tried to pinpoint the direction.

"I make it behind that next clump of bushes," she whispered.

He nodded and moved forward with the camera ready. Flick scanned the ground in a wide arc, then a bright red splash of colour beside a small bush caught her eye. Stepping cautiously through the bracken she crept up on the spot she'd fixed and locked her gaze on, then her mouth gaped open half in surprise, half in horror.

"Eric! Come here, now, quick, it's a child!" she screamed.

"He's soaked through and frozen stiff – what the hell is a child doing out here, alone?" She frantically wrapped their two thick wool sweaters round the sodden, crying bundle and looked up at Eric.

"We need to get him dry and out of here by the shortest route possible, bring him over to these trees by the hillock, the overhang will give us some shelter," he said, rapidly helping her to her feet.

In the overhang they managed to quickly exchange most of the child's useless clothing for their own spare layers, adding one of the woollen sweaters made him look like a cross between an Egyptian mummy and a Michelin man.

"How old do you think?"

"No more than four, five at most, obviously he can walk and now we're here he's talking. He's cold, very scared, obviously, but I didn't see any injuries other than the odd cut and scrape so let's go," Flick answered.

Between them they wrapped him in their survival blanket then Eric hoisted him up into his arms. Flick used the large waterproof bag normally used for keeping wet boots in to cover and fill any gaps between the child and Eric. She calculated a course and held the compass so they could both see it.

"North north-east, say 18 degrees, we should come out of the forest and be able to see a road or some houses. It's a village called Aundorach – ready?"

They marched through the trees singing anything they could remember from primary school. Within ten minutes the sobbing slowed and finally stopped, the boy had succumbed to sleep, driven by the warmth and the rhythmic pace. Flick reached inside the blanket and found a small wrist.

"Pulse feels good." Her hand moved to the fingers. "Warm as toast, great."

Eric glanced up to the tree tops.

"The rain's stopped, I reckon most of this is falling off the trees."

It took roughly forty minutes to break out of the forest; Flick's course had placed them less than a quarter mile from the village. Guided by a column of smoke from a chimney, they reached the road and headed towards civilisation. The door to the stone cottage with the smoking chimney opened to Flick's pounding fist. Two pensioners peered out, taking in the bedraggled trio. She explained the situation, asking if they had a phone to call the police and ambulance. Both turned up in under thirty minutes. One medic took the child into the ambulance for some basic checks, the other asked them how they felt, took their pulse, temperature and blood pressure before pronouncing them sound in wind and limb. Outside more vehicles were pulling up, another police officer came in to inform his colleague the parents were outside in the ambulance. The police asked for the details of their walk in the forest, from the time they heard the cat-like cry. Flick produced the map and together they relived the route from leaving the car park.

The two pensioners made mugs of strong tea, laced with whisky and slices of fruit cake to follow. Once the questions were over, they went outside to find the shocked and distraught parents had now calmed down somewhat. The child – his name was Peter – appeared to be unscathed apart from a few cuts and bruises. Both the mother and father walked their way; with tears streaming over her cheeks and hands trembling the mother embraced Flick in a hug whilst saying 'thank you, thank you, thank you' over and over again. The father took Eric's right hand and shoulder, simply saying he could never begin to repay them for what they had done, they were both grateful beyond words. The ambulance driver came across to say they were taking Peter to Inverness hospital to give him a thorough check-up. The reunited family left the village, and Eric and Flick were given a ride back to the Glenmore car park.

Wolfie was driven slowly back to the camp site. Instead of making a meal, they decided to walk into the village and see if anywhere did food. The events of the day had drained them emotionally and physically, the adrenalin rush earlier hadn't helped either.

Eric put his fork down and looked across at Flick.

"What a day, did you hear how it happened? The police said the family were having a picnic near Loch Garten when Peter just wandered off. They only turned their backs for a moment, it was as easy as that."

Flick was looking tired and seemed to be deep in thought. She turned to him and said,

"I'll never forget the look on that woman's face, never; can you begin to imagine what they must have gone through today, hell and back I guess."

They silently lost themselves in thought. The night air swirled last autumn's leaves round them as they walked arm in arm along the narrow gravel track to the camp site. The day's notes and the photo record lay on the shelf, the biology journal would have to wait. They climbed into bed. Flick took Eric's hand in hers.

"Love you, Eric, to the moon and back."

"Love you too, Flick, to the end of time."

They lay silent for a while. Eric fell asleep. Flick listened to his deep measured breathing whilst watching his chest slowly rise and fall. Finally she reached across for his hand, placing it on her flat stomach before covering it with her own. Her eyes closed soon after.

Tuesday morning saw the sun beginning to make an impression on the cloud bank, Eric was on breakfast duty, Flick was having the best of three falls with her hair, yesterday's rain had done it no favours at all. Over the toast and jam she asked how he felt about children. He paused momentarily.

"I can't manage a whole one and the chips as well – seriously, no strong feelings either way," he shrugged.

"Well I'm sitting on the fence but leaning heavily towards my life being a 'No Kids Zone', let me explain."

She sat down on the side couch with her legs drawn up underneath her.

"When I was about eleven, maybe twelve, the family next door had a severely autistic child. This poor mite was pitiful to watch, there was nothing the medics could do. The parents went through the mill on a daily basis; they split up in the end. I realised later that the sheer physical effort needed as he grew older was more than most people could summon up. The mental pressures must be immense too."

Eric listened and nodded. "I see what you mean, suddenly you have a normal, everyday world with your partner, you decide on a baby, then fate takes a hand and life's turned upside down, never to be the same again."

"What made it more intense for me was the onset of menstruation. I'd started my periods, mum made sure I wasn't in the dark on that subject so I knew what to expect, and the connection with pregnancy is irrefutable. That experience swung me somewhat. As the years passed, I saw my friends' older siblings have kids, then I watched as the child tore the relationship or in some cases the marriage apart. I even saw a couple who used having another baby as a patch to try and stop a mortally wounded relationship bleeding to death – not once but four times, the first three were when I was very young but witnessed by my mother and told to me much later."

"I guess these bad experiences outweighed the good in your mind."

"Sadly yes, it seems so. Yesterday was another angle of parenting I'm not sure I could handle, that mother had been thinking the worst things imaginable, it was written all over her face." She took a deep breath and continued, "I would like you to know, Eric, that deep down I don't really want children, maybe I'm a bit scared or just too selfish, but if you were adamant you wanted to be a father then I will bear you a child. I would do this for no other man – that sounds so old-fashioned, but I love you intensely and I don't want to lose you."

Looking at her the way he always did when something serious was being said, he locked his eyes on hers as he spoke softly. "Lose your fears, love, I couldn't imagine being without you, I'm more than happy to wander down life's highway as a couple."

He reached for her clasped hands, taking them gently in his own.

"I respect you, and your wishes, I love you with all my heart, that's a bit dated as well – let's roll along together and see what the future brings."

A kiss sealed the deal.

T he dramatic rescue in Glenmore Forest didn't make the news until a reporter who was at the hospital covering a different story picked up the details when the ambulance arrived. The paper ran the story the next day, then it hit the lunchtime news on radio followed closely by early evening national television coverage. By this time the camper was in Dundee looking over the river Tay, which was handy as the local Inverness reporter, a radio car and BBC Scotland were desperately looking for them. From the small Scottish village they had phoned their parents before they left to update them on the events of the week not thinking the story would be so newsworthy. They caught up with the continuing events in the pub they'd chosen for dinner. The TV in the bar was showing the news, Peter was smiling, sat on his mother's lap with the father resting on one knee beside them. The interviewer presented a summary of the day's events through the parents' eyes, ending with them thanking the two students who 'saved our child's life'.

"They're looking a lot happier now," Eric commented.

"I should say so, they can put it behind them and so can we," Flick replied as she raised her glass. "Cheers, all's well that ends well as the bard said."

The next morning it was Eric's turn to visit a couple of places he wanted to photograph and make some drawings of. First was the Mills Observatory, a purpose-built telescope to which the public had access free of charge. Next was the rail bridge over the river Tay. The first bridge had fallen in a violent storm in 1879. The site still had remnants showing and he wanted to experience the weather conditions, the wind especially, as the lack of a wind-loading allowance was a principal cause of the structure's failure.

After all the notes had been written, the rolls of film labelled and the rubbish dumped, Wolfie pulled out of the campsite with Flick driving the first leg back to Manchester. The A92 crossed the river then headed for Edinburgh. On the outskirts of Kirkcaldy the road slowed.

"I hope this isn't all the way to the Forth Bridge, bloody tourists," Flick cursed and dropped down the gearbox.

"It may have escaped her Majesty's notice, but we are also tourists."

She turned her head towards him and stuck her tongue out by way of reply. For the second time they found themselves in a queue of slow-moving vehicles then a junction appeared.

"Take the slip-road and drop south, it's a bit longer but we end up roughly in the same place," he said, looking up from the map.

A few miles further on the road turned west again, Eric spotted a signpost.

"Well, that's a name from the past – I wonder what happened to him."

"Who're you on about?"

"A guy I knew in school, five, six years ago, had a weird name, Penley Augustus Dysart, same as on the road sign back there. He left after a couple of terms, they moved to Oxford I think, odd lad, family had similar ideas and attitude akin to Aunt Mavis but with an old money fortune behind them: diamond mining, Africa, I seem to remember. Later on, a rumour circulated that his father was carrying on with his own sister."

"Ah, incest, a game for all the family," she wickedly interjected. "That's really strange, because I knew a Dysart too, Norman, and a name I can't recall. It's a funny, sad and odd tale all at the same time. He seemed to be locked in the Victorian era as far as the way he spoke, he called his parents Pater and Mater, which raised a chuckle in the common room. We're fifteen at the time and all the boys were asking the girls out on dates and all the usual stuff you do at that age. I remember he spotted me coming out of dance class and asked me out for a coffee at Reno's, the place near school we all used. I agreed and we walked out of school, meeting Mr Benson the music teacher who reminded me about band practice and gave me a pair of new brushes for the drum kit. Over the coffee he was oddly quiet, like he was trying to sort something out in his head: it appeared to be bothering him somewhat seriously. He asked if I had a boyfriend, I replied no. Next came did I like dancing, followed by, do you really play the drums. I told him I'd been dancing for as long as I could remember and yes, I really can play the drums. He fell quiet: so quiet you could almost hear the cogs going round. By now I was getting a bit fed up so I said something like, 'what's up, trying to do your maths homework in your head'. Another few seconds passed; it felt like an hour, then he asked if I'd ever had a boyfriend, putting the emphasis on 'ever'. I said I'd had one or two but nothing serious, I'm fifteen remember. More silence and cog whirring, then he comes up with: 'So you've not, sort of, you know, 'done it' then.' I thought bloody cheek, then my wicked side popped up. I'm never going to heaven, Eric, I'm far too naughty, me. I looked at him and said, actually I'm a theoretical virgin, I hope that satisfies your strange curiosity, I said it in my 'Snooty Mavis' voice."

Eric glanced at her and amid his chuckles asked what a 'theoretical virgin' was.

"I'll tell you after. He stared at me as if he couldn't believe what he'd just heard, got up and left without a word. That was the first and last encounter with Dodgy Dysart. Anyway, he took a shine to Janet Crossling at an end of term dance and it progressed from there. Perhaps it was my fault, maybe I shouldn't have asked Mother to donate one of her older, fancier dresses for her to go in that exposed a bit more top half than was wise. He started 'courting' her, his expression, not mine, Janet said. It was the whole caboodle, the red roses, a picnic in a rowing boat on the river, Wimpy burger and chips."

Eric looked on fascinated.

"Within a month the letters started arriving; she read them out to us at break, declaring unending love and so on. For her sixteenth birthday he took her to London, in a taxi, for a meal at a posh restaurant in the West End. On the way back he said he wanted her to meet his parents."

Flick paused to move Wolfie across into the lane for crossing the bridge.

"I better give you some background on Janet before the next bit. Janet suffered from the over-active knife and fork syndrome, no plate must go un-licked, you've probably come across one of the same type before?"

He nodded.

"Not fat, just bigger than she should be. Before the dance, Mother's ball gown had to undergo side seam surgery in needlework or the zipper wouldn't have a snowball's chance in hell of doing up. Janet was also what you might politely like to call 'easy', she'd left an assortment of bedfellows in her wake, ranging from lads in the sixth form to the window cleaner and the milkman."

Flick turned right and headed for Glasgow.

"Part three... I'm not boring you, am I?"

"Anything but, I can't wait to hear what happens to Dodgy and Janet, I can sort of guess, mind."

"Right, the next bit is obviously second hand but goes something like this. It seems he sent a taxi for her – he lived out in the sticks near Hitchin if memory serves – then she got to meet 'Mater'. She felt she was being measured up. Aunt Mavis as you know goes a bundle on 'breeding' and it felt as if her breeding was being assessed. After tea – and don't laugh, it was cucumber sandwiches with the crusts cut off – his mother left them to pick up Dodgy's father from the station. I can't remember the exact words she told us, but it went along the following lines."

Here she adopted a dated, upper-class Bertie Wooster type voice:

"I hope you like Mater, I would like you to see her as your role model when we're married. I come into my trust fund at twenty-one so you will not be finding yourself wanting for life's little pleasantries. I would like to have intercourse with you now please, I feel it is important that we are sexually compatible and that providing the family with a male heir will not be difficult. If you would just go to the bedroom and remove your clothes, Mater has left you a towel for afterwards should there be any bleeding."

She paused to negotiate a tight bend. Eric began to laugh.

"Oh good grief, really, just like that!"

"Yes, but the next bit's funnier," she said joining in the laughter. "I was hard pushed not to wet myself at the time."

Flick continued to recall the breaktime confession.

"Next, Janet says she looked him straight in the eye then walked into the bedroom. The whole house by the way was decorated like it was the 1940s but this room was back to Victoria's day. She thought, 'what the hell', stripped off and lay on the duck down cover stark naked with her legs open, called out to him and waited. His face was an absolute picture, Eric. She said it was indescribable, she didn't think he'd even seen a picture of a naked girl before, never mind one the flesh. After a lot of bluster and flapping he reckoned he'd entered her, coming about five seconds later. In actual fact he'd managed to – he'd actually managed to, give me a second, I can hardly speak for laughing, I'm sorry – I know what's coming next."

After wiping her eyes she continued.

"He actually managed to stick it between the cheeks of her arse!"

Eric, convulsed with laughter, slid slowly off the passenger seat onto the floor.

"Dodgy's expression turned from smug to horrified when he looked at the towel she was lying on. He made some comment about there ought to be bloodstains. 'You're not a virgin, he screamed, Mater will be horrified'. He went ape and told her to get dressed, so she did. A taxi was waiting at the door by the time she'd dressed;

from the rear window she claims she saw him and his mother; he was showing her the towel."

"Oh Flick, that's bloody amazing, where do these people come from? I take it he'd been instructed to find a nice girl to marry, one with no outside interests or influences, to be groomed to provide a male heir then take over from his mother, I guess. You ready for a coffee, there's a pull in a mile away."

Over a hot drink and the last of the ginger biscuits Eric asked what a theoretical virgin was.

"It's quite simple, love, I broke my hymen horse riding when I was about thirteen or fourteen, so I told him that to confuse him. I confessed to my girlfriends and we all waited. I imagined him trawling through the medical books and scratching his head because he'd never have the nerve to ask another girl. If he'd asked Janet if she was a theoretical virgin it would have gone round the whole school like wildfire." She grinned.

Flick piloted Wolfie to the outskirts of Glasgow.

"You never did finish the story about your ex girlfriend, we were both a bit down on the way back from Portsmouth and the tale ended when we found out about Glastonbury and cheered up."

"That's right, I never have filled in the blanks about Neurotic Nancy." Eric leaned against the passenger door and started. "It began when I was almost seventeen. It's not a funny tale I'm afraid, Nancy was more to be pitied than laughed at; however, there were times when it was too crazy to do anything else other than laugh."

"What is it they say, if you don't laugh you'll cry," she added.

"We met at the bowling alley in Bradford. It was a Saturday afternoon, we were both out with friends and the banter soon started. Over a coffee she seemed interested in me even though at first I wasn't noticing her. She was rather skinny, too skinny if the truth be known, I found out later she suffered from anorexia. She sort of invited me out on a date; we agreed to go to the cinema the next day. I didn't notice at the time but looking back the signs were all there. The anxiety, over-sensitivity, the worry and by far the worst problem were the mood swings. Later on, the realisation she was a control freak dawned on me. The minor stuff I could cope with, the serious was unpredictable and at times in certain situations unbelievable. We found ourselves in bed together about six weeks after that first date. Sex itself was almost impossible, she was never in the same frame of mind twice running. We jogged along for a month or so, she began talking about a wedding, babies and what type of house she wanted soon after Christmas. My friend Gina took me to one side for a chat as she'd been seeing me being worn down for a while. Nancy came into the bar and went green with envy. She made a load of sarcastic comments to Gina along the lines of: what are you talking to my Eric for, is there anything you're telling him I should know about."

"Jealousy, on top of everything else," Flick interjected.

"In the end Gina got up and baited the bull by throwing her arms round my neck and gave me a loud sloppy kiss leaving bright red lipstick smudges all over the place. Nancy stormed out two minutes later, bright red in the face and almost in tears. I tried to follow her but she was taken up in the crowd. There was no contact for almost two weeks. Then, as if nothing had happened, she announced that she'd forgiven me for my affair with 'that Italian woman' and asked if I would drop round to help her choose a wedding dress. I hardly had to remind myself I was only seventeen. I never went round and I never heard from her again."

They changed drivers at Glasgow, Eric slid the seat back, adjusted the door mirror and pulled out into the traffic.

"As you say, a strange tale and somewhat sad." Flick made herself comfortable in the passenger seat, put her feet on the dashboard and peeled an orange. "It sounds a bit like my first encounter, he was the one I mentioned on the way back from Portsmouth as well, the 'all boy and no friend' joker."

"Spill the beans, your Majesty, the stage is all yours."

"Like you, seventeen and a bit naive. He was a year older, and modelled himself on some macho guy out of an action movie. I got taken in and viewed life through rose-tinted glasses for about three months. After three attempts he got the hang of intercourse; his idea of a date would be for us to go and see a film or something then he'd leave me to make my own way home while he went and hung out with his mates. I put up with it a couple of times then the rosy tint wore off and I started seeing another guy." She leaned over from the passenger seat. "Open wide, I'll feed you some orange. He found us in a pub in Letchworth one night and went ballistic. For a moment I was a bit worried he'd give Joe, my date, a black eye or something, but as it turned out Joe just stood up and told him to put his money where his mouth was, clenching his fists at the same time. The effect was amazing. One minute acting like Tarzan on acid then whimpering and chattering like Cheetah on speed."

"I take it the romance ended right there?"

"Yeah, I dated Joe a couple of times but nothing came of it. I don't think either of us wanted it to, looking back now. Joe went into the Navy soon after, we promised to write, keep in touch and all that but it never happened. Last I heard he was in Hong Kong. So, that's me up to date I think."

The rest of the journey was spent talking about the band with Dan and Alan and wondering if the media were waiting in ambush back at the flat.

Hyde Road came into view followed by the sharp turn into the tree-lined avenue they lived on. Reversing Wolfie into the parking space nearest the front door, Eric pulled on the brake and turned the engine off.

"OK, shall we get the project work off first then unpack everything else in the morning?"

"Sounds good, I'll get the door open."

She turned the key in the lock and scooped up the accumulated mail before walking into the kitchen. Eric bought the project files, boxes and the camera in, dropped them on the table and sat down next to a steaming mug of tea.

"Anything in the mail, love?"

"The usual, junk adverts, two bills, free newspapers and this, hand delivered, no stamp."

Eric read the note which asked either Miss Bowden or Mr Marstone to contact the BBC in Manchester if they would care to be interviewed about their involvement with the rescue of Master Peter Simmonds in Scotland. They both wondered how the BBC had found them, but really it wasn't important. Flick made a note of the number and said she'd call the next day, then leafed through one of the free newspapers that often carried money-off coupons at the supermarket. As neither of them had a taste for any of the tins and packets bearing strange names on offer, she gave up and started on the crossword. Eric combed through the New Musical Express, now sporting NME on the masthead, looking for any festivals, concerts or tour dates of their favourite acts.

"We need to confirm with Dan and Alan about the band."

"Yes – I'm stuck on the last one, got any ideas, seven letters, first two 'rh', middle and last is a 'b', the clue is – got it! Rhubarb." She put the paper down. "First prize is a fourteen-night holiday going to the first correct answer out the post bag. We could do with one of the minor prizes though, that washing machine's on the way out." She yawned. "I don't know about you but I'm ready for bed."

Eric pulled himself out of the overstuffed chair and picked the mugs up.

"Me too, I'll tidy up, see you in a minute."

He washed the mugs and put the BBC letter on one side then looked at Flick's completed crossword. After filling in the details he placed it in an envelope and put it on the table as well. After all it's Freepost, no stamp needed, he thought, and a replacement washing machine would be really useful.

University life resumed. During the week they had driven to Leeds and picked up Eric's guitar and rig in the evening. The next weekend Robert and Helen came to the flat and brought Flick's drum kit with them. They stayed on the Saturday night, Eric and Flick sleeping in Wolfie to give them a bed. The first practice sessions took place in Dan's father's garage and seemed to be going in the right direction. The BBC wanted to do an interview in their Manchester studios about the Cairngorms rescue. Sadly, the Cairngorms would feature in the news again in November – tragically five school children and a leader were lost in severe weather conditions.

The BBC interview went well; they met the family from Scotland in considerably better circumstances than last time. Little Peter did not seem to be any the worse for his experience and spent most of the programme fascinated by the lights and cameras. At the end there was another round of hugs, applause from the studio audience then suddenly it was over. The programme would go out at the end of July and they would receive a videotape of it in the post. On the way out the interviewer took them to one side and gave them an envelope.

"We don't film this part, some people get the wrong idea. Mr and Mrs Simmonds wanted to repay you for the hiking gear you lost so in here is a voucher for a well-known outdoor clothing shop which they have organised and paid for. I think you will find it more than covers what you lost. I'll let you go, it was very nice to meet you and thanks for coming in."

By the time the programme aired Jim Morrison of the Doors had joined the 27 Club. The band, now named Escapade, were coming along in leaps and bounds. They had roughly a hundred and twenty songs to go at, over fifty were at a standard they could happily perform in public. Gradually the remainder were chipped away at, when the repertoire expanded to sixty-five they agreed it was time to get some gigs.

The last rehearsal was going to be a free two-hour show at a friend's birthday party. The friend had little spare money, it was a case of bring your own beer and was scheduled for late afternoon on a Sunday in the back garden of the shared rented house she lived in with three other students. Alan had made a false bass drum front and using his artistic skills drawn the band's name across it.

"Fingers crossed, I hope it goes well," he said, twisting it slightly to level the letters.

"It looks great, Alan, let's hope we perform good enough to warrant our name," Dan joked, then added, "it'll be great, first time in public or not, you'll see."

Eric joined them on the small rectangle of crazy paving that was doubling as a stage for the day.

"This sun's hot, we could have done with shorts instead of jeans and I'm losing the waistcoat."

Flick was talking to the birthday girl, the heat wouldn't get to her, she wore the denim cut-offs and tight black boob-tube she normally played in. The pair were making their way towards them.

"Let me introduce you to Alice."

Alice shook hands and thanked them all very much for playing. The music started at six, Dan warmed up on his Fender bass, Eric tuned his Stratocaster and Flick checked the individual positions of her kit.

Alice stepped up to the microphone. "Thank you all for coming to my party – it's show-time, so will everyone make a lot of noise for 'Escapade'."

Alan counted them in and hit the first few notes of 'Gimme Some Lovin', his voice ringing out as Dan and Eric stood together sharing their only other microphone for backing vocals. Flick was knocking out the beat with absolute precision, her pony-tailed hair bouncing to the beat. The applause started as the last notes faded away, quickly Alan jumped into the intro of 'House of the Rising Sun'. By the time they took a break the three guys' shirts were wet with sweat, Flick was still cool and grinning.

"I've got a spare towel back here," she said, reaching under her stool into Kenny who held extra drumsticks and a few spare cables.

In the lengthening shadows Escapade worked their way through the running order noting which songs went down the best. At about eight they ended the last set with 'Bullfrog Blues', an old standard which allowed them to do a little solo each before coming to a nice traditional blues ending.

They held a 'post-mortem' over a beer and a plate of sandwiches with slightly curled up edges. On the whole it had been a lot better than they'd expected, so glasses were raised and clinked together. It had begun to get dark when the conversation turned to what made people enjoy music so much. Dan reckoned it was a sort of universal language, understood by anyone with working ears. Alan added there must be something that strengthens imagery, citing the dramatic chords working behind an action movie scene in a battle sequence.

"Think of the tension building up between the two sides before the first charge, music adds to the interpretation by feeding the audience sounds that match what their eyes are seeing. The old silent films, a fast piano piece accompanying the Keystone Cops car chase, there's millions of examples if you think about it," Eric said,

"I think both theories hold up and then there's music therapy, we all know about Nordoff-Robbins," Dan added. Flick chipped in with how music could help to reduce stress and anxiety; she had recently started practising yoga and found music beneficial to meditation. After the subject was exhausted, they packed their kit and said goodbye to Alice.

"One of Kev's mates said to give you this as he had to go early."

Alice handed Alan an opened envelope with a message scrawled on the back.

"Listen up, guys, it says, 'Loved the show do you want a gig at my place, Friday 18th, Irwell Castle. £10' and a phone number."

"He's running the pub with his parents, the place is a bit run down, he wants to keep it open till they retire," Alice explained.

"Fame, fame and fortune awaits," Dan whooped as he swept Alan off his feet, kissing him on the forehead as he did so.

Flick was deep in thought as Eric drove back to the flat.

"Would I be right in thinking your vibe-o-meter's talking to you?"

She looked across at him placing her head on one side and a thoughtful expression on her face.

"I'm not sure yet, I've picked up on this before but tonight has put all the ingredients back in the pan as it were. Before I didn't know if I'd get a pancake or a Yorkshire pudding, now it seems we may have crêpes instead."

"Sorry, love, you lost me there."

"My FI, you know what that is, senses that our dear mates Dan and Alan are gay."

"Hmm, I must say I haven't picked up on that one but if female intuition's involved, especially yours, I'll keep the eyes peeled."

In the darkness of their bedroom Flick lay in Eric's arm and bit by bit she detailed all the signs and nuances that had flitted across her senses over the previous six months.

"I wonder what they feel like, if it's anything like what I feel for you it must be amazing."

"Indeed, we've been together almost a year now, my feelings aren't showing any signs of dimming or diluting either. You don't take any prisoners, do you, girl?"

Zsa Zsa Gábor answered:

"Précisément, mon chéri, you walked straight into my trap, you never suspected those chocolate digestives were laced with my special secret love potion, did you dar'link."

"And I thought I was suffering from acute Deborah-itus."

"You may well be, my naughty biscuits only last a couple of weeks, a month at most and judging by how you look at me I think your diagnosis is correct, Dr Marstone."

"Well if that's the case we had better be prepared, I'm afraid, Nurse MacPherson, all recorded cases are terminal, I shall have this all my life," answered Doctor Cameron with an accent more Irish than Scottish.

The giggles died down and they lay facing each other talking about and trying to imagine how their friends managed to fit into a society that for the most part didn't understand them and wasn't prepared to learn. Matters were difficult enough at times in certain situations with Dan being black and Alan white. If homosexuality was in the mix as well the word awkward was a total understatement. Eric turned the light off as Flick asked him to pass her medicine over.

"What medicine?" he asked.

"My daily injection of Eric please, I can't live without it now, I'm addicted," she sniggered.

13

O n Monday morning the postman had delivered a large letter which had to be signed for; Dennis the landlord had done the honours. When they returned home from college Flick opened it.

"Eric, listen to this, I've won a prize in a competition, it's that crossword you sent in, and it's a – hang on, there's another envelope – Oh bloody hell, it's the first prize! The holiday, it's seven days in a villa on Crete, wait, first is a seven-day cruise round the Aegean, fourteen days in all."

Eric looked up from the floor where he sat among a pile of parts from the washing machine.

"What a clever trousers you are, show it to me, you hold it, I've got greasy hands."

After reading through the details of the prize and the terms and conditions they thought about the practicalities of when they could go and who they could go with. Suddenly an idea lit up in both minds at once. As nice as the prize was, the major problem concerned who did they ask to make up the numbers. The prize said four persons, all the hotel rooms, cabins, flights and transfers were centred round four.

"Why don't we surprise our parents?" they both exclaimed.

During the week two devious plotters hatched a scheme to unveil the prize. In order for the subterfuge to work it had to be surrounded by a plausible reason why John and Avril along with Robert and Helen should find themselves meeting as if by coincidence. When they appeared at the same location it would of course let the proverbial cat out of the bag. By Friday the barrel of ideas had been scraped so clean the wood was wearing thin. Driving out to the gig on Friday night they ran the concept past Dan and Alan. Their best idea was to use what both sets of parents had in common, this they reckoned was the Royal Air Force and aircraft in general. The next problem was the 'where' aspect, Leeds and Letchworth being about a hundred and sixty miles apart. The road atlas had suggested a few places about halfway between the two, Nottingham, Derby and Newark being the biggest places with main road access.

Kevin, the landlord's son, shook hands and opened the pub's back doors. The next hour was spent setting up, performing a sound check then getting changed. Although totally irrelevant to this part of the story this was the rough starting point of Eddy wearing Flick's bra as earmuffs. 'At least I know where the bloody thing is,' she'd said at the time. The band weren't due on until nine so there was plenty of time to relax with a drink.

It was Alan who struck the first blow into the tough nut they had to crack.

"I saw a news programme on TV last week about Newark. The old RAF base is being converted, or to be more accurate, rebuilt, as an aviation museum. They were looking for volunteers, anyone who could spare some time and had wartime aircraft knowledge, I think the guy said it would take a couple of years but if everything went according to plan it would be one of the largest museums of its kind in Britain."

"That ticks a couple of boxes. I reckon we could sell them on going down to see what it's all about and if we say that both sets of parents are going it might just tip the balance, what do you think, Flick?" Eric thought and spoke out loud simultaneously.

"I can see it working, a bit of a gamble but we've got to expect some danger with the deceit. The last bit is where are we going to lodge them for the night, I'm thinking a Saturday night in Newark isn't going to be cheap."

At this point Alice and her friend Tom walked in and waved. They made room for them at the old round table whilst talking about hotels in Newark, a job for the public library where the shelves held a complete set of telephone directories.

"So who's off to my hometown then?" Alice asked.

Flick recapped the story for her benefit and explained the possibilities garnered so far.

"So you need two double rooms for the night, next Saturday, OK, give me a minute, I need to make a call." Alice grabbed her purse and headed for the payphone at the end of the bar.

Tom said how much he'd enjoyed the music at the party and that everyone had been talking about Escapade all week.

"That Allman Brothers track is superb, and the Rory Gallagher cover was mint," he enthused.

Alice returned from the phone smiling.

"Right that's sorted. Two double rooms, next Saturday. Don't look worried, my parents own a commercial hotel on the London Road, on Friday morning the place is starting to empty as the sales reps and contractors have gone home for the weekend, come Saturday the place is deserted."

"Wow, Alice, that's brilliant, what's it going to cost?" Eric asked.

"Zilch, I told them you guys did my birthday party for free so this is payback time. Dan and Alan are welcome too, anytime at the weekends."

It took a while for it all to sink in.

"It never ceases to amaze me how some people can be so utterly kind and caring whilst others..." Flick let the sentence trail off.

"Would you like to get your bods on the stage please, we have a full house tonight and I think you're going to go down a storm," Kev yelled round the door, trying to drown out the hubbub in the main bar.

The first set was a repeat of the birthday bash. After a high energy version of 'Bullfrog Blues' they announced a ten-minute break. Alan was looking at the handwritten set lists whilst Flick was drying his sweating back; she'd already done Dan and Eric.

"It's going to be a very rock and blues night, guys, let's open part two with Sly Stone and take it through to the end of list six, after that the Stones, the Who and we end on Crossroads, as close to Cream as we can get it. OK?"

Alan pulled on a fresh shirt after blasting deodorant under both armpits. His keyboard picked out 'Dance to the Music' and suddenly it was Woodstock in Manchester. The long version of the Robert Johnson classic 'Crossroads' was the last song. The whole pub stamped their feet and shouted 'more, more, more' for almost five minutes, stopping only when Kev went on stage and said if the band were up for it they would do one more song as it was past licensing hours.

Alan stood centre stage and thanked everyone for coming.

"This is possibly one of the most political songs to come out in the last five years. Listen to the words as well as the music, you know what it's all about, thank you all again, we'll see you soon."

Flick raised her sticks above her head and bought them together to do the count in. 'Street Fighting Man' filled the room, Alan strutted round the stage as if he had Jagger's blood coursing through his veins, Dan pumped out the solid bass riffs that underpinned the whole song, Eric adopted Keith Richards' jangling style and Flick pulled off her best ever performance of Charlie Watts. The only word that described the scene at the end was uproar. The crowd loved it, Escapade took four bows and left the stage. Kev put the lights on and asked everyone to please make their way home.

The night had been one of the busiest in a long time, Kev's father said.

"The posters worked well it seems, you'll be wanting a return match I guess, how about ten weeks away, that's a good gap."

Dan put the date in the book with the other four he had managed to grab.

"Here you are, guys, sign on the dotted line please, Dan."

Dan looked up from the dog eared receipt book and pulled a face at Kev. "I thought the wages was £10, it says here £20."

"We did a swimming pool of beer tonight so this is a little slice of the action; next time we're going to sell an ocean, if so, expect a bucket-full instead of a glass."

"It's how I've always done it," his father chipped in, "pay the good bands top dollar and you get the best out of them every time."

The conversation in the camper on the way back was brief but factual.

"We seem to be doing alright."

"Let's hope it lasts a while."

"Our luck can't hold forever."

"Forever is a long, long time, girl."

In the early hours of Saturday the street outside the flat was quiet. Flick and Eric had almost quite literally crawled into bed and fallen asleep instantly. In that silent street Wolfie's exhaust clicked as the cooling metal slowly contracted. Inside Kenny was probably wishing they'd taken the damp towel and three grubby shirts upstairs with them. Stood inside the van out of sight of the windows was a tall being that appeared to be floating a couple of inches above the carpet. It had to bend slightly in the middle as it was some two feet taller than the roof-line. From its side what would have been a right arm on a human un-melded itself from the main body. The elbow seemed to be in the same place as a human's from a scale point of view, the principal difference was at the spot normally occupied by a wrist. Here a second elbow provided a similar movement to the first, then an equal length of arm gave way to a wrist of sorts. The hand could outperform anything human and boasted two opposing thumbs, the second being next to the little or pinkie finger.

The arm articulated itself to reach the top sheet from a stack of posters Alan had drawn. The word Escapade ran across the top in a similar script to that used by Roger Dean. The centre photograph showed Eric, Dan and Alan standing in a straight line facing the camera with Flick lying horizontally across their six arms at waist height. She had her head resting on her right hand with her elbow in Eric's palm. Dan supported her midriff and Alan held onto the thighs and lower legs. The bottom had been left blank for the venue to ink in the date and other vital stuff concerning the gig. What would have been the ring finger on a human hand traced a line across the poster with a small beam of orange light which emanated from the tip. Kenny, now beginning to give off a pungent odour, glowed violet once again.

The being retracted the arm and sent a rainbow from its head area out of the van roof, through the brick wall and into the bedroom. Here it found Eddy on a shelf above the dressing table. The zipper opened and the rainbow halted a few inches from the slit, the orange portion extended into Eddy and remained there for five minutes or so. Eric stirred in his sleep, turned over and settled down again, placing an arm over Flick's shoulder. The orange light retracted, Eddy zipped himself up and the rainbow moved to Eric. For almost thirty minutes the indigo and blue segments shone over their sleeping bodies, paying particular attention to their heads and hands. In an instant the bedroom returned to almost complete darkness, in Wolfie a low pitch hum moved lower down the bass register until it became inaudible. Kenny found himself alone again. Nobody would have been any the wiser that anything had taken place in those early hours. Not in the flat nor in the van. Unless anyone distinctly remembered that three dirty shirts and a limp moist towel should not have been strewn across the floor of the shower, that is.

O n Sunday evening the tangled web of half-truths was unfolded in the phone box at the corner of the street. Two calls were made, Leeds first then Letchworth. Both phones answered after a couple of rings and both recipients rang the call box back as usual. Two very similar conversations took place, a watertight back story first then once the fish was on the hook some precise instructions issued. Both sets of parents were interested in the well-researched spiel about an air museum and once the double lure of a chance to have a night out with friends was mentioned there was little else to sell.

"That, my darling, went better than I could ever have imagined," Eric commented as he kissed the top of her head.

"I thought my mother was going to say they were doing something else on Saturday at one point; thank goodness she had the wrong week open in her diary."

"Shall we drop in for a beer before we walk back, then we better have a recap on what's happening next weekend."

In the flat Flick had opened up the file of papers the research had produced, looking for the address of the hotel in Newark. She began reading from their notes as Eric listened and checked for inconsistencies.

"First, they all believe they're going to a meeting in Newark to learn about and possibly volunteering for the new air museum. Two, the supposed venue is Alice's parents' hotel. Three, we are hiding Wolfie round the back behind the garage which is, fingers crossed, enough to shield him from anyone in the car park, which by the way will have a few spaces already occupied thanks to: Four,

Jean and Neville; Alice's parents, who have been briefed on the scam and have set out the lounge area to look like a meeting room complete with a flip chart. Neville is ex-RAF himself and thinks it's a 'wizard wheeze' so Alice tells me. Lastly, on Sunday morning we sneak out of Wolfie to appear at breakfast and unload the surprise."

"I can only see one problem. I know we sold them on the idea of attending the meeting and combining it with a chance to catch-up with each other, so why not take advantage of the heavily discounted hotel for the night blah, blah, blah. The only hiccup is going to be how come there aren't any other guests in the hotel – what answer can Neville and Jean give them?"

"It can only be a bluff, sort of like 'you're the first to arrive' or 'the other guests have gone into Newark to visit the castle' would hopefully work."

Eric nodded agreement, showing her his crossed fingers.

After the gig on the following Friday night Eric and Flick camped in the pub car park. Wolfie had a full tank of diesel and a well-charged ancillary battery. Saturday morning arrived, Eric made breakfast and Flick tidied up. Being nearer to Stockport than Manchester would make the journey shorter; also it gave them a chance to drive through the Derbyshire Peak District and take in the scenery as far as Chesterfield. Shortly after eleven, Wolfie was round the back of the hotel nestled between two garages that once held horses instead of cars. Neville had informed them that no one had arrived yet and they could disappear without being spotted. Jean had thought of a few answers to tricky questions and shown them the combination of the lock on the tradesman's door set in the rear boundary wall.

John and Avril arrived first, Robert and Helen followed thirty minutes later. After unpacking, the four decided on a walk into town for a late lunch. They spent the evening in the bar with Neville and Jean talking about the RAF, the bar looking moderately busy thanks to a few locals dropping in. Eric and Flick lost themselves by taking a riverside walk near the castle grounds for the afternoon.

In the evening a music pub with a decent R&B band filled in the rest of the day before strolling back up the London Road. Letting themselves in to the car park shortly after midnight, they ducked into Wolfie and climbed into bed in the dark.

Jean had laid a circular table for six to which Neville sat the four victims and served the usual breakfast. Eric and Flick slipped in quietly and hid behind the room divider. Neville gave the briefest of nods in their direction and started his well-rehearsed speech.

"Ladies and Gentlemen, I have a small announcement to make. The air museum are indeed looking for people to help by volunteering time or knowledge; however, this meeting in our hotel has been dreamed up by two people who love the four of you very much and wanted to find a way of showing it. OK, you can come out now."

Eric and Flick revealed themselves and came over to the table wearing huge grins. Robert leaned back on his chair, dropped his napkin on the table, folded his arms and was the first to speak.

"OK, Deborah Felicity Bowden, spill the beans."

"Well, we had to find a way of getting you all together, we have a surprise for you all," Flick began.

John butted in. "I'm sticking my neck out here but this great weekend with Robert and Helen isn't the half of it, is it?"

"No, it isn't, but before we get beans all over the carpet, we have something to tell you, then, something to give you," she replied.

Helen and Avril looked at each other; Helen spoke first.

"I might have guessed this wasn't what it seemed, a certain daughter once hid my birthday present inside her pet rabbit hutch, to stop me finding it, I guess."

Avril nodded in understanding. "Yes, that sounds familiar, I was told my present a couple of Christmases ago had been hidden tightly sealed in plastic bags suspended in the cistern of the downstairs toilet, would you believe; I know exactly where you're coming from, Helen."

"This is a joint speech, we both feel the same about our respective parents, so here goes," Eric read the first part. "Father, Mother, Mum and Dad, whichever way you say it doesn't matter, the fact is both Flick and I realise that since childhood you have always been there for us, always supported us and steered us towards the values and qualities that really matter. This has now extended into the present where you are still providing us with all the help we could possibly want to realise our dreams, that of becoming a biologist and an engineer. We have sat and talked on many occasions, about how often your help both financially and practically has enabled us to climb that ladder of dreams."

Flick continued from her notes. "We also realise that all the help you have given to us both singularly and together has never had any terms and conditions attached to it, unlike the help some of our friends have received. More or less, that is what we wanted to say to you, and that we are so very grateful we are your son and daughter and are loved so much. For our part we love you too, with all our hearts. That concludes the mushy bit, so here's what we have for you. This would not have happened if my mother had not taught me how to solve cryptic crosswords. So, if you don't like our gift, you can blame her."

Eric went on to explain about the puzzle, and the desire to win the washing machine. As the story unfolded four parents looked at each other and started joking about what they would do with half a washing machine or a stereo system, none of the possible prizes mentioned seemed to be shareable. Eric wound up the tale and left Flick to reach into Kenny and pull out a box which she placed carefully on the table and said:

"The box holds some clues, have a go at guessing; if you get stuck we'll put you out of your misery."

Inside the box were five items: a model of a ship, a small Greek phrase and guide book, a little plastic bucket full of sand and a slip of paper with a crossword clue typed on it. John read the clue out to them:

"Goddess has a sacred cat and potassium inside a city."

The last item was another wooden box with a three-reel combination padlock holding the hinged lid shut. Four brains started working as one, using the breakfast table as mission control. Eric and Flick joined Neville and Jean in the kitchen. They both said how very kind it was to do all this for their parents and also to thank them for the band's performance at Alice's party over bacon sandwiches. After several blind alleys had been gone down and some serious over-thinking had occurred, the puzzlers had a conference over coffee and biscuits as to what they had. The model ship had a number three painted on the bottom and by carefully decanting the sand into a spare sugar bowl a tiny folded piece of paper was found which appeared to be blank. Helen spotted the number eight written in sand on the bottom after checking there wasn't anything else left inside. Created by writing the number using glue, sand had then been sprinkled over it and left to dry. The remaining sand simply filled the bucket to the brim, hiding the clue, the blank slip of paper being a red herring. The cryptic clue wouldn't turn into another number and the phrase book had too many numbers. Avril turned her notes over and found the start on the first of the paper napkins she'd written on.

"It has to be something to do with Greece, sand could be a desert, a beach or be connected to a certain amount of time, as in an hourglass. The ship is an ocean-going transport and I think we explored the old film 'The Sea of Sand', so we're left with one number to find and two items to ponder on."

Helen had been filling napkins on her own.

"I think I've got this clue cracked: keeping with the Greek theme we have 'Goddess', that's Hera, and she held the lion as sacred, then, and this was the hard bit, potassium, it's one of the chemical elements and common in a lot of foods, its symbol is the letter K. Put it together and you get Heraklion, which I think is on Crete, which is Greek."

John picked up the phrase book, turned to the index and found Heraklion.

"Page 7," he said, looking up.

Robert picked up the little box.

"Six possible combinations, which one first?"

The lock slid open when 378 was dialled in, there was five minutes of silence whilst the papers inside were read then digested. Four stunned parents looked at each other in disbelief at first then suddenly Avril said:

"We'll have to go shopping, Helen, I have absolutely nothing to wear on a cruise ship and my beachwear collection is looking a little dated."

Afterwards, when Eric and Flick rejoined them from the kitchen where they had been watching the puzzle unfold, the six of them embraced and most of the immediate questions were answered. After lunch Robert and John insisted Neville took something for the food at least. He flatly refused so a suitable amount was 'planted' in the sand-filled sugar bowl which had the model ship cruising round the bottom bearing the words 'many, many thanks', written on a triangular piece of napkin affixed with a toothpick in the manner of a sail.

In the car going back to Letchworth, Helen said to Robert, "It never tells you about this sort of thing in the parenting books, does it?"

"From what I hear at work, most fathers my age consider themselves lucky to get a card from their daughters on birthdays once they've left home."

In Leeds, Avril said she thought they wouldn't crack the code. "I was going to suggest we took those little brass screws out of the hinges and cheat."

"They thought of that one, love, Eric filled the screw slots with solder; they weren't coming out with a nail file or a butter-knife – I taught him too bloody well."

15

Several birthdays came and went, two wedding anniversaries likewise. A few concerts were attended and a steady stream of gigs kept them occupied. Flick and Eric celebrated their first year together with Dan and Alan at an Indian restaurant.

We now move, fast forward to December, but first we have to take a look at the other secret that began in that hot summer. Eric had a secret, shared only with Eddy. The secret had begun one day in early June. Flick had gone with her university team back to the Scottish Highlands to carry out some other research Eric had only a little knowledge of and Eddy had none at all. Taking advantage of her absence he unlocked the old garage that came with the flat – he used it for his engineering projects – and packed several old sacking bags with various random bulges that gave no clues as to their contents into Wolfie. Twenty minutes later he was moving through the industrial area near the river. The sacks were handed over to a fat man in dirty overalls who emptied them on a large set of scales one sack at a time. No words were spoken, the fat man grunted and scribbled on a dirty notepad, ripping off the top sheet when he'd done before passing it to Eric who nodded and walked towards the door. In the office beyond, an anorexic teenage girl took the sheet and read it carefully before counting out the coins to go with a selection of notes. The money and the fat man's scribbled note were passed back through the small hole in the partition separating her from Eric.

Back home he made his way to their bedroom. Eddy was sitting on a chair facing the window; he appeared to be looking out of the window and smiling.

"Phase one completed," he said half to himself and half to Eddy, who just kept smiling. His hand slid under the T-shirt the bear sometime wore and pulled the zipper down. The money from the girl, now in a small plastic bag, was slipped into the compartment inside Eddy's stomach. Over the rest of summer and autumn Eric continued to visit the fat man and exchange the contents of the sack bags for money, usually when Flick was out shopping, which by degrees Eddy ingested with consummate ease.

In November he had to relieve the bear of £10 worth of assorted change before the ursine equivalent of constipation set in. Notes took up a lot less vital space. The next month saw Eric visit the fat man one last time before the end of the year and another twelve pounds joined the two hundred and seventy-four inside the ever-smiling Eddy.

"Happy Christmas," he said, patting the bear's head, "two hundred and eighty-six quid, just for weighing in scrap metal. Not bad at all, but I better find a new home for this little lot." He emptied the bear then returned him to his usual position.

Christmas 1971 saw two things happen; one was nasty and came from nowhere. Just as Eric was loading Wolfie with everything for a trip to Hertfordshire – Christmas was going to be in Letchworth – Dan and Alan turned up with some appallingly bad news. It turned out their landlord had issued them with a notice to quit their rooms in a month's time. They had to be out by the end of January. Then two days later the notice had been shortened to a week.

"In other words, we're out on Friday," Dan said.

In the kitchen they found out the landlord had decided the two of them were 'unsuitable', the word used by the man serving the notice.

"I see," Flick said thoughtfully, "so they found out something – it can't be a colour thing..."

"Flick, Eric, we ought to have told you earlier what with the band and all that, but we're gay, and in love," Dan revealed.

Eric didn't miss a beat.

"OK, so how do we find you guys a new pad. If Flick's cool with it you can stay here while we're down south."

She nodded.

"I've had an idea already if you want to hear it?"

"Go for it, girl," Alan suggested.

"The guy who has the large flat downstairs is leaving after Christmas. If we get in quick maybe we could move in, all of us, together, there's two big bedrooms and a separate lounge and dining room, plus the toilet isn't in the bathroom. I think if we split the rent it's affordable, and Dennis the landlord doesn't give a monkey's if a tenant's black, white or green with blue spots, as long as the rent's paid he's cool."

"Either way, get yourselves moved in here and if you like the idea we can move on it after the break," Eric suggested, putting the last bag in the van.

Dan and Alan watched Wolfie head off down the road,

"I'm convinced both of them would give us their last penny if they thought we needed it, Alan."

Alan looked at the keys Eric had thrown him. "Happy Christmas, dear friends, Happy Christmas."

The second thing to happen in late December was definitely nice and had come about after the Newark weekend. Once the prize holiday had been booked and the tickets and other paraphernalia had arrived a meeting of the 'Cretan Society' – or as John quipped, the 'Cretin Society' – was held in a hotel near Buxton in the Peak District. Once the holiday details had been cross checked over dinner, John sat back and said he had an idea he wanted to run past them.

"I've been thinking about a certain little car I have sat in the back of the garage I got from the Bradford auctions last March. I've been doing a bit to it here and there and it's almost ready to go. It's a Jeep, a little Wrangler, I was thinking about a small off-road recovery truck at the time and this seemed to fit the bill. The guy's a really rugged little fellow, equally at home on the road as halfway up a mountain and that's where the idea comes in." He paused to take a pull on his beer. "Our two kids are using bikes to get to and from most of the week but if they need to go anywhere else it has to be in the Merc' 407. The idea of the van initially was a project for Eric, it became a festival camper, this year it's been on a few field trips for university work and it's taking a big chunk of their money to run it, granted it's exactly right for them in many ways, saving on hotel bills to think of one use; however, I think we could help out here, see what you think." After another pull of beer he continued, "This Jeep is lightweight, reasonable on fuel and can be easily towed behind the Mercedes, which already has a hitch and the wiring. It's got a removable semi hard top, all terrain tyres and a roar from hell when the pedal's pushed to the floor. All I have left to do is an MOT and fit an 'A' frame then the kids have a tow-able for field trips and a runabout for everyday use."

Robert thinks it's a brilliant idea, he asks John to work out the cost and he will settle up with him. The girls think it's excellent, Avril says she had a drive of it already and it's fantastic fun.

"We can tell them they're having a pet 'toad' for Christmas," giggled Helen amid groans from everyone else.

Christmas Day arrived with Mavis and Sydney knocking on the door around 10am. John and Avril, well versed in the ways and customs of Aunt Mavis, were being polite and feigning interest when she approached them. Robert was looking carefully for anything that would 'get the old engine puffing and blowing'. Flick and her mother were making dinner and Eric was chatting to Sydney, who asked him how the band were doing.

"Pretty good at the moment, Alan reckons we'll be earning enough to pay the rent soon. He's been asked to record some backing tracks for cassette decks. Solo vocalists can sing along to them. Some guy with a studio in Salford, I think."

Mavis didn't like the idea of Sydney talking to Eric so much and demanded he poured her another drink, or to pass her handbag, two of the many other excuses used to divert attention back to herself. Robert appeared at the lounge door announcing that a buffet lunch was on the table and presents could be opened.

In between the slices of pork pie and the odd ham roll the presents from under the tree were handed out by Robert, traditionally his job since Flick was small.

"Last one, is for... Sydney," Robert said, reading the label then getting up off all fours and nodding surreptitiously to John.

After most of the wrapping paper was off and many 'thank yous' and hugs exchanged, Helen asked Flick to go and stand next to Eric. Avril came up behind them, as did Helen with a blindfold,

"One extra present left to open, it's yours from the four of us," Robert announced. "No peeping allowed, the ladies will guide you to it."

Slowly the two mothers led their children up to the patio doors; John was ready outside with his camera beside the bushes. Robert reached through and pulled the curtains back before opening the doors. Helen and Avril led them into the garden, stopping just where the grass started. Robert got out of the way to give John a clear shot.

"You can take the blindfolds off now," he said.

Together Eric and Flick stared wide eyed and open mouthed at a very shiny Jeep painted to match Wolfie. They remained stood still staring, hardly able to take it in until Flick saw the card on the door handle.

"To our incredible kids, this is to help you with the work ahead in the coming year and beyond. It doesn't go very fast, but it can go anywhere. Happy Christmas, and all our love," she read.

Eric finally found his voice. "This is fantastic, only last week we were thinking how brilliant something like this would help and now..." The sentence trailed off as he ran out of words.

Flick managed to say, "Thank you, all of you, it's just so, so perfect," whilst hugging her father, followed by Helen then Avril and finally she stood opposite John. "Don't think you're going to get away with just a hug, John Marstone, you must have put in a million hours of work to make this happen."

She put her arms around his neck, lifted her legs and wrapped them round his waist. By lowering her face to meet his she planted a large noisy kiss on his mouth, lasting for about five seconds, enough time to allow the volume to reach the maximum setting. She leaned back against her arms and looked him straight in the eye.

"Thank you, we're going to have a lot of fun with it," she said.

Robert had wandered over. "Sorry, John, I should have warned you, when Flick gives you one of her 'specials' you stay kissed."

Over by the kitchen door Mavis looked on, shaking her head. The afternoon was spent carrying out a full investigation of the little Jeep. After two trips round Letchworth, the first to allow John to explain the complexities of the gearbox and transfer case system, then a jaunt down a country lane to display the off-road capabilities, the second saw Eric and Flick behind the wheel to familiarise themselves with the handling. Back at the house Flick proposed a toast:

"To Jeepy Wranglarious; that's Latin for 'toad', honest, it is; may the adventures never end."

"Indeed, may they never end," echoed Avril and Helen.

The rest of Christmas passed normally, perhaps a little too much food and drink, but generally even Mavis seemed to have 'come off the boil' as Avril said to Helen.

"The go-as-you-please might turn the gas up, mind you," she replied with a knowing wink at the end.

After dinner the furniture was rolled back as usual and Mavis looked agitated already. This year had a theme – all the turns had to be from the thirty years from the 1920s through to the 1950s. Helen began with some jazz piano pieces that started in the 1940s and ended in 1950. Avril did an excellent imitation of Joyce Grenfell's monologue, 'Nursery School', Eric played some Django Reinhardt on his acoustic guitar, John and Robert did a 'Flanagan and Allen' routine, which left Sydney, Mavis and Flick.

Sydney and Flick had been practising a little routine for the evening's fun and games. Flick intended to dress as a ventriloquist's dummy in the 'Alice in Wonderland' style with a pinafore dress, white socks and pink shoes. Mascara would allow her to draw the 'wooden joints' on her knees and elbows, the 'jaw lines' were in lipstick. Mavis decided to visit the bathroom while Flick changed, John held the wicker hamper open for her to climb into by the kitchen door. Robert helped carry it into the lounge where Eric had placed a chair. Sydney introduced himself and asked them if they wanted to meet Alice.

To pantomime cries of, "Yes please, Uncle Sydney", he opened the lid and slid his arms round Flick's 'limp' waist, sat down on the chair, then pulled her into a sitting position on his knee. Flick kept the lifeless limp pose until he placed his hand on her back, at which point she sat upright with her legs dangling from the knee down. He informed the audience they had been to the greengrocer's, but some things had vanished from the hamper on the way home and Alice was going to look for them. After several vegetable jokes, along the lines of 'where have you bean' and 'I could do with a pea', they moved on to double entendres involving the popping of cherries and the squeezing of lemons.

With tears rolling down her face, Avril nodded in Mavis's direction and whispered to Helen, "Gas Mark 9 and rising."

Helen nodded as she couldn't speak for laughing.

Back at the hamper Sydney said, "I can see you found the two pineapples, Alice."

Flick responded by looking down the front of her dress then wrinkled her nose up and placed her teeth over her bottom lip before saying silently and in sync with Sydney's spoken voice, "An I think I found the cucumber too," as a wide smile slid across her face.

The pair got up and took a bow. When the hubbub died down Mavis had left the room.

Midnight arrived, Auld Lang Syne was sung and 'absent friends' were toasted. With glass in hand Robert addressed the room.

"Please top your drinks up, I have one other toast. Although I have been elected to speak, the sentiments include Helen, John and Avril. Over the years we watch our children grow, we have expectations for them, as time passes these expectations change as they mature and realise what they are capable of. They say pride comes before a fall; in this case we're prepared to risk it. Nothing in those years has ever matched the pride we felt watching on television our two kids telling their story about the onerous rescue of a small child in the Scottish mountains. The toast is to Eric and, just this once, sweetheart, Deborah."

"Here, here," said Sydney.

The light went out, Flick managed to get mascara on the top sheet, Eric's leg and the pillowcase. Mavis was snoring and an owl sat on Jeepy's roof looking, but not understanding why, a small brown teddy bear and a larger one with tangled straps round the back were effortlessly gliding between the big metal box and the smaller metal box. There was also the problem of this beam of violet light, dancing between the two; it made the mouse it had its eye on a totally unacceptable colour, mice were sludge grey in its book, and no matter which way it swivelled its neck the low pitched humming noise invaded its head.

And so ended 1971. In many ways it had been a full and busy year with out of the ordinary things happening to ordinary people. The visitors were continuing to amass information, one group noted the Apollo 14 and 15 space flights, the Mariner 9 vehicle that had successfully reached orbit around the red planet and Mars 3 which actually managed to land on the surface. A second group were concerned about the race riots in New Jersey and similar events across the world. They also took an interest in the rise to power of Idi Amin and continued to record the political wrangling and terrorist activity alongside the skirmishes and power struggles.

Dan and Alan had spoken to Dennis the landlord after moving into the flat and worked out a deal for the larger ground floor apartment. By the first week of January everyone had settled in. Later that month the college issued the list of field projects for the year. Flick had hoped that Portugal was on the list and it was, the area near the south-west corner of the Algarve was home to some rare breeds and species. As she explained to him:

"North of Sagres is a National Park where roughly 50 plant species that are only found in Portugal, about a dozen of which don't grow anywhere else, can be found. Also I think it's home to over 200 species of bird, wild cats, otters, foxes, oh, and the last remaining ospreys in Portugal."

"I remember you mentioned it before," Eric said as he took her empty mug.

"I would dearly love to go but it's beyond us. I've calculated the cost, it's too many miles therefore too much money, sadly, even if we include all the earnings from our gigs," she said, looking a little disappointed.

"I think there's a few quid in Eddy, have you taken that into your calculations? We had money off Mavis and Sydney, is that included?"

She looked in the little note book she used to keep track of their funds.

"Here it is, I banked the cheque on the 29th. I don't know about Eddy, mind, it's not going to be that much though."

He reached up and passed the bear over to her before announcing he was going to put the kettle on and headed for the kitchen.

She opened Eddy's zipper where she found their passports tucked against a small cardboard box wedged inside with not much room to spare. Removing the passports first allowed the box to be manipulated so it just squeezed through the open slot. She found it was tied with a piece of ribbon attached to which was a small tag. Written on the tag was the word 'INGUZ' with two capital letter 'X's, drawn one on top of the other, below it. On the bottom line was, 'Where there's a will there's a way'. She pulled the loose end of the ribbon and removed the lid. On top was a paperclip holding some receipts, below that was an old folding wallet containing £200 worth of travellers' cheques and £90 in escudo notes. On the bottom was a Michelin map of Portugal and a student discount voucher for the cross-channel ferry. For the first time in her life she was truly speechless, she just looked at the contents of Eddy's secret compartment feeling slightly stunned.

After reading the tag for the second time, realising it was actually folded in half, she opened it and found the words, 'I love you to the moon and back, and to the end of time – E'. Walking slowly into the kitchen, she wordlessly took the two mugs of tea from his hands, put her arms round his waist and pulled him to her.

"Eric, you're bloody amazing, I'm so happy I found you." Wiping away a tear she kissed him. "I don't know how you manage to do things like this but I'm oh so glad you do. I can't tell you how much I love you – I haven't the words, I'm overwhelmed." A few more tears of happiness ran down her cheeks. She gave a little sniff and a laugh. "Bet I've got panda eyes now."

He kissed her and nodded.

By April 1972 Escapade had a full book of gigs, so the bar work was given up, which allowed more time in the weekday evenings to tackle the increased workload their studies demanded. Most evenings were spent communally in the dining room or lounge,

Dan and Alan entrenched in law books, Flick waded knee-deep into plant and animal structure and function, and Eric, who had decided to focus his studies on the design and building of new technology machines, was tackling robotics. The trip to Portugal would be taking place at the end of July, Wolfie was given a service in Leeds and the ferry crossings were booked from Dover.

On Wednesday 26th July Eric and Flick were stood arm in arm outside on the upper passenger deck of the 8am ferry to Calais looking back at the white cliffs just visible in the morning mist. Five decks below, Wolfie and Jeepy were in Lane 3 and therefore among the first vehicles allowed up the exit ramp in ninety minutes' time. They wandered slowly across France, choosing to avoid Paris by taking the road to Rouen then on to Le Mans, Tours and Bordeaux. They crossed the Spanish border and headed towards Salamanca then at Badajoz the border with Portugal was in sight. The next morning they went shopping to stock up the fridge and replenish their dry goods. Fruit was cheap and looked good, so they treated themselves to a couple of pounds of grapes; some cherries and olives worked their way into the basket as well. Eddy had the change put back in his little drawstring bag and gave up his hold once more on their passports. Kenny was keeping the camera and rolls of film safe, and unbeknown to Eric, providing a hiding place for a couple of birthday presents from home.

The camp site was near a small town and not too far from the coast. They had opted for a place with an electric hook up as it would keep Wolfie's fridge running and continually top up the ancillary battery. The low wattage electric kettle meant the propane gas tank could be used solely for the oven and rings. Now they had Jeepy to go round the sites in, the fuel bill would drop as well. Looking at the map, Flick reckoned Wolfie would not have made some of the access roads, he was far too wide. In the evening Eric had a go at making paella; all things considered it worked out reasonably well but the frying pan took a lot of scrubbing afterwards. The campsite manager, who turned out to be the owner, came across with an invitation to a BBQ, held at the Rancho, which doubled as his house, the campsite office and a small taverna with a cafe during the day and a bar at the weekends.

"Says the food starts at seven, the bar likewise and the local band will be onstage at nine." Eric passed the leaflet over.

"That's good for 500 escudo, we can get tickets tomorrow." Flick put the leaflet on the dashboard as a reminder.

"I'm ready to crash out, how about you?"

He nodded, yawned and turned the light out. They lay side by side listening to something small and probably furry scurry across the roof, highly likely a squirrel – the cork oaks were alive with them. A dog barked in the distance but they didn't hear it.

The next day Jeepy took them through the National Park on dirt tracks to the various points indicated by the notes from the university. They were sharing the track, a Citroen with French plates and from the image in the mirror it looked like a young couple who followed them down to a lake near a ranger station. Eric noticed later they weren't following anymore but paid no notice. It was only on the way back they found the Citroen at a crossroads on the trail with what turned out to be a broken clutch plate. Flick spoke enough French and the petite blonde girl enough English to bridge the language barrier, whilst the two men rigged a rope for towing the stranded Citroen back to a garage. Simon steered the car whilst Nicole jumped in the Jeep. Thankfully the local repair shop had the right part on the shelf and promised them it would be ready in the morning. Flick asked Nicole where they were staying – it wasn't far so they took them back to their hotel. On arrival, Simon, who had been talking to Nicole, asked them to dinner as their guests in the restaurant on the opposite side of the road. Over a pleasant meal enough information changed hands to ascertain they were on honeymoon, they were from Lyon and had an apartment in the city.

After another night of distant dogs barking and assorted small animals practising tap dancing on Wolfie's roof, the sun came up illuminating Kenny through a gap in the curtains.

Flick called out from the bedroom, "Throw my bra and shirt over, will you."

Eric left the bacon to its own devices and found the shirt hanging on a doorknob. The bra was a bit harder to find – it was eventually located balanced on Eddy's head, he was wearing it as earmuffs; Eric had forgotten.

The first job was to pick up their new French friends and drop them at the garage where they were informed the car was fixed and ready to go. They watched it disappear down the road on the homeward trip to Lyon.

"They appear to be happy, but..." Eric said thoughtfully as Flick waved.

"I'm not so sure either, my FI's saying something isn't right, but we'll never know. We've got their address so if a postcard turns up one day we might find out."

"True, I gave them ours as well, so let's see what happens, I think though it will be like most of these chance meetings, nothing will come of it. Let's get going to site 33, end of the road turn right."

That evening they decided to have a walk down into the town and find a little bar for a couple of beers.

"It's your birthday tomorrow, Eric, so I can now get these out of Kenny and give them to you; no peeping or squeezing."

The two presents from home were placed on the front table. Eric was quite amazed she'd managed to smuggle them over without his knowledge.

"I'm just going to get washed and changed, ten minutes, no more," she said, hooking Kenny over the wardrobe door. She asked him from the bedroom what he'd like as a birthday gift from her.

"Just to be with you, to see your face, smiling, every day," he replied cheekily.

She put the finishing touches to her lipstick, checked her hair in the mirror and walked through to the front. Eric just stopped in his tracks and stared. Before him was the most beautiful woman he had ever seen. The sparkling eyes, shining hair, and scintillating smile held him in a spell. Flick had brought with her a dress that managed to show everything about her as a woman with a radiance that he would never forget. The long lissom legs, one peeping through the side slit, the large gently rising breasts with just the right amount on show to fire the imagination, the slender neck with a black satin choker at the throat, the perfectly flat stomach and slim waist all came together in one moment.

"Smoke and mirrors," she said with a wink as she saw his face.

Walking into Odeceixe, the town near the camp ground, she felt she had to stop him drifting away.

"I'm floating on air, love, you look absolutely stunning, so very, very beautiful, I'm such a lucky guy," he claimed with a huge smile.

They found a bodega that served food, and here they celebrated Eric's 20th year on the planet. Back in Wolfie, Flick put the change from their meal back into Eddy before turning to him and asking if he would like to open his present now or in the morning.

"I'll just put this here for a moment." She lifted the cassette player down from the shelf, placing it on the table.

"I didn't expect a present from you, what is it?"

"Me," she answered as the dress slid off her shoulders onto the floor. "I couldn't wrap it any better, it's not the sort of outfit you can wear anything underneath."

She pressed play on the cassette recorder. 'The Witch's Promise' filled Wolfie as she danced naked for him, up close and very personal to the rhythm of Ian Anderson's flute. The dance ended abruptly after the third chorus, as Eric couldn't take anymore, he pulled her tight against his chest.

"You're bloody incredible, you know that, don't you?"

"I do it to please you, I couldn't do it without your appreciation though, the way you look at me and make me feel so loved and wanted. Also, it's partly my way of saying thank you for this amazing trip, you're so good and kind to me."

He took her in his arms and placed her gently on the bed, spreading her long red hair across the pillow then lying down beside her.

"It's way after midnight, you can play with your present now if you want," she giggled, wriggling out from under his arms and climbing on top of his thighs. "I'm driving, so lay back and enjoy the ride."

About ten minutes later a loud, erotic, deep-throated howl that gave the local dogs a run for their money echoed through the trees and across the valley – Eric hadn't bothered putting his hand over her mouth.

The next day was the last of the trails in the National Park, according to the itinerary, also as it was Saturday they had the BBQ to look forward to. Most of the day was spent keeping to the back roads and investigating as far east as Silves, putting the last day in the park off until Monday when the roads would be quieter. They could smell the BBQ when Jeepy pulled into the space alongside Wolfie. Making their way over to the Rancho and the mouth-watering smell, Eric sorted out a couple of large cold beers and Flick exchanged the tickets for a huge plate of steaks, chops, chicken, burgers and sausages.

"There's enough here to feed the five thousand, you think I'm dying of starvation, girl?"

"I promised your mother I would keep your strength up," a mischievous smirk appearing at the same time as the reply.

Several of the campers were undoubtedly friends or family enjoying a holiday together; they invited Flick and Eric over to the large table they'd commandeered, and introduced themselves. One of the women said Flick reminded her of a girl she'd seen on 'the telly' last year:

"About that wee bairn lost in the woods, ye ken."

Flick shrugged and made light of it. Thankfully the rest of the group were happy to let it go so the party started gathering speed as more campers strolled into the Rancho.

Meanwhile back in Wolfie, Eddy and Kenny were having what humans would call a serious talk. They had both heard odd noises too close to Wolfie for comfort. At first they put it down to a demented squirrel trying to bury nuts under the van. They didn't like it but agreed to wait and see what happened next. The interconnecting orange beam linking them dimmed. Outside, Miguel Santos, a thirty-three year old petty thief, came out from under Wolfie empty handed. His search of the underside of the camper had failed to find any secret hiding places where tourists often stashed their valuables. He moved to the next camper. Miguel worked to a system. Saturday nights were best – all the tourists were at the Rancho having fun; secondly, he took the line of least resistance. Experience had taught him about how smart these rich tourists thought they were by hiding money and travellers' cheques, even jewellery sometimes, in phoney water tanks, pretend electrical junction boxes and even stuffed behind the rear bumper in a magnetic steel box. If this failed to work he increased the risk level and actually started trying windows and doors, forcing them if he felt there was something worth having. This method had paid dividends, the biggest one being that in most cases he was twenty kilometres away when the first victim phoned the police and he had friends who could give him an alibi.

An announcement was made to the party-goers by the band's vocalist that their friend's car was trapped in a long line of traffic following an accident in a nearby town. The bass player and vocalist had arrived earlier, but the phone call from their stranded friends confirmed tonight's gig was a non-starter. Eric was already at the bar when Flick came over.

"That's a blow, I was quite looking forward to them; do you think we can do anything to help out?"

Eric went over and asked the vocalist if a drummer and a guitarist would be enough to get something going until their friends arrived. The band were short of a keyboard player, a drummer and a trumpet player. The vocalist covered the guitar work. After reading their set list and scratching about fifteen songs, they agreed to give it a shot.

The line-up was more rock than salsa but as Sal the vocalist said:

"Who's a-gonna notice after three more beers?"

Miguel was toying with the problem of spending another hour under several more campers without finding a single note. Sitting on a rock he decided to keep going as the music hadn't started and there were still a few people making their way over to the Rancho. He reasoned it would be best to stay out of sight; keep to the system, he told himself.

Flick collected her hair into a ponytail, undid the bottom buttons of her shirt, gathered the spare material and tied it under her bust to give her midriff the air it would need. Eric rolled his sleeves up and found a pick in his jeans pocket. It took a few minutes to adjust the drum kit to her liking and Eric needed a few seconds to change the guitar strap length.

"You two OK?" Sal asked then took the microphone, explained what was happening then introduced the three other band members.

"On bass guitar Rodrigo Silva, on lead guitar Eric Marstone, in goal on the drums Flick Bowden, I'm Sal Ferreira, tonight we're called 'Here Goes Nothing', one-two-a-one-two-three-four."

Eric knocked out the chords to 'I Hear you Knocking' and the evening was underway. Just over an hour later Sal ended the amended set list with 'Maggie May' which the audience joined in with. The applause was appreciated and Sal thanked them profusely.

"Thank you all very much, as we said at the beginning, we have now played every song we all know, so it's time to say goodnight."

A German voice from a table near the stage stood up and asked to use the mike.

"I think you have performed extremely well all things prevailing. May I ask if you would consider please playing more songs, some that are a bit strange to you. I am trying to say, are you prepared to improvise, I think the words in English are 'a jam session' – a rocky jam session would be excellent."

A round of nods answered his question. Eric and Flick together launched into 'All Right Now', Rodrigo jumped in and Sal came through right on cue. Five minutes later 'Brown Sugar' drifted across the road calling in at a local bar. Not long after 'Shapes of Things' along with 'Tumblin' Dice' and 'Get Back' popped in to see what was happening. Most of the drinkers had started the exodus to the Rancho; suddenly the bar keepers were a lot busier.

Miguel was not a happy man. The thought now crossed his mind that he would have to start trying doors. He stubbed out his cigarette and made a start. Eddy and Kenny were listening. The orange glow was changing colour, moving into the red end of the visible spectrum. It was just a matter of waiting, they agreed, about half an hour at most. Kenny sent out a small green ray which focused on the lever that locked the sliding door. Slowly it moved from left to right with a faint click indicating the door was now unlocked. Eddy sat back wondering how to play the next part. While he thought, the zipper opened and a yellow glow filled the inside cavity illuminating a roll of notes held in an elastic band. He looked round the camper for anything that might help.

The last time he had had to do something like this was when he arrived in a small child's bedroom. He recalled looking round her room for information and inspiration. The picture books were read, the toy box rummaged through and the girl herself observed. He had no memories of this room or the little girl as he'd only just arrived. After working through the possible forms he could take, the solution presented itself in one of the picture books. It had to be a shape that wouldn't frighten the child, ideally something she felt safe and happy with. His duties were to observe her and offer protection if needed and was practical. So, by deducing the girl must be completely happy with her surroundings, or she wouldn't be asleep, and the shelf had three teddy bears, two dolls and a monkey that banged a drum on it, he copied what he saw and adapted it to fit the desired size he needed to be. This is how a zipper-fronted teddy bear arrived on the shelf. As a finishing touch, he opened a drawer in the dressing table and inserted a nightdress inside the cavity. The following morning the child woke and tried with reasonable success to dress herself. She spotted him on the shelf and by standing on the bed reached him down. Ten minutes later he was named 'Eddy' and sporting freshly brushed fur after being the recipient of several hugs and kisses.

This time the opposite effect was needed. Eddy was not allowed to dispense violence but protection was in the job description. The methodology was the same: he needed to morph into something that would stop what he and Kenny were now certain was going to happen very soon. Searching round the van again he looked on the table by the side of the bed. An orange and a banana, one of the girl's chiffon hair ties and a few black grapes lay in a bowl. On the ceiling was a large spider with very long hairy legs, the bed held a book of artworks by Escher and a peacock feather. The only other things were a bottle of shampoo and a pair of nail scissors sat on the same shelf as him. The next thing to do was replay the recent memories he'd recorded; they might be useful. Viewed at a thousand times faster than reality, Eddy soon had the whole day's events to go at.

Back at the Rancho the place was filling up and hotting up at the same time. The audience had taken to asking for particular songs, a lot of which they were able to manage. The time slipped past and the last song was announced. The crowd, now mainly locals, went wild when Eric began the opening of 'Crossroads' – this was a song Rodrigo knew but they had discounted as being a shade too bluesy for the audience. The guitar solo went down a storm then Flick hammered the ending into submission. After the last few glasses were collected, the barman brought a tray of beers over for them. Four glasses chinked.

"Hail hail rock and roll," they chorused.

Eddy watched with interest and silently communicated with Kenny. He saw a light coming closer with a figure behind it in the shadows. For a second he pondered on the next action he was going to take. He heard Eric's guitar in the middle of a song, then Flick's drumming confirmed what he thought and answered the question he was trying to solve. The song was 'Crossroads', it had something to do with a character called The Devil, now what did a Devil look like, the name was familiar, he had heard it this morning. Referring to the morning's memories he soon found what he was looking for. The girl was lying on the bed with the man on top of her, straddling her legs, he seemed to be using a large bird's feather to stroke her skin round a small hole in the middle of her torso. She was laughing and trying, but not too hard, to wriggle away from him. He heard her say, 'You're a devil, Eric Marstone, a bloody devil,' amid the giggles. The man stopped and after putting the feather down slowly lifted himself off her before opening her legs. A prong projecting from the lower end of his body made its way towards the girl then disappeared inside a hole between her legs. Eddy had seen this event many times in the past, but this was the only time it had the word 'Devil' attached to it.

Miguel tried the door of the blue Mercedes; it had a colour co-ordinated Jeep parked next to it – they must have a load of money to afford this rig, he assumed. Perhaps if he'd had a little more knowledge of the English vehicle registration system he might have noticed the vehicles were a lot older than the electric blue paint suggested. He placed a gloved hand on the sliding door; it yielded under his touch. Climbing into the lounge area he quickly flashed a small torch around the inside of the van. On the second sweep he spotted Eddy with his zipper down. The torch shone inside the opening. Miguel's fingers felt itchy, he reached in to grab the roll of notes but stopped dead before his hand had hardly moved.

Behind the money something was moving; it was luminous pink, pulsating, and covered in red and blue veins. He watched transfixed as the thing began to slither its way snakelike towards the fur-lined opening. It was halfway out of the teddy bear now, growing at an alarming rate, dripping slime from two huge pointed razor-sharp fangs which had materialised from the bottom of what looked like a deformed turtle's head. The jaws were opening slowly until he reckoned they were wide enough to swallow him whole. He began to shake and tremble, he wanted to turn and run. Ten or twelve slime-covered spider-like legs unfurled from the dripping body, two bat-like wings opened out of the back, beating the air. The thing had now grown to the point where the turtle head would have hit the roof of the van had it not stooped forwards towards him. The remains of the teddy bear was nothing more than a tiny square of brown fur. As his petrified eyes watched, the creature sucked the sodden hair into one of several quivering lipless mouths. This was impossible, the insides couldn't eat the outsides, that was insane.

The black wings flapped slowly and silently as Miguel became transfixed to the spot, mesmerised by vacuous, lidless, watery, empty eyes, all totally beyond his understanding. The spider legs were moving towards him inch by inch, he reached for his rosary and began to recite the prayers he was taught as a child while fingering the beads. The creature's eyes locked on his own and held them just as securely as if they were in a vice. The fang-filled slavering mouth was inches from his; for some incredible reason his mind managed to find the time to inform him that the thick drool spilling from the lower jaws smelt like shampoo. A manic laugh escaped from his quivering lips.

The creature issued a silent invitation for Miguel to look down, he did and almost passed out. From between the spider legs a yellow banana shaped object was growing, he backed away until he reached the sliding door that Kenny had thoughtfully closed. With sweat streaming down his face and a strangled scream frozen in his throat, he watched as the banana grew to about three feet long, covered in black ovoid blisters and starting to reach for his groin. From the end what could only be called a glans had formed, resembling an impaled rotten orange, with the juice dribbling from the slit.

Almost wild with terror Miguel clamped his eyes shut, opened his mouth but still nothing came out. He could feel the creature's hot breath on his face. Suddenly he heard a female voice, 'You're a devil, a devil, a devil', it echoed away then light laughter filled the van's interior. He cautiously opened his eyes and found himself looking at a stunning, completely naked girl with long red hair, holding an elegant bird's feather. The pink pulsating demon from hell had vanished. He began to relax slightly as she appeared to be smiling at him. He took in the large full breasts with erect nipples and the flat stomach, then instinct demanded he looked at her crotch. This time the scream did come out. Roughly where her Mons Pubis should have been, the grotesque yellow penis sat waving at him, a pair of reptilian arms with long fingered hands were shooting out of the slit in the rancid orange tip making straight for his throat. It was the final chapter of his own personal horror movie.

He turned and ran, over the fields and into the woods, then kept running until his legs could carry him no further. He dropped to the dirt, whimpering and shivering. The torch shone into the sky, held there by a hand that could not let go, rather like his mind was incapable of letting go of the images he'd just witnessed. In the morning light a dog walker found him on the side of the track. The torch had stopped shining a couple of hours ago; the battery was almost dead, rather like his brain.

Miguel Santos was sent to a mental asylum where he spent the rest of his life. Several specialists examined his case notes and visited him. No one could fully understand why the only words he seemed capable of saying with enough clarity to be understood were 'teddy bear'. More perplexing was his reaction when the doctors gave him the bear they thought he was asking for. Every time a smiling little furry brown bear was taken out of its bag his bowels liquefied and urine flowed like a breached dam. Further observations revealed the same acute reaction occurred if he saw a banana, grapes and an orange together in his fruit bowl.

Once one of the male porters carelessly left a soft porn magazine in the patients' toilets open at a page showing Roz, a nineteen year old dental assistant, who apart from a black chiffon hair band was totally naked, showing her large breasts to full advantage. The photographer had also fanned out her long red hair over the bed and placed a peacock feather on the pillow next to her. Three male nurses were needed to restrain him. From that point no female staff were allowed to work in his room.

Eddy had resumed his usual shape and consistency whilst Kenny had dealt with closing the sliding door and relocking it. He also rearranged the banana, the orange and grapes in the bowl and wiped a trace of shampoo off the scissors. Eddy hadn't tidied up too well and Kenny was a stickler for details. The spider had climbed up out of the air vent and the black hair band along with the Escher book were returned to their rightful places.

Eric and Flick arrived back from the Rancho and flopped onto the captain's chairs.

"Well that was a night, love, I really enjoyed it," Eric said, locking the door.

"Yeah, count me in, a great night."

Flick undressed and climbed into bed, Eric made a last check round the van and joined her. Her hand made its way slowly along his thigh then dropped between his legs.

"You're a devil, Deborah Bowden, a wanton devil," he said to two cheeky brown eyes twinkling at him over the top of the sheet.

With the project assignments completed there were four days left to spend in Portugal before the homeward journey commenced. The entire campsite was completely unaware of the covert nocturnal exploits of the unlucky Miguel. Flick drove the Jeep down the coast toward Lagos where they became tourists for the day. Their second day was spent in the mountains around Monchique and the next was a visit to the Lighthouse of São Vicente.

Feeling the need to stretch their legs Jeepy was left on the roadside whilst they struck out north along the cliff top tracing one of the many off-road trails used by the farmers. About six miles out they stopped at a particular spectacular viewpoint to have a drink. Flick repacked the rucksack and Eric threw it across one shoulder. The return leg was tackled hand in hand over the sandy grasslands. They walked along the cliff top in silence, looking at the wheeling birds and hearing the sounds of their calls mixed in with the breeze. Suddenly Flick stopped and shivered, just the once, from head to foot.

"Oh, that was weird, you know that saying 'someone's walked over my grave', well it was like that but, but, like it's trying to tell me something. Like when my vibes start demanding attention, but stronger, a hell of a lot stronger."

She continued to stand still, looking down at the sea lapping against the rocks below. Eric held her hands and looked straight at her bowed head as if he could read her mind through the portal.

"You're shaking, tell me what you're feeling."

"I sense danger, soon, right here, exactly when I don't know, but soon, Eric, very soon."

They looked around them; the cliff top was deserted apart from the birds, no other living thing could be seen. She calmed herself and the walk continued, the lighthouse slowly getter larger with each step. The noise of the motorbike began as a faint buzz then rapidly increased in volume as it drew nearer. A small red and white off-road machine appeared to fly over a dune, the engine screaming as the rider failed to adjust the revs. The bike hit the sandy dirt, skidding round a clump of bushes before shooting forward towards the edge of the cliff. At the last moment the rider tried to pull the bike round in a tight turn but shockingly failed. They watched in horror as it went over the edge.

Running towards the rim, fearing the worst, they immediately saw the remains of the trail bike embedded in the sand below. Flick saw the young rider first, hanging by the straps of his dungarees on an old root poking out of the cliff face. He looked unconscious, not responding to their cries.

"Not again, Eric, once was enough; hold my arm, I can almost reach him. Damn it, let's try it another way," she said.

She lay on the grass, arms outstretched whilst Eric held her ankles firmly. When her hands managed to reach the denim straps her knees were just about at the edge.

"Got him, pull, Eric."

He needed no second telling and began backing away from the stony brink. As the rider became unhooked from the root he found the increase in weight almost too much to hold when the full realisation of the predicament they were in came home. Determination took over with rising anger and frustration coming along to help. Taking a deep breath, he summoned every last ounce of strength he had in his arms, dug his heels into the dirt and pulled like never before. Suddenly the load became lighter, Flick was mostly on the grass and was wriggling her way backwards trying to help, another pull and the unconscious rider was on the cliff top as well. Flick sat up, getting her breath back.

"The lighthouse must be the nearest place to get help, the guide book said there's a cafe and gift shop."

Eric pulled his shirt off and wiped his face.

"You stay with him, I'll start running, it's two miles tops, hold onto the sack." He blew her a kiss and started out at a faster pace than normal.

Fifteen minutes later he jumped a small dip and sprinted for the lighthouse. Inside the cafe a waitress spoke good enough English to work out the seriousness of the situation and rang the emergency services. Fifteen minutes later a helicopter clattered overhead and a police Land Rover pulled into the service yard. Using the waitress as an interpreter he outlined the story leaving out the bit about Flick's 'vibes'.

Back on the cliffs Flick had begun to worry about the young rider. She estimated he was a well-built eleven or twelve year old and had a large gash down the right side of his face. One eye was starting to swell and she didn't like the look of the way the left arm was hanging. The pulse felt weak and the breathing looked shallow. After covering him with the spare layers from the rucksack she sat beside him watching and waiting. Her mind went over the events of the last hour asking questions and creating doubts. Should they have tried to rescue him? Would it have been better to just go for help? How long would that thin gnarled root have held out? Why didn't he wear a crash helmet? She stood up and looked cautiously down to the swirling water below, the root had broken off, the bike was now half submerged under the waves. Moments later she could just make out the engine of the helicopter. As it drew nearer she grabbed Eric's blue shirt and began waving it furiously whilst running up and down the trail. They saw her and changed course, landing on a wide patch of dirt a hundred yards away from her. A flight-suited medic was charging across the grass before the wheels hit the sand, a second medic asked Flick how she was feeling and carried out some general checks on her. The police Land Rover arrived along with Eric and the Jeep ten minutes later, they hugged each other and then the shock hit them.

The rider was airlifted out and the police asked them to come to the police station in Vila do Bispo to get the full story in the form of a statement. The paperwork took an hour, then Jeepy took them back to the campsite.

"I have no idea where I got the strength from," Eric said simply.

"Sheer determination, I guess. My arms were beginning to give out once we had the full weight of him at that angle, I felt you gripping my ankles harder then next thing I know I'm trying to wriggle back over the edge, my tee shirt's going over my head so I can't see too well."

"They say when people are in a tight spot they can do things way beyond their normal capabilities – this must be one of those situations."

In the back of the Jeep Eddy and Kenny were glowing faintly. About the time the rider went over the top they had sat in the car park with a bright strong violet light emanating from their bodies.

Thankfully there was no one around to see anything, the last traces showing on the ride back were almost undetectable.

"I wish I understood my vibes more, it's the unknown aspect that's hard to handle," she remarked, looking out of the window, watching the trees flash past.

"You seem to have developed an unerring accuracy these days, love."

"It's a little on the scary side to be honest with you, thankfully I have you with me, I'm not entirely sure if it's vibes, FI or I'm turning into a fairground fortune teller – no that's not right at all, I do know, I'm not being logical enough. FI is probably nothing more than girls looking at things in a female way with perhaps a dash of mystique thrown in. Vibes are definitely a gut feeling with a warning bell accompaniment, but this is totally apart from the rest. This is stronger than vibes, it made me shiver, the warning side is amplified, it feels more like watching a newsreel that hasn't happened yet. Oddly enough you absolutely know it's all in the future, the picture is in your head, not behind the eyes, nor is it like a dream, there's no surreal situations involving impossible events with people who look strangely familiar but aren't – if you get my meaning."

Eric swung the Jeep into the space next to Wolfie.

"Let's grab something to eat and relax, we've both had a harrowing afternoon, you more than me."

By the time the sun had sunk over the horizon they were both feeling a little less fraught.

17

Their last day was spent taking a lazy walk along one of the lesser-used beaches. Eric asked how she was – he was expecting her to reinforce the case for not having any children; it had crossed his mind on the run to the lighthouse. She looked at him and said the evidence was certainly stacking up but she had no intention of going back on her word. Eric repeated that he was perfectly happy as things were. They exchanged a hug and a kiss and the sunshine did the rest. Back at the campsite they made ready to move, Jeepy was hitched up, the fridge packed with enough fresh food to last four days and at ten they went over to the Rancho for a meal and a last beer. At three am Flick awoke and sat up in bed. She had been mumbling in her sleep for ten minutes or so. Eric woke as she moved.

"What is it, love, you dreaming?"

"I reckon, very odd, it was like the shivery vibe but without the shiver, very odd indeed."

"What'd you see – not more kids to rescue, I hope, two is more than enough for one lifetime."

"This was like a thin strip of paper, the ones you see in old movies when the news is coming in – a ticker tape, only it wasn't one thin tape but ten or more stacked up on top of each other moving from right to left across my eyes. There were no words, or letters, just runes, like Tolkien's."

"I don't know what to make of that other than you had a lot of cheese tonight and that's supposed to make you dream."

Flick had reached over to her rough book and drew a line of characters.

"This was the only bit clear enough to make out, I'll see if it's in the book when we get home, perhaps it's a subconscious thing."

"Makes sense, my beautiful Elvish Queen, now come here and be cuddled."

The homeward journey was similar to the trip down. There were no problems except for a delay on the road to Rouen a few kilometres north of Le Mans. The dreams stayed away and the miles slowly passed. They managed to find a few things to do each day to give themselves a break from the slog of the road. Even a simple walk in a park was enough, everywhere they went happiness radiated off them. Anyone watching and learning the English language would have found the right word in the 'B's – bliss covered it nicely. The weather in England was reasonable; however, they both slipped on an extra shirt as the Portuguese climate had acclimatised them to warmer air.

The first stop was Letchworth where they let themselves in and relaxed in the garden. The next day Robert and Helen arrived from the airport. The prize holiday had been an amazing experience and for most of the afternoon the conversation was of little else other than Crete and Portugal. The story of the motorcycle rider was left till last; up until leaving France nothing had been heard about the young boy. Flick had been talking to her mother about the strange premonition-like feelings she had experienced less than an hour before the accident. Helen listened and sympathised on hearing how intense the 'walking over my grave' sensation was. She had nothing to offer in the way of an answer though.

The next morning they set off on the penultimate leg, the Great North Road to Leeds. John and Avril welcomed them and had a dinner waiting. Both the holiday and the adventure in Portugal were relived again. Avril had the same thoughts as Helen as to the cause of the 'Very Bad Vibes' but was intrigued with the runes Flick had pencilled into her book. Reaching for a copy of 'The Hobbit' and from the next shelf, 'Lord of the Rings', they started comparing symbols. After an hour they drew a blank; it was almost midnight so everyone made their way to bed. The next morning John had already looked over Wolfie and Jeepy, reporting they were both in good shape. Leeds to Manchester is an interesting trip as the Pennines have to be crossed, affording beautiful landscapes and some spectacular views. Often Saddleworth Moor was the route taken, a high, wild lonely spot with a dark side to it, being the burial place for the victims of some of the most evil murders of the twentieth century.

Dan and Alan were there to greet them and could hardly wait to hear the details of the trip. For the third time the adventure was relived. They were amazed how the locals had enjoyed the blues and rock numbers the impromptu band had played. The accident was the downside, of course, they hadn't seen or heard anything on the TV or radio. Life returned to normal, the band played more gigs, the university workload increased and the world went about its business. One evening in November at the end of the nine o'clock news the presenter closed a programme almost entirely devoted to the Watergate scandal by announcing that a young Portuguese boy had awoken from the coma he'd been in for three months. Alan, the ardent news watcher, called out to the others who surrounded the TV as the boy appeared with his smiling family in a hospital.

Christmas and New Year were celebrated in Leeds, Robert and Helen came up country, Dan and Alan went to Dan's parents in Altrincham. Alan had no family as such – both parents were alive but his mother subscribed heavily to the Aunt Mavis school of thought, homosexuality only happened to other people's sons and certainly not in Cheltenham. He had a sister in London who had left home at sixteen and disappeared into the swirling throng that makes up the East End never to be heard from again, or so it seemed. In 1976 she was found bruised and naked with the hypodermic that killed her still stuck in a toxic-veined scrawny left arm at the north end of Epping Forest in the undergrowth close to Theydon Bois.

Mavis and Sydney were spending the holiday alone in Stevenage. Avril had invited them – however, they politely refused. The go-as-you-please was quite a gentle affair with the principal victim probably glaring at Sydney over the turkey down in Hertfordshire. Early on Christmas morning Flick awoke with the urge to use the toilet. As she sat up in bed her sleepy eyes closed for a moment as another ticker tape of runes marched across her field of vision. She dreamily drew them in the margin of a magazine. Eric transferred them later into her notebook. After lunch they were shown to everyone for an after-dinner puzzling session. The rest of the day passed as Christmas Days all over the country do.

Between Christmas and New Year they visited the Moors and Dales, the Lake District and rural Bradford. Helen was particularity taken with the high rolling hills of the Dales whilst Robert found the Moors enchanting. During a walk round Keswick the conversation turned to the runes.

"Did you manage to do anything with them," Helen asked, "was Tolkien any use?" Flick said despite spending a while on it they were none the wiser.

"Just a lot of twaddle, I guess, I'm just curious, that's all, it's not as if there's another prize holiday to win," she joked.

"I was thinking about Jules Verne," John interjected, "only there's a rune puzzle in one of his books, 'Journey to the Centre of the Earth'. I think we have a battered copy back home."

Robert and Avril were beckoning them over to a quaint stone-fronted cafe with steamy windows.

"Last one in pays," shouted Avril before chasing after Robert with indecent haste. After the cakes were eaten Flick and Eric waited for a gap in the conversation and said they had something to tell them. Flick started the ball rolling.

"You know we're living with Dan and Alan now and the band's doing really well."

"Also the backing tapes we've recorded are selling like mad. In short, dear parents, that means all of you, will you please stop paying our rent on the flat, we can manage it ourselves now."

Eric quickly jumped in. "Our calculations are good, Flick accounts for all our incomings and outgoings–"

"Apart from some scrap metal dealing that we won't talk about," she added in mock innocence.

"Well, not including the ancillary funding for extra-curricular activities derived from the recycling industry, we can manage, and we know if a big problem comes up we can always ask for help."

"Well, that's a relief, for a moment then I thought you were getting married, phew," Robert feigned mopping his brow with a napkin.

"Funny you should mention that," Eric said quietly.

Getting up out of his seat he turned to face Flick taking a small box from his pocket at the same time. He opened the box to reveal an engagement ring sparkling on a velvet pad. With the café's customers now giving them their full attention, he dropped down on one knee in the middle of the cafe, looked up at her and said:

"Deborah Felicity Bowden, would you do me the honour of becoming my wife?"

Holding his face in a steady gaze, she pushed her chair back and stood up slowly, tilting her head slightly to one side as she often did. After placing both hands together so the fingertips covered her lips, her eyes were saying, 'you've managed to do it again, haven't you'. The hands came down to show a wide smiling face.

"Yes, I will, Eric, I most certainly will." She moved forward and kissed him as he stood up.

The ring fitted very well.

"I took your dress ring to the jeweller's to get the right size," he whispered.

"Oh, you engineer, you," she whispered back.

After the applause died down, the customers and staff joined in as well, one old lady wiped a tear away from her eye whilst another old couple sought out their bony gnarled hands under the table.

"I'm going to have to be very careful from now on, I seem to have managed to attach myself to a man who is so full of surprises he ought to explode. This is the second time you've left me speechless, Eric Marstone and I've got a teeny weeny feeling it isn't going to be the last."

Robert looked very pleased; he winked at John and said in the Jewish accent he'd copied from him:

"Maurice, Maurice, my boy, I'm ruined, ruined I tell you. The cake alone will cost a fortune, and the dress, my life, oh the money, Maurice, think of the money, I'm ruined I tell you."

John turned and put an arm round his shoulders.

"Hush now, Manny, the good people of Keswick are watching, wedding, smedding, your problems are solved, just sell your grumpy Aunt Mavis to the BBC, she'll go down a storm on 'Till Death Us Do Part', that Warren Mitchell's a lovely boy, he's making lots of moolah."

This little skit resulted in mass laughter through the cafe.

Back in Leeds a few serious questions were asked. Can we tell people you're engaged, when are you thinking of getting married, and are you really sure about managing on your own were the main ones. The answers came in the same order: Yes you can tell people, At least five years away, we want to finish our studies and get good jobs, and yes we can stand our own two feet now, and that's thanks to you four.

Helen sat back in her chair and started to laugh, silently, shaking her head as she did.

"Share the joke, Helen," said Avril.

"I was just trying to picture Mavis's face when we tell her, she'll freak out."

"Don't worry, my dear, we're sworn to secrecy, she'll never find out about 'Till Death Us Do Part' from any of us, on my life, on my dear mother's grave I tell you this," The Jewish Robert replied.

And so ended 1972.

18

The new year began. Dan and Alan were overjoyed at the news of their engagement. Dan treated them to dinner at their favourite Indian restaurant and Alan presented them with a watercolour painting of Stanage Edge, one of the places they had all enjoyed hiking over on many occasions.

Aunt Mavis snorted saying it was high time he made an honest woman out of her. Robert replied that their daughter wasn't dishonest, she'd told them at the first opportunity she was fornicating with Eric on a regular basis. This nugget of news got another snort and a look of disgust that had last been seen when Helen informed her that she and Avril sunbathed topless on the beach in Crete most days. This wasn't actually completely true, they had in reality also sunbathed totally naked in the villa's secluded garden, but she thought this additional information would be more than her sister could cope with.

Thankfully there were no more children to be rescued, and no more crossword puzzles won. The field trips were local so if expeditions were required, they used Wolfie and Jeepy for anything with an overnight stop or longer to save money. The band kept playing and the world kept turning. In March, 'Pigpen' of The Grateful Dead applied for membership to the 27 club and was accepted. The Yom Kippur War began and ended, Watergate was still in the news, The Vietnam War was beginning to wind down and space exploration projects increased.

On June 30th a total solar eclipse lasting over seven minutes occurred, this gave the watchers plenty of time to send a large explorer ship deep towards Mars – humans were becoming interested in the red planet. Eric and Flick both celebrated their twenty-first birthdays in the autumn even though the age of adulthood was now eighteen.

Nothing happened for most of the year until a week before Christmas. It started with Flick having another dream involving runes on ticker tapes. The legible ones were added to the rest; however, the proximity of Christmas meant there would be no time for puzzling over the three lines of symbols. It was John and Avril's turn to spend the holiday down in Hertfordshire; they arrived early on Christmas Eve. Sydney and Mavis arrived in the afternoon, Eric and Flick were last, pulling into the drive as the short winter day was becoming dark.

The days passed customarily, with lots of food and drink, again perhaps too much as these occasions often give rise to over-indulgence. Memories were relived in the evenings, starting with John showing the cine film of the holiday the two couples had spent in Italy. Mavis was on the edge of her seat, no doubt poised to distract Sydney if so much as a single bare breast showed on the screen. Flick and Eric told them about the walks they had taken over Yorkshire's wilder country – they were both looking to increase their navigation and orienteering skills. Mavis stayed quiet as Sydney spoke about the two weeks they had spent in Cornwall that summer – he had enjoyed the quaint Cornish villages and judging by her expression Mavis had not.

Boxing Day slid by in much the same way then Sydney announced he would have to go and work for a few days on a major new contract his firm were starting the first week in January. He explained it was unavoidable and he would be away until New Year's Eve.

After he left the next morning Mavis rose later than usual and wandered into the lounge to find Flick sitting cross-legged on Eric's back and shoulders attempting the Times crossword as he was doing press-ups.

"What on earth are you doing?" Mavis ejaculated.

"The cryptic crossword, Auntie."

"I am referring to where you are sat, young lady."

"Ah, I'm providing extra load for Eric to lift, also with a slight modification it's page 72 in the Kama Sutra." She smiled sweetly.

Mavis moved off towards the kitchen in disgust.

"Naughty naughty, Deborah, don't start stealing Father's thunder so early in the day," Helen reprimanded. "By the way I think 12 down is 'nemesis'."

The day was spent walking off too many excellent meals and feeding bread to the ducks in Stanborough Park before calling in to exchange gifts at one of Robert and Helen's friends. After dinner John and Avril said their farewells and headed off for Leeds. Their garage business was trying to cope with a much higher than normal number of broken down vehicles, the police had kept their recovery trucks busy almost non-stop since Christmas morning. The duty manager had phoned asking for help – he reported every hand was already on deck. This was the principal reason why it was easier for Robert and Helen to come to them at Christmas – there was no way of knowing when bad weather would cause a massive increase in road traffic accidents.

The early hours of the morning were shattered by the telephone ringing. Helen took the call, listened and made a few notes before hanging up and returning to the bedroom. Waking Robert, she relayed the message from the hospital in Maidstone.

"They said Sydney's had a serious heart attack and they've taken him to Maidstone as Sittingbourne aren't equipped to deal with it. I should come as soon as possible – the situation doesn't look good."

"What time is it, darling?"

"A few minutes to four."

"OK, we better wake Mavis and break the news; why you, I wonder, surely they meant Mavis."

Robert sat up and tried to wipe the sleep from his mind.

"They said was I his sister, I'm guessing they're assuming our telephone number is that of his sister instead of sister-in-law; no matter, at least we got the message."

Robert nodded and began to look for his trousers.

"I'll dress and get the car out."

As expected, Mavis took the news badly. Flick and Eric woke as activity in the house increased. Helen filled them in as to what had happened then Eric suggested he had better drive as Robert would still have too much alcohol in his system to pass a breath test.

"I only had a glass of wine with dinner, that will have gone through long ago."

The Volvo made its way to Maidstone, a difficult journey even at five in the morning during the Christmas holidays. Finally, Eric swung into the car park and they walked into the main entrance. The receptionist instructed them on how to get to intensive care and gave them a photocopied map. Flick navigated through the maze of identical corridors and doors until a nurse saw them and ushered them into a small room next to her office.

She introduced them to a tall thin woman who shook hands and asked them to call her Elaine. Flick and Eric went in search of the vending machines to buy some badly needed coffee. Elaine was thanking them for coming so quickly, she feared he might not last the night. She addressed most of her remarks to Helen who nodded and commented that it was good of her to let them know.

"I understand you were quite close, Sid has told me a lot about you and your family. I would have liked to have met you before, but Sid said with you living in Leeds it wasn't all that simple."

Robert looked at his wife and said in a puzzled tone, "We live in Letchworth, it's our daughter's fiancé Eric, his family live in Leeds."

"I must have it wrong somewhere, getting my 'Ls' mixed up," Elaine replied.

"So how did this happen then, was it at work?"

"No, Robert, he sat up in bed and said he felt really strange than clutched at his chest, he whispered to me that I was to phone his sister then he flopped back onto the bed. I knew straight away he was in serious trouble so I called 999 for an ambulance. It only took five minutes, I just had time to get dressed. The hospital rang you, the number was in his wallet."

"Please don't think I'm prying, Elaine, but what you're telling my husband is rather confusing. Would I be right in thinking you were in bed together when this happened?"

"Yes, dear, we'd been, well you're a married woman, Helen, indulging, you know, a bit of hanky-panky and then almost straight after he goes all wobbly on me."

Mavis's legs buckled under her; Eric was just in time to stop her hitting the floor, thankfully Flick was light enough on her feet to avoid the six coffees she was balancing from spilling over her.

Whilst the nursing staff administered to Mavis, now sat on a low couch, Helen, with increasing amazement, interviewed Elaine about her relationship with Sid or Sydney. The beginning of the tale went back four years. Sidney had been working away from Monday through Friday in Bearsted, using the pub she worked at to lodge in. One night in the bar they got talking. The chat grew into friendship then to something a bit more intimate. She suggested he came to stay with her in Sittingbourne and soon he was a permanent fixture. After a while he said the contract had ended and the next one was in Birmingham. He would only be able to come down a few days at a time as he now had to find lodgings in the West Midlands.

"All my family and friends think Sid's wonderful, some of his jokes are hilarious."

"And all the time I thought he was beavering away in Birmingham," snuffled a now compos mentis Mavis through her handkerchief.

"Instead he's been shagging in Sittingbourne," sighed Robert.

Somewhere around seven the hospital had a change of staff. All the deceit and white lies had been found out and explained when the six of them found the refectory. Those who could face it had breakfast. There was a lot of explaining to do to a lot of people. A doctor in the traditional white coat found them a little later, Mavis and Elaine were allowed into his room to see him one last time. He died shortly after ten.

"Looks like the funeral could be interesting," remarked Helen. "Oh bloody hell, what a mess."

Robert took Elaine home then came back for the rest of them. The ride back to Letchworth was awkward and humourless. In bed that night after spending the rest of the day helping Mavis get over the shock of what had happened to her, Flick lay in the crook of Eric's arm as she normally did. They had been talking in low voices for almost an hour, going over the clandestine life of the late Sydney trying to make order and sense of the events that had just been revealed to them in a maelstrom of disconnected bits and pieces. Flick looked pensive.

"Penny for your thoughts, Your Majesty?"

"I was thinking I didn't get any vibes about poor Sydney, that and I remembered the old rhyme, 'Oh what a tangled web we weave, when first we practise to deceive'," she said though half closed eyes.

Eric turned his thoughts to the absence of foresight; he admitted it hadn't crossed his mind at all until now. Sleep claimed them.

19

974 would be looked at in later years as the time when Dan and Alan's relationship began to set itself in stone. Living in the flat together at ease with two friends who understood them was the first step. The constant need to be on guard diminished. It wasn't a matter of feeling shame, the violence meted out by skinheads and far right factions that often dominated the news was the main issue. The acceptance and comfort found in the Manchester Madhouse made the difference.

Eric was unconsciously helping Dan by striding right through the invisible barriers people erect around themselves if they live life on the defensive. Being in the band added to the effect, guitarist and bassist would often stagger into each other to prevent falling over in some of the crazier moments on stage and when the music gave them an opportunity they would lean together back to back at a slight angle to fight a musical duel of riffs and fills. It wasn't a man thing or a gay thing, it was a musician thing.

Flick for her part was also unknowingly helping Alan who had since his sister left home led a sheltered boyhood right through school and beyond. His confidence level wasn't quite where he would have liked it to be, dominant characters often undermined what self-esteem he had; however, in other areas he was extrovert, full of life and appeared happy. How she helped was the way in which she lived her life and the total lack of inhibitions about anything she did or said.

It started simply enough – she had always wandered around the flat in one of Eric's shirts, usually just long enough to prevent her receiving an indecency charge, instead of getting dressed in the morning. All was well until she needed something out of the bottom drawer or had to reach up on top of a kitchen cupboard, things she did without thinking. Alan happened to be in the kitchen when Flick stood on tiptoe to get a large saucepan. As the shirt rode up he saw more then he'd ever been used to. Flick picked up on his red face and asked what was bothering him. After he explained she took hold of his hand and told him not to worry, she didn't mind he'd seen her naked bottom half, she was built the same way as every other girl. The most important part of this encounter was that she didn't tease, laugh at, or ridicule him.

"I'll find a longer shirt," was the parting shot.

A week or two later Alan came back from the library looking somewhat strung out and stressed. Dan managed to get out of him what was wrong – it seemed despite his heterosexual cloak one of the students in his group had seen through it and was hassling him. Alan had politely refused the advance but his antagonist was persistent. Eventually Alan had won through by standing his ground but it had taken a lot out of him. Flick told him to come and lie down on the fireside rug. She pulled herself into the lotus position she used for meditation and yoga then asked him to rest his head on the small cushion she'd placed between her folded legs. In the quiet of the room Alan slowly unwound his knotted muscles as he listened to her gentle voice talking to him about his breath, asking him to unwind his fingers, then his arms before moving on to legs and toes. By the time she'd whispered about clearing his mind of all thoughts it was obvious the soothing voice and the gentle massage of his temples had caused him to drift off to sleep.

"Told you he wasn't listening," Dan joked to Eric.

Soon after, Alan began to feel increasingly confident in several other areas that had been bothering him. A week later when they were all in the lounge, he plucked up courage and casually asked if he could touch on a personal subject, looking at Flick as he did so. The others looked up as he turned to Flick and enquired what it felt like to have a bust. Flick thought for a moment then replied that it might be easier to demonstrate than describe the answer. She excused herself and went out the door. Dan asked him what the question was all about – as an answer Alan showed them the brochure he was reading about sex change operations. Eric was looking at the pictures with his engineer's head on when Flick came back into the room. She asked Alan to pop his arms through the straps of one of her bras. A piece of elastic was knotted across the back straps to make up the difference in chest sizes then she filled the cups with socks and old tights to get the shape right.

"Go look in the mirror, that's a G-cup by the way."

He stood and looked at his reflection and turned sideways, first one way then the other. The conversation turned to how amazing breasts were. Eric made them laugh by saying only Mother Nature could have designed and built such a perfect feeding system, being totally portable, thermostatically controlled and all models having an automatic refilling valve. Dan added that they came in all colours and a range of models from a 500cc to huge V8 six litres. Flick made them chuckle when she told them how hers had started growing at the age of ten.

Alan was looking down at his sock-filled chest and seemed to have another question. Although the size and shape part of the question had been answered, the weight and sensations side of things was a little difficult to imagine. Flick said she could obviously only describe the sensations she felt, but if he was all right with it, and Eric and Dan were too of course, she would undress and let him hold her breasts.

Dan and Eric said it was fine by them. Alan nodded, so she pulled the tee shirt over her head, unclipped and slid out of her bra and stood before him. With a slightly apprehensive look he slowly reached out and slid a hand under each breast then lifted them gently; the weight surprised him.

"Yes, unsupported they do make my back ache after a while," she said, anticipating his question.

"Thank you," he whispered whilst sitting back down in his chair with a thoughtful expression on his face.

He remained silent for a while, lost in his inner thoughts. Flick slipped her shirt back on and scooped up her bra.

"At 14 I needed a 'C' cup and they were arrested by the boob police, both were convicted to stay behind bras."

"I see, Mrs Malaprop, was it a life sentence?" Dan asked in his prosecuting lawyer voice.

"Yes, there's not a chance of parole but they do get to come out into the exercise yard most weekends." Flick tittered whilst wiggling her bust under the shirt.

"Thanks, Flick, all of you in fact, for giving me the opportunity to resolve something I would never have managed on my own. I think that I can sort the rest of the questions out for myself," Alan remarked from the chair, having made his decision.

The socks and tights bra came off and Flick put it with her own. A couple of days later Dan confided to Eric that after weighing up the pros and cons Alan had decided not to proceed with surgery. Flick had provided exactly the information he wanted, her description of the sensations she felt and allowing him to feel for himself what a real breast felt like had answered all the questions.

"It would be all show and little sensation he thinks. That's our feelings, but mainly his, on the subject anyway," Dan had commented.

The following month Alan came back to the flat armed with a poster inviting entries into an art exhibition in a popular Manchester gallery. Artists were to submit their work by the end of September, any medium was acceptable and the judges would pick the top one hundred pieces for display in November. The small print went on to explain the themes the artists were to depict and how to fill in the entry form. He'd decided to enter a picture and started thinking about the content, but as he explained to the rest nothing concrete had emerged from the old brain box yet.

Later in the week he emerged triumphant from a pile of art books he'd looked through. Work began in earnest, Dan was to be part of the picture, and if possible would Flick mind lending herself to it as well. His idea was to do a surrealistic piece woven around all six of the themes the gallery had listed.

"The themes were in groups: black and white, good and evil, hard and soft," he explained.

"And you reckon you can combine all six elements into one picture?" Eric asked.

"With surrealism, yes, there are no limits to the imagination and therefore reality can be completely absent, perhaps limited to the smallest of anchors so the viewer has a clear understanding of the root of the picture. Take for instance Dali's 'The Persistence of Memory', most people know it from the melting pocket watches on a normal beach. It could be his interpretation of hard and soft. In a similar world the concepts of good and evil give rise to a vast store of possible subjects to depict. Then consider black and white, this can be taken to mean several different things as well, from the saying, 'it's all down there in black and white' to the lack of any colour in a photograph as an example. I have got an image in mind that uses all six and would like you to help me with it."

Dan spoke next.

"I've started my bit already, here are the pencil sketches, I'm being depicted as a muscular, black angel with wings furling round me."

"The meaning here is Dan can represent the 'hard' theme with his muscled body. Also 'black' is covered by his skin colour, the angel wings cover the 'good' part. Flick, would you be prepared to pose in the lotus position for me wearing a bikini, and I also have a task for you, Eric."

"I've no problem with that, Alan, why the lotus position?"

"Firstly, I know you can do it, I've seen you often enough practising yoga, and secondly, it means the practitioner is meditating, trying to find understanding in what is often a crazy world and to live with it in the present. Trying to achieve mindfulness. It's thought to help in many areas of human life, I think you told me once it helped you deal with some of the more difficult things you've had to experience."

"Indeed it has, looking back to when I was trying to console my friend, the one who lost her father, I wish I knew then what I know now, it would have helped."

"The reasoning and connections stem from Flick being 'soft' in her skin and many parts of her body and she needs to be flexible; a synonym for soft, in order to achieve the lotus position without injury. Also in contrast to Dan she is 'white'."

"Where do I come in, Alan, not the evil, half-cast, flabby, slayer of good men and transcendental woman," Eric joked.

"No, my friend, it's your engineering head I'm in need of. I want you to build me the canvas I can paint on, it will be a little out of the ordinary hence the use of that engineer's brain of yours. I'll explain, but first I'll put the kettle on."

Alan returned with the tea tray and biscuit tin.

"The finished painting is going to be about eight feet by five feet six. It has to be this size to make the effect I have in mind work properly. The surface has to follow a shallow arc that will allow me to bend perspective enough so that anyone starting from the left hand side of the picture can, by moving sideways across the whole width to the right, experience an illusion. That's the theory anyway."

"When do you want me to start posing, Alan?"

"Whenever you can please, I'm going to do several pencil sketches first to get the twist in perspective right, which means dividing the subject into several sections. It's a little complicated to explain."

Flick left the room, returning five minutes later in a blue bikini, carrying her revision notes. Pulling herself into the required pose, she opened the book and began reading. Alan began sketching her from the knees up. He'd given Eric a rough drawing of the frame shape wanted for the painting. He and Dan had begun to study it. Twenty minutes later Alan asked if Flick could put the book in the other hand. When her notes had been read and a few extra comments pencilled in the margins she looked straight at Alan while he drew her face several times. Lastly, he made rough outlines of five or six positions her hair could hang in.

"Lots of options there, thanks, Flick you can unwind now – literally," he laughed as she uncoiled herself.

They all looked through the drawings and saw how the finest details of muscles and curves had been captured.

"You have an incredible eye for detail, Alan, I reckon you could enter this and get in the hot one hundred," Dan said.

"I'm looking at this one of Flick's abdomen, you can actually see the definition of each rib through the tight skin, the muscles bunched up, every little thing is captured." Eric put the sketch down.

"I think this is bordering on unbelievable." Flick held up a picture of Dan's left upper body where the angel wing morphed out of the skin at the shoulder. "Just look how the muscles and sinews have been adjusted to allow for the wing."

"I cheated there, the library has a book on bird anatomy."

Over the course of the next few weeks Flick did some of her home studying in a bikini whilst in the lotus position in the lounge or on the kitchen table with Alan sat on the floor. Getting the perspective exactly right was his reasoning. She was also drawn sitting at the bottom of the stairs with the artist sat precariously on a tread halfway up. She became quite used to being fed cups of tea, biscuits and the odd beer by anyone who was passing.

The canvas, or more accurately a curved frame, was coming together in the old garage. Dennis the landlord had donated some wood that had once been a couple of cold frames and the odd lengths they had found in the rickety shed. The frame was the easy part; what was not so simple was the bending of the long sections evenly to achieve the shallow arc Alan's plan demanded. The art of wood bending is not a simple one, and the results are often unpredictable even for the experts using the right type of timber. Dan and Eric were working with old pine and some deal, soaking it in the bathtub, their expertise being read out from the book they'd borrowed from the university library. Eventually it came together with any inaccuracies compensated for with judicious saw cuts and copious amounts of glue.

"I think I'll put this into my project book, it's one the others aren't going to be covering, I'll bet."

Dan answered with, "Perhaps I should have been studying the laws of physics as applied to wood rather than the laws of taxation; at the moment both subjects are very 'taxing'."

The slight boredom of cutting and making over eight hundred spheres of pine was secretly welcome as they could make silly jokes, like, 'wooden it be nice to see the frame saw-ted'. Like falling off a log became a catchphrase in the garden for a week or two.

Inside the house Flick was going through the facial contortions only normally used on demand by character actors. Alan couldn't get the right look he needed. Matters grew more complicated as he needed three separate looks, one for each stage of the illusion. By the end of the evening she'd managed to pull off the looks he wanted and discovered some extra muscles in her face she was unaware off. Alan looked a little pensive as he put his pad and pencils down.

"Flick, would it be alright if I did your breasts next?"

She smiled at him. "That's not a problem, I was talking to Eric a week ago and we both thought it was going to come up, in fact we wondered if you'd like me naked but were fearful of asking. We agreed that if you can handle it we were OK too."

"My, my, what absolutely amazing friends I have, far better than I deserve. A million thanks to you and Eric, you're both brilliant."

The next day after Flick's final pose the three friends agreed that Alan had an amazing gift. They all said it was as sharp and precise as a photograph and the detail was out of this world. The finished picture of Dan was equally as amazing – he was portrayed as the black angel with enveloping wings, looking over the page to a stunningly attractive girl meditating with a slightly smiling face returning the angel's glance. The general feeling was he should enter both these drawings exactly as they were, that he was bound to win a place was agreed upon unanimously. The 'contraption' as it been named was manoeuvred into the front room along with the spheres in sacks and three old buckets.

"Bet it wasn't like this in Picasso's studio, mate," Dan retorted to Eric, who giggled.

"Cold beers are waiting to be drunk, gentlemen, I shall await you in the garden," Flick announced in her posh voice.

Alan hit the artist's equivalent of writer's block six days later. He checked and double checked his calculations and couldn't discover any errors. He became frustrated that his idea worked well in theory, but when he'd started to paint the spheres the illusion wasn't as smooth as he'd hoped. The experiment he'd played with two months ago had worked but now, in the top left hand corner of the frame he was using as a test area, the increase in detail has gone against him. He went to bed around midnight puzzling over what he had to do to make it work. Three days later he was no nearer an answer and was on the point of taking his friends' advice and submit the draft pictures instead. He nodded off in the armchair that night for an hour then went to bed, sliding carefully under the sheets to avoid waking Dan.

Around one in the morning a red light illuminated his partially completed canvas. The beam washed over the two images then dropped to the pile of notes and calculations. Finally, the beam moved into the orange segment of the spectrum and made its way through the sketch pads and loose pages. When the last page had been scanned the beam retracted into Kenny who was hanging on his normal coat hook by the door. A green beam then shot off at a tangent to the first and sought out Eddy, who was also in his normal place on the shelf in Flick and Eric's bedroom. A yellow beam came out of Eddy, passed through a couple of walls then hit the sleeping Alan's left ear and disappeared inside his head. Roughly four minutes later the coloured beams dissolved together and outside the lounge window a squirrel watched uninterestedly from a tree as a single drawing of Flick's hair lifted off the floor and slotted itself into a notepad.

In the early hours Alan awoke with all the answers to all the questions. The others found him in the lounge trying to turn the frame through ninety degrees.

"I'm so stupid," he said. "It will never work like this, it has to move – not the viewer, the tilt has to be top to bottom not left to right and–"

He stopped, out of breath with talking and heaving on the heavy frame.

"Alan appears to have had a flash of genius," Eric mentioned to Dan; both had heard the commotion and wondered what was happening.

Flick poked her head round the door.

"Well as we're all up and about nice and bright and early I'll go and put the kettle on, shall I, anyone for a four o'clock coffee?"

Three voices shouted in unison at her retreating figure: "Any chance of a chocolate digestive with that?"

Without stopping or turning she extended the middle finger of her left hand and jabbed it at the ceiling.

Eric mounted the frame on a stand that allowed it to tilt about the middle of the arc. He also devised a mechanism that slowly tilted the frame through roughly a hundred degrees starting with the bottom nearest to what Alan called 'the viewing point', ending with the top nearest the 'viewing point'. By pressing a button the motor, salvaged from the old washing machine, would go into reverse and rapidly reset the frame to the starting point. The final job was to apply a thin film of machine oil to the pins set in the spheres so they wouldn't stick as the frame turned. Alan asked if they would mind waiting to see the finished picture working as he wanted it to be a surprise if he won a place. A tinge of disappointment hung in the air but he got his wish.

"Will you at least tell us the title?" Dan asked.

Alan looked at them and said the title did not reflect in any way the fantastic efforts the three of them had put in. He asked them to remember that the painting was a surrealist work.

"It's called 'Evil Beyond the Veil', I hope that it won't offend you."

They all looked at him. Flick broke the silence.

"Alan, I know you have a tough time with certain emotions—" here she smiled at him and the big brown eyes twinkled— "please understand you're a good friend to all of us, we know you well enough that to even contemplate you were going to insult or upset us isn't going to happen. Use that to strengthen your weakness and come and give us all a very big hug."

Alan posted the entry form off and they did the only thing left to do. Wait.

Sometimes situations get out of control. There are times when words will solve a problem or diffuse and calm a tense situation. As Churchill said 'Jaw-Jaw not War-War'. Sometimes the words are diplomatic, offering the opposition a way out without losing face, and there are times when the words are an ultimatum. Sometimes the ultimatum is silently delivered, or perhaps in a structured roundabout way. Also in cases like this it's extremely handy to have a back-up that can protect the speaker against violence; some of the people we meet in life consider their opinions and rationale are the only viewpoint. These people are very dangerous, especially if in a position of power. Sometimes we meet corruption and instances of power in the wrong hands on a lower level; not everything plays out on the world stage. One day a situation unfolded at the Manchester Madhouse that reflected some of these aspects.

Around seven just as they had finished dinner the front door flew open and two police officers marched in uninvited. They made straight for Dan and wrestled him to the floor. Alan wasn't home yet but Flick and Eric came in and demanded to know what was happening. One officer, the Sergeant, took Dan to the van outside whilst the plain clothes man managed to inform them in a very offhand way that Dan was being arrested for a violent robbery at a jeweller's in the city earlier that day. Eric explained it could not have been him as the two of them had been at home studying. He leered at them and said they better not try and say that in court, he knew about the dope they were dealing and to enforce the lie produced a plastic bag full of cannabis from his pocket.

"Look what I just found – tell you what, I'll let you off this time, be seeing you."

As he turned to go Flick shouted at him, "You fucking turd-brained mother fucking son of a whore's asshole. You're as bent as a fucking rusty nail."

The man turned and slowly walked towards her and at the last minute he raised his right arm to strike. Eric, however, saw it coming and took the detective's fist in his own, bringing it to a dead stop.

"You don't want to do that, she bruises rather easily," he said calmly, tightening his grip to such an extent the detective had nothing else to think about other than the intense pain of his fingers being systematically crushed.

Flick had put the packet of brown crumbs in her bag using eyebrow tweezers.

"Perhaps the real police will find some interesting fingerprints on this," she opined as the detective tried to block the pain.

She sat down and smiled at the wincing plain clothes man.

"I think we can start with the warrant to forcibly enter these premises, will you be so good as to hand it over please. Oh, not in your pocket then, so we can say you don't have one. Now then, we're going to ask your nice friend the Sergeant to come in and we'll sort out if he's straight or a nasty, squirming pile of fetid, pus-filled shit like you."

Flick went out to the police van and said the detective needed to speak to him. She went back in and sat down. As the Sergeant entered she spoke in a clear calm voice.

"Don't even think about doing anything silly like attacking either of us or running away because if you do Detective Fuck-Wit here will be an arm short."

The Sergeant took in the scene and stayed calm. "OK, Miss, what's the game?"

"Ah, mordant humour, the game as you call it is very simple. You have to convince me that you are – please note I said you and not him – are a straight police officer. I already know shit-for-brains here is as phoney as a nine bob note so now it's your go. Have you got a warrant?"

The Sergeant said the detective told him they had one.

"Who are you looking for concerning this alleged robbery, the suspect's name please? I see, you're not going to tell me."

Flick glanced at Eric and nodded. He changed his position slightly, he still held the crushed hand firmly whilst his left hand had a purchase just below the detective's armpit. By exerting just enough pressure to make an audible crack of something breaking heard by everyone the game changed slightly. Sweat was now pouring out of the injured man's face. The Sergeant started to move forward.

"Stay where you are or his arm will come off!" she growled.

Something must have been written on her face that suggested to him she wasn't playing.

"OK, Miss, we're after a black guy, goes by the street name of Benji T."

She went over to the shelf and tossed a passport at the Sergeant.

"That's the guy you have in the van, Daniel William Lavigne, please note the passport is French and that he's a citizen of France; he's here reading law at university."

The Sergeant decided his suspicions gathered over the last year were now looking to be more than just suspicions. The detective suddenly realised his power was slipping away and found a desperate voice.

"Wilson, you prick, arrest them both now, you two are in so much shit you won't live to see Christmas, I promise you that."

For Wilson the outburst was enough to convince him the detective was as he and the girl suspected, bent.

"Shall we all go out to your van and I think I can convince you that Dan is not Benji whoever?"

Wilson and Flick made their way to the van. Dan was somewhat surprised when the door opened. Flick started the conversation.

She asked Dan his name followed by where and when he was born whilst Wilson checked the answers against the passport.

"Do you have a profile on this Benji bloke, if so what does it say in the bit about distinguishing marks?"

Wilson said he didn't know, he'd have to radio the station. The answer came back as none.

"Mr Lavigne has a star-shaped birthmark on his upper left arm to the rear near the shoulder blade."

Wilson pulled at Dan's shirt to reveal the mark.

"So, can we go back inside now and finish this?"

Wilson nodded and released Dan from the handcuffs.

Back in the flat Wilson formally arrested his superior officer and arranged for back-up to arrive. Now Eric had released his right arm the detective was swearing they would all have to start looking over their shoulders from now on. Wilson told him to shut up. Evidently now his flimsy cover was blown he was becoming frantic and starting to panic. The second police van arrived without fuss or bother, no lights flashing or sirens wailing. Two uniformed officers strode towards the detective who now had full confirmation his world was about to fall apart lunged away from Eric and flattened himself against the back wall. Reaching down his desperate fingers sought for a weapon, anything would do, even if his hand was hurting like hell he wouldn't go down without a fight; the underworld who bribed and corrupted him would see him as a diamond geezer and not a soppy bollocks as the east-enders would say. He managed to put his hand on what felt like a stout wooden stick, he grabbed it clumsily, his hand sliding in his own sweat down to the metal part where the moisture helped the two hundred and thirty volts make an excellent connection.

In less than a millisecond the electricity had gone up his right arm, across his chest and exited via his left leg, which was pressed against the radiator, stopping his heart in the process. The old porcelain hard wired fusebox in the kitchen went 'fizz-phut' a second or two later but it was too late for him. The ambulance crew reported him as dead at the scene.

Once a degree of normality had returned to the flat Wilson told them everything that had happened here would be subject to a government cover-up under the office of the Home Secretary, a matter of national security. The hushing-up would ensure they were not going to suffer any revenge attacks and they could get on with life. A woman in a business suit arrived later along with a French speaking man whom they guessed was attached to the embassy. Wilson returned with another man who asked them to sign the official secrets act. Compensation would be calculated and delivered within the month, he announced.

Alan came in just as they were all leaving. Dan had to keep closing his mouth for him as the tale unfolded. Flick sat with her legs folded under her.

"I'm so weary. I don't know how I stood up to that man, all the names I called him, I was burning up inside, I wanted to beat him with my fists but swearing seemed to help. Right from the start I could see through him, I seemed to sense it, the bent copper hiding inside the fake outer shell. I have no idea how I managed to stay so cool and logical, I should have been scared shit-less – oops, sorry, there I go again."

Eric was leaning on the door jamb.

"I could have carried out your threat Flick, so easily, too easily. I felt the anger and strength surging through me, in fact if something hadn't been present inside my head I would have tore him to pieces, effortlessly, I felt so strong. But, and here's the odd part, a message was repeating itself over and over again, just the one word, protect, protect, protect." He ran a hand through his hair and sat down.

"All I can say is thank you, I'm a bit numb but I didn't see any of this, I was only thinking something was very wrong, way beyond mistaken identity," Dan said wearily.

Alan closed the debate.

"I guess now we'll never know what it was all really about, why they needed to frame Dan, how they were going to make sure he was convicted of a crime he didn't commit, even if the crime was true, which I suspect is just another pack of lies. The case wouldn't hold up, that detective must have built up a lot of fake shit as far as I can see and judging by his rash actions he was getting very close to being found out by his superiors. The only thing I can work out is they needed a fall guy to keep this Benji T on the streets, at any price. Looks like wrong place, wrong time and thanks to you two guys, wrong people."

Lying in bed an hour later, sleep was a little elusive that night. Eric kissed the top of Flick's head – it was in easy reach as she had burrowed and wormed her way into the crook of his arm as usual.

"I thought I'd killed the power to the motor on Alan's picture frame, I'm sure I did. I was working on the switch wiring, Dan was reading one of his law books and I'm ninety-nine point nine percent positive I turned it off." He didn't get a response – under a pile of red hair were two closed eyes.

From his shelf Eddy shone a green beam into the sleeping pair. In the morning Eric wasn't so sure about turning the power off and Flick had returned to her calm collected self. Eric found her sitting on top of the bed in the lotus position meditating. He kissed his fingers and placed them over her lips then slid quietly out of bed and wandered towards the kitchen. Kenny was looking sanguine.

21

ife returned to normal again. Humans are remarkably versatile at enduring hardships especially the shorter episodes. Disturbing as it was the incident faded into memory in a few weeks, albeit into an area that could be brought up quickly. Once the danger had passed the routine of life showers on the fires of troubles, the smouldering debris can last a while though. The next incident was nowhere near as vivid or dangerous; in fact, it was decidedly tiresome but still it presented a problem to Alan, who despite his recent increases in confidence and understanding of emotions, was struggling to deal with it.

On Thursdays Flick picked Alan up from the courts where he often spent the afternoon hearing cases and adding to his notes. She would swing the Jeep into a loading bay to let Alan climb in. On this occasion he was talking to a man of medium build in a business suit. He seemed to be friendly so she waved as she pulled up.

"Who's the suit?"

"That, my dear, is Patrick; he's still after me I'm afraid. He isn't exactly sure about me though, I still keep up the heterosexual appearance in public. I know I should chill with it, but I don't feel that safe yet. Anyway, he's quite openly gay and perhaps the body language is filling in the gaps, he's becoming a right royal pain in the ass, whoops sorry, wrong choice of words there, I just wish I could get shot of him."

The next Thursday Flick spotted Patrick as she turned the corner. Her devilish imp was sitting on the right shoulder whispering in her ear as she pulled up and got out. Chancing no traffic wardens were lurking near Woolworths, she walked slowly, smiling, with exaggerated swinging hips towards Alan. With her chest pushed out as far as it could go, she gave him one of her 'special' kisses complete with legs-wrapped-round-the-waist extras. Alan responded as best he could – there aren't many options available when you're the target of a girl with spider-like qualities in the limbs department who seems be wrapping you up for consumption later. Several people gave them peculiar glances and quickly found a reason not to go to Woolworths; after all, whatever they had come for could wait till next week. She released her prey and smiled at him. Mae West took over the vocal chords.

"Well hello, honey, is that the judge's gavel in your pocket, or are you just pleased to see me?"

Alan left Patrick on the roadside, the pair climbed into the Jeep and Flick hit the ignition.

"You do know, Deborah, that your chances of obtaining a ticket to pass through the pearly gates dwindle when you perform these stunts of yours. Any more like that and you're going straight to the fiery pit downstairs, girl, straight to the halls of hell, do not pass 'GO', do not collect two hundred pounds."

"Nice and warm down there, a girl can sunbathe naked all year round," she teased.

Alan reflected. "Joking apart, thanks, it might make him rethink the situation."

Flick being, for want of a better word, 'helpful' was the reason Wendy knocked on the door the following Monday. Wendy and her boyfriend Colin were regulars at many of Escapade's gigs. Sadly, Wendy had a bit of a problem with her lifestyle and when she first saw Flick putting a hundred and ten percent into drumming for a rock band she saw a threat. Colin positively stared at her especially when this red-haired siren had both arms and legs hammering out a complex pattern with a body motion and matching facial expression which she misinterpreted as sheer lust. It didn't take much imagination to substitute a man for the snare drum sat between her pounding legs. The second part of the problem was

Flick's apparent lifestyle, within the band at least, was the exact opposite of her own.

The next step she decided on was to understand the enemy – this took the form of chatting to her when the band took a break. Ten minutes into that first meeting Wendy discovered the threat was actually a very nice person who was engaged to the guitarist.

She arrived with Colin a good hour early at the next gig and managed to get her on one side after the sound check. After spending a while talking about a charity gig she asked her first meaningful question.

"Do you mind all the men looking at you, the cut off shorts and boob tube are rather sexy?"

"It's no problem, I'm a tall girl with long legs, big tits and a mane of hair – men are going to look at me. We four live together, it's the same here as it is at Uni, out there, anywhere really, I've got used to it and secretly I get a kick out of it sometimes. Remember, Wendy, thousands of men can look at me, some maybe lust after me, but I'm only interested in and lust after the one man."

The answer was both enlightening and direct but also prompted another rather personal question.

"I hope you don't think I'm a weirdo or something, but I have a lot of problems with keeping Colin interested, I don't mean the sex thing, we don't seem to be a couple anymore. Coming to your gigs is just about the only thing we do together. So what I'm asking is how do you keep your Eric interested – just by looking I can see you have no problems."

"I have to go, it's time for the first set, tell you what, bring that charity walk entry form round to the Manchester Madhouse on Monday, I'll sort out some posters for the fund raiser, we can continue our chat then."

Wendy sat down and placed the entry form on the table. A local children's care centre they were involved in needed funds, so a charity walk along Hadrian's Wall was one of the events they'd come up with. Flick walked in with two steaming coffee mugs and rolled up band posters under her arm.

"We try and put thirty out for a new venue, try and get them in the local shops and bus shelters. If you're selling tickets don't forget to throw a few comps at the shop keepers."

Once the details of the forthcoming gig were confirmed and the charity walk entry form filled in and handed back, the girls got down to talking about Wendy's worries.

"In a nutshell, Flick, I think things would be better between Colin and me if I were more like you, I mean your lifestyle, your attitude and how you manage your life, not your physical resemblance, but I wish I could be as bloody sexy, if only a little bit."

Flick put her cup down and thought for a moment before replying.

"One of the problems is that deep within us all the sex angle tends to rise to the top in certain situations. Sex is incredibly deep rooted, it's strong, that's how we survived as a species. It's animal and can cause as many problems in today's society as you could shake a stick at. They say comparisons are odious but in this case I think it might help. If I were to tell you about a situation I experienced a week ago and you think what you would have done in that situation then we might begin to understand the differences that we're trying to help you with – does that make sense, it came out a bit higgledy-piggledy?"

Wendy nodded so Flick carried on.

"Last week is actually a very good example. I do most of the cooking here and in return the guys do all the housework, running repairs et al. A while back I'd done a Baked Alaska, not the easiest dish but my mother taught me the secret; I don't like it personally, it's far too sweet. Tuesday evening the guys come up to me asking for Baked Alaska. I get all the funny voices, the mock begging, kissing of feet, clasped hands praying, kowtowing, grovelling and all manner of crazy things. My devil imp appears on the right shoulder as always and I look down on them kneeling at my feet and in a toffee-nosed voice I said 'You're getting limp crackers and mousetrap cheddar, there's no way I'm doing Baked Alaska tonight'."

Wendy looked thoughtful, peering at Flick over her coffee mug.

"Here's what happened next: Dan changed character to a German SS officer and tells me in a cod-German accent that if I don't obey and go to the kitchen immediately I will be held down across the lounge table and tortured. There's no time to answer, I'm laughing too much, so Dan picks me up and lays me full length on the table then pins my legs down at the ankles while Alan takes my trainers and socks off. Eric has my shoulders secured, then Alan takes one of the peacock feathers out of that vase in the corner over there and starts tickling the soles of my feet. I'm squirming and wriggling in between laughs and convulsions as I'm very ticklish in a fair few places. A couple of minutes later Alan stops and Dan's German major asks if I'm now going to go to the kitchen or the torture will continue. In between giggles I say go to hell, you can tickle me to death, I will never surrender. The guys are still holding me down so Alan comes round the table and pulls my shirt up to just under my boobs before getting two feathers going in my navel and round my stomach. That did it, I lasted about two minutes, no more, 'OK, OK, I'll do it' I cried out, with tears of laughter running down my face. I went into the kitchen and made a start. So, Wendy, how would you have reacted to that scenario?"

Wendy thought for a moment.

"I'm not sure I would have handled it like that, I don't have two friends as close to me as you do and I've no idea as to how Colin would fit in. You're just friends then, no bed hopping?"

Flick shook her head.

"I can see there's a lot of trust, a depth of understanding I've never reached and might never manage to. You obviously have no fears with any of them. What happened next?"

"Obviously I would have done it for them, my mischievous side just teased them, they of course knew that the odds of me saying, 'OK guys' would be slim after all the comic capers and banked on me reacting as I did. We're always trying to be witty and get laughs, bouncing off each other. When I was allowed off the table, I feigned being forlorn, pulled my shirt down and said in a low voice, 'you big bullies, it's not fair, three onto one', then I skipped down to the kitchen giggling. A few minutes later they all came into the kitchen after setting the table. Alan, who was nearest the fridge, opened the door and from the back pulled out a bottle of Moët and Chandon, my favourite champagne. 'This is for you,' he said, 'we know you like it, from the three of us, to say thanks for being you.' The Baked Alaska hit the table, the three of them sat with spoons poised, drooling. Dan got up this time and went to the fridge, pulling out a 'death by chocolate dessert', another favourite of mine. 'As you're not keen on this wonderful dish we got you another little treat,' he said. It was a nice feeling listening to their appreciations of my efforts as the dish vanished in a tenth of the time it took me to make it. Alan tapped his glass to call for silence. He stood up and said the toast was to their wonderful friend, meaning me. They had all agreed I was the most amazing woman they had ever known, they adored being so close to me, sharing life's journey and each in his own way loved me very much. I got up, hugged and kissed each of them in turn, words failed me, my head was spinning."

Wendy took in the story. "It's obvious from that they do absolutely adore you."

"For what I am, Wendy, for what I am. By turn it seems I'm an enchantress, a chef, a musician, a nurse, a princess and a friend, among another things. On certain nights, with a certain person, I'm a complete and total whore. Different things to different people, these guys say I'm positive, honest and a bundle of fun, but mostly I'm one hundred percent female, that's their way of saying I'm sexy. I try and find time for the people I care about, where I can help I will, and I'm not scared or ashamed of my credo or my body, I guess I'm very lucky it all seems so very natural to me and comes easy."

"You don't have any hang-ups, everything just flows I take it."

Alan popped his head round the door. "You two want a beer?"

They both said they would stick with coffee.

"No hang-ups at all, most of them went at school, so yes, it flows. My thoughts on this are a little fuzzy but from what I do know about you I'm going to guess your biggest fear is Colin's going to go walkabout soon if things don't improve between you."

Wendy nodded.

"Then you have to ask yourself a few questions, most of which are double edged; what you ask of yourself applies to Colin as well. Am I putting enough effort into the relationship, is he doing the same? This is the sort of thing I mean by double edged. Then think how you could improve the relationship, based on where you're at now. List what areas of life aren't at the level you want. So, if you think Colin is becoming tired of the life you're leading, try a new approach. For instance, if you love the guy, don't just tell him, show him, then he might get the hint and show you back. Let me tell you about Eric's birthday in Portugal."

Flick recounted the story by first explaining how Eric had started the ball rolling by saving up some money because he wanted to make one of her little dreams come true. How he kept it secret, how he let her find out and finally how he'd written of his love for her on a little gift tag. She then began to tell of how she packed a very elegant, sexy dress, a couple of classy accessories and a pair of high heels. The effect it had on him when he saw her was told next then finally the extremely erotic dance that blew his mind. Wendy was visibly taken aback with the whole thing.

"I don't think Colin would dream up anything like that and I could never do that dance, I wouldn't know where to start."

"If you want to do it then make the effort, learn. Remember, where there's a will there's a way. You could start simple and work up to it. An hour ago you said you would like to be as sexy as me or at least a little bit. A lot of sexiness can come from your clothes. As an example at the last three gigs you've turned up in jeans and a tee shirt. Fine, but not very sexy. Go buy a low neck one and for the next gig try losing the bra. If you can afford them, get a tight pair of jeans with the big brass buttons instead of a zip, the sort that stand out. Now let's look at the other weapons in our female armoury. Do your hair a bit differently, back combing is popular, then look in the fashion mags for make-up hints. Make sure though whatever you do doesn't cross the Tart border. Sexy, Slag and Slut are all under 'S' in the dictionary, you're looking for the first entry. Come out the bedroom and wait for the bomb to go off. New hair, super make-up, nipples poking gently through thin cotton and a denim crutch magnet, you're home and dry, girl. Make sure you're aiming all this sexuality on a narrow beam in his direction, no bouncing it off the gawkers in the pub – the first commandment is, 'thou shall not flirt'. But you can still enjoy it."

Flick imagined Wendy went down the road with a slight spring in her step. She went through to the garden.

"I'll take that beer now please," and she flopped down on the grass.

Eric passed her a bottle.

"It took a bit of sorting, the gig and the charity hike, any problems?"

"Not with the hike or the gig, the trouble's with Wendy and Colin. Wendy doesn't make a lot of effort at life, so habit and routine gnaw away and their life gets dull. I don't think Colin works at it any harder either. When we play the Crown and Compass on Saturday night, look out for her. If she's got a new hairstyle and make-up, a low-cut top, maybe bra-less, and tight buttoned hipster jeans, it would be great if you told her she looks cool."

They all spoke together as they often did when she asked them to do something for her.

"Your wish is our command, your supreme Highness, our radiant flawless jewel of the midnight lamp, our Queen of the Cordon Bleu, our–"

"Enough! Princess will do fine: slaves, peel me an orange."

On Wednesday Dan left for France – he had to see his grandparents somewhat urgently about arrangements for the making and signing of new wills and a trust fund. Alan's white tie dinner fell on the Thursday, so Flick stepped up to the plate and volunteered to go with him. The tuxedo rental company delivered on time and she collected her dress from the dry cleaners. Eric was on hand to photograph them to show family and friends, but especially for Dan. Alan looked extremely dashing and handsome, Flick wore an ice blue floor length backless gown with a halter neck, she had one of her mother's ball gowns in reserve but thought the fit was not as good. Her red hair was billowing out across the shoulders and cascading down her bare back.

The taxi arrived and they sped off into the dusk. The gala was a great success, the only blot on the horizon was Alan's disappointment to discover Patrick, 'the pain in the posterior' was also there with a rather thin girl, her face expressionless.

"I reckon it's his sister," Alan spoke quietly close to Flick's ear.

"I think he recognises me; whatever, let's ignore him and have some fun."

The evening ended about eleven, taxis were waiting on the rank outside and 'goodnights' filled the air. Flick had followed the sister into the ladies' powder room but no contact had been made. Outside Alan was telling Patrick he was not interested in him at all, he had a girlfriend and if he didn't stop harassing them he would report the matter to the police. Patrick seemed to be of the opinion he wouldn't have the nerve and the girlfriend was nothing other than a cheap tart he'd hired from an escort agency. This comment wasn't timed too well. Alan became the most angry Flick had ever witnessed and she didn't go a bundle on the cheap tart bit either, being on the fringe of the conversation as she and the sister joined them.

"Say goodbye to Prickless Patrick, it's home time, darling," Flick said in her upper-class voice, "my tits are throbbing and my pussy's positively pouring, you need to give me a damn good, long hard fucking tonight, sweetheart."

Patrick's mouth opened to speak but nothing came out. Flick's parting shot was directed at the sister and came as they climbed into the next taxi.

"You could try wanking him off, if you can find it, darling; many have tried and failed I'm told, bye now."

Alan had ran from incredible angry to laughter-ridden shaking wreck in under a minute.

"Oh Flick, you're bloody marvellous, did you see his face, a picture, an absolute picture."

"I think the sister must be a deaf mute or something, she never said a word and the vacant expression didn't change, not a fraction," Flick chuckled in reply.

Back at the flat Eric almost fell on the floor when they re-enacted the taxi rank scenario.

"Well there's one thing, he won't be harassing you anymore, Alan," he said.

Flick quietly thought through the incident, although humorous, it was the second time her anger had turned to a foul-mouthed torrent. On Friday when Dan returned from Paris Alan climbed back into the rented tuxedo and she slipped into the ball gown. They performed it all over again for his benefit, Dan almost wet himself he laughed so hard.

The Saturday gig was going to be a full house. They'd played it twice before and the audience was definitely into rock and blues. The day had been warm and the inside of the pub would be hot. In preparation the band had got into lightweight cotton multi-colour sweatpants and loose vests, Flick abandoned her cut-off denim shorts for a thin wrap round skirt and the usual boob tube. The venue found her a large electric fan to place on the back wall behind the kit. The audience erupted as the first eight bars of 'Jumping Jack Flash' left the PA. An hour later 'Walking the Dog' closed the set with a ten-minute jam session on the end.

In the interval Alan spotted Wendy and Colin by the bar as he made his way back from the toilets.

"They're both here, and – you're gonna love this, Flick – she's gone bra-less under a scoop neck shirt and a black mini skirt, sexy but not sleazy. The hair style has transformed her, but, wait till you clock the make-up, it took me two goes to be sure it was her."

Flick asked if Colin was looking OK.

"He seems to be, she's not attracting too much attention, but he's loving it judging by the smirk on his face – look out, they're coming over."

Eric welcomed them and commented to Wendy how great she looked before asking Colin how the fundraising was going. Alan excused himself to talk to friends at the bar. Dan told Wendy the hair style was a knock-out and she was looking great. Wendy winked at Flick who smiled back.

The second set saw a lot of the crowd's favourites played, the last twenty minutes filled the small dance floor completely. They ended on 'Street Fighting Man', it had become a staple track and closed most shows. The crowd wanted the traditional encore and made it known with whistles, clapping and shouts of 'more, more' until Alan walked up to the microphone to thank them all for coming.

"One for the road, then it's time for night-nights, we can't have Peter missing out on his beauty sleep, he needs all the help he can get," this last remark being aimed at the landlord.

A voice from the back shouted 'Toad, do Toad', the crowd voted with their voice, Toad, Toad, Toad became a chant. Alan held his hand up.

"One second please, Flick, are you ready for this?"

Even without a mike her answer came out loud and clear: "I'm ready, I was born ready!"

Drums, bass and guitar began together. Once the theme had been established, Eric and Dan joined Alan at the side of the stage. Flick worked her way through the Ginger Baker solo as close as she could manage. The crowd hushed to a murmur then fell into silence as the rhythms pounded across the room driven by a red-haired girl whose body seemed to be under the command and control of four different spirits. The hypnotic beat rose, fell, rose again, patten followed patten until finally, lathered in her own sweat, guitar and bass jumped back in to close the song off. Eric and Dan took an arm each and hoisted her off the stool and over the cymbals. Alan screamed over the thunder of applause:

"On the drums, Flick Bowden!"

Flick bowed once then together they lined up for the second. To round it off they struck the pose from the posters hung on the walls, a horizontal drummer smiling and waving from her six-handed perch.

With the doors locked and the lights low it was hard to believe the scene of twenty minutes ago. They'd cooled down and changed into fresh clothes then Peter had bought four drinks over. Alan had just packed some cables away and sat down.

"Well that was interesting, the crowd here get right into it, don't they?"

Everyone agreed it was one of their hottest venues, a fair hike from home but it paid well. Eric put his glass down and spoke to Alan.

"I bet we can work a keyboard part into Toad, by the way where'd you go, mate, while the solo was going down?"

"Colin called me over to say they'd had a brilliant night and they were heading home as soon as it finished. I got the info pack to go with the map of the walk too."

After the rig had been torn down and packed into Wolfie they set off on the hour's run back to the flat. On a moorland road about halfway to Manchester the headlights picked out a car on the grassy edge. The windows were steamed up and the whole car was rocking.

"Someone can't wait to get home," Eric quipped.

When the chuckles died down, Alan said, "It looks like Wendy's miniskirt's done the trick – that, my friends, was their Volkswagen."

22

The next week saw Alan's picture accepted as one of the hundred winning exhibits submitted to the art gallery in the city. Wendy called in to say the date of the charity walk had been fixed for the last weekend of September. She told Flick things were picking up between her and Colin. Patrick has fallen off the radar and Colin had dropped by to say the fund raiser was booked at a large pub near the children's care home. The posters were out and over two hundred tickets had been sold so far. Whenever possible Dan and Alan walked the streets and public parks building up their stamina for the cross-country hike across northern Britain; they were feeling pleased about doing the walk – many of their friends had sponsored them. Eric and Flick took them into the Derbyshire High Peak during the day at weekends, the evenings were spent on stage playing more rock and blues, the middle of the road stuff was dropped from the play lists completely. Wendy told them the care home were overjoyed about how much effort was being put in.

Flick woke up around two in the morning. She slid out of bed and found her notebook, a fourth set of runes joined the others. Sleep reclaimed her ten minutes later.

One evening they all met at the city gallery where Alan showed them how his picture worked. When you stood in front of the bowed screen, the distance was very important, so much so a red tape line marked the limit of where you placed your feet. With the top edge nearest to you the picture appeared to be that of a naked girl sat in the lotus position just outside a veiled cave mouth. This was in the bottom section. The girl was looking up and wearing a face of innocence. Directly above her, beginning at the top edge and ending near the centre, was a muscular naked black male with a pair of feathered angel's wings. The arms held the wings open as if in flight. The motor hummed and the frame shifted on its pivot. As the tilt increased the illusion began as the picture seemed to move as the spheres turned. The girl now started to levitate and slightly unfold her legs, the hair shifted as it might do as if in flight and the expression lost some of its innocence. Above her the angel looked down and noticed her, the wings began to furl as the arms arced inwards. Further tilting of the frame saw the girl rise towards the angel with her body almost in a straight line as if diving upwards into space. The black angel continued to fold its wings, dropping down the picture to meet the ascending girl. At a point just over the halfway mark the girl was directly under the angel's open legs with the closing wings taking on the appearance of two feathered doors ready to close over her. The girl was now heading straight up into the lower torso of the angel with long strands of hair pinned by the pressure of the implied slipstream.

The next part of the frame arrived at the exact angle to allow the viewer to witness for a few milliseconds the girl, wearing an expression of pure lust, with arms outstretched disappear into the slit in the angel's penis. The wings folded over themselves shielding the entry site as he slid down towards the bottom of the frame.

As the motor turned the last few degrees the veil parted as the angel dropped into the cave the girl was originally sat outside. Closer inspection revealed this was actually an almost three-dimensional picture of the entire female vulva. The motor stopped for ten seconds then rapidly rewound the frame to the start position.

Dan spoke first.

"How in the world did you manage to work this all out? The mechanics of it are simple enough; I mean, I helped Eric build it."

Eric looked carefully at the huge collection of spheres and the seemingly abstract lines of colour painted on them. Close up it was a nonsense, from the far wall it was the same story, an incomprehensible mass of disjointed shapes, shades and colours.

Some spheres shifted at one angle some rotated in another. A crazy kaleidoscope that seemed to break all the laws of optics probably including the ones humans hadn't discovered yet.

"I can comprehend the illusion and the way in which you've painstakingly placed every tiny little detail is fantastic."

"This has to work by tricking the brain into seeing what isn't there, obviously, but this also tricks it into actually believing what isn't there," Flick said over the fingertips of her clasped hands. "I have one question: I cannot work out why you wanted me to do the lotus pose at the bottom of the stairs where you drew me from above. My lotus pose is only in the first viewpoint, by thirty percent of the frame's travel I've transformed into the high board diver pose going up not down so the pose from the stairs isn't any use – or is it?"

"The image of you where you should be when the frame is at the start of its travel is used in the original placement, the illusion depends on the brain requiring an anchor to sort out what it's seeing as against what it thinks it's seeing. As we have to tell the viewer this is an illusion, the brain is sub-consciously scanning the whole thing trying to find out how it's done. Rather in the same way a magician will use distraction to fool you, the brain is engaged in looking for the slip up, to this end by putting the image of you from the angle and position at the top of the stairs in that totally 'wrong' place the brain sees it, says, that's OK, right girl, right pose, right position forget it, let's keep looking for how it's done. This millisecond of eye-scanning is just enough to allow the impossible image to become the true image in the brain's opinion."

Flick smiled. "So if you filmed the whole thing and played it back it becomes as Eric said a nonsense, the illusion depends on the brain not seeing as well as seeing. Smoke and mirrors, just smoke and mirrors. Bloody good ones, mind, Alan, I think it's magic – there's almost a pun to be had there."

"Will you tell us about the title next, we can't work it out," Dan asked.

"OK, we better go to the nearest pub, they want to close in a few minutes."

Over a beer Alan started to explain the title.

"I've written this down as a handout but they're not printed yet so I will have to bore you to death. This isn't a full explanation, I want the viewer to read the blurb and using what they have just read form the final experience according to what they saw, or think they saw, and all according to their particular credo. You may have noticed in the title the two key words are anagrammatical, now the leaflet adds three more, so we have Levi, Live, Vile, Evil and Veil. The viewer has to think about options. We have to deal with Levi first."

Alan took a deep pull on his beer and started on Levi.

"The Torah suggests that the name 'Levi' refers to Leah's hope for Jacob to 'join' with her, join in this case meaning to become pregnant. In Genesis Levi and his brother, Simeon, exterminate the city of Shechem in revenge for the rape of their sister Dinah. They seized the city and killed the men. Here we see what many will interpret as a totally over the top act of violence. They had misled the citizens earlier by making a deal concerning Dinah's rapist, basically if he married her in exchange for all the men of the city being circumcised. Jacob hears about their destruction and berates them. We move now to Levi on his deathbed where he gathered all his children to narrate the story of his life. He prophesied what they would do, and what would happen to them until judgement day. He also told them that, 'God had chosen him and his seed as priest of Lord unto eternity'. Levi is described as having had two visions. The first vision covered the seven heavens, the Jewish Messiah, and Judgement Day. The second vision portrays seven angels bringing Levi seven insignia signifying priesthood, prophecy, and judgement. Please note there aren't any black angels as far as I can tell, fallen or otherwise."

Alan took another pull and launched into the 'Live' segment of the title.

"This means 'to exist' not 'as it happens'. Live is what the lotus girl is doing. Meditating enhances life, Meditation has roots in Buddhism. To live is to have life and a life is a creation between male and female. The life begins in innocence and may change to lust and wickedness. Vile comes next, apart from being a synonym of evil it's an adjective with over eighty common word entries in a thesaurus. It's a very widespread word so one has to be careful where one uses it."

Dan and Eric went to the bar for another round then Alan carried on.

"Three down, two to go. Evil is a tricky subject; much has been written about it throughout the ages. We can start with a couple of the more controversial pieces, 'If men were born free, they would form no conception of good and evil so long as they were free' and 'According to the guidance of reason, of two things which are good, we shall follow the greater good, and of two evils, follow the less'. In his writings Guru Arjan explains that, because God is the source of all things, what we believe to be evil must also come from God. And because God is ultimately a source of absolute good, nothing truly evil can originate from God. Martin Luther argued that there are cases where a little evil is a positive good. He wrote, 'Seek out the society of your boon companions, drink, play, talk bawdy, and amuse yourself. One must sometimes commit a sin out of hate and contempt for the Devil, so as not to give him the chance to make one scrupulous over mere nothings'. And what is the root of evil? 'Desire is the root of evil, illusion is the root of evil' – so said Gautama Siddhartha, the founder of Buddhism, I think. Finally, my long-suffering friends, we come to 'Veil'. We all know of the uses of the veil as worn by humans, but here I want to direct the viewers' thoughts to this piece, 'the removing of the veil as a symbol of the temple veil that was torn when Christ died, giving believers direct access to God, and in the same way, the bride and the groom, once married, now have full access to one another'. The actual handout has more details, also the explanation is fuller than my brief speech, but I don't think I've made any errors so you should get the gist of the text. Hopefully it encourages the viewer to apply their own thoughts to the piece; there may be many different ways it can be seen. Can I shut up now please?"

Eric started the debate.

"I'm truly amazed, Alan. Using what you've just told us I feel I have a direction to assemble my thoughts in. I'm thinking four or five things at the same time, everything seems to point one way then the whole stack of ideas collapses because another concept has burrowed underneath the first and popped its head up."

Flick interjected, "Which is fine until another pile of thoughts comes screaming in riding a Harley straight through all of the previous possibilities, backfiring lumps of fantasy and paradoxes into the soup bowl as it goes."

Dan sat quietly, drained his glass and leant back.

"As I see this, at first glance that is, the theme here is life. Natural life, life lived by doctrines, life by science and academia, even life in reverse. There must be over a hundred ways of fathoming this amazing piece. I am going to watch this exhibition closely, I think we're going to get some amazing reactions."

Flick had returned from the toilets and sat down next to Alan wearing her mischievous face.

"It just crossed my mind that if, as Dan thinks, the picture will attract a lot of publicity it might just come to the attention of dear Aunt Mavis, who would be mortified if someone told her Alan modelled the 'cave' on my intimate sexual organs?"

Alan, who had learned to recognise and now understood Flick the Naughty Elf, turned to face her and said, "Well, my dearest Deborah, we won't tell and if the question is asked as to who owns the magnificent vulva on display we will all keep our collective mouths shut. I can guarantee you one other thing as well, your father will have a bloody field day winding her up."

The resulting laughter was enough to make people turn and look at them.

Before they knew it the Hadrian's Wall walk was upon them. On the Tuesday before, Escapade had played at a huge pub with a function room normally used for weddings that held over eight hundred seated at tables. The fire officer had permitted the same number if people were standing instead and so far the venue had never exceeded it. The gig was expecting to attract about three hundred and fifty. Pre-sales accounted for three hundred and fourteen according to Colin, and Wendy guessed there would be another fifty late sales they didn't know about.

Wendy had a chance to chat with Flick and told her that things were on the 'up and up' between her and Colin. She decided she wasn't going to die if she got on the back of his 750cc Norton Commando, so they'd started going for ride outs. She'd also bought some new clothes that went with the new image; however, the same mini skirt was making another appearance and a shirt unbuttoned to the bust with the remaining material knotted underneath was on its first outing. Flick asked how she was getting on going bra-less only to be told she wished she'd had the courage years ago, it was so comfortable. Eric wandered over and they chatted about the number of people already coming through the doors. Colin joined them and said another eighty tickets had been accounted for. While the girls talked about hair and make-up, Colin showed some pictures of his Norton. Eric told Flick later that a few of them had Wendy lying across it in a bikini, rather like the one she had, three small triangles and a couple of bits of string.

"Making up for lost time I guess," she commented.

The gig went very well considering it was a Tuesday, with the final ticket count hitting four hundred and thirty-one, representing a good chunk of the thousand pounds they were aiming for. Alan got Colin and Wendy up on stage just before the last number to say on behalf of the care home how thankful they were to the audience and to Escapade for donating their time and effort to the project. The last number was 'Gimme Shelter' with Wendy helping out on backing vocals, assisted by two more beers than she normally drank.

Wednesday evening saw the maps of northern England come out and the information pack about the route. Starting at Bowness on Solway, the path followed a roughly straight line across the countryside finishing at the appropriately named Wallsend near Newcastle upon Tyne. At seventy-two miles long, it was usually a three-day hike if you wanted to take in some of the Roman sites on the way.

Thursday night saw Escapade back at Kev's pub by the river. The brewery had said the place was going to close down in the following April – the whole area was earmarked for a housing development and some commercial units. The gig went down well and Kev paid them the 'beer bonus' which put a smile on their faces. Wendy and Colin came back to the flat after the gig and helped unload the gear before putting all the equipment for the hike back onto Wolfie. Colin had an eight-berth tent which he and Wendy would put up at the two overnight stops along the route; they became an unofficial support crew. He was also moving Wolfie down the route from Solway. Colin and Wendy slept in Wolfie that night so they could have an early start on Friday.

Slipping out of Manchester at six in the morning saved a good hour on the hundred- and forty-mile journey. The hike started close to ten, on the sandy estuary of the River Esk. Wendy and Colin moved to Rickerby Park, the first checkpoint just east of Carlisle, bagged a good parking space and waited. The four were making good time, arriving at the rendezvous around two-thirty for a light lunch. The second leg took them to Walton where the tent had been pitched and a hot dinner awaited. Feet were soaked and blisters attended to. Weary legs were witness to the twenty-six miles they'd covered.

The second day began with an early breakfast then whilst the four slightly stiff hikers trod the path east, Colin and Wendy had to move everything another twenty miles or so and make another camp. This of course came after the lunch stop at Cawfield Quarry. Alan was beginning to feel the stresses of walking over a wide range of terrain. A lot of the route is on well-made roads, some over fields, some through undergrowth sheltering under plantations. Dan was cheering him on, Flick and Eric did what they normally did to combat fatigue, they sang. Camp at the end of day two was near Walwick. This left roughly twenty-two miles to Wallsend. Both Alan and Dan were determined to carry on and complete the event, even though their feet were blistered and attacks of leg cramps had forced them to take a couple of unplanned breaks. Flick and Eric, being used to hiking, were in good shape, and wolfing down the sausages, mash and onions like it was their last meal. Dan was surprised how hungry he was; thankfully Wendy had done plenty, working on the theory that breakfast could be sausage sandwiches if there were any leftovers. That theory went out the tent flap fifteen minutes after the knives and forks started work.

Sat outside watching the moon rise gave rise to small talk and idle chatter. Flick was leafing through her notebook and stopped at the pages the runes were written on. The last set were different to the others. After ten minutes trying to work something out, she gave up just in time to hear Wendy say:

"Look, you've all done fantastic, there's twenty-two miles left, this time tomorrow we'll be done."

Eric leaned over to her. "Dan and Alan have the fatigue blues, they've hit their personal wall so to speak, we're got to do some morale boosting in the morning."

She put her mug down and told him what she had in mind. "I foresaw this so it might be time to start doing some team leading. I'll go up front and set the pace, you sweep from the back. I'll get Colin to call in at Heddon for an extra tea break as well as the riverside stop near Newcastle. It's now, as you know, they're going to suffer the most and if the weather changes as well it might looking at the forecast we may have to cut the last leg off short."

Eric nodded. "Let's get them bedded down, we'll start an hour later, so they can warm up before the start."

They were all deep asleep by ten. The good night's rest had papered over some of the aches and pains, the psychological side of things was looking better than the previous evening.

Setting off soon after seven they made fair progress towards Heddon. After the hot drink and bacon sandwiches Wendy had pulled from the magic frying pan morale was better than when they arrived, but still not good. The next stage took them towards the north bank of the river Tyne. Flick told them they were less than four hours from Wallsend and to keep looking at her rucksack if they felt their determination slipping. As the hike progressed Dan couldn't stand it any longer, he had to catch her up and find out what was written on the large card stuck to her straps. It took him almost a quarter of a mile; she realised what he was doing and slowed her pace imperceptibly so two minutes later he reached out and held her pony-tailed hair away from the rucksack. When he read it, he laughed and fell back a couple of paces. She'd written in large letters with a felt tip pen, 'Tuesday night menu, Roast Chicken with jacket spuds, for dessert, BAKED ALASKA, collect your meal voucher at Sedgedunum.' Underneath was a picture of the dessert in question cut from a magazine. Alan caught them up and shared the sudden lift it had given Dan. At the riverside stop they were in better spirits; also the promised rain hadn't materialised.

Wendy was ready for them, Colin had the teapot ready and waiting. She'd been feeling guilty that Dan and Alan had suffered quite a bit of pain and would not recover fully for almost a week.

"I've been thinking, guys, I don't reckon anyone would complain if you stopped the walk right here. No one would even know."

Alan answered her first: "Sorry, Wendy, I'm not giving in. It would be cheating the people who're sponsoring us, but above all we'd be cheating ourselves."

Dan nodded and added, "I'm carrying on too. This cunning vixen has found my weak spot and I'll be dammed if the minx is going back to Manchester with my dinner voucher in her bag."

Eric grinned and added nonchalantly, "Oh, the power of a Baked Alaska, we had better hope our Duchess of the dining room remembered to bring them with her."

Flick looked quite serene as she spoke. "I always keep my promises, as indeed you're doing now by walking the last leg, all of us, together."

"Hear hear, nice one. Look at it this way, guys, you won't have to torture her this time to get the goods," Colin chipped in.

"You have to be joking, this lot pass up on a chance of tickling me silly. They'll be dreaming up something on the way to Wallsend, they're totally without mercy, you know; thankfully I've never done them Beef Wellington, I'd probably end up tied to the kitchen table stark naked while those six peacock feathers reduce me to jelly."

Dan rubbed his chin. "Beef Wellington, you say, that's the one in a luscious pastry case, isn't it?"

Alan looked at Eric. "I guess we better prepare the torture chamber then, if Beef Wellington's at stake she'll hold out against foot tickling, the navel's good but will it be enough?"

Eric pretended to be thinking. "The small of her back is very sensitive, and just behind her knees. The lower abdomen also produces large wiggles and almost hysterical giggles. To be on the safe side, let's take all her clothes off, then we can see if there's any other ticklish spots we don't know about."

All the time Alan is nodding and miming making mental notes.

Wendy had still not entirely worked out life at the Manchester Madhouse; she looked at Flick and said, "I don't believe it, they wouldn't, would they?"

"I'm afraid they will, Wendy, I'm actually rather looking forward to it," she answered as Flick the Naughty Elf. "I haven't tried a Wellington since I was at school. Don't look worried – at least Eric didn't tell them about my inner thighs – oops, I shouldn't have said that."

Eric, Dan and Alan couldn't keep their faces straight any longer.

"The look on your face, Wendy, yours too, Colin," Alan spluttered. "You're both invited to dinner, Flick can do her Beef Wellington, just bring some wine."

As the joke sank in Wendy asked if she could help her in any way. Flick couldn't resist one last crack:

"If you like, come early enough you can join in, are you sure you want to be ticked silly as well, the table can take two, there's enough feathers for Colin to join in and we may as well be naked in the kitchen together."

This brought another round of chuckles. With that she picked up her rucksack and yelled, "Get fell in, you miserable wretches, we have an appointment with the Romans!"

Morale zoomed back up the ladder.

"Hi ho, hi ho, it's through the trees we go," Flick sang out; the others soon joined in.

The last leg ended late on the Sunday afternoon. Flick handed Dan his dinner voucher, written on a gift tag wishing the bearer a very happy birthday. Alan collected his too, it wished him a Joyous Noel, both of them were dead beat and flopped into Wolfie. Wendy was quite emotional once it dawned on her they'd finished.

"I'm so happy," she cried, tears rolling down her face.

Dan and Alan were fast asleep by the time Colin turned onto the A1 at Gateshead. Flick and Eric watched the world go by, cuddled up on the front couch sharing a bottle of home-made wine and smiling at each other a lot.

The daylight hours were getting shorter when the controversy over Alan's 'Black Angel' broke. It made the local paper first, then a radio debate added to the ruckus. The art gallery were defending their position against several representatives of the church who had demanded the piece be withdrawn as it was blasphemous, pornographic and corrupting. The art gallery teased the argument along, enjoying the unprecedented free publicity taking it up to national level. In the end Alan agreed to be interviewed by a local art historian to be recorded for broadcast as part of a popular arts programme. Interest grew for a while, the expected extremists had a good yell, and eventually most people who were up in arms against it finally managed to get their heads round the two most important words surrounding the whole thing: Illusion and Surreal. Eventually it fizzled out and died as most of these things do when the vast majority of people fail to be caught in the back-draught of the affronted few. The whole affair ended on a sad note, however, when a fanatic with an oddball persuasion hid in a closet until the gallery closed and destroyed the whole thing before making a clean getaway out the fire exit.

Alan said that in many respects he was glad he did paint it, but mainly he felt sad about the destruction. He went on record later as saying he would not be repeating the process. Soon afterwards a trickle of similar pieces were announced in the art world but none managed to display the full illusion like Alan's original. He'd been asked on the programme where his inspiration came from to which the reply of, 'I really don't know – it just came to me' had stymied one particular bishop who was hoping the answer would fuel the argument up to the white hot level.

Colin and Wendy accepted the invitation to dinner and just to remind them of the prank the dining table was laid for six with peacock feathers stood in the wine glasses. As the evening wore on and Alan's hobby of wine making was beginning to make its presence felt, Wendy asked about the cute bear rucksack hanging on the hook. Eric told them the story of their first meeting and Flick added she wasn't sure how she'd come by it.

"It must have been a present, birthday or Christmas, from one of the family. Nowadays we use him to put important stuff in, you know the expression – 'I'll put that in a safe place so it won't get lost' – Kenny's that safe place."

Colin was looking out of the window probably for the fifth time in twenty minutes, Wendy asked him what was so interesting out in the street. He said there was someone walking up and down looking at the house and he didn't like the look of him.

"He's looked at the house four times now, I can't work out if he's waiting for someone or he's not sure of which house to go to, either way there's something dodgy about him."

They all peered out into the night but there wasn't anyone to see anymore. The conversation turned to the children's care home and how the target of a thousand pounds had been shattered. Wendy told them the total raised was over sixteen hundred and it would make a fantastic difference to the children. Alan went to the kitchen for more wine and was out of the room when the knock on the door came. Eric answered, the others heard a muffled dialogue then Dan looked round the curtain.

"Shit – it's bloody Patrick, he's still after him."

Colin and Wendy looked a bit puzzled. Alan came into the room and took Flick's hand when she explained what was happening at the front door. Eric returned and reported that he had left him on the doorstep under the pretence that he wasn't sure if Alan was in the house.

"I've got a couple of minutes, I can tell him you're out, but he'll be back."

Flick looked at Alan. "We've got to get shot of him permanently. He still thinks I'm a rental tart and he won't believe you're not gay. I've got an idea, will you trust me on this?"

Alan nodded, all of his previous fears were flooding back after thinking the episode was dead and buried.

"I trust you, Flick," he mumbled, looking down.

She started issuing orders:

"Dan, go to your bedroom, hide behind the curtains, he might turn violent. Colin, Wendy, stay in here, listen out for a scuffle, if there is I'd like Colin to come through as quick as possible. Alan, go to your bedroom, strip off, everything, and I do mean everything, then get into bed. Eric, give me a minute, two if you can stall him, then let him in and bring him through, knock on the bedroom door then open it a crack. You all got it?"

"What are you doing all this while?" Wendy asked.

"I shall be in bed with Alan, also naked and providing an interesting soundtrack to go with what we're doing. If I'm right this will prove to that warped brain of his that Alan is not for him."

"Ah, 'in flagrante delicto', sort of," Dan chuckled.

Flick and Alan pulled their clothes off, got into bed and adopted what is known as the missionary position with Alan supporting himself on his arms. Flick arranged the sheet so it just covered Alan's upper thighs, her wide open legs showed as two bumps in the cotton, a foot hanging out each side. They waited a few seconds then as Eric's footsteps were heard outside Flick began a very convincing rendition of a woman on the brink of orgasm. Alan caught Patrick's reflection in the mirror as he swung the door open and strode through. As Flick rolled out her imitation climax his face turned from shock through disbelief and ended in horror as she arched her back and pushed herself towards Alan's chest. Dumbstruck as he was, with legs that ignored the brain's frantic messages to leave, he stared open mouthed for a good five seconds.

Finally he said with a voice full of confusion:

"What on earth do you think you're doing?"

The Naughty Elf propped herself up on her elbows and addressed Alan:

"You're right, he's totally stupid."

Patrick turned and fled down the passage, slamming the door behind him. Dan stepped from behind the curtain with tears of hysterical laughter running down both cheeks. Eric was more or less in the same position; they both held their sides as they started to ache. Colin and Wendy appeared at the door.

"Is it OK to come in?" Wendy asked.

"Only if you've bought the wine bottle with you," Alan answered.

He sat up and let Flick retrieve her legs, they just looked at each other shaking in silent mirth. Twenty minutes later Wendy and Colin had been bought up to date with the troublesome Patrick, including the re-enactment of the gala ball parting shots complete with posh voices.

"And you said there was no bed hopping, that, Deborah, was a little white lie, wasn't it?" Wendy admonished.

"No, it wasn't," Flick answered. "Tonight was the first time ever that I've been in Alan and Dan's bed."

Colin was the only person who spotted the slip.

"Alan and Dan's bed, that means – what exactly?"

Dan looked at him. "It means, Colin, that Alan and I are lovers, in much the same way as Eric and Flick are. Flick and Eric did what you have just witnessed to help Alan in his struggle to keep his sexual persuasion hidden, partly to avoid violence from the thugs out there on the streets, partly to make sure his tutors and fellow students aren't biased against him, and also because he's not quite ready to 'come out' yet. Now you know do you feel any differently towards us?"

Almost immediately Wendy said it didn't change a thing for her, they were both great people.

Colin took a moment to think then agreed. "I've just ran through my memories from the first time I saw you at the Star and Garter to the charity gig, the hike, tonight and I can honestly say it don't change a damn thing."

The third bottle of wine was retrieved from the fridge and the conversation moved more towards Alan and Dan's relationship; Colin and Wendy swore they would not say anything to anyone. Alan looked round the room and announced that as of now he was going to 'come out', once again he had learned a lot and it was time to stand up and be counted.

Only one thing bothered Colin, it was his lack of understanding how Eric could let his girlfriend, who was actually his fiancée, firstly pose naked for Alan's picture, and also let her have intercourse with another man whilst he and his friends looked on. Eric smiled then chuckled. Out of the corner of his eye he saw Flick's face split into a wide grin; it was almost possible to see the wicked imp materialise on her right shoulder.

"Let me answer you in a roundabout way, Colin. First I have a question for you, in your relationship with Wendy do you own her, do you think you're the boss? I don't own Flick, Flick owns Flick, she shares herself with me because she loves me and she knows that I love her. Dan and Alan feel the same way about each other. You may well have asked the same question to Dan: why can he bear to see Alan in bed with Flick? If you can understand the fact that nobody owns anybody else, we consent to share, then Flick will provide you with her side of the story."

Colin nodded.

Flick asked him to tell everyone what he saw from the moment he came through the bedroom door.

"I saw you two straight away, I knew Eric was stood in front of the chest of drawers and Dan had been there all the time behind the curtains in readiness I assume." He paused, the others sat silent, taking that as his cue to continue he carried on. "Automatically I focused on the bed, Alan on top of Flick, there had been this wolf-like howl that rang through the whole building a few seconds ago and I was looking at two naked people who had just finished making love. I remember Flick raised up on her elbows, both breasts exposed, legs wide open, Alan wedged between them, propped up on his arms. The sheet was across them, it ended just by Alan's buttocks. There is no doubt in my mind you two had just had intercourse, not for many minutes I grant you, but it was the real McCoy of that I'm sure."

Colin refilled his glass and waited for Flick to say something; he thought his recollection was correct and accurate but hopefully, as they were all their friends, wrong as well.

"Although there are many 'slips 'twixt cup and lip' please consider Phaedrus: 'Things are not always what they seem; the first appearance deceives many; the intelligence of a few perceives what has been carefully hidden'," Flick said slowly. "Let me run you through what you just recalled, only this time I'll provide you with some footnotes instead of an erotic howl. After you entered the room, you immediately noted the position of the other men in the room as I would expect you to do as I asked you to be a back-up to Dan and Eric if violence erupted. Nothing happened on that front, but it didn't stop you becoming charged up in readiness. Then your male instincts went into action again. You now looked at the scene on the bed and assessed what you thought was happening. At this point you had to face two things at the same time and you're struggling to assimilate somewhat. The overwhelming bit right in front of your eyes is a naked couple who are familiar to you. They are, however, in a role or position that is not right according to your previous experiences. A googly has been bowled. The second problem is that you have never seen either of us naked until that moment. If you're with me so far I'll move on. As a heterosexual male you're naturally drawn to the female first, which is handy because it distracts you from the actual action happening at groin level. Whilst you're busy looking at my tits, which by the way I was shaking and wiggling for all I was worth, and you only came in at the end of my performance, you could not differentiate between Alan's position, just resting on my belly and the proof needed that actual intercourse had taken place, it was shall we say, tricky? The illusion is added to when you look down and confirm we are really completely naked. At this point the information in your head has reached the point where the brain says, enough info, I've got that, by then the laughter had started so you now try to put what you've just seen alongside this madcap maniac situation and weird questions like the one you just asked start popping up. To finish off my little lecture, I did take a gamble, that's one reason for the heavy mob on stand-by, I had to assume that Patrick was a dominant character and had enough 'maleness' in him to be distracted by a writhing female with her tits bouncing to the extent the fun going off lower down would not be analysed in greater detail. It's just the same as transforming how I look with lipstick, powder and paint as the saying goes, it's all smoke and mirrors, Colin, just smoke and mirrors."

Alan looked at Flick and said, "Shall we let him into the secret of where the old 'John Thomas' was, Princess?"

With a puckish smile she winked. "After you, Sir Lancelot."

"I found my member tucked firmly between 'les joues d'elle derrière' as Dan would put it."

Wendy had to laugh; she apologised but soon everyone was chuckling too.

Colin still looked a little ponderous. He was still trying to get his head round the fact that he was sitting opposite a girl and a man who had not the slightest qualm about what they had done. Flick read his mind as she often did to people who seemed to be on the point of asking a question but were unsure if they could.

"It wouldn't have made any difference if it had been Dan," she said. "I would have done it for him too. Our little flat got called the Manchester Madhouse because that's how a lot of people would perceive it, always thinking and fearing the worst, their stupid little prejudices blinkering their eyes. Carbon copies of my Aunt Mavis and sadly found the world over. Have you heard the one about the Christian, the Jew and the Atheist who met up with a Muslim on their way to visit a Buddhist temple? They looked round, chatted and nodded to each other then the four went to a café; here they talked about the visit and later told stories and laughed a lot in between the coffees. It isn't a joke, it's what happens when you're not an asshole."

1974 drew to a close. The Christmas period was busy with gigs and studies, exams were looming and arrangements were made to go to Letchworth over the holidays. Helen reported that Mavis was turning into a rather 'cantankerous old bitch' to put a finer point on it. Robert had made matters worse by telling her to lighten up and start living in the twentieth century as well as winding her up even more than usual. She was sure he was sick and tired of having her around, but Mavis was now such a pathetic creature showing her years well before her time that his tolerance grew, well, a little bit. Patrick never showed up again, rumour had it he had left the area, taking the thin girl with him.

Just before Wolfie took them down to Hertfordshire, Flick sat at the table with the strips of copied runes in front of her. She had looked in all the university library's sections that dealt with languages and couldn't find anything that resembled anything she had carefully scripted onto strips of vellum, cut from a page Alan had given her from an artist sketch book. Around eleven she put the strips carefully back in her notebook and returned it to Kenny for safekeeping. The light went out and darkness fell on the dining room of the Manchester Madhouse, except for a faint violet glow coming from Kenny hanging on his hook.

lthough it sounds out of character, between January and April of 1975 not a lot disturbed the residents of the Manchester Madhouse. Friends came and went, midnight oil burned almost every night the band didn't have a gig. Alan was a new person now he'd overcome his fears and 'come out', Dan said he couldn't believe the changes in him. In March Escapade were the last band to perform at the Irwell Castle before it closed; also John and Avril sent out the invitations to their twenty-fifth wedding anniversary celebrations. Alan consulted his notebook and announced both his strawberry and rhubarb wines would be ready by then. 'Oh shit' was Dan's teasing comment.

The Easter break saw the four friends pile aboard Wolfie and head off to North Wales. Early on Saturday morning the roads out of Manchester were reasonably clear; however, they dropped in on Dan's parents in Altrincham for a coffee break as Alan was having difficulty getting his eyes unglued and Flick wasn't far behind.

"Who invented six in the morning anyway," he grumbled.

After two mugs of extra strength espresso he had eyeballs out on stalks. Most of the holiday traffic had arrived in Snowdonia on the Friday evening whilst Escapade were playing a blues club near Oldham. Wolfie wandered his merry way down the A56 towards the Welsh border, Kenny swinging on his straps and Eddy sat on the bed holding onto Friday's gig money. By the time they arrived at the campsite in Capel Curig, Colin and Wendy had pitched their massive tent and sandwiches were just asking to be eaten. At half past ten, six well-fed and watered hikers set off for the Pyg Track to the top of Mount Snowdon.

Thankfully there were no wandering children or reckless motorcyclists to worry about, the only problem arose when Colin's boot disappeared in a boggy section of grass, sinking so far the water went over the top, waterlogging his sock. He had to squelch his way to the summit and dry off at the mountain railway station out of the twenty mile an hour wind.

That evening the conquest of Snowdon was celebrated in style. Around the BBQ set up in the disused barn where a camp fire had been lit by the owners, beer and wine flowed and plans were made for Sunday. Eric and Flick were taking Jeepy off-road through part of the Coed y Brenin Forest to see the waterfalls. The others were going to have a day on the island of Anglesey.

As the evening wore on, the scent of pine wafted across the barn as the fire crackled, sending short shadows across the floor. Eric reached for his old acoustic guitar and Flick filled empty beer and wine bottles from the standpipe. After spending five minutes threading them with bailing twine along a long forgotten scythe handle found in the straw and 'tuning' the bottles her 'booze-a-phone' was ready. Soon the campers were treated to 'Mannish Boy' followed by 'Who Do You Love' arranged for guitar, bottle xylophone and six almost harmonising voices. By the time they'd slaughtered 'Get Back', fellow campers were coming over with folding chairs. Somewhere near midnight, 'I Shot The Sheriff' wandered over the mountains marking the first and probably last time the song would feature a Welsh-ish choir. The music ended there, Flick gave her temporary 'sticks' to a small terrier which had been watching them intently from its undisputed place, that being as close as possible to the camp fire without scorching its fur.

"Well that rounded the day off nicely." She smiled.

"Just like being at an Eisteddfod, boy'o," Dan replied.

Jeepy made good progress along the narrow tree-lined forest tracks taking the water-filled potholes and mud patches effortlessly. Flick looked up at the map she'd wedged onto the steering wheel.

"I make it a left here then a drop of a few metres to the clearing we can park in."

Eric was leaning out of the window, photographing a stunning landscape of trees and rolling hills. Turning and looking at her finger on the map he asked, "I take it that's the first waterfall?"

She nodded. "Then we walk on this track here to the second – just here," stabbing the waterfall symbol just above the next brown contour line.

The Jeep made light work of the incline. At the bottom a wide circle of scrawny grass and bracken marked the end of the drivable trail. The first waterfall was about a mile and a quarter away; they were approaching it from the more difficult access – normal tourists would choose the simpler route. Eric was busy shooting the scenery including a self-timer one showing them hand in hand on a large rock with the falls in the background. After a quick hot drink, they moved on to the second set, a leisurely affair with the early sun gaining strength as the morning ticked past, raising the temperature a couple of degrees. Despite being the Easter holiday, the forest and the waterfalls were deserted; this may have been in part to the cold weather – the forecasts had predicted snow in many areas which is unusual at Easter. On their way to the second falls, they'd seen two people heading towards the road, two dots in the wooded valley below. They sat on a large flat rock which served as both seats and table for their lunch break, the sun as high as the month of April would allow and already the chill was noticeable as they walked back to the Jeep.

Eric was leading when Flick told him to stop, he held a branch out of the way of the path as she caught up; she had a vexed expression on her face and was studying the compass.

"Take a look at this, it's been swinging for almost a minute now."

Eric looked down at the needle as it swung between the north mark and about fifteen degrees east then fell back towards north before repeating the anomaly again.

"Magnetite can do this but even if there is a large deposit here why didn't it show on the way up? Look through the gap in the trees, this is the sharp bend at the junction of the narrow ridge where you can either drop down the hill, the way we're going, or stay on this track towards Ganllwyd."

Eric couldn't think of any other reason the compass should show inaccurate readings.

"At least it keeps moving, so we can't follow a wrong direction and thankfully we can retrace our steps from memory. Let's tackle the descent and have another look at the bottom."

Ten minutes later the compass seemed to have settled down, but when Eric held the map against it the needle was almost five degrees out. On their return home it would have to go to their local outdoor shop and be checked against another. The bottom of the hill was out of the wind and felt warmer; they knew the Jeep was only a half mile away so the last of the coffee was shared and a nearby squirrel inherited the crumbs from the sandwich box. They froze when they heard the howl – after a couple of hours of nothing but birdsong and flowing water to listen to it surprised them.

"What did that?" Eric asked.

"Well, it wasn't a bike or a kid thankfully. My best guess would be a very large dog but there was something about it that says no, it was too drawn out. If I didn't know better I'd go for a wolf."

Eric looked at her. "Just as a matter of interest, how's your vibe-meter?"

She smiled and held out her hand. "It's OK, no spikes or troughs, just ticking along – hold on though, I'm getting a weird sensation now, but not so intense this time."

Eric held her hand tightly. "You mean the 'walking over the grave' feeling? What are you sensing?"

She was concentrating hard, both eyes closed, breathing the deep controlled breaths she used when meditating.

"I see a small narrow branch of a tree, stripped of twigs and leaves. There's an image of a woman in a long flowing dress, she's raising the branch over her head with both arms; it has to be six foot long at least. At her feet are a pile of leaves and two swans. A rabbit – no, a hare sits next to her, the image is fading: gone."

She opened her eyes and looked intently at Eric's troubled face.

"I'm fine, there's nothing to fear, I think this is a good thing not like last time, let's get back to Jeepy, I'm getting cold stood here."

They set off; the squirrel, realising there were no more free handouts coming its way, scampered off up the trail ahead of them; however, a much larger furry animal padded out of a thicket blocking their way. They stopped dead,

"Eric, that looks very much like a wolf, bloody impossible but certainly the closest to the pictures of wolves I've ever seen. Canis lupis, extinct in Britain since the 1500s."

"You sure it's not a huge Husky, what's it got in its mouth?"

She looked hard. "At this distance I'm not sure, it looks like a stick of some sort, it must be someone's dog."

They stood side by side on the stony trail and watched as the animal sat down, dropped the stick, then eased itself back onto four legs in one fluid movement. Quickly it turned and vanished into the undergrowth. On the trail in front of them lay a large wooden stick, one end slightly thinner than the other, it looked as if someone used it to hold back overgrown branches, or in the autumn to persuade elusive blackberry brambles to submit and bend toward the holder.

"It must belong to somebody; we're near the car park, let's see if anyone's lost a stick – and a dog."

The Jeep stood alone in the circle of grass; no other tyre tracks entered or left the circle.

"Nothing's been here since we arrived, not a single print anywhere," Eric said as he carefully walked the circumference of the glade. "There's no houses or anything down here for a good two miles or so."

Flick had got into Jeepy and started the engine; Eric joined her with the stick.

"It's all a bit odd, love, but I'm not picking up anything sinister or bad; in fact, it feels good, very good." She smiled.

"We better not say anything to the others about this till we find out what it means." Eric nodded. "They wouldn't believe us anyway, they'd think it was another of our crazy jokes."

Flick smiled. "Like the boy who cried 'Wolf!' perhaps."

Dan had a meal on the go when they arrived back at the camp site. The staff was left in the back of Jeepy, it would later be explained as a branch they found near the waterfalls and would make a good walking pole for Flick. The evening ended round the barn camp fire again, the weather was changing for the worse so they had an early night – the tenters climbed into warm sleeping bags, Eric and Flick lay together in Wolfie. They fell asleep talking about the impossible wolf and the odd vision. The wobbly compass was totally forgotten about.

Easter Monday morning saw the sky turn greyer than previously but the remains of Wolfie's fridge still tasted great at breakfast. The last day would be spent having a look round the ancient city of Chester before taking the back roads to Manchester, objectively avoiding the holiday exodus. Once the tent was down and packed, the site cleaned up and the Jeep hitched, they said goodbye to the others. Colin and Wendy were taking Dan and Alan back, Wolfie was bringing all the gear home. The tent fitted into the Jeep with the rear seat folded down, the staff came into Wolfie and then, just because they could, they undressed and got back into bed again. For the second time in twenty-four hours a wolf-like howl resounded across the Welsh hills.

The rain hit near Chester. They waited an hour then abandoned the idea of walking round the old city with its two-storey shops. The wipers stayed on all the way back to Manchester. Flick was unpacking their clothes and hiking gear whilst Eric put Escapade's equipment back into Wolfie and unhitched the Jeep. Alan and Dan were at a comedy night in the city so they had the flat to themselves.

Eric had taken the staff and washed it down; it had a few odd knocks and scrapes but still looked to have the smooth brown bark intact. It was more ovoid than round in cross-section and measured six feet two inches in length. It weighed no more than a kilo, he estimated. The thing that troubled both of them was the vision and the meeting. Flick's books told them wolves were persecuted in Britain to the point of extinction, in the sixteenth century in Wales and by 1760 the last recorded wolf in Scotland had been slain. They both realised they weren't going crazy as they had both seen the exact same animal. If it was an exotic breed of dog, looking more like a wolf than a wolf and as close to one as the pictures they had available, it was going to be an identification job for the library. Nothing in the vision made any sense, especially now with the strange compass reading had been bought into the mix as well. In the end they reasoned there wasn't anything bad to worry about unlike the previous vision in Portugal so they would just wait and see what happened. The weather wasn't getting any better and snow was still figured for many parts of the country on the TV forecast.

Eric came in from the kitchen with steaming mugs of tea and a packet of chocolate digestives.

"Oh that's a mess, what happened?"

She was holding a piece of limp soggy paper between thumb and forefinger, gently trying to lay it on the coffee table.

"It must have come out of my notebook and something managed to spill on it or the rain's got in. They're the four strips of paper with those runes on, I kept them pressed flat in the book."

Eric touched the vellum carefully.

"They may just separate when they dry out, I can have a go at easing them apart with a craft knife blade."

Flick supped her tea and Eric opened the screwed up end of the biscuit wrapper.

"Now I have a cunning plan to claim these few naughty chocolate biscuits for myself," he said in one of his home made silly voices. "You may have one chocolate digestive for each piece of clothing you remove entirely in fifteen seconds starting... now!"

Flick pulled off trainers, socks, jeans, pants, shirt and bra in under twelve seconds.

"Eight items, I think, so eight chocolate digestives please," she said with a smirk.

Eric counted the remaining biscuits. "There's just eight left," he sighed, "another good idea down the tubes."

Flick accepted the packet and carefully put one in her mouth before handing him two back.

"I think it ought to be six really, after all it was a pair of shoes and a pair of socks." Eric smiled and sipped his tea whilst munching the two biscuits.

"In that case you owe me another one as you also had a pair of jeans, so the total was five."

Flick looked at him with twinkling eyes. "OK, I concede, hold on a minute though." She took one of the biscuits in each hand and rubbed them over her breasts, chocolate side down, making sure most of it went over her nipples. "Come and get them."

Eric chuckled and leaned forward.

"You used two, I was supposed to have one, now I'll have to give you one."

She opened her legs slowly. "I was rather hoping you would, the other three are down there on the dessert trolley. Dinner is a little topsy-turvy tonight: appetiser, dessert, then entrée to finish."

Reaching down to take the crumbling remains from the chocolate-coated right breast, he looked at her smiling face, saying, "One helluva menu in this restaurant."

Two days later Eric tried separating the four slivers of vellum. He had looked at them twice a day since carefully placing them on a piece of toilet paper on the chest of drawers. Thinking they were dry enough to lift away from each other, he slowly eased the thin blade of a model maker's scalpel between the layers. Teasing the strips apart was a delicate job working from what looked like a loose edge and sliding the blade inwards. The wad parted between the second and third layers, leaving two more operations to perform. This second part was not so easy; no matter how he tried the halves of either piece fail to move. Flick picked one up.

"The ink's run – it's difficult to tell what was on which slip now." She tried the other sliver. "Same goes for this one, I guess this ain't going to work, love."

Eric put the scalpel down and looked at the first piece.

"With the ink running it won't make much difference if we do get the four slips apart."

Over by the window Flick was trying to see if the daylight shining through the paper would make it easier to see what was ink and what was stain. Suddenly she saw something, not on the pieces of paper but in the reflection on the glass. A thought hit her like a sledgehammer.

"Oh, you stupid girl, if I had a brain I'd be dangerous," she admonished herself on the way to their bedroom.

She rummaged in a cardboard box and eventually found the notebook with the original drawings of the four lines of runes. She copied them out onto a sheet of Alan's tracing paper, chopped it into four then putting two slices together she checked the reflections of the combinations in the hall mirror.

"Eric, come and look at this."

The reflected image wasn't undecipherable runes anymore. She held up the first two strips – looking back at them were a string of numbers. Eric held up the other two slivers to reveal a string of numbers with symbols separating the groups.

"I'll write them down, for the symbols I'll name them what they look like."

The first set of numbers read 32, diamond, 17, sun, 8, moon, crook; the second set were 104, diamond, 5, sun, 48, moon, waves.

"I have 9, 29, 29 on this piece, with no symbols," Eric called out.

Six symbols were in use, the one after 32 and 104 were identical, it resembled a diamond shape styled like a playing card. Following 17 and 5 another sign which could only be described as a childish drawing of the sun, a rough circle with lines cutting through the rim to represent rays of light, the third was a crescent moon sitting after the 8 and 48. The fourth came after the 'moon' following the 8, it looked like the top of a shepherd's crook; finally, the fifth was located after the 'moon' following the 48 and looked like a wavy sign used to denote water on maps.

Dan and Alan arrived after they'd spent two hours pondering and getting nowhere, they were just about to recap on what they knew when the pair walked in.

"So what have we here?" Dan said, picking up the strips. "Our elf's gone mystic again, she's casting spells on Aunt Mavis. When we get to this party in Leeds I wouldn't be at all surprised if she turned her into a frog or something worse."

Alan leaned over her shoulder to see what she was drawing, kissing the top of her head as he usually did. Eric brought them up to speed.

"We were just about to rethink what we have, so any ideas from you guys would be good. Taking this slip first, the other seems meaningless, we have the numbers with symbols, not a lot you can say about them but here goes. Point one, the two sequences are even, odd, even. Two, you can add, divide, multiply and subtract till the cows come home, nothing makes a patten you could say really holds up. There are six numbers in total so a magic square's out. Now the separators, if that's what they're supposed to be, are a diamond, a moon, a sun, a shepherd's crook and water. This is rife throughout mythology all over the world, from Egypt to Native Americans."

Alan thought for a moment then mentioned Plato. "He talked about the axis mundi being diamond."

"Runes have the diamond as a symbol of creation, it represents the woman's birth canal," Eric added.

Dan was concentrating hard; finally, he scribbled something on a piece of paper and went to a pile of books in the corner of the room. Pulling out a thick atlas of the world he opened a page at random, then closed it again. The thoughtful expression slowly turned into a wide grin that split his face apart.

"I think I may just have this one cracked, try this on for size. First, the symbols, a diamond, the hardest substance on earth, and as Alan says Plato talked about the axle of the world. Around the world we have lines of latitude and longitude, drawn geometrically around the axis. The other symbols are the sun and the moon, so if we said diamonds equal degrees, the sun is minutes and the moon is seconds we have two co-ordinates. The crook I think is actually a crook and flail, meaning the health of the land and is either north or south as latitude is written first. That leaves water, the other part of the world that isn't land, to be east or west. The 104 sequence has to be longitude because latitude only goes up to 90 and finally the remaining four numbers are all under sixty."

Flick looked at him with wide open eyes.

"That deserves a beer if nothing else."

Alan and Eric were thumbing through the atlas and making notes.

"OK, so we have four possible locations for Dan's theory. One is off the coast of Australia west of Perth, the next is in the South Pacific near the Pitcairn Islands, number three is in the north-west mountainous region of China, and last but not least is a small community in New Mexico near the border with Texas. We need a map of the States to define it in greater detail but at least we can say this looks like the most promising of the four."

Flick got up and made her way to the kitchen. Eric was still looking at the remaining slip.

"So has anyone got any thoughts on this one?"

Silence fell as the three friends pondered the three numbers.

"There's not a lot to go on, 9,29,29, no symbols, nothing at all," Eric commented.

"How about hexadecimal, look at it upside down and you get b5b5b, what's that in decimal?"

Ten minutes later the answer turned out to be as meaningless as the question, 744283 didn't do a lot for anyone.

"Dinner is almost ready," Flick said.

"What have we tonight, O' Goddess of the Sumptuous Repast?" Alan asked.

By way of an answer she lay across the table pulling her shirt up as she did so.

"Not telling," she said with a cheeky look on her face.

When the peacock feathers had done their work, a giggling elf brought in a large steak and kidney pie with roast potatoes, mushrooms and a veritable bucket of gravy.

"I think it may be something simple like a date," Flick mentioned between mouthfuls. "Excuse me, I need to take pudding out the oven."

It takes a while to get used to Flick's portion sizes, having fed Eric in the manner to which Avril had bought him up and being a Yorkshireman didn't help. Apple and rhubarb crumble with chocolate ice cream arrived in under five minutes, she didn't believe in keeping hungry people waiting. Eric had been thinking about New Mexico when it hit him that Americans wrote the date differently – it was month, day, then the year.

"I reckon Flick could be onto something here, it could be September 29th, 1929."

The library was going to be busy that week. As it turned out, apart from the Wall Street Crash the date had little to show in the way of historic events; however, Dan came back with a smile on his face a mile wide.

"None of you are going to believe this, and I promise it's all true and checkable. The New Mexico coordinates take us to the township of Loving, in Eddy County."

Three bemused faces chuckled at him then he produced the photocopies from the library.

"Well there we are, my dreams have taken us across the Atlantic, all we have to do now is wait for September 29th, 2029 and go there to collect my fortune in diamonds," Flick giggled.

As the weeks marched steadily onwards towards the examinations there was room for little else other than revision and keeping Escapade supplied with enough gigs to pay the bills. The compass had been taken to the store for testing and it appeared to have righted itself. There weren't any further dreams about runes, the vision of the woman in a long dress never repeated itself and finally no impossible wolves turned up at the Manchester Madhouse looking for sticks or steak and kidney pies.

Eric spent part of a Saturday at their landlord's house doing some odd jobs that were getting beyond him. Dennis, in return for all the free labour he'd received over the years, never put their rent up. Alan and Dan give him legal advice on the clear understanding they were still unqualified. Flick simply fed him tea, coffee and biscuits to the extent he always managed to be 'just passing' on Tuesday evenings when a cake was being made. He rather enjoyed chatting to her as well.

"My two sisters drive me crazy at times, one's always complaining, the other's always about to do something but never gets round to it. It's like your cakes, I told her your date and walnut's to die for – 'I'll make you one, Dennis,' she says – still bloody waiting, aren't I."

When Eric returned he told her, 'Patti Cake' and 'Mona Lott', as Dennis called them, were about eighty.

"Patti is always in the kitchen – doing nothing – she cleans the sink a dozen times a day, Dennis reckons she just rearranges the germs; Mona, on the other hand, is almost deaf, when things get too bad Dennis pulls the batteries out of her hearing aid."

The exams arrived and once over, the lack of tension in the flat was noticeable.

"Sunday next we have a freebie gig if you want to do it – Wendy and Colin are trying to fundraise again, they've been asked by a different charity this time," Dan asked.

The venue was a large rambling house in the middle of a parkland. The charity had received the freehold to the house but not the entire grounds. The problem was whilst a free property was a wonderful gift, the upkeep was costly to say the least. Wendy said they were booked for the nine o'clock slot, the penultimate act. The weather was set to be quite warm, some people said hot.

The day arrived, Escapade pulled in around ten and found Wendy wearing her organiser's hat.

"All is going exceedingly smoothly Wendy informs me," Dan reported. "We only need instruments, the P.A. is on loan from a music shop. They've knocked up two risers for drum kits, when we're due on the crew will pull one riser out and put ours in, Alan's gear's going on a pallet ready to lift."

Eric looked at the stage.

"It all looks very professional and organised, I guess they've got a lot of volunteers."

Colin nodded. "Muscle is one thing we're not short of, some of the bands are a bit lacking but as it's all for free..."

Alan looked over the edge of the stage. "Beggars can't be choosers, my friend, whatever, let's hope the audience like it."

The first band began at noon and played a standard one-hour slot, their repertoire being limited to middle of the road chart hits from 1972 onwards. More of the same followed then Wendy came over to bring them some drinks and a tray full of sandwiches. The band sat behind the stage whilst Alan tried to sort out a set list. So far the crowd had applauded but not very enthusiastically. In the end they decided on the same approach they used for Alice's party – try one, try another, work it out as you go along.

"I'll just shout the next number out as we go," he concluded.

By the time 9 o'clock arrived the show was running roughly twenty minutes late. Flick got behind her kit then waited for the announcer. Alan counted them in then Dan and Eric powered into 'Street Fighting Man' opening the set and it just got better from there on. 'Rocky Mountain Way' closed the one-hour slot, the crowd were demanding an encore but the announcer made it clear the next band were due on in under ten minutes. Flick's kit arrived backstage on the number two riser; they sat with a cold drink and relaxed.

"The crowd liked the rock stuff alright, I think we did well to keep the blues side turned down," Alan commented.

Colin came over with more drinks.

"Great set, guys, just perfect," then he disappeared into the house.

"Shall we go round the side and watch the last act?" Dan asked.

By the time they gathered up their drinks the last band were halfway through their first number or so they thought. A fraught Wendy caught them by the door.

"Can you help please, they've got a big problem."

Seeing four faces saying, 'what's the problem', started her off in full flow.

"The last act refuse to go on – this is a tape you're hearing. They're saying after your set the crowd will probably boo them and they have an A&R guy from the record company that's interested in signing them watching in the audience. They're saying anything to avoid losing face."

Dan looked outside at a crowd that were getting a little restless.

"Surely they can't be that bad, the organisers have put them at the top of the bill, they must be good enough or it's a mockery."

Colin had come over looking for Wendy. "They're not going on, and that's it. The charity have been given a donation to put them on last, seems they can't hack it."

A frantic announcer came across and asked the question Wendy hadn't got round to.

Alan answered, "Get out there and tell them we'll be back as fast as the crew can get the riser back up there – got that?"

He got it.

"Hello again, here's something to dance to," Alan introduced Escapade for the second time whilst playing the opening bars of

'Dance to the Music'.

The next hour passed rapidly, Alan shouted the last number and started 'Gimme Shelter'. Flick noticed the announcer and another couple of men in suits were talking on the grass behind her. She also noticed two police officers next to them. The crowd were looking for an encore; the police officer looked at his watch and nodded.

"You've got ten minutes," Wendy told them.

Alan walked up to the edge of the stage. "We've just enough time for one more, we're going to wind it down now, lay back and relax, look up at the summer sky and start imagining, we'll see you all again soon, good night."

Eric pressed the effect pedal he needed then began the haunting tones of Fleetwood Mac's 'Albatross'. The song ended to a cheering crowd who kept it up for almost five minutes. Thankfully there were plenty of helping hands to pack everything in Wolfie, Eric closed and locked the door after the last bag of leads were wedged inside. Dan had managed to find coffee somewhere, the men in suits were still nearby as were the two police officers.

One of the suits was talking to Alan who was shaking his head and holding a hand up as if to stop oncoming traffic. Later he told them the man was from a small record label and wanted to sign them up.

"As soon as I mentioned 'students' he got very excited and started talking money. Strangely enough when I mentioned 'law student' he toned down a bit and when I said we're just a covers band he went a bit limp."

"Does anyone know what happened to the other outfit?" Eric asked. If a shrug is an answer that was it.

Dennis arrived on Tuesday as usual with a broken vacuum cleaner and the hope it was date and walnut's turn to go with the coffee. Eric was already in the garage when he came through the door. By the time the overstuffed bag had been prised out and a mountain of hair removed from the rollers, the motor stood a chance of sucking.

"That's cat hair, but we ain't got a cat, or a dog; probably why Mona's looking a bit thin on top," Dennis mumbled with a mouthful of crumbs.

Flick had arrived with coffee and a cherry fruit cake, which in Dennis's eyes was an excellent substitute for his beloved date and walnut and cheered him up no end. After they both left, Eric turned his attention to what he had come to the garage for. On the bench was the stick from Wales. In the week surrounding the exams it had been left untouched after its brief clean up in the back of the Jeep. The wood wasn't as dirty as it looked – either polish, oil or varnish had been applied. As the surface dirt washed away, the shine on the wood was obvious. Closer inspection exposed a deep layer of oil had been worked into the wood. Looking at it he decided somebody had made it from a branch cut from a beech tree and spent a lot of time on it. Sighting along its length he found it looked completely straight, rolling it along the bench confirmed his findings. One end was naturally thinner than the other, the top was cut square and shaped slightly to keep the bearer's hand free of splinters. About four inches from the top he could see a slight discolouration. Reaching for a cloth he tried to buff the surface in the hope it was ground in dirt. He wasn't exactly sure how it happened but as he twisted the cloth round the top of the staff it started to unscrew. Easing the thread backwards and forwards alternatively with a little machine oil dripped onto the exposed threads ensured the thing came apart without breaking. The inside of the staff had been hollowed out, a six-inch deep hole according to his depth gauge. Using a small flashlight he saw a scroll of paper close to the outer wall of the wooden chamber. Pointed nose pliers extracted it, then carefully the roll was unfurled. Written in faded ink were the following lines.

The staff of Hyndla passes to you
Völva, daughter of the Bows of Dene
Clear shall be the vision now
No mist obscures what is foreseen
Forever Ruler protects the seer
With strength of Mars and senses keen
Wood and heart will find the way
And thus prevent what might have been
For wand in staff is yours to wield
In times of darkness grasp and lean

Eric read it several times, he wasn't at all happy about showing this to Flick, but they had never kept anything from each other before and this was no time to start living lies. That afternoon they walked down to the library, Flick took the staff with her; she refrained from naming it 'Sticky'. There wasn't a lot about Völva, but Hyndla came up trumps in spades. A book on Scandinavian mythology drew them to an old Norse poem. Hyndla being a Seeress in the Poetic Edda, she was also referred to as 'prophetess', 'staff bearer', 'wise woman' and 'sorceress'. The titles of 'witch' and 'enchantress' often turned up in the tales as well. Another section explained the swans and hare in Flick's vision and the painting of Veleda by Lenepveu accounted for the woman in a long flowing dress. The library was closing when they decided they had enough information to work with, the main part of the verse was now meaningful but some of the details were a little sketchy.

"As far as I can understand it, the staff is passed to you, a seer, by birthright. Your name being Bowden is not a million miles away from 'Bows of Dene'. It suggests that your visions, the 'walking over my grave' variety, will be easier to understand if you are holding the staff. Next I think it's telling you to use your feelings to avert disasters, and you're protected by a strong ruler, a forever ruler whatever that is?" Eric commented as they walked back to the flat.

Flick had already picked a rhythm to swing the staff to.

"I agree, but what a forever ruler is I have no idea. Also, the line about the prevention of what might have been suggests I can use the staff and do something, or an idea will come to me through it, to avert a disaster that I have a vision about. All I can do is take the staff with me on our hikes and see if I have any premonitions."

Eric opened the door. "I'm rather glad you won't be doing any slitting of throats or leaving bags of entrails in the fridge."

Flick gave him one of her special sideways glances, the one that often turned out to mean 'watch this space'.

Dennis turned up on Tuesday as usual, reported the vacuum cleaner was doing fine, neither of his sisters had managed to break it yet – and asked Eric if he could change the lock on his back door as the old key had broken off inside the barrel. Over coffee and a slice of orange sponge cake, he managed to fill in the two blanks they had concerning the verse. Somehow the conversation had steered itself to people's names and Dennis turned out to be a fount of knowledge. Eric was a Norse name, it meant eternal ruler, a type of warrior chief or king. Deborah was from the Old Testament, the only female judge and prophetess mentioned. He also told them Alan meant handsome, a little rock, and Daniel often meant beautiful or 'God is my Judge'. When he had gone with six bottles of Alan's blackberry and apple homemade wine they sat and considered the verse again. In the end the only thing to do was exactly what they'd decided on, wait and see what, if anything, happened.

26

The days passed without incident. John and Avril had booked a large room in a hotel that had flower gardens and a swimming pool, two tennis courts and a gymnasium as well as a small stream running through a wood on the southern edge. Escapade were providing the music, Alan had pencilled in a list of easy-going numbers that everyone could get on with. Sunshine poured through the lounge window of the flat; it looked as if the day was going to be a hot one. The four friends climbed into Wolfie and set off for Leeds, two hours later the gear was offloaded and set up on the small stage at the end of what was, in the 1920s, a ballroom.

"I didn't think places like this existed any longer," Dan said to John.

Robert was chatting to Alan.

"Ah Alan, this is my sister-in-law Mavis, I don't think you've had the opportunity to experience the unforgettable pleasure of not meeting her before."

Alan managed to unravel the sentence and grinned.

Flick moved between her father and John to suggest there could be some extra mileage to wind-up Mavis a little tighter in the form of the boys' homosexuality, a situation guaranteed to provoke her. John commented to Robert that his daughter is full of little subtle surprises, like providing ammunition for his hobby of annoying his sister-in-law. Robert replied that Helen is exactly the same. John then asked if Eric is aware of what a naughty bundle of fun his girlfriend is.

"Perhaps," said Robert, "I rather think so by now; however, I've no intention of tipping him off, he'll just have to find out for himself about her more wicked habits as I did with Helen."

"Ah, we should stay tuned to this channel then." John smiled.

Helen and Avril had been to the pool, Eric and Alan were talking music near the outside bar whilst John and Robert sat discussing the next adventure they were planning in Cornwall. Twenty minutes later Mavis blew a fuse when she first found Flick, then Helen dancing with Dan.

"Robert, it really is too much, I almost expected to see your half-naked daughter cavorting with a black man on the lawn in full view of the guests, but for your wife to indulge as well. No, don't say anything, Robert, I don't want to hear any excuses. What the devil is Felicity wearing anyway? You do know what these blacks are like – before you know it he'll be seducing the pair of them, at the same time I shouldn't wonder."

"I doubt that, Mavis, I really do; after all, everyone, but you it seems, knows he's gay, that's his partner Alan, over there talking to Eric, oh and I see Avril has joined in the dancing too, she's not wearing a lot either."

Mavis looked horrified when she rechecked the dancers and spotted a bikini-clad Avril had joined in.

"Flick is wearing the clothes she plays drums in, a pair of home-made denim shorts, the red top is called a boob tube. You could be next, why don't you slip that cardigan off and join in the fun – yes?"

John steered her to a nearby garden bench.

"I think you'd better sit down, dear, it's rather hot out here."

Mavis spent ten minutes fanning herself before she could bear to look at Helen and Avril sauntering around in bikinis, this on top of discovering that it was possible to be black and homosexual as well.

"I must say, Mr Marstone, I find this promiscuous behaviour quite upsetting, I shall have to have one of my pills. Would you be so kind as to fetch me a glass of water."

John returned a few minutes later with a large vodka. The afternoon wore on, more guests arrived in readiness for the eight o'clock party. A buffet had been laid out in a side room, the main room with the stage had large tables and the dance floor as well as the bar. Escapade waited for John and Avril to give their speech. Several others stood up and spoke fondly about them, family and friends alike wished them well and hoped the next twenty-five years were as good as the first. Robert was sitting by the side of John's cine projector which had a black and white film of their wedding in 1950 ready to roll.

Alan went up to the microphone to introduce Escapade and suddenly the evening was underway. They were only doing an hour then a disco was taking over for the evening. About halfway through Alan told the audience there would now be a short commercial break. Dan placed a home-made 'A' Board saying 'RAVI-SHED – best quality log cabins and dog kennels made to order', at the front of the stage, took the mike and introduced himself as Mr Ravi Lecher, Managing Director of Ravi-sheds Limited. Meanwhile, Alan; now dressed as a Chinese mandarin, had come forward and stood next to Eric who had a Red Indian headdress on. Flick carried a photo album under her arm whilst wandering round the back of the stage like she's looking for something.

Dan started his lines.

"I'd like to take this opportunity to tell you about our fantastic special offer, for this week only we have 10% off sheds, 15% off log cabins and a free dog kennel with every order for a..."

"Hello, is there anyone there?" Flick called from the back as she walked forward to join Dan.

"Can I help you, madam, only I'm a bit tied up at the moment."

Flick read from a newspaper cutting:

"The ad said ravished by appointment, so I thought, well it's been a while now so why not get the album out and see if they have anything new to offer, although I don't think this tied up thing's for me, bondage, isn't it?"

Dan did a double take and offered his hand.

"Well let's see if I can be of assistance Miss..."

Flick shook his hand. "Miss Givings, well I've been ravished many times before you know, I was there at the West Yorkshire sessions in the Bradford Co-op." She showed Dan the photo album. "I'm the one in the tinned fruit and veg aisle and that's a nice close-up of me after the bodice has been ripped open, bent over the cut price peas, it's a bit blurred I know, poor Jason was shaking quite badly I seem to remember."

Dan was looking at the pictures goggle eyed, turning the album round and looking back at Flick, then he turned a page. "Now that one's in Rackham's furniture department, it presented a few challenges as I had to put both legs behind my head in order to balance on the tea trolley. And opposite is the pièce de résistance, a full colour glossy taken in Harrods, I had to learn to do the splits for that one."

Flick nodded.

Dan turned to another page, totally stunned.

"I'm taking it you're not here to buy a summer house then."

"Not at the moment, thank you, I find that I don't have much use for a shed living in a Bradford council tower block; I want to book the sexy looking chap with the feathers and the gorgeous Chinese guy next to him for my nan's 80th birthday."

Eric and Alan are now looking very pleased, grinning and smiling whilst making thumbs up gestures to the audience. Dan takes out his notebook as Flick gives a nonsense address:

"4 Canal Side, near Safeway, yes, the one I got arrested in."

Dan asks if she wants to be ravished in any particular order.

"I don't think it'll matter too much, Nan likes them any colour, black, red, yellow or white – they're all good, it'll make her day."

Eric and Alan dive off stage fast with horrified faces while Dan faints.

The applause echoed round the room. John signalled to Robert who joined him on the stage. Together they stood next to Alan's mike; John spoke first.

"You know what, Manny, we're in the wrong business, my boy, all these years toiling away mending cars and vans, for what, Manny, for what; me and you, we should have teamed up years ago."

Robert leaned over. "You think you got troubles, Maurice, I've been working my fingers to the bone, to the bone I tell you, and for what. We could have cleaned up in this ravishing business, made a fortune, Maurice, a fortune."

On cue Alan started to play 'Underneath the Arches' as Robert and John slipped into Flanagan and Allen. Another round of applause bounced off the walls. Escapade started their second set and the dance floor filled up.

The disco played afterwards, which gave the band a chance to relax and mingle. Several of John's business associates were interested in Dan and Alan, they asked for contact details and to be informed once they'd graduated. They told John how amazed they were so many people had asked about them, it had them thinking about forming their own company instead of looking for positions in an established legal firm. Robert added that if they did, he would recommend them to all his business contacts as well.

Dan and Alan were sat near the doors leading to the garden when Mavis appeared with a large grin and a larger vodka. Dan watched her as she wobbled up the crazy paving pathway.

"She's absolutely stoned, where the hell has she been all evening?"

Alan couldn't help but laugh. "Oh my life, Robert's going to love this one,"

He got up and approached her. "Would you like to dance, Aunt Mavis?"

The wobbling stopped, Mavis ground to a halt, well most of her did. She looked up at him, smiled and replied she would love to. Alan got a grip on what might loosely be called a waist and waltzed her into the room. 'Stand by your Man' was playing. Helen couldn't believe her eyes when Dan pointed out Alan looking for a gap in the smooching couples. He swung Mavis onto the maple wood floor as John and Avril came over. Robert had already spotted the unlikely pair and was sporting a huge grin. He ambled across to the others.

"Well don't that take the biscuit, after all that spouting, she's dancing with a gay Chinaman, looking like Catherine the Great in a pink parachute."

Alan steered his ship over to a side table where it berthed reasonably gracefully.

"I see you're finally enjoying yourself, Mavis?" Helen asked.

Mavis beamed the smile of the utterly drunk. "Yes, dear, have you met Mr Wu, he's a window cleaner now, you know."

Robert explained about the George Formby song from the 1930s before he and John took her up to her bedroom. Helen took her shoes off and pulled a sheet over her. Downstairs they looked at each other, Robert started the giggle, then the rest followed in a laugh that rapidly turned into near hysteria.

"This is going to be fun in the morning," John spluttered.

Eric and Flick had taken a bottle of wine and strolled down the garden to where a small copse of trees stood on a slight hill. Underneath a horse chestnut lay an old iron bench that had seen better days. They'd sat on the rusty slats for a while, talking about the last five years they had spent together. It was going to be exactly five years next Thursday. There was no Glastonbury Festival and they had missed Knebworth. For almost half an hour they sat in silence, deep in their thoughts, broken only by odd comments as things came to mind. So far nothing had come of the curious message in the staff, it was as if the whole thing had faded away, but in the quiet moments it didn't take long before the staff knocked on the mind's front door. Eric had wrapped her in his arms, she laid her head against him and looked up into the night sky.

"The moon looks full tonight," she said softly.

Eric looked up too. "New moon and a new era, my darling; who knows where we'll go from here."

They got up and made their way back to the party, talking about the applications they had made for jobs as the examination results would be arriving any day now. Eric opened the door for her, they were just in time to hear all about Mavis.

Wolfie sat at the back of the hotel car park, out of the way. Using very thin rainbows instead of eyes, Eddy and Kenny were also looking at the moon.

Mavis surfaced about ten, after Helen had knocked on her door to remind her about breakfast. Robert had two slices of toast and a pint of fresh orange juice ready for her along with two paracetamol.

"Sunday won't look quite so tragic if you can get these down, Mavis," Avril said softly.

The letters they were all on tenterhooks for arrived on Tuesday. They opened envelopes and read with joyous faces the wonderful words inside.

"Yesterday I couldn't spell ingineer now I is one," Eric told the others as Eccles from the Goons. There were telephone calls to be made and important letters to write; this is how on Thursday 28th August some five years to the day that Eric and Flick had met on the Isle of Wight, the four friends had a double celebration in their favourite restaurant. They all realised that the end of an era had been reached. The days of the Manchester Madhouse were almost over, and Escapade would have to be put into mothballs at best or disbanded if the distances made it impractical. As it turned out, their last gig was performed at the same large venue the children's care home had used. Their last show was for them, this time they sold the place out.

Dan and Alan announced a decision had been made about what they were doing for a career. They had been following up on the contacts made at the party and Robert had passed on. Leeds was undoubtedly the second biggest business centre outside the London square mile, being at the other end of the M1 and connected by British Airways to Heathrow, also it was a third of the London price for office space. John found them a cheap shop with a flat over the top to rent, which would start them off in their own business. Both Dan's parents and grandparents backed them with enough money to get things rolling. Flick and Eric were getting a little desperate – they both had offers but in two different cities. Eric was working for his father in the garage and Flick found a job with a local veterinary surgery. It wasn't till late in October the break came. They had moved everything from the flat into the spare garage at Leeds and were living with John and Avril to save money.

Two large envelopes, one addressed to each of them, dropped through the letterbox on the last day of the month. Inside was an invitation to attend an interview at the Queens Hotel in Leeds on Thursday November 6th at 11am. A bound presentation folder gave information on how to get there and a brief outline of the positions available. The company were called Qwendos Biotech and based in Cambridge, England, the parent company were in Sacramento, California. The brochure went on to outline the company profile, they were deeply committed to the field of medical bionics, particularly in the improvement of prosthetics. They both looked at the list of prospective employers they had written to and Qwendos wasn't on it.

"It might be a referral, or the company have been trawling this year's results," Eric said. Whatever the reason, they were going to Leeds on Thursday.

David Widders introduced himself as the Managing Director of Qwendos Biotech UK and asked them to make themselves comfortable at the conference table. He apologised for the delay in contacting them – the scout agency had given the Manchester address but fortunately they had obtained their forwarding address from the landlord. He then went on to ask a few personal questions to make sure everything he already knew about them was up to date and accurate. Once he was satisfied, he proceeded to tell them about the opportunities they were being offered.

"Qwendos is one of the major organisations in what we all feel very sure is going to be a huge global market in the coming decades. Bionics is the means of transferring the technology in a life-form to manufactured technical devices," he explained. "We're heavily involved with the medical fields and in computer science. One of the major differences between our company and its competitors is the understanding that communications between the engineer and the biologist are poor at the present time. We're striving to forge better awareness levels by interlocking our biologists with the engineers to make a dual talent team capable of driving forward the exciting projects we have in progress."

A knock at the door revealed a man with coffee and biscuits.

David continued, "We've seen your examination results and reviewed your entire coursework, furthermore the incident over the wrong address has actually worked to increase our confidence in you. We found out from the landlord that you're engaged and have lived together for roughly five years. This stability is another excellent reason why you were chosen, your understanding of each other both on a personal and subject level is already far in advance of all the teams we want to put in place. I better tell you about the projects we are currently working on. It's a long-term research effort; if successful it will result in the building of much-needed medical devices. You're probably aware of the progress made on the bionic ear, the Cochlear Implant. Work by organisations like ours covers the designing and building of an artificial heart, replacement eyes and other human organs that can wear out or become diseased, and that's the tip of the iceberg. We're also involved with developing prosthetics for amputees, I can't promise we're going to make everyone into a six-million-dollar man, but, we are trying to make a significant improvement over what we're having to offer people now. Finally, the human race is going to explore space, of that we have no doubt; we need life support systems and a whole raft of tech to do this. Are you excited?"

Eric and Flick looked at the various booklets and decided to say yes. David smiled and outlined what he wanted from them. The company labs and workshops were in Cambridge, the company would like to engage them on the projects as a matched pair. They would pay the costs of moving house to Cambridge and provide a company flat rent-free for one year while they became established. When David handed over two employment contracts that also included a pension plan and private health care along with an unbelievable salary, they both thought they'd hit the mother lode.

"There's no rush to sign, take them away with you and read through. The phone number on the bottom is our personnel department, ask any questions you like. Anything they can't answer, call me direct." With that he gave them his business card.

Avril and John were almost as dumbstruck as they were. Robert and Helen reacted in a similar manner, Dan and Alan were equally amazed even after they'd read through the contract and pronounced it perfectly legitimate in every respect. After the Christmas holidays they moved into a two-bedroom flat in Cambridge and began work with ten other two-person teams.

1976 unfolded slowly. Dan and Alan's enterprise made steady progress and by September had reached the break-even point. Flick and Eric had started work on one of the prosthetics projects and found a few new friends both at work and near the company flat.

The year was also eventful for Colin and Wendy – they'd decided to get married; the invitations went out in February, the ceremony set for May. Robert, Helen, John and Avril went on holiday together in July – after a lot of research and several planning trips they decided to fly to Chicago and do Route 66 all the way to Santa Monica in a motor-home.

Eric was in the shower when Flick had another 'walking over the grave' sensation. This time there were highly charged emotions attached to it and a mystery to unravel. Once the shudder subsided she went to tell Eric.

"It's a bit worrying as I know the person in the vision, it's Dan, only he's laying on the ground with a hole in his chest," she sobbed.

Eric reached out and held her close, saying, "Try and keep calm, love, what else was there to see?"

Flick sat on the bed next to him and composed herself.

"I saw a man with a small gun, he was on the other side of a wide street, there was a tall building behind him with a flag flying, France I think, three vertical stripes, blue, white and red."

Eric held her trembling hands and looked her straight in the eyes. "We'll call Dan and Alan, now, tonight, to make sure he's OK, we can use the excuse that we're coming up to Leeds to see family and can we take them out to dinner on Saturday night. The staff can come with us and perhaps if you hold onto it when you see him, something positive may come to you."

She nodded and leaned forward to kiss him. "I feel very small and insignificant right now, thanks to you though I know I'm going to be fine. I feel so safe, but slightly scared, it's the not knowing that makes it hard to deal with."

Eric held her face in his large hands, using his thumbs to wipe a couple of tears from her cheeks as he returned her kiss. "Never forget I'm here for you, always and forever. There's no power on Earth that will stop me protecting you, until I draw my last breath I'll be beside you."

They walked through to the lounge so Flick could use the phone. Eddy and Kenny were faintly glowing violet. A low hum seemed to be coming from the washing machine.

Flick was a lot happier once she'd spoken to Alan. Dan was also in the shower at the time, but Alan confirmed for both of them that dinner in Leeds would be absolutely wonderful and they were very excited to see them again. He also wondered if Escapade could play at Colin and Wendy's wedding – it would solve the 'what-to-get-for-a-present' problem. Flick said she would ask Wendy's mother – she was in charge of the arrangements. The next day being Friday they set off straight from work for Leeds, arriving at John and Avril's just before nine o'clock. After a late dinner they brought them up to date with what was happening with their work and in particular how they were making some progress with the prototype of a new arm for amputees who had lost an entire limb from just below the shoulder. On Saturday they went out in Jeepy to Malham Cove, spending the middle of the day walking the footpaths and trails around the limestone pavement and Janet's Foss. Flick stopped at several points along the tracks, clutching her staff, hoping for anything that might help or explain the vision of yesterday. Sadly, nothing came. Jeepy took them to an Italian restaurant on the outskirts of the city. The meal was a relaxed affair, the conversation consisted mainly of their work in Cambridge and the small triumphs of the newest law firm in Leeds. Although Flick tried to make a vision happen, nothing materialised. It was only back at the flat over the shop that matters erupted.

After accepting a coffee from Alan, she asked Dan what was happening in the next month or so, using the forthcoming wedding as an excuse. She was stood by the door when Dan began to reel off what he and Alan were doing, within easy reach of the staff she had sneaked in with her. The wedding date was not going to be a problem, Alan was going to Cheltenham to have a final attempt at establishing contact with his parents after almost six years, and he was going to Paris in the second week of April to see his grandparents. As soon as Dan mentioned Paris, she felt the compulsion to grasp the staff. The image of yesterday flashed into her head; this time, however, she was totally calm. Eric sensed what was happening rather than having to ask; he moved closer.

"Dan, you know in the past I have asked you both for trust in something I have either said or done, I am going to ask again, now, I think it's very important, but you can laugh if you want to."

Eric took that as his cue to explain the events of Friday evening.

Flick walked up to Dan holding the staff and looked directly into his eyes without blinking and wearing a serious face said, "I sense it would be better if you didn't go to Paris, but I cannot force you. I will do the best I can with the skill I have. Firstly, while you are in Paris, please avoid coming close to any buildings that are flying the flag of France. Secondly, I want you to take something of mine with you. You're to wear it night and day until you return safe to England. I cannot give it to you, for if I do it will not work. You must take it from me, here and now, and return it when the time is right."

Dan took in the serious face and knew this wasn't the Naughty Elf from the Manchester Madhouse. Calmly he answered her, "OK, Flick, what is it I need to wear?"

"Open your shirt, then open mine. Take the chain and pendant from round my neck and place it in the same position across your chest."

Dan did as he was instructed. Flick looked at her medallion, the silver roundel shining on the velvet black skin.

"I'm sorry to be so mysterious but this is the best I can do. I haven't managed to work it all out yet; in fact, Eric and I don't know much at all."

The friends parted company and Dan promised Flick he would wear her medallion and heed her advice. He arrived in Paris on Tuesday 13th April to spend a few days with his grandparents who lived near the Jardin des Plantes. On Friday another demonstration was taking place on the left bank of the Seine – confrontations between the students and the police were happening on the streets near the river. Dan was making his way to the Metro station when he noticed a scuffle on the opposite side of the road. A large building flying the Tricolore caught his eye and Flick's warning jumped into his mind. As he turned to walk away, he felt something hit him in the chest, knocking him down. Out of the corner of his eye he saw a police car had stopped and two men had wrestled another to the ground. He sat up as a medic came running over to him – from the look on the doctor's face he gathered 'surprised' would be an understatement. After letting the man check out his chest, Dan discovered Flick's medallion was rather bent and an interesting bruise was forming underneath it already. He was dispatched to hospital for a check-up along with several other officers and students suffering anything from cuts and bruises to tear gas exposure symptoms. He was allowed to leave after the hospital pronounced him fit and well and commented on how lucky he'd been. If he had not turned away and been wearing the medallion he would still have been in the hospital, but three floors lower down in the morgue.

"Even a .22 calibre can kill, thankfully this was a ricochet and the silver did the rest," the doctor had said.

He returned to his grandparents and rested over the weekend before returning to England. Alan rang Eric with the news late on Friday evening just as they were returning from watching a band in the local pub. Flick sat and listened with wide eyes when the details of the event were relayed to her. Almost ten minutes ticked by before either of them spoke. They sat, slightly stunned, hand in hand on the sofa, thinking about the whole event, pondering on how it all came about and being very grateful that Dan had remembered her words of caution. The following Saturday the four friends met in Newark, about as close to halfway as possible. Neville and Jean were ready for them and insisted on providing free rooms for the night. They accepted, with the proviso they paid for dinner that evening. Before they changed to go out, Dan and Alan knocked on the bedroom door.

"I think it's the correct time to return this to its rightful owner," Dan said.

Flick looked at the bent silver and then at Dan as she reached for her staff. She held it by her side and after a moment with her eyes closed said, "The procedure is the reverse of before: open my shirt first then yours. Place the medallion back in the same place on my chest."

The act was carried out, then Dan and Flick came together and embraced.

"I have no words, Flick."

She shook her head. "Me neither, I'm just so happy you're alive and here with us now." Then her tears came.

"Good job I didn't put my mascara on. Come on or we'll be late."

Six people went into town and had an amazing time. The lights were still burning at one in the morning.

"There's nothing to get up for," Jean had said, stifling a yawn.

Alan had forgotten to tell them about his visit to Cheltenham as he had precious little on his mind other than what state Dan was in. After breakfast he reported his parents were no closer to accepting him back into the family fold and they had also lost all interest in his sister. Eric and Flick agreed that he seemed to have accepted it and thankfully it would not be too hard for him to bear.

"I think living with us at the flat has helped him enormously, I dread to think how he would have handled the situation otherwise," Flick commented from the driving seat.

"Personally, without your help I don't think he would have summoned up the courage or confidence to even go down there," Eric replied.

She shrugged.

Saturday May 29th arrived, Colin and Wendy's wedding was upon them. Wolfie was driven up to Leeds on Friday evening and loaded with Escapade's rig from John's smaller workshop. Close to midnight the four friends pulled into the hotel car park where the reception was being held, and checked in. After the traditional breakfast, the one that's always more enjoyable in a hotel as you haven't cooked it, as Alan commented, they moved into the ball room and set up the gear. The church was booked for two o'clock, Eric unhitched Jeepy then joined the rest getting into their wedding outfits. Flick had taken to bringing the staff along every time they left home. Mainly it stayed in the vehicle unless they were hiking. Today it was lying across the back of Jeepy, rattling a little as they made their way to the church. The ceremony went off smoothly, the weather held up and although the photographer had insisted the wind would die down, it didn't.

Eric was driving the return leg to the hotel and commenting on how beautiful Wendy looked in her long white dress, Dan sat next to him leaving Flick and Alan in the back. The staff was rattling quite loudly as the Jeep bounced over some of the lumpier country lanes so she reached over to try and wedge it behind the large umbrella they always carried. As soon as she grasped the head of the staff a vision appeared on the back of her eyelids. She smiled and jammed the staff between the umbrella and the seat back. The photographer wanted another shoot in the gardens of the hotel; by the time the family had been safely captured, the wedding breakfast was almost ready to eat. This delay gave her enough time to explain the circumstances of the encounter with the staff on the journey back.

"I have a surprise for you, but it's going to be a shock to Wendy, a nice shock I hope, but I want to sound it off you three first. You see, I know something they don't. Wendy, my darlings, is about seven or eight days pregnant."

Three faces looked at her, first in disbelief, then slowly the possibility that she was right overtook the doubts.

"The middle to end of February next year then?" Alan calculated.

She nodded.

"What are you going to do?" Dan asked.

"Bloody good question, any ideas?"

Eric chimed in, "Let's think about it for a while, perhaps nothing is the right answer."

Wendy had put Escapade on a six-setting table with Kevin and Alice, who in the last six months had gelled together into a couple. After a three-course meal with champagne and wine, the speeches started, then the party moved into a smaller bar whilst the staff prepared the room for the evening's entertainment. A disco was due on first to entertain the children and the older members of both families before Escapade who were slated to go on from roughly eight o'clock. Eric went round the room doing some table magic and a few card tricks. As the afternoon became the evening more guests arrived, many of them were friends of the band as well as Colin and Wendy, so eight o'clock arrived a bit quicker than it might have done otherwise. Alan came over and said the bride's father had requested they get ready.

A small, cramped dressing room was rather a treat for Escapade, who usually had to settle for the toilets at most venues or out in Wolfie if the place had a car park close enough. The four were dressed and ready, the guys had gone with the standard blues band uniform of Levi's, button up shirt and waistcoat rescued from a three-piece suit found in a charity shop. Flick had her normal chopped off denim shorts and a bright blue boob tube. She stood the staff up in the corner of the room and immediately received another vision. She asked Alan to look into her eyes.

"You know that old wives' tale about seeing if the mother's eyes have any black flecks in the irises?"

Alan shook his head.

"It's supposed to foretell the sex of the baby. Can you see any flecks in mine, Alan, you have the sharpest vision of all of us?"

Alan shook his head again. "Nothing but the normal sparkling brown, sweetheart."

Flick blinked a couple of times. "The child will be a girl, they will name her Stephanie. Oh shit, what am I going to do with that gem of information?"

Halfway through the evening the bride's mother solved the problem for her.

The best man called for order from the stage and asked Wendy and Colin to come and join him to introduce the band. The newlyweds began to tell how Escapade had supported the children's charity they were involved with, not only with the band but also taking part in the Hadrian's Wall hike. Alan took over the mike once the applause had died down.

"Good evening, everybody, as the lady says, we're Escapade and this is the time when we're gonna dance to the music."

The familiar chords swelled from the stage as one of Colin's favourite numbers launched the party. As the set list dwindled and the dance floor became more crowded, the clock continued its measured beat forward. Around ten Alan said after the next number they were going to take a fifteen-minute break. Muriel, also known as the bride's mother, asked to borrow the mike. She spoke about the charity Colin and Wendy supported and asked if the guests would indulge in a silly lottery. She explained the entrance fee was set at one pound per attempt. The guest was to write the birthday and name of the happy couple's first child on the slips of paper she held in her hand. All the envelopes would be sealed and only opened after the child was born. The one and only prize would be a framed picture of the two proud parents with the new baby and a bottle of champagne.

"Brilliant," said Eric, "problem solved."

The second set leaned more towards the old Escapade, mainly due to the amount of beer being drunk, the children going to bed and the older members making use of the side bar. A lot of Wishbone Ash and Santana were requested by Alice and Kevin; the Stones and Fleetwood Mac filled up some holes with other standards including Cream papering over the cracks. By eleven thirty the hardcore fans had started asking for blues numbers then right at the end they heard a familiar voice.

"Toad, do Toad."

Flick got up and borrowed Dan's mike. "So, Kevin Harris, it was you all the time, wasn't it? You can't fool me with that phoney southern accent. You want Toad, do you?" She walked along the edge of the stage asking, "Anyone else want Toad?"

A loud cheer went up.

"I can't hear you, does anyone else want Toad?"

Dan reckoned everyone, and he meant everyone, stamped and chanted, 'Toad, Toad, Toad', the loudest voice being Kevin with support from Alice. Colin and Wendy conducted the stamping and clapping.

"Enough, we submit,' said Alan, holding his arms out. "Ladies and gentlemen. On lead guitar, Eric Marstone, on the bass, the one and only Danny Lavigne, on the drums, our inimitable powerhouse, Flick Bowden; I'm Alan Courtney, and this is Toad."

Flick played the Ginger Baker solo the best she'd ever done according to Kevin and the rest. About halfway through she appeared to be so totally engrossed the building could have been on fire and she'd have ignored it. After a seemingly endless ovation, Peter, the bride's father, took the mike and spoke to the audience, bringing the evening to a close.

Back in the dressing room Flick filled in the hastily photocopied slip with the date and name of the newborn child of the future. Eric placed a pound note in the envelope and sealed it. She wrote her name on the front.

"So what did you write?" Alan asked.

"Stephanie, 23rd February 1977," she replied.

Back in Cambridge the work on the Qwendos project continued; there were a few small successes and a fair few disappointments. Being eternal optimists, Flick and Eric tried to keep morale high in the fellow workers as they did with everyone else. Little hand-drawn cardboard notices appeared on desks and benches. Things like 'If at first you don't succeed, try and try again. If you still don't succeed go down the pub and have a beer, then come back and try F***KING harder!' Several people laughed and morale lifted a notch; David Widders started making notes about them in his files. Route 66 postcards arrived, one from each state their parents passed through. Flick held her staff each morning as she waited for the kettle to boil. The communication channel was assumedly closed for the summer.

In September the Qwendos teams did the Yorkshire Three Peaks, a challenge hike for a local Cambridge children's charity. Eric and Flick had been training the non-walkers and Qwendos had hired a local coach company to transport them to the Yorkshire Dales. Dan and Alan had borrowed the large parts van from John to use as a support vehicle. The whole event was an amazing success that not only raised money for the charity, it made several participants realise the power of positive thinking and teamwork. Eric asked David to present the cheque on behalf of them all. He also sent a long report to Sacramento about the event to be added to their personal profiles.

The next vision Flick received was the most unpleasant she had ever experienced; however, something was happening to her emotional controls. This time she was able to bear the imagery and also to feel the brutality and despair it generated without any distress to herself.

"It's as if I'm being taught: and I mean taught, not controlled, to channel the information and preserve my own, shall I call it, sanity?"

Eric sat down next to her at the kitchen table. During the kettle boiling ritual she had grasped the head of the staff as usual and been subjected to a distressing scene: a young naked girl, unhealthily thin with a hypodermic wedged in her arm. There wasn't any other information needed, she knew exactly who it was and where it was. She told Eric as she lifted the phone.

"It's Alan's sister, she's either overdosed or been killed, can you get me the road atlas please."

Eric opened the pages to Essex and passed it over.

"Theydon Bois is near Epping Forest," he pointed with his finger.

Flick sat for a moment then looked at Eric. "I need to hold this stick of mine twice a day, if I had then this might not have happened. I can handle that, just, but how do I tell the police?"

He covered her hand with his, gently lowering the receiver.

"This time we're going to think it through, rather than freak Alan and Dan out and draw what might be a lot of unwanted attention to ourselves. Remember the woman in Portugal who spotted us from the BBC interview? A lot of people know us from Escapade, not everyone will keep quiet like Dan and Alan."

She agreed, nodding then bowing her head.

"Are you OK?"

She nodded again and reached for the toaster. "I'm a bit mixed up inside but not upset. Two slices?"

Flick established that the girl in the undergrowth was well and truly dead; the vision seemed to be 're-playable' on demand; this helped her in a small way – she realised that there was nothing to be done to save her. Eric came up with a solution which although not without problems looked the best way out of the situation. He explained as they drove to work.

"Firstly, I am with you completely when you say the girl is dead. Secondly, the radio and TV haven't reported anything yet. Third, you can get the vision anytime so we can afford to wait to see if she's discovered. Four, if we hear nothing by Friday evening we check the vision again and set off on Saturday morning for Essex. When we get there, it may be possible to 'find' her or engineer someone else to."

Saturday morning arrived after three days of tuning in to radio stations and keeping an eye on the news. The staff confirmed the vision so they drove down towards Theydon Bois. As they approached Epping, Flick pulled into a piece of waste ground. Eric took the Jeep south along the Epping Road towards Woodford then Flick started issuing directions with her eyes shut. Jeepy arrived at Piercing Hill.

"We have to walk from here, through the trees to a clearing, she's hidden in a thicket."

Fifteen minutes later they arrived at a grassy open space; coming towards them were a couple with a Labrador carrying a stick. As they drew closer, the dog trotted forward to investigate if they had any treats. Eric stopped and patted the dog's head. Flick took the stick and hurled it towards the bushes, the dog took off before she'd even let go. Eric had struck up a conversation with the man about what a great dog they had. The woman spoke to Flick then after a couple of minutes called the dog who barked but didn't appear. All four walked towards the bushes and found the dog sitting alongside the corpse. The dog-walkers lived nearby so the woman took the dog home and made the phone call. Twenty minutes later the police met them in the clearing. After the preliminaries were recorded and the ambulance had departed, Eric looked thoughtful and spoke to the officer in charge.

"I'm not exactly sure about this but you may like to contact a friend of ours who has a sister – she's been missing from home for a few years now, and although the photo I've seen of her was taken a couple of years ago, it looks very similar to this girl here."

Flick said she thought the girl looked a lot like Alan's sister too; it was the shape of her nose which jogged the memory, adding that Alan, who had the same shaped nose, hadn't actually seen her since he was a child. She gave the police the address of the practice in Leeds, explaining that Mr Courtney was a solicitor with family in Cheltenham.

Once the scene returned to normal they drove the Jeep to Letchworth and recounted the whole episode to Robert and Helen, missing out the actual 'vision' part of the tale. The medic assessed the corpse had been dead for almost three weeks and a post-mortem would confirm the time and nature of death. Helen mentioned to Flick that Mavis was becoming withdrawn and rarely came to see them these days. She was keeping an eye on her but it was difficult.

"We will have to see what happens."

They left about eleven, driving the thirty miles home in the dark. Helen had suggested they could stay but there were things to do and Alan might need them. Flick sat in the passenger seat holding the staff, angled to thread between the seats.

"I wish it wasn't quite so cumbersome, it needs a seat to itself," she joked.

Eric thought she was right about taking it everywhere. "It really is a bit big though."

The answer arrived in her head as the Jeep pulled up outside the flat.

"Eric, I'm an idiot, I can take the staff everywhere we go, it'll even go in my handbag. The answer's in the last lines: 'For wand in staff is yours to wield. In times of darkness grasp and lean'. I can use the wand on its own, I only need the staff for the solution, the wand will give me the vision."

During the week Eric took the wand section of the staff and thought about how to make it into a pedant. It weighed roughly 100 grams although it looked a lot heavier. At 75 millimetres long it wasn't going to look out of place; the only issue was its appearance – it could hardly be called artistic or aesthetic from a jewellery point of view. Flick had stopped wearing her St Christopher medallion a day or two after Dan returned it. She'd said it had done its job, there was nothing left for it to do.

"In a way you could say it took the bullet for him," she commented when Eric asked her for it.

After melting it down and casting it into a small circular peg he cut a thread on the outside to match the wand's inner one. From the cuttings he made a wire that became, after some bending, a new loop to take the original chain. After a clean and polish to the metal and the wood he came in to show Flick the results of his labours. He placed it round her neck and clipped the chain together. The bottom end hung slightly above the swell of her breasts.

"It's perfect, thank you so much, you're amazing." She smiled, looking at it in the mirror.

28

The funeral took place at the end of November in Cheltenham. Apart from Alan, his parents, Dan, Flick and Eric, there was only one other mourner who turned out to be Sarah's flatmate. His parents kept to themselves at the church. Alan had arranged for drinks and a bite to eat at a local pub; his parents arrived twenty minutes after the rest of them. Eric was talking to Dan at the bar when Stella, Alan's mother, moved over to Flick. She introduced herself and asked how long she had known Sarah. Flick replied that she had never met her daughter, then went on to explain she was Eric's girlfriend and how she knew Alan.

"So you were the model for that dreadful picture, I don't know how you could bring yourself to sit in that position without a stitch on while he drew you and then to have everyone look at the result."

Stella, having made one mistake, slid imperceptibly into her second. She gravely misjudged the red-haired girl in front of her, thinking she was a pseudo-intellectual with a degree in something vague and useless. It never occurred to her that after ten years of Aunt Mavis she was going to be a walk in the park for the Naughty Elf.

"To answer your question, Stella, I actually enjoyed letting Alan draw and paint me. If you bothered to look hard enough you would have noticed his incredible eye for detail. Also, and again for the record, I don't give a monkey's about it going on display for the world to look at."

Alan had wandered over the second he realised the Naughty Elf had infested his friend.

"Have you met my father, Flick?"

He managed to stifle a giggle as his mother looked at him with an expression somewhere between disgust and bewilderment.

"Mother, Father, this is Flick Bowden, the drummer in our band, an excellent chef and a very good biologist. She also happens to be the best friend a man could ever have."

"You're no man," his mother hissed. "If you were, you would have found a nice girl to settle down with instead of a black Frenchman."

Flick turned slowly to face her; she had been taking some extra deep breaths as some anger was rising, it also made her breasts appear to be expanding and contracting with a mind of their own. Edgar, a facsimile of the late Sydney on the outside at least, looked Flick straight in the bosom. Stella was quick to notice and was about to take action when Flick made her move. She reached out and, placing two fingers under Edgar's chin, lifted his head up until they had eye contact. She smiled.

"I'm Flick, glad to know you, nice aren't they, 36G, if you want to make a note of the details."

Stella bridled whilst Edgar grinned, then laughed, as people often do on the point of panic. The wicked imp was obviously whispering furiously in her ear, Alan reasoned.

"I take it you don't go a bundle on Alan being gay. I have wondered in the past why that was, I'm not all that good at differentiating, after all it's not that he doesn't like women, he was absolutely brilliant in bed with me..."

Stella was almost at the point Mavis had reached when Sydney and Flick had done Alice in the Vegetable Hamper and was starting to splutter. Edgar had his mouth open for a few seconds before he became acutely aware his wife was turning red.

"We were faking it to get rid of a pest who'd been hounding him – it worked a treat, didn't it, Alan?"

Eric and Dan had wandered over. Alan decided he may as well be hung for a sheep as a lamb and said she had performed magnificently, the fake orgasm was incredible. Dan put his drink down and started to speak.

"I know this may not go down too well with you, but this is going to be the last chance you ever have to build a bridge between us. If you don't take our olive branch then the door will shut forever. Also, whatever opinion you may have formed about Flick, I can assure you she is, perhaps with the possible exception of her mother, the most honest, sensible, complete woman I have ever met. I am extremely proud and thankful she's my dear friend."

Stella, although not boiling, was still in the red section of her personal thermometer, and rasped, "And what, I dread to think, has she done for you? Something as sordid and filthy as what we've just heard, I imagine."

Dan looked at Stella then turned to face Flick, reached out and took her hand. "She's done nothing like that, Stella, nothing like it at all; the main thing Flick's done is to save me from being killed by a madman's bullet."

With that he kissed her forehead then her fingers before turning back to Stella. "You have until the end of the year."

Alan had the last word: "We mean it, the end of December."

They left and ambled slowly back to their cars. There wasn't anything to say; this time the sober atmosphere had taken the edge off the humour – not only had Alan buried a sister he hardly knew, it was also the time he might be saying farewell to both living parents.

"Thanks for coming, we'll see you at Christmas," Dan said as Alan got in the car. "He'll be OK, I'll look after him."

The Christmas period was going to be a little different this year. John and Avril were determined to return to Letchworth for Christmas and, if the garage workload could cope, stay for the New Year. Eric and Flick were planning to announce the arrangements for their wedding and Mavis was an unknown factor to be dealt with as it happened. Wendy was showing well, being over seven months into her pregnancy, Colin was clucking around her like a mother hen. Flick had a vision whilst at work in the first week of the month. Behind her eyes she saw a newborn baby sleeping peacefully. She smiled and fingered the wand round her neck before wondering if she would receive anything from Cheltenham.

The next day they decided to treat themselves to a meal in a romantic Italian restaurant they'd heard about from work friends. Flick emerged from the shower, drying her hair and yelled at Eric, "You seen my black bra anywhere?"

From the bedroom Eric suggested she tried looking on Eddy.

"I think Eddy must be in Wolfie, I can't find him, though I'm sure he was wearing it."

Eric came through and together they looked for Eddy and the missing bra.

"Hold on, didn't you just ask me to put a load in the washer? There was socks, pants and stuff in there, perhaps I gathered up your bra as well?"

Flick thought back. "Yes, that sounds about right, the trouble is my other three are in there too. Ah well, can you cope with me braless for the evening, Mr Marstone?"

Eric nodded vigorously, scooped both breasts out of the towel and started fondling her nipples.

"You're a bloody devil, Marstone, they'll be stuck out like chapel hat pegs all night if you do that for much longer."

Eric released her. "Cover them up, they're more addictive than cocaine, and put some pants on or we'll never get out the door, the table's booked for eight."

Eddy was sitting in a straight thin rainbow close to Cheltenham. Flick's bra was looking more like a flying helmet than earmuffs – he'd pushed his arms through the straps and the lacy bits looked quite fetching as the wind slipped past. The rainbow found the area known as Charlton Kings, then the correct house and finally the right room. Edgar and Stella were intently watching the news, so they never noticed a yellow beam of light hit the sideboard behind them or the walnut brown teddy bear that arrived with the slightest of thuds. Eddy listened and waited. Eventually the conversation turned to the ultimatum Dan had issued. Eddy pulled what looked like a short steel tube out of his compartment and pointed it at the woman on the sofa. Thirty minutes later the rainbow lifted the bra-helmeted bear out of Cheltenham, and deposited him back in his usual spot in Wolfie thirty seconds later. Kenny took the bra off him and returned it to the washing machine, the place where it was almost nearly supposed to be. He passed the bedroom and heard the usual sounds – the girl was just about ready to start making howling wolf noises again, three down, two to go, he calculated on his way back to the camper van as the clock struck midnight.

Christmas Eve arrived in Cambridge after work on Friday, which made them the last to arrive in Letchworth. Mavis was looking a little happier, actually smiling from her usual seat nearest the TV. The evening passed pleasantly enough, made all the more so as Mavis seemed to have lost her fire and just listened to the others. Christmas morning was the usual flurry of presents, breakfast and dinner preparations. Mavis soon returned to the TV, then the topic of the wedding came under the spotlight. Flick knew some of the July wedding plans she had might not be easily accepted, so she and Eric were ready to compromise if they hit a problem. To summarise their side of things, neither of them wanted a large lavish white wedding and they had opted for a simple non-religious ceremony as they didn't agree with much the church stood for and as they had been living together for over six years they didn't want to appear to be hypocrites, in some people's eyes, either. The parents were understanding and wanted to know a little more about certain aspects, so they had answers for family or friends that might be a little put out.

"I'm thinking of Mavis for one, Uncle Jethro and Aunt Maud on our side," Robert said.

"We have three, possibly four on our side as well, it's not so much the non-white wedding as the non-religious side of things that's going to stick in the craw," John added. "Some folk don't have much lateral play in their bearings when it comes to God."

"We knew this was going to be a problem in certain quarters; this is why we want to talk it through with you. Our stand is that the modern church is still attempting to hold on to enforced ignorance, preaching the ancient fears of history that elevated them into a position of power. A power so high it took royalty and science – think Copernicus, Galileo – to overthrow and disperse some but not all of that power, it's still out there today. We look at history and see more wars and deaths fought in the name of religion than any other cause. We hear of men of the cloth preaching violence, children molested, women suppressed and whole nations forced to convert or face death," Flick said her piece.

Eric followed her.

"It isn't that we don't accept religion, it's the church that controls religion we cannot abide. They're the owners of more land than anybody else in this country, they have abundant money and seem to delight in adjusting religion to suit their particular slant on it. At university we met and befriended a lot of people, from places all over the planet, who believed in one religion or another. They might have been strong in their faith, or it could have been something they just put a tick in a box against on hospital information forms. The important thing is we all got on together. Although church preaches goodwill to all men the reality is well wide of the mark."

Flick took over.

"While we're on the subject, we're not too sure about God either, we think the accepted versions are not quite right, so the best way of saying what we feel about it is that we're not sure it's a case of who God is, but what God is. Until we accept all the common areas of all religions and start treating every human as equals and being the same under the skin we aren't going to progress as a species. We're going to have to seriously start doing things for love not money."

Eric finished off.

"We also need to fully understand Quantum Physics a lot better than we do now and the same goes for our understanding of time.

Master these three topics and we may just move forward enough to save ourselves from disaster."

Helen spoke next.

"I've been talking with Avril about the wedding for a while now obviously and we both had a feeling this matter was going to come up. The first inkling of modern thinking came when we saw Alan's picture, that amazing piece had so many ways of looking at it I for one could see four meanings in it. Flick was always asking questions as a youngster – when she started at the vets I can remember her looking at the anatomy books they'd loaned her and commenting there was no way this lot got done in six days."

Avril continued: "Eric was always questioning church and religion from being a child. Apart from the simple ones that every kid asks, he began to study the whole subject from another perspective as he went through school. 'Chariot of the Gods' probably set all the religious books and their theories on fire."

Robert thought for a moment then asked, "So, what's your angle on the subject, what do you believe in, if anything?"

John nodded and added to the question. "I think I know what you're going to say but it will be good to hear it from the two of you. Why do you want to get married anyway?"

Eric began.

"First we want you to know there's been no fights or threats between us over this. We don't seem to fight or argue at all, over anything. We're both of the same mind in all the major areas – there's a few differences of opinion on minor issues, but we're agreed they won't matter in the long run. We want to marry because in our minds it's a way of showing everyone how much we love each other. We tell each other almost every day. As to what we believe, our version if that's the right word, thinks there is a power or a force that created this universe. We don't know how long ago, how long it took or why it was done. It happened. Both of us believe that we cannot be the only planet in this universe that has life on it. Just using the law of averages makes for a mind-boggling number of possible planets, even if the ratio or co-efficient is microscopically low. We think that religion was taught to the human race to stop them fighting and killing each other by aliens from somewhere out there in the universe. Our main bone of contention is that whilst many members of many churches of many religions all across the world spanning all of recorded history are full of good intentions, the controlling heads of these churches are nothing more than power crazy dictators who rule by maintaining ignorance, spreading fear and inciting violence. From the fear of burning in hell for eternity, to selling tickets to heaven on a TV show, the concepts of life, living a good life, what the aliens taught, has been manipulated and engineered to suit the power-hungry and financially-greedy at the expense of the common people. The ideas the aliens sowed will never reach maturity, blind faith or belief is not enough – humans need proof, even then the dominating powerful outweigh the caring powerful."

Flick took up the story.

"We're striving at work in Cambridge to make life better for unfortunate people who have suffered, suffered for whatever reason by trying to give them back something they lost. Even our work has a side to it the power and money crazy are keen to exploit. Stem cell research might one day allow us to grow a human organ, say a liver or kidney, under lab conditions and implant it as a replacement into a suitable donor. Instead of going through the agonising wait of hoping a human donor can be found before the patient dies. The dark side of this research is if it ever does leap from the pages of science fiction, it has already been posited that some evil power will use it to build the universal super soldier, once they have one, they'll start cloning. 'Let's play God' is not impossible."

Eric returned to the room with a drink of water.

"Can we go into the dining room please? Mavis has nodded off but we don't want her to hear what we have to say next."

Flick sat at the end of the table and began her speech.

"I have to take you back to 1972 when we were out on a field trip in Portugal. The incident with the young boy who rode his bike over the cliff has a few more details than we first let on about. You may remember I told you about the odd premonition I had about an hour before the fun started, you had just returned from Crete at the time. It concerns our emotional state, mine in particular. Mentally several things have happened since that have acted as a diffuser or a limiter and made both of us a lot more stable. Well, there's a lot more to tell now and I can only hope you can see why we're of the mind we are."

Eric recounted the story of finding the staff in Wales last year and how they had unravelled the verse inside. The story of the vision involving Dan and how the chunky thick St Christopher had helped save him followed. Flick continued with Colin and Wendy's pregnancy and the additional vision of the sex and name of her baby. Finally, Eric told them the full story of the discovery of Alan's sister in Epping Forest.

Robert broke the silence. "To start with, can we see this staff, and also are you two OK from a stress point of view? This sounds an awful lot of weird stuff to bear."

They assured them all they were fine, as each event occurred the impact seemed to lessen emotionally; this was the other matter which had been withheld. Flick went to fetch the staff from their bedroom and mated the wand round her neck to it. She'd withdrawn the verse from the compartment first, passing it to Eric to open out on the table.

"You know everything now, we hated having to hold things back but please understand we needed to know in our own minds what we were dealing with, even now we're not completely sure," Eric said.

"The hardest part is simpler as we said, each vision is easier to interpret and the emotional shock is now down to a minimal level," Flick added.

John spoke for them all when he told them their secret was safe with them, they understood that Dan and Alan knew and the number of people who didn't know should be kept that way. He also asked if there was anything they could do. Eric answered his father by saying there wasn't anything any of them could do until Flick cracked the secret of the vision, the rest was a matter of trying to avert disaster by protecting the persons involved, if it was that type of vision.

"The wand alone allows her to see, when coupled to the staff, as it is now, the methodology can be found."

John picked it up and ran his hand down its length.

"This all fits with Norse mythology, I take it?"

Eric and Flick nodded.

"Norse and Roman, Look up Hyndla in Norse legend and Mars in Roman mythology."

Avril had a thought after reading the verse. "So this could indicate that you might be a witch or a seer, that adds to the reasons why you see the church as you do. They used to burn witches."

"Do you know that in the Bible Deborah is a prophetess, and Eric's Norse name means 'Forever Ruler': coincidence?" said Flick.

The phone rang and pulled everyone out of their reverie. Helen took the call, Dan and Alan wished them all a Happy Christmas. Helen passed the phone over to John who returned the compliments from Avril and himself. The rest of the afternoon passed, dinner arrived about four. They left Mavis asleep in the TV chair afterwards and went to burn some calories off along the river Ivel. Back in the car park, Flick had separated the wand from the staff and was fastening it back round her neck when a vision appeared. Eric had just laid the staff in the back of the car, he sensed the signs and went to her. She smiled, so he relaxed.

"This is how it happens," he said. "If she smiles, it's a good vision, a scowl is a bad one, that's the code we agreed on since they don't stress her emotionally anymore when they arrive."

She opened her eyes and gave a puckish grin.

"Guess what? Edgar and Stella are on the outskirts of Leeds, I saw a road sign go past their car window."

Back at the house Mavis opened the front door and announced that Alan had phoned and asked her to tell them Edgar and Stella had arrived in Leeds.

"Bloody hell," Robert said.

The rest of the evening revolved round 'Flick's Stick' as Robert managed to name it. Mavis dropped back off to sleep as Avril and Helen made supper, whilst Flick served drinks.

"I have to ask, Flick, this isn't another of your little pranks, is it? I remember all too clearly some of the jolly japes you've pulled in the past," Helen said.

Flick closed her eyes for a second. "I'm not conning you, Eric isn't either – wait." Flick held the wand under her shirt. "This may prove it, if you'll trust me and believe in me then I might be able to prove it."

In the middle of the lounge the parents formed a square round their two children. Robert faced John and at right angles to the men Helen faced Avril. Flick sat in the lotus position on the floor, facing her father, with the staff fully assembled and held aloft.

"Ladies, if you will take an end each, rest it in the palm of your hand, there's no need to grip it. Eric, stand behind me facing your father, look him in the eye as I am now doing to mine. Helen, my Natural Mother, close your eyes; Avril, my future Law Mother, close your eyes too."

Flick lowered her arms so the staff lay supported in the two mothers' hands. Taking the first finger of either hand she stroked the wood with arms outstretched, working outwards from the centre. Avril and Helen saw the same image form behind their eyes, a newborn baby. Flick and Eric never broke eye contact with their respective fathers.

"Meet Stephanie, she will arrive on February 23rd next year," Flick spoke out loud, softly.

"I guess that answers the question," Helen said.

For the rest of the evening the families planned the forthcoming wedding and began the process of accepting what had happened to their children, beginning with the realisation that they were facing a completely unknown set of circumstances brought about by an impossible object that belonged to the world of myth and legend. At first fear had played a part in the judgement, the demonstration had shown them something that could soon be proved to be an indisputable fact and knowing the people concerned had led to an uneasy belief in Flick's Stick. The factor that helped the most was that nothing had hurt or harmed their children, and their acceptance of it aided the belief too. They also discussed the Portugal incident and the risk they had taken to recover the boy motorcyclist, if the staff had been in their possession then perhaps a less traumatic way might have been found.

The next morning it was Robert and John's turn to reveal something which the parents had been working away on in the background. After breakfast Mavis asked to be taken home. Helen took her sister back to the empty house in Stevenage she still insisted on staying in after Sydney's death. Once Helen returned, Robert began to unveil the plan the four parents had hatched some three months ago.

"We half guessed you wouldn't be looking for lavish wedding, so we wanted to find a present for you that would last a lifetime and also be fruitful during that time. This led us to your company flat in Cambridge which I understand you are now going to rent as of January and that you have managed to save a fair amount for a deposit on a house of your own. I'll let John explain the next part."

John opened a thick folder he'd brought downstairs with him.

"We looked at the way house prices are rocketing and did some thinking; next we engaged a well-known legal firm in Leeds, you may know them, nice guys, just started out this year."

Helen added to the story: "We've formed a company, there's four owners and the business has start-up capital of roughly ten thousand pounds. This has enabled us to make a start in the house restoration business, our first two properties are in Cambridge."

Avril opened the folder and pulled out a set of estate agents' documents advertising a pair of semi-detached houses, close to the colleges, in need of modernisation.

"We purchased this pair in September, Dan and Alan acted for us, they also formed the company; number 33 is almost ready, number 35 will be started on after the holidays."

Robert told them the idea was to let them move into 33 and give the flat up. It would be rent-free, so they could keep saving their deposit money at a faster rate.

"The next stage is when number 35 is ready, we intend to sell it and use the money to buy another two similar houses, hopefully another rung up the ladder, and repeat the process. When the first one's finished you two move into it and we sell number 33. This repeats itself making money each time we buy and sell. We reckon in three to four years' time there will be enough money in the business to reimburse the original capital and pay a dividend to the four owners."

Eric looked at the house. "This looks like there's a load of room for improvements, I'm keen to see it."

"And we can live here rent-free and save more money for our own house, that's a fantastic present," Flick said.

John pulled some more papers from the folder. "Alan's done a projection, Dan's ran a model through the tax laws and we can safely say by 1980 at the latest we will have hit our first goal. Here's the figures."

Flick looked at the neatly written columns of figures then wrinkled her nose up in an attempt to work out the section at the bottom.

"I don't see what the last part is, what's an owner's dividend?"

"It works like this, Flick," her father said. "By 1980 you will have lived in hopefully no more than four houses rent-free and managed to amass enough money to put down a deposit on a house of your own. Also, the four owners are John and myself, we're taking 5%

each, and you two who are slated for 45% each. When it all adds up if the targets are met, you'll be able to buy and furnish a rather nice house as the projection says, your share will allow you to live comfortably and mortgage-free. In order to avoid tax, the house you buy will be an asset of the company and not your personal property, but as you own 90% of the company it's yours anyway. Us old fogies are more than happy to have our original investment back and 10% is a tasty slice of the action as our American friends would put it."

John took over. "The other angle is that we can keep the company rolling, this time it will provide you with another pension fund and we're going on a lot of holidays."

They had to let the information sink in.

"First the Mercedes, then the Jeep, now this; we thought the four owners were you guys, not us." Eric looked thoughtfully at their grinning parents. "Flick, I'm speechless, help."

She looked at the four in turn and reached out for Eric's hand.

"This is beyond words. I'm as stunned as if I'd had an electric shock. The opportunity this gives us is way above fantastic, it's off the scale. Thank you all so very, very much."

Eric looked at his father and asked, "Who's doing the renovation work? Where did you find them?"

Helen supplied the answer. "We were told about the builders; and when we come up in January to help you move in, you can meet Terry and his business partner Albert. They're both good tradesmen, we met them earlier and they showed us some jobs they'd recently completed and some photographs of other people's work they'd put right."

"Terry is Jean's brother, you know, Neville and Jean, from the hotel in Newark. When we were up there on one of our 'halfway house' weekends he mentioned they were having cash flow problems, a customer had engaged them on a big job and defaulted on the invoice. It's going through the county court, but in the meantime they have to keep going so we stepped in and said the job's all yours," Avril added.

Robert provided the last details. "They live near Saffron Walden so it's not a long daily journey for them. Our company has opened some trade accounts and it's been agreed that if the project extends past 1980 and the market is still buoyant, then they can either increase their workforce and stay as contractors or we can appoint them to the board. So, what do you think?"

"I just thought, what about the money we've saved for a deposit, shall we invest it in the company?" Eric asked.

"There's no need to do that exactly, we've had a word with Dan and he's recommended a couple of nice little investment schemes to slip your money into. Offshore, with no risks," Robert answered.

"You've thought it through right down to the last detail: Oh Daniel Lavigne, you're in for it when I see you next, you think Beef Wellington's good, oh have I got a surprise for you, and as for Alan Courtney, Baked Alaska, my feet and navel, I'll tickle your taste buds so much they'll explode."

The rest of the days between Christmas and New Year were spent lazily, a trip into London to see the lights with a meal in the West End to follow managed to take up the whole day, a trip to Southend for fish and chips and a walk on the pier wrapped up warm also went down extremely well. Eric phoned Dan to ask how Edgar and Stella were doing and found out they were still at the flat. Flick took over the call and said to Alan they would still like to take up their offer of stopping with them for the New Year, they would pick Wolfie up on the way north and sleep in him round the back of the shop. New Year's Day's dinner was on them, she'd said, Alan replied the strawberry and apple home-made was rocket fuel, his mother had loosened up considerably after a few glasses.

They left Letchworth after an Avril-size breakfast and called in at the flat to exchange Jeepy for the camper. Eric loaded up whilst Flick grabbed recipe books and packed tins and packets into a cardboard box.

"Put Wolfie's fridge on, love, we need to stop at a supermarket somewhere near Leeds, it could do with being cold by the time we get there."

Eric drove whilst she read her recipe books and wrote out her shopping list; evil grins appeared over the top of her notebook.

"This is going to be so much fun, culinary ecstasy for six coming up."

When Flick came out of the supermarket, she had to take all the shelves out of the camper fridge to get the purchases in and be able to close the door.

"As long as these three stay cool, we're home and dry. I can put them in the boys' fridge, the rest won't spoil."

Eric moved out of the car park, nudging his way into the lane for Leeds city centre.

"So what's on the menu, love?"

The wicked imp was already halfway through his instructions, but Eric had been too busy driving to notice.

"What gives you the idea I'm going to tell you, my dearest? If this goes well Dan and Alan will be loyal and devoted slaves to my cooking skills for life, not that they aren't already. I intend to have them eating out of my hand, well... not exactly, but there won't be any pattern left on the plate, put it that way. I can't have you spilling the metaphorical beans, can I?" She smirked mischievously.

"You have remembered they've two of the peacock feathers and the old dining table from Manchester. And I doubt the presence of Edgar and Stella is going stay their hand." Flick looked at him, eyes sparkling and cheeky grin in place. "A chance I will have to take."

Wolfie managed to tuck himself into the parking space reserved for the shop and half of the one allocated to the shoe repairer's next door, a trailing lead hooked him into the electrical supply to run the fridge. The four friends greeted each other then Edgar and Stella were 'reintroduced'. Stella was at pains to apologise for their last meeting in Cheltenham and hoped she could be forgiven.

"I've learned a lot this last month and a great deal more since we came to Leeds."

Edgar smiled and wished them both well for the New Year, hoping they'd had a good Christmas with their families. Alan came in with glasses and a bottle of 'Château Manchester '75', his attempt at faux champagne.

Dan handed out the flutes and proposed a toast: "Good health, good luck and happiness to us all."

"I've been brought up to date with a lot of things," Stella said to Flick as she repacked the contents of Wolfie's fridge into the huge American model in the flat. "It's not been easy. It began a while back when we were at home one evening talking about Dan's words at the funeral. Something came over me, I felt that I had to make the effort; Edgar is a lot more broad-minded, so I've tried to think more like him and even though some things were difficult to accept, I think I can honestly say my viewpoint has changed, and for the better."

Flick leaned back on the kitchen wall and sipped her drink.

"That has to be a plus, the main one being you can handle Alan and Dan as a couple."

Stella looked at her with a slight splash of intrigue in her expression.

"Indeed, I can see the importance of their relationship, and that brings me to something I would like to talk to you about."

Flick nodded, jumped up onto the worktop then folded her legs under her.

"You may know this or you may not, I have been told of an amazingly wonderful red-haired girl, who looks a lot like you by all accounts; it appears she was a Princess in a Manchester palace, she seems to have woven a spell round the people who lived with her." Stella took a sip and with a sly twinkle in her eye, continued her tale. "Furthermore, this Princess and her guardian save wandering babies and rescue children who have met with accidents. She also appears to know and understand much about how people think and act, she injects confidence into those who are lacking, and showers wit and humour as if it were apple blossom in April. Lately I'm told she saw fit to save a man from a bullet and now I'm informed she was involved in the unpleasant task of discovering my daughter."

Flick reached into the fridge and pulled out a bottle.

"Blackberry and apple?" Stella offered her glass.

"An intriguing person, Alan tells me she's gone far beyond the borders of friendship and transcends moral boundaries as if they were made of bubbles without losing any sense of right or dignity to herself or anyone associated with her. Dan added that she has the strength of ten in her mind when it comes to fortitude and optimism. I understand she has a weak point though, her life is often influenced by two imps, one good and one not so good shall we say, and for some reason she can be controlled by, of all things, a peacock feather." Stella was smiling now. "Sound like anyone you know?"

Edgar arrived at the kitchen door with an empty glass and a full-on smile. "This a private party, or can anyone join in?"

Flick passed the bottle. "This one's on the go at the moment, we used to call it paint stripper. It's just me being me, Stella, nothing more, I'm made that way. Eric makes a lot of seemingly impossible things work because of his unswerving faith and trust in me and as he never, ever gives in, neither do I."

Back in the lounge the conversation was light and cheery, the plans for New Year's Eve were debated until the clock said midnight and their beds called to them.

The daytime hours of December 31st were spent taking Edgar and Stella round the Yorkshire Dales in Wolfie. The six of them piled into a hearty-looking pub in the middle of nowhere for a lunch of beer and sandwiches around midday, then the tour of North Yorkshire continued till the sun went down. Edgar remarked he had never seen such countryside and asked Stella if they could come up for a holiday. Eric told them there were thousands of places to visit, a week was the minimum time to spend here.

"Be warned though, if you do come and stay don't be surprised if it pulls you back time and time again, this part of the world could almost be magnetic," Dan ventured.

John and Avril had introduced them to a private club in Leeds, mainly used and frequented by business people, in order to give them an opportunity to find more clients for the company and also provide a place where it was possible to hire the function room or a smaller meeting room for a much reduced rate. Tonight they were having a party, Dan had six tickets in his pocket and by eight they were sitting at a table ready to be entertained. The evening unfolded in the manner these type of parties often do. Auld Lang Syne echoed round the room then people started wishing each other well and hugging rather over-enthusiastically. The moment was rather poignant for Stella who shed a few tears on the way back to the flat. Edgar sat in the lounge and told them about the hard battle she'd had after the body was discovered. Each day it had been a little easier and then one morning the realisation she would lose her son as well provided her with the drive she needed to make the changes.

When breakfast was out of the way and New Year's morning had opened its eyes properly, a question was asked by Alan that was in a way rather overdue.

"Well, Princess, we're noticed nothing's been mentioned about this dinner you're rustling up, are we going to be enlightened as to the menu for the evening?"

Dan was standing next to a small vase with two peacock feathers in it, pretending to arrange them, with an expression of thinly-spread innocence on his face. Eric was propped up against the door jamb, grinning.

"Told you so."

Flick looked slowly round the room, Edgar and Stella were half wondering if there's an action replay of the tale they'd heard about due or something different was in the wind. She was wearing the mischievous face she pulled out for special occasions and spoke in a slow measured voice.

"It's a little different this year, boys – as we have guests, I've made a little puzzle out of it. Your starter for ten, pardon the pun, and first course tonight will be French onion soup with grilled cheese croutons–"

Dan looked straight at her. "Oh Flick, that's a dish I dream about, my mother's soup is to die for. If you can get even close to hers I'll hug you so hard!"

She continued, "Hopefully not so hard I fart. The details of the main course and dessert are written down and hidden somewhere in the flat. When you find it, you'll know the full menu, except for the wines which Alan will be in charge of. So, whilst I prepare matters in the kitchen you five can start looking. I offer no clues."

With that she disappeared through the door. Edgar and Stella concentrated on the magazine rack, Dan and Eric started looking through the four shelves of books and videotape boxes. Alan thrust a hand down the side of sofas, chairs and looked in drawers and cupboards. He lifted rugs and ferreted about inside cushion covers. Apart from becoming thirty pence richer on finding three fluff-covered ten pence pieces he only found the remains of a long dead biro, a cuff link and a piece of jigsaw. Dan and Eric had an interesting pile of temporary bookmarks to show for their time working through the shelves. From a train ticket dated April 1972 to a taxi receipt and the discovery of a long-lost set of notes on tax rates in the Bahamas, there was nothing that hinted even slightly of food. A menu for the local Chinese takeaway had raised false hopes and despite everywhere else being searched there was no sign of a menu. Alan held a meeting on the sofa.

"Right, we're looked everywhere, there's not a single item we haven't checked and double checked. We know that Flick plays by the rules, she never lies or cheats. Any ideas, anyone?"

Dan suddenly had a flash of inspiration. "The ceilings, we've been looking down all the time, not up."

With manic glee the five of them looked at all the ceilings and examined every light fitting.

"It was a good idea, Dan," Eric told him after they retired back to the lounge empty handed.

Minutes passed, then Alan stood up. "Oh, you cunning vixen, you naughty little elf, where haven't we looked, of course it's here – we've all walked past it a dozen times if not more."

At that moment Flick walked in and asked if there was any wine open, she'd got everything ready and under control. Alan issued orders like a field marshal.

"Eric, shoulders; Dan, legs."

He moved the magazines off the table as Flick was carried giggling across the room and held down on the table.

"Right, fellow searchers, I will unveil the evening's repast."

She wriggled as Alan pulled her shirt up. Written in lipstick just above her navel was the word TURGOOKIN, below they saw the word SOUFFLÉ.

"Ah mon cherié, soufflé I understand, you will tell me what is the Turgookin, si vous plaît?" Dan dropped into his native language whilst rolling the peacock feather between thumb and forefinger.

She looked up at him with a very naughty sideways glance radiating out of her eyes.

"Not telling, you'll have to find it, it's written down somewhere."

Alan started the feather going round her navel, the giggles rose to near hysterical levels.

"Do your worst, I'm not telling," she managed to say between her involuntary chuckles and chortles.

"Turn her over please, gentlemen," Alan asked. Once she'd been rotated through 180 degrees Alan pulled her shirt up a little further to reveal a thin strip of paper wedged in her bra.

"It's a three-bird roast, a turkey stuffed with a goose that's stuffed with a chicken that's full of bacon, sausage, Paris brown mushrooms, onions, peppers and breadcrumbs."

Flick had been released from the torture table and given a large glass of Strawberry '75. Edgar was laughing fit to kill.

"You lot are crazy, totally mad, but amazingly funny with it. Oh boy, wait till our friends back in Cheltenham hear about this." He managed to stop laughing long enough to collect a glass of wine from Stella.

"Do you go through this 'torture' every time you do a meal like this?"

Flick brushed her tousled hair to one side and nodded furiously. "Yes, it'd be rude not to, really." She grinned.

Sometime near six the meal arrived on the table. The soup almost made Dan explode with joy, the roast was eaten in total silence, twenty minutes later the big serving dish was almost empty, second helpings had given way to thirds, and in Edgar's case, after a quick check round the table for any other candidates, fourths. Flick had used the time to keep visiting the kitchen; finally the soufflé arrived.

"I've died and gone to heaven," Alan said.

"There's three spoonfuls of soup left in the pan if anyone's got room left," Eric called from the kitchen.

There were no takers. Edgar asked if it was OK to undo the top button on his trousers, Stella told them the dinner was without doubt one of the finest meals she had ever eaten. Dan told her the soup was indistinguishable from his dear mother's and would she give him the recipe she used.

"I've got a couple of ends of lipstick I'm not keen on, so pull up your shirt and I'll write it on you," she joked.

"Touché!" He grinned.

29

Colin made a phone call on February 24th, after he'd caught up on his sleep. Wendy and the baby were doing well, he excused himself after five minutes as there were a lot of phone calls to make. A week later Eric answered the phone to Wendy who was obviously feeling elated at being a new mother and wanted to tell them their entry into the 'baby stakes' was incredible.

"You got the date and the name exactly."

The champagne and photograph arrived in April. Flick smiled.

"I told her I just picked a date at random and forgot what year it was. Stephanie's a popular name at the moment so I got away with that one, a weak excuse I know but what else can I say?"

In May the second batch of houses were purchased in Cambridge, the first selling at the price expected of it. Qwendos gave them a pay rise and David said the American side of the operation was very impressed with their performance and attitude. The four parents spent a lot of time together at weekends, taking in parts of the country they'd not seen much of previously; Helen mentioned Scotland and Avril opted for Ireland for the longer weekends.

Without too much fuss, July and the wedding arrived. The register office held the small party of family and friends. Neither the Bowdens or the Marstones had large numbers of family; along with a few of Eric and Flick's friends plus Dan and Alan acting as 'best men', the room was about three-quarters full. Robert had booked a hotel for the reception where most of the other guests joined them later. The photographer finished off the formal pictures and left, the party spilled out onto the lawns and relaxed.

Dan and Alan had changed into schoolboy outfits supplied by the fancy dress shop and placed a large sign next to a long table.

"Tweedledee and Tweedledum's BBQ is now open," John announced. "There's no need to rush – help!"

He feigned panic and skipped out of the way of the hungrier guests stampeding towards the food.

By nine the party picked up its drinks and headed indoors. Colin, Wendy, Alice and Kevin had set Escapade's kit up behind the stage curtains. It had been a little tricky keeping Eric and Flick occupied whilst the kit migrated from John's parts van to the hotel side door; thankfully, several people were in on the scam and difficult situations were avoided. Robert climbed the steps to the stage and asked for quiet. His speech, he said, was along the lines of Churchill's:

"It's like a woman's skirt, long enough to cover the subject but short enough to make it interesting."

John followed him in a sense, he simply ambled up alongside him then both started talking about the bride and groom in their bogus Jewish accents. Alan climbed the steps next, Dan joined him and together they recalled a few of the incidents from their days together in the Manchester Madhouse. When they had finished and the laughs had died down, Colin took the microphone.

"I've got some bad news, I'm afraid, the disco is going to be late, they're stuck in a traffic jam in Tottenham."

Kevin waited whilst Flick talked to Dan, then Alan ambled over to Eric. The four friends chatted for a couple of minutes then Alan nodded at Alice who blew a kiss to Kevin.

"Do Toad, do Toad," the phoney southern accent bounced round the room.

In seconds many of the guests pulled off formal shirts to reveal Escapade t-shirts bought at the children's charity gig. As they shouted 'Toad, Toad, Toad', Colin and Wendy pulled on the ropes to open the stage curtains. Alan handed a completely stunned Eric his guitar, whilst Dan gave a wide-eyed Flick her red boob tube, cut-offs and sticks.

"If you'd care to get dressed, Princess, battle can commence."

She opened her mouth, closed it, opened it again then finally formed a very wicked expression that used twinkling eyes and the corner of a turned-up smile.

"Nice one, guys," Robert and John said between giggles.

Whilst Flick changed, Eric took the mike and thanked everyone for coming to their wedding-gig. Flick returned and surveyed the guests.

"I did wonder why our female friends had opted for two pieces rather than dresses. You're all very naughty, devious little friends, or should that be fiends. OK, here we go – if you're very good we might, just might, do Toad at the end."

The first number acted as a sound check, a few knobs were tweaked then the set unfolded properly. Around midnight Toad bounced round the room, then almost as quickly as the surprise gig started, it ended. Sometime after one, they said goodnight and went up to bed. Edgar and Stella both said they had never been to a wedding quite like it. Mavis had a smile on her face not a hundred miles away from the one Eddy always wore; however, this was down to vodka input rather than the skill of a seamstress, not that Eddy knew what a seamstress was or had ever been near one. The four parents sat downstairs in the bar reliving the early days of their children's relationship and comparing it to their own.

"A brilliant day," Eric whispered in her ear. "Love you, Flick, so very much."

She smiled at him and asked if he would like her to dance for him, she wanted to show her love for him as well as tell him. Without waiting for an answer, she slipped into the bathroom, appearing two minutes later naked but for seven scraps of material.

"The dance of the Seven Veils, one for each year we've been together and for the sevenfold times my love for you increases each year."

The cassette player play button let the music start; four veils in, the dance stopped, Eric couldn't stand it any longer.

"I appear to have overdone it, haven't I?" she whispered afterwards.

He raised himself up on his arms and nodded.

"Perhaps you should have made it the Dance of the Three Veils."

She folded her arms behind her head and looked up at him lopsidedly.

"You do know it's against the law to have rampant sex with a dancing girl twice in one night in Hertfordshire, I take it?"

Eric lowered himself just enough to plant a delicate kiss on each nipple.

"In that case I will ravish you again shortly, then if you'll be so kind as to give me a few minutes to catch my breath I'll give you one of our long slow ones, we can fall asleep after that and having managed it three times I haven't broken the law."

She arched her back slightly. "Perfect, I knew you'd think of a way round it."

Wolfie and Jeepy found themselves once more in the bowels of a cross channel ferry bound for France. The plan was to drop Alan and Dan on the outskirts of Paris so they could visit his grandparents. They were driving down to the south coast for their honeymoon, spending a few days in one place then a few in another before heading back to Paris and their friends roughly two weeks later. On the outskirts of Reims, they found a suitable spot to unhitch Jeepy. Alan and Dan waved as the little Wrangler pointed its nose towards Paris. Eric carried on as far as Troyes, this was going to be home for the night. In the morning they walked into the ancient town and spent most of the day arm in arm sauntering round nowhere in particular. Around six they decided to have an early night and set off before the sun came up.

From her usual position nestled in the crook of Eric's arm, Flick said she was rather surprised the staff had been inactive since last Christmas. He asked if she'd had even the slightest suggestion of a vision only to see her shake her head.

"Sometimes I feel it's trying to teach me how it works – does that sound stupid, I've said before it's not like possession or domination, I feel it wants me to learn."

Eric had wondered if the staff was capable of more than they were aware of but for the life of him nothing came to mind other than crazy stuff that belonged in the world of science fiction.

"I honestly don't know, love, the only thing I can suggest is why don't we try some experiments with it and see if anything happens. So far it seems to be able to foretell events up to a month away, if we take Dan's situation, nine if we consider Stephanie. Next, it appears to foretell good and bad events. Also, your emotional reaction has been, for want of a better phrase, 'turned down' so there's a possibility it can monitor you. Next I suppose is the way in which you managed to relay the vision to our mothers. Finally, I think you discovered the vision can now be, again for want of a better word, 'replayed' on demand for a while at least."

She had reached over to pick up the staff and held it carefully, stroking the polished wood with her thumb.

"I think we would have to be careful, I'd hate to do something that made anything worse by being stupid. We could try thinking of something that would help and playing through all the things that could happen... no, that would be too involved, the number of possible outcomes is huge. I don't know, Eric, how do we communicate with it; so far it communicates with me but now seven months have passed without a peep never mind a vision."

He took it from her and kissed her lightly.

"Let's get some sleep and talk about it as we drive south in the morning,"

Kenny held the staff for the night, he glowed a shade of deep violet very faintly in the dark.

Wolfie made his way towards Dijon, Flick had the window open, enjoying the early morning breeze.

"My first problem is the way in which the staff teaches. I'm never too sure if it's a lesson or not. The sporadic nature is not helping either, so if we try something we can only talk to it or think it. Well, I will, we're not sure if it even knows about you, do we?"

The conversation continued investigating various scenarios as the French countryside slid past. Since Tourus, the road had followed the river Saône and would take them to Lyon. The confluence of the Rhône and Saône is bridged at the southern end of the city; the Mercedes continued steadily south to Vienne where they decided on lunch. Eric had a thought as he made a drink.

"Do you remember that French couple we met in Portugal? They lived in Lyon – try and think of them and see if you get anything."

Taking the staff from its place under the bed, she screwed in the wand optimistically hoping the entire staff would respond, or do anything, as a whole thing rather than in two pieces.

"Nicole and Simon," she said, looking in her address book. She closed her eyes. "I'm trying to remember what they looked like and holding tight on the wand."

The kettle boiled and Eric started on slicing the baguette to put some of the smelliest camembert he had ever experienced in with the pastrami.

"Nicole, Simon, where are you?"

He heard her faint whisper in the quiet of the van.

"Eric, I have a picture, I can see them. They are a long way apart, I don't think they live together anymore, that's it, the image is fading."

She looked up and found a steaming mug next to a smelly plate.

"Well, that's something – do you think it worked thinking about them or speaking out loud? Help yourself, they'll walk to the trash bag unaided if you don't."

Between mouthfuls she said it was doing both, she was sure of that.

"That's how the lesson works, I experiment and if I get it right the staff works and confirms the method. So... if nothing happens, we have two possible scenarios: one, the thing I'm asking is outside the staff's powers; or two, I asked incorrectly. Does that sound roughly right?"

Eric nodded as he had his mouth full.

"There's something else I noticed – have you picked up on the style of language I use when the staff is, shall we say, active? I called Avril my Law Mother, not Mother-in-Law, I think it uses an older language than we do."

Their drive ended in Beauchastel, a small town near Montélimar. Wolfie headed out of the main streets and found a nice little spot under the trees up in the hills. That evening they discovered if they took an end of the staff each and Eric looked at a playing card, Flick could see it. Later on, after a bottle of local wine, they tried it with Eric holding the staff and Flick the wand. Finally, they tried it with Eric out in the trees and Flick inside the van. Sitting on a fallen tree trunk they wondered if it would work with anything else other than playing cards.

"You do realise we can never tell anyone about this, perhaps we can include our parents and the guys, but that's the lot," Eric mentioned.

Flick looked across the valley.

"I know, love, it'll be our secret to the grave. Even if we could show someone they'd think it was a magic trick, a new type of illusion – or candidates for the loony bin."

Wolfie emerged from the side road and turned south once more. As the day progressed, quick glimpses of the sea flitted past, flashes of blue in the green and brown. Their plan was to find the access road to the Giens Peninsula, a small stub of land jutting out into water near Hyéres; thanks to a good bit of map reading and spotting the road sign, this part of the proceedings was accomplished easily. They agreed on a camp ground near the beach, finding a place almost at the western end of the cape. The afternoon was spent setting up the van and taking a walk along the totally deserted pure white sand beach. Twenty minutes into their walk they found a small cave the sea had washed out.

"A certain type of man could have his wicked way with a girl in here," a playful voice echoed round the rock walls.

Eric slid a finger down her bare belly stopping at the denim waistband.

"Rape, rape, help," a tiny voice said close to his ear.

"Why are you whispering?"

She kissed his cheek.

"I don't want anyone to hear me."

Eric patiently waited for the BBQ to heat up, inside Wolfie a salad of sorts was submitting to Flick's way of doing things. Next to Wolfie was another Mercedes; this was a custom-built model presumably belonging to a couple of senior citizens from Austria if the licence plate and the two people sitting under the awning were to be believed. The woman came over to them, asking if she might borrow their corkscrew – she couldn't find theirs anywhere. Flick obliged and introduced herself and Eric. The girls began talking, and soon the four were sitting in the space between the two campers, getting to know each other. Hans and Heidi were from Göfis in Austria – this little headland was where they'd spent their honeymoon in 1911, making them 86. The afternoon slid along; by the time the insects were clamouring round the citronella candles, they'd decided next day to hire a four-seater dune buggy and have some fun.

Although the cape wasn't easy to get round, they managed to cover almost all the beaches and most of the inlets by dodging round the lanes and tracks. Lunch was in a small bistro where the conversation turned to the Austrian couple's home town. It seemed Hans and Heidi were the odd ones – most of their neighbours couldn't understand why they kept travelling around Europe like they were in their twenties. According to Hans they were all sticking to the mud: the English idiom isn't the easiest part of the language to master. Heidi told them she went to yoga and keep fit twice a week, she visited the hairdresser once a month and still used make up if she intended leaving the house.

"This, my friends say, is crazy, why bother at your age? I laugh at them and say if I didn't do these things Hans would find another woman. They don't understand the joke either," she said. "They do not see that life is what you make it, and some effort and love is needed to make fun and games. Young people are not to be entertained, they do not want to know about anything other than complaining and being miserable."

On the way back, the buggy crossed the beach Eric and Flick had walked along the day before. Hans asked Eric to go towards the cave.

"We came here sixty-six years ago and the place was as deserted then as it is now. Being a lot younger we were rather daring and at the time the thought of being caught wasn't entering our heads. I think we spent a good hour in there, didn't we, my dearest." Heidi gave Flick a sidelong look.

"Thankfully no one spoiled the fun, there's a large flat rock inside at just the right height which I remember was on the left as you looked out to sea."

Flick nodded as she looked into the cave mouth.

"It's on the left, I can tell you that, we were in there yesterday afternoon, luckily we didn't have any interruptions either."

The four started to laugh as Eric put the buggy in gear and headed for the rental shack near the camp ground. Hans announced they should now have a beer in the garden then change for dinner. Eric and Flick were more than welcome to join them – it would be their way of saying thanks for the hard work they had put in driving the buggy all day, and making them evens for getting the lunch.

"I do like to shower and put fresh clothes on in the evening, I cannot stand these people who sit down wearing the same shorts and shirt they've slopped around in all day," Heidi said.

Flick said they would join them in the restaurant at seven and now it was her turn to buy the beers. Hans grinned at her and slapped his knee.

"Poor Manfred, wait till I tell him a red-hair English beauty bought me a beer! He will turn green with the envy!"

To provide some circumstantial evidence to support his claim, a waiter took their photograph holding large glasses of Kronenbourg.

Flick slid into the long evening dress she had bought just in case a situation arose that demanded it. As Helen had spent a lot of time teaching her daughter what dresses looked fantastic and which ones could make her look like a cheap tart, she knew what suited her, which colours went best and what accessories added to the glamour. Hair and makeup did the rest. Eric went with a simple white shirt and lightweight trousers.

"Ready when you are, love. Oh wow, you look amazing."

She dropped her bra over Eddy for safe keeping and walked towards him.

"Down, boy, save it for after dinner, the zip's in the left side on this one, that's all you need to know." She winked and blew him a kiss.

Heidi had also pulled out the stops; the two girls might have had over sixty years between them, but for sheer class, style and elegance the gap was down to micro seconds. To say heads turned in the restaurant was to pass up on the chance of using the word rotated. Eric ordered a bottle of wine as Flick asked Heidi how the dress stayed up.

She replied, "A little concealed elastic and a large helping of will power."

Over coffee Hans announced they were going to have an easy day tomorrow and asked what they intended to do. Eric told them they were having a bike ride round the peninsula and said if they found a good bouchère they would bring a BBQ back with them. Hans asked if they knew about the shared problems of sexual intercourse and riding a bicycle. They shook their heads.

He explained, "In both cases once you'd learned how to do it you never forget, but by the time you get to my age it's difficult to get your leg over either."

Back in Wolfie, Eric eased the zip of the dress down, letting it slip to the floor. As he suspected, there wasn't anything else to remove. Flick had a thoughtful look on her face.

"I wish I could ask the staff to give them a little bit of their sex life back, I guess it's wishful thinking."

"Foresight seems to be the key point of the staff, I doubt we could help them on that score," Eric agreed.

She climbed into bed and waited for him to join her before playfully pulling him onto his back.

"Time for me to do my wifely duty, Mr Marstone. Whilst the way to a man's heart is said to be through his stomach, I am started a little lower down this evening."

Eric grinned at her. "Can you get your leg over, Mrs Marstone?"

She looked at him coyly. "Silly boy, there's no cross bar on a girl's bike."

Eddy and Kenny were debating if what they had in mind would be classified as interference or not. They'd agreed it certainly wasn't protection – the argument ran if they didn't alter the course of history then it was allowed; however, the reasons for doing it were to be honest a little difficult to find a name for. In the end they decided to do it and think about where to file it in the system later. Or perhaps if no one noticed, forget about it. They set to work and made a few adjustments to some processes in the human body and tried a few test runs with the internal equipment. Eddy used a sequence he'd seen before and to his way of logical thinking this would be the safest way to get the function working smoothly. Kenny double checked the pressures required and the time needed as a recovery period. By the time they'd watched the first test and were both happy the clock on the dashboard said two. Kenny resumed his position hanging off the wardrobe door, Eddy sat on his usual overnight perch, adjusting the bra draped across his head as he sat down, the last traces of rainbow light faded into the night sky.

The next day was eventful as the staff revealed another angle on the complex matter of how it worked. They'd arrived in a small village and found a café when Flick found a short vision coming up in her mind. The imagery depicted a small cobbled square with a butcher's shop in one corner; she saw two bicycles leaned up against the fence nearby that looked like theirs. By touching the wand Eric could see it too.

"Well, I think this is new. We said if we found a butcher's we would bring a BBQ back, so now the shop's found us."

She studied the vision again, looking at the edges rather than the centre to try and find more detail. The only thing that seemed to be of use was the name of the street – looking round, Eric discovered it ran from the square they were at. By cycling along the named road it connected with a second square with the shop in the corner.

"Built-in street map – that's oddball."

Flick thought for a moment and slowly mentioned it could be a form of foresight.

"We had this thought in our heads and when we're almost on top of it the wand fills in the details – mad."

They cycled back with food for the five thousand.

"I didn't know a BBQ pack for four would be this big. I hope Hans and Heidi have got big appetites."

Flick grinned back.

"They said they were having an easy day, so perhaps they didn't do much for lunch."

At the site they found them in the communal space between the vans, smiling and beaming at each other. Hans asked where they'd been as he helped take the bags off the handlebars. Heidi passed glasses of wine over, then she and Flick began preparing the usual salad.

"We haven't been up long," she confided. "It must have been the visit to the little cave yesterday, it bought back some lovely memories, the whole day was one long beautiful memory, we sat in bed last night looking at the old sepia photos we have, and just being so happy to have come back to relive our youth."

Flick chopped tomatoes and asked, "So you didn't get to sleep till late then?"

Heidi glanced over to her. "No, dear, we turned the light out about midnight, then in the dark I felt something pressing against my leg, something I haven't felt in a long while, I think you know what I mean. Anyway by the time Hans had agreed three times was enough at our ages it must have been about six in the morning."

Flick's face cracked into a smile. "I'll have to ask him he wants to have a go on Eric's bike."

They couldn't stop the laughter that poured out, no matter how they tried.

Flick didn't as a rule sunbathe, but they were moving on tomorrow and they wanted a day doing very little. Hans and Heidi walked with them to the beach then carried on to the little cave.

"We'll keep a look out, I'll whistle if anyone comes near," Eric offered.

They exchanged addresses, making the usual noises people who meet on holiday always make. This time it was slightly different – Hans and Heidi made it very clear they felt Eric and Flick had made this holiday the very special occasion it had turned out to be; they would send them a Christmas card and would be overjoyed if they did the same.

Heidi explained, "We always send a card with a picture inside and ask our friends to do the same. That way we always know what you look like as the years go by. So far we have about six hundred friends who write to us each December, we'd love to add you to our list."

After promising they would love to be on the list and would definitely write, Wolfie pulled out onto the gravel road as they waved goodbye.

Voreppe was the end of the day's drive, a spot was found in the forest under the mountains. Flick had driven most of the day,

Eric had done the first hour then the last two. While she put her feet up, he managed to make a dinner from what was left in the fridge. The next day they had to go shopping, or starve. Lying on the sofa at the back with notebook in hand, Flick had listed all the attributes of the staff and wand as well as the possible other and as yet unknown powers it possessed. After they'd eaten a combined dinner and supper, the forest began to come alive; small furry animals probably watched from the carpet of bracken, birds cast sideways glances at the two humans who sat on a huge stone that had been used to prevent traffic going any further up the narrow dirt trail. They talked quietly.

"Do you think I should talk to it, sing to it, or maybe even dance with it?"

Eric looked at the list of notes and answered that if they were to eliminate anything it had to be tried, preferably at least twice before drawing a line through it.

"I don't really know what to ask it, shall I say 'tell me the future' or is that too direct?"

Eric passed the staff to her. "Hold it and just say it, see what happens."

She held the staff in one hand and touched the wand with the other; nothing happened. She tried again saying 'show me the future' after realising the staff didn't communicate via speech. Again, nothing happened. Lastly, she sang the words, in the highest voice she could reach; this time an image formed in Eric head – he was holding the staff for her as she held the wand close to her chest with both hands.

"I saw you, here, right now, but you're not wearing jeans and a shirt. You're in a white flowing dress like the one we saw in the picture at the Manchester library."

She thought back. "I remember it, Veleda was her name. We're going to be hard pressed for a long flowing dress out here."

Eric looked thoughtful then started searching through one of Wolfie's boxes that held spare parts and tools.

"Is it possible to make a dress, rather like an Indian sari, out of a long length of material? Only I have both of those massive white curtain linings you brought up from Letchworth when we were building Wolfie left over, I intended to use them as rags. Would it wind round you enough?"

She looked at the material. "Nothing ventured, no, what's the word, Eric, INGUZ, where there's a will there's a way."

The material held in place with some careful wrapping and a couple of safety pins from the sewing kit.

"If this works I shall have INGUZ tattooed on the back of my neck. I owe it to you for showing me to never give in whatever the odds."

Dusk had fallen some time ago when a red-haired girl in a makeshift dress sang and danced in the middle of a small clearing at the bottom of a mountain in south-east France whilst holding a six-foot wooden staff. She finished the folk dance – it was a little difficult without the right music; Eric had improvised as best he could on his old acoustic guitar, she could remember the steps from her childhood. Eric joined her in the clearing; the moonlight bathed her in a shaft of light sliced by the surrounding trees. The forest was incredibly quiet now. Nothing stirred, no creaking boughs, no bird sang, the leaves and undergrowth moved silently in the breeze coming off the lower slopes.

"Back to the drawing board, love," she said a shade despondently.

"Wait, I can sense something, take my hand."

Eric moved closer to her, his arm suggesting an invisible armour-plated shield to protect his lover. Red pinpoints of light formed in the darkness between the tree trunks. Slowly a wolf entered the clearing, slinking towards them with eyes fixed on the wafting hem of the white dress.

"Eric, that's a wolf, not a fucking husky."

About ten feet away the animal stopped and dropped its front legs down, laying its head on them once they reached the grass.

"I think it's OK, I don't think it will attack."

Eric was not so sure.

"I'm going to offer it the end of the staff, I feel that's the next thing to do."

As she did so the animal inched forward until its nose was touching the end of the wood.

"You have come to me, Fenrir, I thank you. I have my Eternal Ruler with me in all ways at all times. Go in peace, I will call if I need you."

The wolf stood up, looked at Eric and almost imperceptibly bowed its head at him before backing out of the clearing, turning only when under cover of the lower branches of the trees.

"Shit, where did I get that language from?"

Eric held her hand and smiled. "I'm thinking more and more the staff is teaching both of us. Let's go inside, I'll make us a drink whilst you get out of the curtains."

She smiled and gathered up the loose material. "I have to hand it to you, Mr Marstone, you'll stop at nothing to get my clothes off – do we have any chocolate digestives, by the way?"

Summoning a wolf went into the notebook after the biscuit crumbs were brushed off the pages. The drive to Limoges took two days, due to keeping on the rural roads that passed through many of France's forests and parks. There was very little traffic on the roads, at the end of the first day they found themselves in Saint Germain – l'Herm. Eric spotted a stream running through the village – there was supposed to be a camp ground on the main road, but all they could find was the remains of an old wooden sign with faded paintwork. On the other side of town, a restaurant was just about to open so the van pulled up outside. Whilst they were scouring the atlas for another place to stop, a waiter asked them if they wanted dinner as well as a site for the night. By seven-thirty they were sitting outside with wine and three courses, the plat du jour being trout.

The second day on the road took them further west, the green lanes still deserted. Slowly Wolfie ate up the miles, always with his nose pointing at Limoges. Lunch was taken parked under the branches of a huge elm tree. In the heat of the day a stream alongside a disused mill provided a place to wade knee-deep in mountain water. A campsite on the eastern edge of Limoges turned up as the guide book suggested and became home for the next two nights.

Paris was a slow drive north; they'd arranged to meet Dan and Alan in the Jeep at Versailles. The tourists were flocking to the palace and gardens. To keep out of the way just enjoying each other's company, they discovered a campsite in a nearby village which offered everything they needed. It was possible to walk to the palace down wide, tree-lined avenues past small intimate bistros and a traditional French restaurant in which they treated themselves to dinner on their last evening. The next morning the familiar roar of the Jeep was heard shortly after ten o'clock. After hitching up the 'Toad', Dan took the wheel and steered them through the Paris environs using roads that only a native could have known about. Most of the journey up to the ferry terminal was spent bringing each other up to date with their adventures.

30

The forty days between August 12th and September 20th, 1977 where littered with events that would change the direction of Eric and Flick's life and career path.

On August 12th the NASA space shuttle Enterprise completed the first of five Approach and Landing Tests where the ship was in free flight.

August 15th turned out to be a busy day at SETI in Ohio University as the WOW signal was detected by the radio telescope known as Big Ear. It bore the hallmarks of extra-terrestrial origin seemingly originating from the constellation of Sagittarius.

August 20th saw the launch of Voyager 2; Voyager 1 followed on September 5th. Both craft were designed and built to leave the solar system and begin exploring deep space.

The last date was September 20th when the Petrozavodsk phenomenon occurred in the USSR and Scandinavia. The cry went up: UFOs! It was soon shouted down though.

In October the American parent company paid a visit to Cambridge. For the first three days the six black-suited executives remained ensconced in David's office. On Thursday morning both Eric and Flick were asked to join them for an informal meeting. David made the introductions and began by informing them of the high regard the company, on both sides of the pond, held them in. Their work had been reviewed and it was his pleasure to ask them to consider joining a new project called 'Space Exploration Life Support', or SELS to use its acronym. This branch of bionic engineering would be centred on making machines and environments that humans could interface with. They were equipping a new lab and workshop with the latest tools and computers. It would be housed in a purpose-built unit next to the existing Qwendos site.

He gave them a large envelope of information to study at their leisure. All six executives made a small speech, saying how they were exactly the sort of people the company wanted, how the rewards and job satisfaction would increase as they progressed through the ranks. There wasn't any ceiling on where they could rise to.

Over a bottle of Alan's '3G', also known as 'Grape, Ginseng and Gasoline', they read through the information David had supplied. Apart from another sizeable increase in salary, they would be working alongside two other biologist-engineer teams, one from Belgium, the other from Italy. NASA were deeply involved and the work was considered to be under the auspices of the military and the FBI. On Friday morning they arrived at work with the papers signed, and everyone smiled. The new project would be ready for October of 1978. Everything they'd heard about the specifications and brief from the end user would be available on the latest computers; they would be getting one to use at home as well.

December arrived, as did Christmas cards. Hans and Heidi's was the first to drop through the door. Among the pictures of robins, Santa's sleighs, snowy villages and trees laden with baubles and parcels was a wedding invitation from Alice and Kevin. Flick added the date to her diary. It went without saying that Escapade were on the bill for the reception in Newark. Christmas was spent in Letchworth and the New Year in Leeds. Mavis came to the Christmas festivities at Letchworth but didn't want to travel to Leeds. Helen told them she was getting worried about her as she had gone very quiet and seemed to be spending a lot of time at a friend's house a few streets away.

As the months passed, the staff continued to reveal other aspects of its capabilities or put another way, its powers. In February 1978 Flick and Eric were invited to the one-year-old

Stephanie's christening in Manchester. Flick had a vision of a road traffic accident somewhere near Leeds and told Eric to leave the motorway. This advance information avoided a five-mile tailback and a four-hour delay. The radio announcement asking people to stay away from the area came an hour after the vision.

March being the month Alice and Kevin had decided to get married saw reasonable weather and although cold promised to be bright. The church and reception were in Newark, so Alan and Dan loaded up Escapade's gear, borrowing John's parts van again. They were set up by the time Eric had parked Jeepy in the London Road hotel car park. Flick being a Matron of Honour had gone to the hairdresser along with the two Bridesmaids and Alice. The ceremony went well, the reception started with an excellent lunch then got better when the speeches became funnier as the afternoon wore on.

Alice introduced Escapade, 'for the second time' and the evening was well and truly underway by eight o'clock. The last song was Eric Clapton's 'Wonderful Tonight', the encore was 'Bullfrog Blues'. By special request of the groom's father they did 'Toad', complete with an improvised keyboard part for Alan.

Fenrir made an un-summoned appearance in June. Wolfie had taken them to the Black Forest in Germany for a well-earned break. Leaving Jeepy in the car park with Kenny on the back seat, they had managed to hike about eight or nine miles into the dense black trees when Flick sensed the presence of the wolf before either of them saw the animal sitting by a large rock next to a narrow, fast flowing stream. They stopped a few feet away from the stone, Fenrir walked towards them with something in its jaws. Laying the object at her feet first, the wolf made the same almost imperceptible nod to Eric before turning and disappearing behind the rock then crossing the stream. Eric picked the object up off the grass; he estimated it to be about nine inches long, tubular and made of a material he'd never encountered before. On one end was a coarse thread, the other held a violet gem, certainly not an amethyst, and unknown to either of them.

"This looks as if it would fit the staff. What, I wonder, is it, and more to the point what does it do?"

Flick looked at the shining jewel and fingered the wand round her neck.

"I know what it is but I'm at a loss as to how it works."

Eric had examined the surface for any buttons or switches – engineers do that type of thing – without finding either.

"What's it do, love?"

"It's a communicator; don't laugh, we're not talking Star Wars here, it's more like an interface than a light sabre. I think it might be a bridge between the staff and us."

"No 'beam me up Scotty' either then?"

"Afraid not, you're right about it fitting the staff though."

"This is really strange material. It's so smooth I can hardly feel it, light doesn't reflect off it and the colour is amazing, I've never seen anything so black."

"What do you make of the jewel?"

"Solidly attached to the material. It's a dodecahedron when viewed from the top, the colour is violet, I can't see how deep it goes though. By the way, the main section is completely devoid of marks, scratches and dents of any description."

Flick offered the object up to the staff and screwed it into the place normally occupied by the wand. Not only was it the same thread, it sealed itself to the wood of the staff so accurately it was impossible to see the join.

"Perhaps it has to be held up to the sun and the light refracts..." Eric's voice trailed off.

"Maybe, it's as good an idea as any. Have you noticed how cold the surface is? It doesn't absorb heat very well either."

Back at the camp site in Schenkenzell they made a meal and sat thinking out loud till the insects showed up for their dinner. In bed the conversation turned from 'how did the interface work', to accepting the staff would show them when the time was right.

Kenny was glowing violet again as he often did when he needed to communicate with Eddy. On this occasion it had nothing to do with Fenrir or the new object, but something was bothering him and Eddy would have the answer. He'd detected something nasty was about to happen over in Cambridge later that night. Searching back in the records he found what he was looking for filed under Portugal, sub-folder, campsite, sub-heading: BURGLAR.

Eddy waited until he was sure the humans were sound asleep. Kenny joined him in the van and sat at the top of the bed, listening first to the girl then the man breathing deeply. Carefully he moved the girl's hair out of range of the man's mouth – it wouldn't do to have them wake up in the night. Together they turned to face the window then sent out rainbow beams through the roof. Seconds later, the two bears vanished out of Wolfie only to reappear instantaneously on the kitchen table in Cambridge.

Outside in the street Ronnie and Tommy, two teenage thieves, were waiting for midnight. They'd been watching the house for some time; finally, the disappearance of the Jeep and the camper van was considered a signal that the owners were on holiday. They made their way round to the rear of the house; Eddy saw them through the kitchen window whilst Kenny carefully and quietly unlocked the back door. Ronnie slid the steel tube he carried over the door handle – one push usually broke the lock mechanism – only to discover the door opened to his touch.

"This is going to be so easy," he said to Tommy.

Eddy was playing on home turf; he watched as the pair slipped into the kitchen, closing the door behind them.

'This is going to be so easy,' he thought to Kenny.

To make matters a little more interesting, Kenny, who liked to play with electricity, made sure all the lights didn't work. Ronnie made his way to the lounge while Tommy investigated the dining room. Kenny did his trick with all the doors in the house – he closed them tight in their frames regardless of if they had locks fitted or not. Part one of the 'protect' operation was complete, divide and conquer was a good maxim.

Realisation slowly dawned – they were trapped in separate rooms. Both burglars started pulling and pushing at the doors only to discover the handles still worked but the hinges appeared to be seized solid. After a few minutes, Ronnie; the brighter of the two but not by much, decided to open the lounge window. This wasn't moving either as Kenny had dealt with the windows immediately after the doors.

Eddy was sliding down the banister, having finished his handiwork in the bedrooms upstairs. Ronnie, meanwhile, was getting angry and a little bit worried. Picking up the steel tube, he threw it as hard as he could at the TV in the corner of the room. He became a fraction more worried when he saw the steel tube fail to break the glass; it seemed to him the screen actually absorbed the impact. It even looked like it stretched inwardly for a second before springing back into shape, forcing the steel tube back at his head. With a bruise already forming and a broken tooth floating around in his mouth, he never noticed Eddy returning the packet of elastic bands to the desk drawer – rubber morphed excellently into anything he could imagine and had come in handy many times in the past.

Tommy fell into the lounge; the door had suddenly unlocked itself.

"What happened to your face?"

Ronnie told him.

"This place is weird, let's hit the bedrooms – any jewellery will be up there."

Nothing could have prepared them for the sight Eddy had manufactured. Together they entered the master bedroom making their way in the dark to the centre of what appeared to be an empty room. They had just reached the conclusion they were in the spare room when Kenny turned all the lights back on. The two turned and stared at each other then noticed the light fitting near their feet. Looking up they discovered the entire room was upside down.

"This is a madhouse," Ronnie said.

'Wrong', thought Eddy, 'the madhouse was in Manchester.'

The thieves tried the second bedroom only to discover all the furniture preferred standing on the walls rather than leaning against them. The third room had stuff everywhere, on the floor, the ceiling and all four walls. If they'd looked harder, they might have noticed the chest of drawers in bedroom three actually went through the wall into bedroom two. Eddy got a bit slapdash sometimes.

The bathroom gave them some serious doubts about their sanity. Everything in the room with the exception of the toilet was plumbed onto the ceiling. Ronnie cautiously turned a hot tap towards what should have been the on-position before staring wide eyed at the spouting water running upwards into the basin where, after whooshing round the porcelain, it gurgled up the drain.

"Come on, Tommy, let's get the hell out of here."

"Right, mate, bloody aliens must live here."

'Well, he got that part right,' thought Kenny whilst locking them in the bathroom.

Ronnie was the first to hear the rumbling of the drains. They both watched, first in fascination, then in abject horror, as the toilet bowl began spewing all manner of filth into the bathroom. Soon they were knee deep in a whirlpool lake of excrement with sanitary towels, condoms, vomit, baby-wipes and toilet tissue floating on the pool of urine in an insane dance which was reaching the floor or ceiling, depending on your viewpoint, rather rapidly.

Just as they thought they were about to drown, the gurgling stopped, an eerie peace filled the room, then the sea of shit began to drain back down through the toilet. They both had the feeling they were shrinking, like Alice in Wonderland, as they were sucked through the toilet into the Cambridge sewage system. They regained consciousness half in and half out of one of the filtration beds at the sewage treatment farm.

"What the hell happened, Tommy?"

"I haven't got a clue. Let's get home and get out of these clothes."

A bright light shone in their faces.

"Don't move, we want a word with you two," said a disembodied voice from behind the bright white lamp.

Two confused burglars were taken to Cambridge Care Centre – it used to be the hospital – in a hydrogen-powered ambulance. Here they discovered that instead of being June 21st, 1978 it was still June 21st but inexplicably it was now 2066. Instead of being eight hours adrift they were eighty-eight years into the future.

Eddy liked the number eight, it reminded him of the human's symbol for infinity, something he was very knowledgeable about.

Kenny returned the house to normal, replacing the collected works of Lewis Carroll in the correct place on the book shelf, then joined Eddy for the return trip to the Black Forest. They communicated at length about making their own 'black hole' to solve the problem and hoped, paws crossed, they hadn't messed up the course of history.

Around nine Eric and Flick woke up; Eric put the kettle on.

"Pass my bra over, love."

Kenny had just enough time to slip it on Eddy's head.

Over the next few months Eric began to research radio transmission and unusual materials as well as peculiar jewels. There was a lot to learn about radio but information on the other topics was scare. He started experimenting to try and discover more about the object Flick had called a communicator. Magnets had no effect on the smooth surface, a close proximity to heat, water or ice revealed nothing of interest at all, it remained at eleven degrees Celsius regardless. It didn't conduct electricity either.

Frustratingly for Eric, there wasn't any visible way of taking it apart. Pulling, pushing and twisting the tube achieved nothing. Turning his attention to the jewel, he shone a light into one of the dodecahedron's facets; the jewel refracted the beam, redirecting it outwards from the facet opposite the entry point.

Flick had tried more subtle approaches, starting with stroking and rubbing it, perhaps hoping for a genie to appear; that ended in failure. Holding it next to the wand did nothing either. Eric was on the point of saying it was similar to a telephone, not much use unless you had two of them, when they had a little triumph. In the evening of August 18th a full moon shone in the night sky. Flick was sitting on the bench by the garden wall, writing in her journal. Eric had passed her a mug of tea when she noticed the staff propped against the end of the seat. They both heard a slight humming sound, just audible above the leaves rustling. The jewel was pointing directly at the moon but there wasn't anything lighting up, it was the black tube that had reacted. A low hum emanated apparently from inside and if a finger rested lightly on the surface a minute vibration could be felt. Flick commented it sounded like a seashell held to the ear. Despite trying again when the remaining three new moons were in the sky, they were no further forward by the end of the year.

The wand, staff and communicator working together or separately continued to give Flick visions, many of which were simple or helpful. The built-in traffic bulletins and road maps continued to the point they rather missed them if they didn't occur. In May a serious vision presented itself and thankfully the person who managed to save the situation knew about the wand and staff. Flick had just got out of the car in the company parking lot. The vision was crystal clear, knowing instantaneously it was Mavis who was involved and where she was. She phoned her mother, telling her to go to Mavis's house as quickly as possible – her sister had fallen down the stairs and was unconscious. Helen knew her daughter would be right and lost no time in driving to Stevenage. The ambulance arrived, Helen went with her to the hospital. Thankfully she made a full recovery. Later that evening she told her mother how the vision had unfolded; afterwards she replayed it for Eric using the wand. This time the violet jewel on the communicator glowed but there wasn't any humming noise or as far as she could tell any vibrations.

Another event in May concerned Kevin and Alice. Flick had a series of visions that all linked into one larger picture. This was totally new to her, and it took both of them a while to understand what was happening.

"It's like watching a serial on TV, except the instalments are a single picture," she said to Eric.

"I think this is another lesson, the staff is showing you something more complex, so it's doing it in easy stages, baby steps perhaps," he answered.

The first picture she received was of Kevin and Alice, they were holding hands and smiling, looking like they were standing in a wood or copse. Picture two focused on a newborn baby, asleep in someone's arms; the person doing the holding wasn't visible. Next came an image of two children playing in a grassy field; the girl was taller and older than the boy. On closer examination Flick thought it was Stephanie in about four years' time but she couldn't be sure. Following on from the playtime vision was a sideways shot of Kevin talking to Colin whilst Alice was deep in conversation with Wendy. All four looked a little older, Eric estimated about twenty years into the future.

A gap of almost a week followed, then another four visions followed. Starting with a couple who had obviously posed for their wedding photograph, that came first, then a picture of Colin and Wendy followed by Kevin and Alice all dressed for a wedding. The final image was two numbers, 08062000 and 143000.

"I think what we have here is the date of Stephanie's wedding – she's going to marry the as yet unborn son of Kevin and Alice on June 8th, 2000," Flick told Eric.

"OK, and the other number, how about 2:30 in the afternoon as the time of the ceremony?" Eric added.

They replayed the sequence several times and agreed this was the simplest answer to the puzzle. The post arrived next morning with a letter informing them Alice was three months' pregnant, which added weight to their speculations. In late November the Harris family had an early extra Christmas present: Nicholas was born on the 30th.

31

I n 1984 an incident involving Eric and Flick took place in northern California whilst they were attending a bionics convention in San Francisco. Someone with a plant-based biological problem had noted the pair and instigated a risky plan to try and solve the very pressing issue that threatened to put them out of business. This part of the tale shows how over the years life with the staff had instilled a strange confidence and unusual instincts in both of them. What was about to unfold would, for most people, have been fearful, distressing and very hard to cope with mentally, both during and afterwards.

Juan Casperio grew a lot of cannabis in the dense forests between Ukiah and the Pacific coast. His problem was the competition, one of them, or perhaps several of them, had managed to infect his entire crop with a blight that wasn't in the book. His own experts had drawn a blank and the matter was escalating daily as he had just heard that the plants in the nursery were also showing signs of infection. He knew Qwendos Biotech had some of the top biologists and bio-engineers on the planet, and a trusted source had informed him the convention had some of them as speakers. For three days his gang waited and watched as the convention drew to a close. His man in charge phoned him with the result he was looking for. The best bio-team were without a doubt Eric and Deborah Marstone.

Juan had a slice of luck the next day. With the convention over, the Marstones had hired a car and headed north up the Pacific Coast Highway. One gang member had tailed them to the rental company office and overheard them asking about the route. By the end of the first day, they were in a Mendocino hotel. At six in the morning the gang, wearing clown masks, slid into the room, kidnapped Flick and left one of their members guarding Eric. After a two-hour car ride wrapped in a sheet, she was taken into a large room where Juan sat behind a glass-topped desk. The man who led her into the room told Juan neither of them had been harmed in any way, then he left.

Juan offered her coffee and toast, when she accepted before asking what was going on, which totally surprised him. She said the man who had brought her to the house had half explained, mainly reinforcing the original instructions which amounted to keeping calm, doing what you're told and nobody will get hurt. Juan expanded on the problem he had and how he needed Flick to look at his plants and tell him what was wrong. She listened then asked how was she supposed to carry out any tests with no equipment and more importantly no clothes. A knock on the door preceded its opening, the same man had a sports bag with Flick's clothes in. She took it from the table, went behind the room divider and got dressed.

Juan took her through the house to a large well-equipped laboratory; he asked if everything she needed was there. Flick asked to see the infected plants. He nodded to the man who had followed them, who left the room only to return with a wheeled trolley containing some of the smaller specimens from the nursery. Juan told her the main crop was in the hills behind the house – he would take her there when she was ready. Flick looked at the plants under a strong light and began to examine the leaves. It was obvious something was very wrong.

"How good is security on the plantation and in the nursery, can you trust everyone on the payroll?" she asked.

"Assume it's OK," was the blunt reply.

"When was the first time you spotted the problem?"

While he answered her, she began collecting samples and mixing chemicals for analysis tests. As these developed, he mentioned she was incredibly calm under the circumstances.

"I know it won't be too long before the answer you need arrives and then, if you're as good as your word, I can go back to the hotel," she answered.

He grinned and let her carry on. Two interesting things happened mid-morning. The first was a positive result on some of the plants from the nursery, and then when Flick saw the crop in the fields she knew almost without doubt what Juan's problem was.

The second interesting thing happened back in the hotel in Mendocino. Eric had waited for his moment and planted a massive uppercut on the guard's jaw. The jaw split in two, driving two halves deep into the roof of his mouth with such force the blow fractured both cheek bones and almost severed his tongue. Several teeth came out and fell to the floor at the same time as the guard. Eric dressed, picked up the hire car keys and the crumbled guard after placing his gun back in his limp hand and putting the odd teeth in his bloody mouth. He then checked out. In the car park he closed his eyes and using the communicator turned slowly in a circle, stopping when he felt Flick's location in his head. Noting the direction, he sped off away from the coast into the tree-covered hills. At each crossroads he stopped, got out of the car and repeated the circular turning to establish a new bearing. Inside an hour, two more interesting things were about to happen.

Flick had managed to discover that the problem with the plants was being introduced through the irrigation system in the fields. She had isolated it in the nursery plants as well; the irritant was a mixture of peroxide and an enzyme.

"The plants appeared at first sight to be infected with a nematode parasite but without the outside appearances usually associated with that type of infection. Someone, and it was definitely a human intervention, has chemically mixed a liquid solution that mimics the infection without anyone being able to detect the presence of the parasite under a microscope. This is what had thrown your in-house workers," she reported.

"Are you absolutely certain about this? Because if you are, will you give me some form of proof."

"I cannot give you proof, you don't have the equipment to analyse the samples to that depth. Can I go now? My husband is here to collect me."

He laughed and leaned back in his executive's chair, calling her the coolest chick he'd ever met.

"Have you checked the hotel recently?" she asked, with her head on one side and the faintest traces of a smile showing.

The confidence radiating from her face was enough to make him lift the phone and dial. Flick could hear the other end ringing out. He pushed a button on his desk, ten seconds passed before he pushed it again.

"Perhaps he's having a siesta," she smirked.

Juan opened the door at exactly the wrong moment: Eric had decided it was precisely the right time to come in. The door swung round hard and fast on its hinges, slamming Juan deep into the plasterwork. Eric shut the remains of the woodwork and held him round his neck just below the chin with one massive hand.

"Juan, meet my husband Eric, he takes protecting me very seriously. He makes Rambo look like a cub scout; please don't make any sudden moves or something might get broken or drop off."

"You OK, Flick?"

"Absolutely fine, love, I think you can relax a little now, he's going blue."

Juan collapsed in a heap and offered no resistance when Eric tied him to the desk.

"It seems you've managed to lay waste to eleven of them, some are more damaged than others, I take it they were the ones who tried shooting at you?" she said, returning from the hallway.

"You got it, actually there's twelve, I brought the one from the hotel with me. Oh, I checked out as well."

Flick sat down in front of Juan and gave him some instructions.

"So here's the way we're going to play it. We're off now, the gang's all here, most of them will be in need of some medical attention, so once we're clear of this place I'll stop and phone the police and paramedics. In case you forgot, it has been a little hectic round here after all, you have the answer to your problem. The only cure will be to burn the entire crop and plough the land to a depth of about two feet. It will have to be extensively watered and lay fallow for at least two years – I would recommend four – before replanting even potatoes. Whoever did it knew exactly what they were doing, that in itself may give you a clue as to who's the culprit. Please don't think about following us or getting revenge, in a short while you will be able to witness first hand what happens to people who get in my husband's way. Also, you haven't seen what I can do yet."

Juan nodded and looked away.

Outside, the twelve gang members who had successfully managed to get in Eric's way as he looked for his wife were lined up unconscious in the hall.

"Come on, I'll treat you to a big ice cream, you've had a busy morning and I bet you didn't have breakfast, did you!" She winked at him whilst kissing his nose.

"I have never experienced anything like that, I was as cool as a cucumber and knew you were unharmed the whole time. The oddest thing is I knew exactly what to do and how to find you. I had perfect control of the situation, except for the hitting people bit, I need to work on that, if it ever happens again, which I hope it doesn't."

"Once again, Eric, you've took the words out of my mouth. I felt so bloody calm and in control, I never felt any danger, I didn't even start swearing like a trooper – why? I have no idea. I could see you every step of the way. Juan just seemed so insignificant and pathetic; that sounds crazy, but do you know what I mean?"

"I know exactly what you're saying, there's a phone booth on this corner, let's make that call."

The police and paramedics arrived and put it down to inter-gang warfare, which in a way, it was. Juan didn't contradict them. They also assumed one of the gang had made the call. The incident died there, nothing further ever came of it, they heard and saw nothing on the news either.

Back in Cambridge there was a soft thud and a splash. Kenny landed on Jeepy's roof, slid down the windscreen and made his way over the grass to the pond. Eddy had touched down in the middle right beside a large lily pad. They had left at the same time Eric and Flick had driven away. He joined Kenny, leaving little puddles of water on the crazy paving as the pair made their way to Wolfie.

'That went well, they seem to be getting better at controlling their emotions and sorting their skills out I think,' thought Kenny.

'I don't think we're needed in situations like that anymore, we did nothing this time; but orders are orders, we'd better keep observing and protecting. I think I'll have to sit in the sun for a while and dry out,' Eddy replied silently while inspecting his dripping fur.

The next day the thirteenth member of the gang and perpetrator of the crop failure returned and quickly set fire to the house. By the time the fire department arrived it had spread to the crop fields, there wasn't anything left of the house, or the crop. That did make the news, Juan was out of business in more ways than one.

Threw the computer sat at the back of the large partners' desk they shared at home, Flick was writing up her notes; over the years it had amalgamated the diary, a to-do list, address book and countless other things she managed on a day-to-day basis as well as a secret folder that only she had the password to. It was vital Eric didn't stumble across this file, so she hid it several layers down in a folder full of test results from the experiments she carried out in the lab. This secret had only another two months to run then she could play him at his own game and unveil the results of three months' planning. Dan and Alan were in on the scheme and sworn to secrecy. As the calendar moved steadily through July 1992, she could hardly contain herself.

In Paris their two friends had put the French end into action, a hotel had been booked in Calais for the evening, a table for four at the restaurant and two train tickets from the Gare du Nord. In Cambridge, Flick had been surreptitiously loading Wolfie with clothes and bedding for four, making sure the water tanks and toilet were all charged and ready, and on the Thursday evening managed to sneakily fill the fridge she'd turned on two days before as well as stocking the food cupboards. She had just enough time to lock the camper's door and return to the couch in the lounge before Eric came downstairs from the shower.

Over the years Eddy and Kenny had picked up on quite a few human traits and wore them as a sort of mantle. Flick's secret folder wasn't secret to them, they knew all about the surprise she had plotted and were in their own way as excited as she was. The two bears were transferred from the shelf in the master bedroom and coat rack in the dining room, their usual places, onto the rear bed and wardrobe door knob in Wolfie on the Thursday; there was just the Jeep to hook up.

'Looks like we're going as well, this could be a lot of fun,' Eddy telepathed to Kenny.

'Are you holding the passports and tickets?'

'Correct, what's she put in you?'

'Two cubes wrapped in shiny paper, they're for the other two from the Manchester Madhouse if I'm reading the tags right. There's a plastic bag with seven bits of blue cloth in as well. You any idea what this is all for?'

'They've all been around for forty Earth years, this is an adventure to celebrate it I think. The seven bits of material mean she's going to have another go at doing that dance again – the one that ends up with wolf noises all night.'

'I remember, she's not very good at it is she? The first time she managed to take off four bits, then she got to five before he grabbed her, she managed to do it all the way down to six before it went wrong last year. They were up half the night that time.'

'Chances are she might get it right this time after so much practice, then we can all get some rest.'

Friday morning began as usual in the Cambridge house. A normal day at work unfolded; Flick left at lunchtime with a wink in David's direction on the pretext of dropping off some documents at the archives. Back home she coupled Jeepy up to the tow hitch, double checked she had everything on Wolfie and made a last sweep of the house before locking the door and driving the rig back to work. Parking round the back by the loading bay meant Eric had no chance of spotting the electric blue Mercedes from the laboratory.

David came over close to two o'clock and said they could have an early day, there was no point starting another sequence of tests at this time on a Friday. They walked out into the sunshine, Flick telling Eric she had parked round the back in the shade.

Eric was somewhat bemused when he saw Wolfie; Flick opened the camper door and went inside.

"I've been a very naughty elf, love." She smiled a wicked sultry smile at him. "I've been doing a bit of plotting and scheming to surprise you. Would you like to know what's going on?"

Eric looked at the lopsided grin and mischievous smile, knowing she was at bursting point to tell him.

"OK, your Highness, bare your soul."

"I've planned a little trip to Italy, the Amalfi Coast. David has given us three weeks off, everything's packed, we just have to be at Dover for five-fifty to get the ferry."

Flick drove as Eric asked his usual thousand questions. The terminal lanes weren't crowded, they sat in the first one some fifteen vehicles from the front with just over an hour to kill. Eric led Flick into the rear bedroom and undressed her very slowly.

"Naughty elves have to be punished," he said, laying her across the bed at the same time.

Although there weren't many people about, he remembered to kiss her full on the mouth twenty minutes later. They had just enough time to put their clothes back on as Wolfie was called forward and clattered up the ramp to the high vehicle deck with the buses and trucks. The stern doors closed and the ferry left port exactly on time.

'Is this what humans mean by starting things off with a bang?' Eddy asked.

'Perhaps, it was the oddest punishment I've ever heard of though. You all right after that fall? They thrash about a lot, I could see you bouncing and slipping towards the edge, next second I heard the thud.'

'I'm fine, she picked me up and put me back on the bed again afterwards. It's going to happen again in a while, he doesn't know about the other half of the surprise yet.'

'She's going to get it big time for that one, of that you can be absolutely sure.'

Two hours later Flick slid Wolfie into a hotel car park.

"We're in here just for tonight, I thought we could both do with a shower and dinner; this place can provide both."

She pulled a small holdall out of an overhead locker and led the way into reception. It might as well be placed on record that in all the years they had lived together Eric had never managed to resist the feelings that welled up inside him when he watched Flick taking a shower. This was no exception.

"I must be a very naughty elf if I'm being punished again," she chuckled. "Come on, get dressed, the table's booked for eight-thirty."

Reluctantly he released her and with a last kiss told her he loved her so much he was ready to explode with happiness. The waiter took them through to the restaurant and sat them in the window; she made sure he sat with his back to the door. Five minutes later, Dan and Alan snook into the room and whispered 'surprise surprise' in his ear.

Eric's face was an absolute picture. No words came out. The threesome giggled and smirked. The waiter brought champagne and flutes along with the menu. The toast was 'Happy Birthday, to all of us'. As the evening unfolded the full story came out, the secret planning, the near misses where they all thought Eric had rumbled them, details of the route they were going to take and where they were headed. Eric was almost drunk on information overload by eleven o'clock.

In bed Flick squirmed her way into her usual spot, snuggled up inside a large right arm which held her tight against his chest.

"Enjoying it so far?" a cheeky face with twinkling brown eyes enquired from within a shock of red hair. "You're going to punish me again now, aren't you, please, pretty please."

"Wanton doesn't come close to describing you, Deborah Marstone. Turn on your side, your majesty, this is going to be a slow, long drawn-out punishment."

"Oh goody goody, my favourite end to the day," she whispered as she turned over. "Don't be too gentle with me, will you, I'm a very horny naughty elf."

"I worked that out all by myself a few years ago, darling."

After breakfast had been demolished, the four began the drive to Italy, working as two teams – each pair did two and a half hours' driving and navigating then the team changed over. On the second shift the driver became the navigator so each driver had two and a half hours on and seven and a half hours off. As it turned out by the time Wolfie had covered almost 700 miles when the first shift ended, they'd left Switzerland behind and parked at a motorway services for the night. Food had been flowing freely all day, Flick had assumed her role as chef once more and managed to provide tasty treats all day. Each driver had been spoon- or fork-fed as the wheels turned.

Throughout the day memories of adventures in Wolfie and Jeepy came back, giving rise at times to near hysterical laughter and many fond recollections. Eddy and Kenny listened in and smiled internal smiles; after over twenty years of being with them they decided humans weren't so bad after all, well these four weren't.

The village of Ravello is high in the hills above one of the most picturesque coastlines in Italy. Wolfie was shunted up the narrow roads to the hotel where the management had reserved a corner of the car park for him. Jeepy was unhitched and the four checked into two suites on the top floor which Dan and Alan insisted was their birthday present to Eric and Flick. After the crazy journey they decided to spend a couple of days doing nothing, so the hotel garden and pool were investigated, Dan found the outside bar and Alan the ice cream stand. Before breakfast the next morning they all plunged into the pool seriously swimming fifty lengths side by side. Eric and Dan had a round of miniature golf while Flick and Alan sat on loungers in the garden under a tree reading.

"You fancy an ice cream, Alan?" She was rummaging inside Eddy for the purse with the cash in.

"That's a nice idea, I'll go."

As he walked over to the stand, she quickly checked inside Kenny whose job had now expanded to being the holder of the factor 50 sun cream, insect repellent and antiseptic among other things. Some people might have thought an adult using a teddybear rucksack was somewhat juvenile; however, when Flick wore it most people weren't looking at the rucksack. After she was sure the two gift-wrapped boxes were right at the bottom under her bandana, she closed the bag, relaxed and lay back. Alan passed her a large 'gelato al cioccolato' – he was picking up the language already, he said with a grin. Flick managed to get a dribble down her front, and Alan being the brave soul he was did the decent thing and licked her clean whilst she giggled as it tickled.

"Don't look now but we have an Aunt Mavis clone sitting to our left, she's most put out by what you just did, face like thunder; her husband's beaming like a Cheshire cat, mind," she whispered in his ear.

Eric and Dan walked across the grass from their game just as Flick had another blob run down her cleavage. This time Dan nonchalantly did the honours complete with overdone sound effects, reducing her to a giggling heap. Mavis Two went red and the husband burst into silent laughter, Flick's reactions being very contagious. Alan filled them in on the details of the prior event half-heartedly saying with loaded mock seriousness he hoped the Naughty Elf wasn't going to appear. A 'watch this space' look appeared on the only female face.

As it turned out the afternoon wore on with Flick doing nothing at all other than lie on her lounger. The men, however, took it in turns to apply her suntan lotion, fetch drinks and snacks, massage her back and generally behaved as they did back in the days of the Manchester Madhouse waiting on their Princess of the Kitchen hand and foot. Mavis Two and Husband, however, were taking it all in.

Eddy sat in the sun next to Kenny.

'This is nice, I can cope with this lifestyle.'

'I like it quiet, you picking anything up?'

'Nothing, they've been sensible, all the valuables are in you.'

Mavis Two was agitated. She was looking on the grass all around her as was her husband. Eric told the others it looked as if she'd lost something. The search intensified taking in the space underneath their loungers and side tables. A look of deep concern was growing across her face, Eric called out to them,

"Have you lost something?"

The husband, introducing himself as George said his wife, Mavis, had lost her wedding ring. Eric managed to keep his face straight, but Alan wasn't so successful – he had to feign choking on his drink to cover a laugh.

"Shit, there really is two of them," Dan murmured.

Eric had walked over and joined in the search.

"Apart from here have you been anywhere else since you last remember seeing it?" he asked.

Mavis said she had been in the pool twice, other than that she had remained on the lounger all day. Flick got up and asked what the ring looked like to be informed it was a plain band of yellow gold. George offered his hand.

"A smaller version of mine," he said.

Flick held the ring between her fingers whilst pressing the wand to her chest and closing her eyes. For ten seconds or so they all watched her saying the words 'smaller, smaller' over and over. Finally, she strode to the pool and dived in, striking out for the bottom. A minute later she pulled herself out and placed the missing ring into Mavis's hand.

"It was on the bottom, your suntan lotion probably made it loose."

'That was nice of you, Eddy, you're just a big softie at heart.'

'I'm a Teddy Bear, me.'

Flick sat down and pulled Kenny towards her to get a dry towel. George came over and thanked her profusely, Mavis did the same after she'd recovered from the shock of being reunited with her jewellery. Flick smiled. Mavis nudged George who then awkwardly asked if they would care to be their guests at dinner tonight. They politely refused but would love a long fruity drink from the bar instead. The afternoon turned into early evening. At dinner Eric called for order in the usual way by tapping his fork on a wine glass.

"It falls to me being the victim of my wife and friends' little scam to carry out the only part of this delicious plot I actually knew about. Dan and Alan, you have your fortieth birthdays next month when Flick and I will be in California. We hereby with intense pleasure aforethought present you with our gifts."

Flick reached under the table and took the two boxes out of Kenny, read the labels and passed them one each. Two faces burst into huge smiles as the paper came off the boxes.

"Oh, this is too much, you shouldn't have," Alan said.

"You two are bloody amazing, I don't know what to say," Dan echoed.

"Nonsense, friends like you are hard to find, how you've managed to put up with us for over twenty years warrants them anyway." Eric smiled.

Flick went round the table and hugged them both.

"We got them in the States on our last trip," she told them and in a lower voice added, "we smuggled them in."

The two Rolex watches looked perfect on their wrists. Alan was caught playing with the buttons on his several times throughout dinner, Dan kept telling everyone what time in was in various parts of the world. After the meal they wandered through to the terrace and found George and Mavis Two as she'd been unanimously labelled. George insisted on getting drinks and the conversation started off with them all finding out about each other. George was interested in the combination of an engineer, a biologist and two lawyers all being on holiday together. Flick filled him in on their university days; the wicked imp appeared when George started becoming excited about them all living in the one flat, the lascivious look was visible in both eyes. Accumulated drinks were giving his imagination free reign and his eyes had nothing else to do other than be transfixed by Flick's dress, or to be more accurate, the contents of Flick's dress. Whilst it was a classic and sophisticated number, it didn't leave a great deal to the imagination, Mavis picked up on that fact straight away and began watching George closely. Alan was the first to overhear the Naughty Elf start a wind-up her father would be proud of; he tipped the others off.

'Listen up, Eddy, this should be interesting,' Kenny transmitted to the bedroom from his place under the table.

"The newspapers made a big deal of it back then, they all supposed we were hopping from one bed to another, running around naked all the time, it was a miracle anyone managed to get any studying done at all never mind obtaining a degree. I must admit I did my yoga exercises and meditated in the garden nude, but we didn't bed hop as such," Flick teased before picking her next words carefully. "If the guys wanted anything from me they just asked, I usually said yes."

George's imagination was now making him a little embarrassed. Flick continued with Alan in earshot and ready to contribute.

"The parties were great, at the end of the night you just flopped into any bed with anybody, I've woken up next to all three of them on so many occasions," she recalled.

"The end of term bash was brilliant, you did that amazing belly dance, the one that turns into the dance of the seven veils, remember – then we all took it in turns to hold you down and tickle you with those huge peacock feathers," Alan added.

"Yes, I remember, you lot do that every time you want something exotic out of my little recipe book, you naughty boys," she giggled. "Weren't Colin and Wendy in on that one as well?"

Alan nodded whilst grinning devilishly. Eric had been talking to Mavis whilst the wind-up was progressing and deliberately keeping her from listening too hard. George was getting hot under the collar and had little difficulty relating what he was hearing to what he was seeing, even though his wife had now joined the audience.

Dan chipped in with more slightly adjusted versions of the truth.

"The one I remember best is when Patrick burst in on you both right at the wrong moment. I was with Eric by the window when he opened the door and couldn't believe his eyes, oh that was so funny, I don't think he'd ever seen two people doing what you were doing; as for Flick's orgasm, that just blew him away."

Flick let him off the hook, figuring that he'd had enough input for the evening and Mavis was ready to make steam as her father would have said. She couldn't resist one last parting shot, however; stretching her arms above her head as she stood up, she asked in an innocent voice, "I forgot, whose turn is it tonight?"

What she was actually referring to was the bill for dinner, was it theirs or Dan and Alan's, not that George knew that. The straight faces cracked and the laughter started in the lift up to the top floor.

"That was extremely naughty, Deborah, but exceedingly funny," Alan spluttered with eyes streaming.

"Did you see his face when you asked whose turn it was. His jaw dropped a foot," Dan chuckled.

"I was looking at Mavis Two, she couldn't make anything out, from the events of this afternoon starting with the ice cream dribbles through to the recovery of her ring, then to be told in such a matter of fact way we're all crazy ex-hippies and Flick's our willing sex slave just about took the proverbial biscuit. She's having a hard time understanding our albeit slightly adjusted lifestyle, and George, poor sod, is dreaming away in fantasy land," Eric added.

Flick went into the bathroom whilst Eric tried to make the TV work. She came out wearing the seven tiny pieces of material and pushed play on the Sony Walkman. Eric managed to hold out until the fifth veil hit the floor, but by speeding the dance up she managed to quickly remove the sixth and seventh in record time before he swept her off her feet and onto the bed.

'She's getting worse if anything, certainly not better; never mind, better luck next time,' Kenny mentioned. 'I'll turn the

Walkman off or the batteries will be flat in the morning.'

Over the course of the next few days Jeepy roared his way round some of the narrowest but most spectacular roads in Italy. They went to Sorrento, Amalfi, Vesuvius and Pompeii doing tourist things, including buying far too many gelato tutti-fruttis in Alan's case.

Eddy and Kenny contributed to the adventure by suggesting the roads that didn't have too much traffic on them and steered the Jeep away from accidents and grid-locked mountain passes. Flick's wand was never busier than the day they went to Naples, city of a thousand traffic jams. They had both started wearing snazzy sunglasses, but nobody remembered actually slipping shades on the bears. It was assumed someone had done it for a joke whilst they were left parked in the Jeep.

Most evenings they went down to the poolside bar, George and Mavis were sat at the same table every evening; they waved them over one night for a chat. George wanted to know how Flick had known exactly where the wedding ring was. He'd also figured out there was a connection between the wand round her neck and something he wasn't quite sure about. His initial fantasy involved her as a voodoo goddess with three men under her total spell; thankfully, he kept this one to himself. Sensing they had to divert attention away from the wand, frantic ideas leapt into their minds. Alan simply announced she had incredible eyesight and the pool was the logical choice. This might have worked; however, the matter of Flick holding on to George's ring mumbling to herself didn't do the excuse any favours. Dan went for the crazy approach, building on the previous wind-up. He leant forward into the centre of the table and lowered his voice.

"It's best if as few people know what I'm about to tell you, promise me it will go no further."

George and Mavis nodded; George looked as if he was about to be told who stole the crown jewels.

"The story begins forty years ago – you've worked out we're all forty, I guess. Our beautiful Princess is actually the high priestess of a little-known African tribe living in the central Sahara desert. They're nomads, and wander constantly, making them exceedingly difficult to keep track of. Otanga here–" Dan paused and pointed to Flick– "is the eighth daughter of an eighth daughter which enables her to do things like tell the sex of unborn babies, find lost items and other normally impossible things. My grandfather rescued her – she was going to be sacrificed on her sixteenth birthday – smuggled her to England where my friends and I have sworn to protect her for the rest of our lives. The wooden Nazar amulet is her protector from the dark powers. You saw first-hand how the Nazar works; without it she couldn't have found your ring, Mavis – her eyesight's good but not that good."

Dan took a drink of beer then looked round at Eric who was trying hard to keep a serious expression on his face. Alan took up the story.

"You can see we're all devoted to Otanga, she has to be served unconditionally as a royal personage. This is why you have seen us attend to her every need so she can concentrate on keeping the Nazar under her control. If it goes out of control there's a possibility terrible things will happen to her and probably us as well; we don't want that. A few nights ago when we were talking, you asked about our living together in Manchester and we had to tell you a light-hearted version of events to cover the real reasons behind the situation we're in. Do you understand?"

Eric estimated George was about half sold and Mavis was open-mouthed ready to say something but thought better of it.

Dan stepped up and continued, "Is there anything else you've lost recently, it might be she can locate it for you?"

"There is but it's not here, I lost an old fountain pen belonging to my father; it has more sentimental value than worth," Mavis answered.

Flick asked her to concentrate on what the pen looked like, closed her eyes and held the wand. A minute passed, then her mouth creased into a smile.

"I see it. You drive a Ford Escort, a light blue one – if you look under the rear seat, on the passenger side right at the back, it's lodged behind a ruck in the carpet – it rolled out of your brown handbag, the one with big brass rings, when you were coming back from – Shrewsbury, I think, does that make sense?"

The pair stared in amazement at her, one hundred percent sold, Eric thought.

"That was unreal, how did you know?" Mavis asked, wearing the face of the totally stunned.

Flick shrugged, Eric came to the rescue informing them she was born with the skill and they had all been lucky enough to be in the right place at the right time to be with her.

"I'm very fortunate to have three men who look after me; although my life is quite normal in almost every way, I do have to be made love to rather more than most women. Thankfully with three of them I can remain continually satisfied and keep the Nazar stable," the Naughty Elf added, shaking her head in mock sadness. "It's hard work but it has to be done."

George almost choked on his beer and Mavis just looked on in astonishment.

"This has to happen every day?" she asked.

"Indeed, we have worked out if I can orgasm eight times a day I remain on top as it were; if one of those climaxes ends with me howling like a wolf then we can all have a day off. If you do hear a wolf in the night, don't worry, it's only me."

Alan and Dan had to go to the bar, the pressure of keeping from erupting into laughter was too much. Eric looked at the grass so nobody could see his face until he had it under control.

The next day the friends went to Paestum to visit the ruins of the Greek city. As Jeepy rattled along the dirt roads, Alan had to ask, "Did Princess Otanga get her eight orgasms last night? Eric looks too bright and bubbly in my book and we didn't hear any wolves howling from our room."

"Our Princess stripped off, fell into bed and started throwing zeds at the ceiling inside five minutes of me opening the door. Naughty Elf didn't even clean her teeth," Eric answered, grinning at her as he did so. In the back Eddy and Kenny seemed to have gained a small baseball cap apiece.

The remaining days of the holiday passed quietly, then Wolfie was brought out of the car park to start the drive back to the ferry. The return route was different and more leisurely, they headed for Milan and took the autostrada towards Switzerland. They'd been on the E62 heading north from Milan for an hour or so when Flick asked Alan to pull over into the Verbano service area. They all knew a vision was coming in, Flick had her eyes closed and looked puzzled. Dan and Alan made a drink and some sandwiches whilst she sat on the back bed still deep in thought with her eyes firmly closed. At last she smiled and accepted a mug of coffee.

"Well that one was certainly strange. It came across as a miniature movie, about fifty seconds, no more, I ran it five times but what it was I have no idea."

She picked up the communicator and pointed the jewelled end at the wardrobe door before closing her eyes again and frowned in concentration. The movie projected itself onto the door, it depicted a broad expanse of water, either a small sea or a large lake, there were several boats on the right-hand side of the picture, the land behind them rose steeply out of the frame. On the left was a large object, or it seemed large in comparison with the boats, the like of which they had never seen before. The closest thing it reminded them of was an aircraft carrier seen broadsides with four large, squat, round oil storage silos at each end. The movie finished with the odd shape sinking under the water. They watched it four times without gaining any further information, though Eric spotted the only other clue: at the point where the hills joined the water an old van could be seen on what might have been a road running alongside the shoreline. Using the knowledge gained in his father's garage he thought it was from well before World War Two, about the mid-thirties. As Wolfie made for Bern, they pondered and puzzled about what they had seen.

Dan and Alan were dropped off in Paris, Eric and Flick made their way to Calais, no fresh ideas or theories had been worked out. As the ferry pushed across the Channel, they sat on the rear deck looking back at France.

"Brilliant holiday, love, and a fantastic surprise, thank you so much." He leaned sideways and kissed her.

"I'm so pleased you enjoyed it," she said softly. "I love you so very much, Eric."

"The feeling is entirely mutual. What did we say back in 1971? Love you to the moon and back."

"Love you to the end of time was the other one. Hard to believe it's been over twenty years." She snuggled up to him and rested her head on his shoulder.

Down on the vehicle deck, Eddy and Kenny were sending a rainbow out of the boat; on the deck the passengers who saw it thought it looked wonderful.

33

For Eric and Flick the years were passing peacefully and excitingly at the same time. Their careers were fulfilling and enriching, their happiness with each other never seemed to dim, they were still very much in love, with life and each other. No life ventures its entire course without problems and sadness, and theirs was no exception. Mavis had died in 1993 – although this was expected, it still came as a shock when it happened. Robert had said that it was a great shame that she had never managed to see life from a more relaxed point of view.

The mystical side of life stayed mainly in the background. The staff sat in the house in Cambridge until a hike or holiday was planned. The wand stayed round Flick's neck and didn't do anything out of the ordinary very often. Several times there were brief glimpses into a future that was becoming increasingly obvious. The deaths of Robert and Avril were revealed gently and calmly and only when it was certain the end was near. John and Helen comforted each other; their partners' deaths falling within three months of each other in 2010. In the autumn they decided to spend the rest of their days together, having known each other for forty years. In 2012 they too 'conked out' as John would have put it. The wand had shown four peaceful painless endings.

In 2022 they held a small seventieth birthday party. Dan and Alan came over from Paris, many of their old friends had gone down different paths and contact had been lost. Soon afterwards they were sitting in the garden when the communicator, the third part of their mystical life, turned itself full on.

Eric was sat in Wolfie, having just restocked the fridge. The old camper van had been retired in 1995, having covered over a quarter of a million miles in twenty-eight years. It now sat at the bottom of the garden under a large horse chestnut tree where it performed as a summer house. They often spent the night in the rear bedroom with a bottle of wine and the photograph albums, reliving adventures. Near the pond an equally well-travelled Jeepy looked as if it was about to drive in – the Wrangler had been repurposed as a store for the garden chairs and cushions; it had a small green painted stone toad resting on the roof.

Flick was sat on the bench near the pond, reading a paper on the subject of ageing. She was making a few notes in the margins, cross referencing with the laptop on the table and looking rather ponderous. She glanced up at the full moon as Eric walked over with two glasses of something rosé coloured. Suddenly a loud hum came from the communicator making the staff vibrate. The jewel on the top was glowing bright purple. She picked it up as Eric sat down beside her. After a few experimental sweeps they discovered the vibration and intensity of the violet light reached the maximum levels when the tip of the communicator pointed at the moon. Eric wedged the staff so they had their hands free to do anything else needed. As the evening wore on, the beam glowed through to a muddy red colour before the humming decreased in volume as they were reading Flick's paper and sipping wine. Ten minutes later, the red light split into a rainbow and illuminated the water in the pond. For almost an hour they watched as scenes from their life together played out like a newsreel, dancing and skimming over the water; muddled sounds jumped in unexpectedly, Flick recognised the garden of the Manchester Madhouse, Eric knew the run he took over the cliffs in Portugal and they both remembered the truck stop north of Birmingham. There were snippets of Escapade gigs, an odd view of Hadrian's Wall and a very old clip showing them in bed in the first camper at the Isle of Wight. The impromptu movies stopped around midnight. They sat back with a contented but quizzical look on their faces.

"Any ideas what that was all for?" Eric asked.

"It's a communicator, so I guess it's communicating. But why it's showing memory lane is beyond me."

"Judging by the way the soundtrack was mixed up, I'm going to go with a test run."

Eric looked over the staff again for any buttons or switches, it was a half-hearted attempt as he'd done the same thing many times in the past without finding so much as a scratch. In bed that night, Flick finished telling him about the paper she was reading. The thing that had triggered it was her observations about themselves. Their seventieth party with Dan and Alan had added to her thoughts. Had Eric noticed how their two friends seemed to be ageing faster than they were. It was the same with some of the younger people they knew – their neighbours were a good eight years younger, but acted older than they did and looked it as well. Eric told her to remember Hans and Heidi who defied the years; she agreed but asked him to think about some of the more subtle things that made up their lives, things that perhaps should have ended, changed, or at least calmed down.

"Take my hair, for instance, it's still very red, your hair hasn't lost any thickness and it's more or less the same colour as when we met. Our skin is still supple and almost wrinkle-free, and compared to others our age we aren't losing anywhere near the amount of muscle, plus our energy levels are good. I don't need to say anything about our sex life, do I?"

Eric had to admit she had a point. The conversation wound up around two in the morning with him also conceding that after fifty-two years of lust and love he was as obsessed with her now as he was then. She nodded her agreement. Then he went and proved it, as engineers do. In the morning they decided that nature was being kind to them, and they were wearing better than most.

Roughly a month later, the moon was full again, so around eight in the evening they took the staff outside and fixed it to align with the jewel upwards. This time the newsreel was nothing to do with them. From what they could make out a lot of the clips were from the Vietnam War and battles in Africa and South America. Jungle fighting and long lines of people carrying rifles were seen walking through desert cities. There were scenes of air battles and ships firing huge guns across the water. Both world wars from 1914 to 1945 figured in the clips as well as possibly the Boer War and the Napoleonic battles. Later there were medieval armies hacking each other to pieces and fighting off the backs of elephants. The display ended with an atomic bomb explosion out at sea.

"War, and bloodshed, a potted history of human activity," Eric commented.

"Makes you wonder about our peace and love generation; it never prospered, did it, love?" Flick murmured, staring into the water as the last flickering images died away.

The next month was devoted to race riots and the parts of the world affected by famine. By December the subjects were the population explosion and global warming; they didn't think there was anything sad or depressing left to show them after this. At Christmas they went to Paris to see Dan and Alan. It was here they sat round the table and discussed the staff, wand and communicator in depth. They started off with listing its properties. Dan and Alan were looking as curious and baffled as their friends when the communicator's 'newsreels' were related to them.

"All very negative, war, famine, population controls and the health of the planet. And after showing you a brief history of your life together since 1970, which I would have said was a positive, happy thing," Dan said.

"We're all aware of the many aspects this staff and its components have. Foresight, in various formats, appear to be its strongest point. The fact that it seems to have a built-in traffic warning system and road atlas as well is unexplainable; just like this wolf that arrives from time to time. I take it you're nowhere nearer to finding out why it only worked when you danced around wearing an old pair of curtains?" Alan added.

"That is going to be part of the larger mystery," Flick answered, shaking her head. "We'd spent a lot of time that evening, the combination of my speaking and singing whilst dancing in my mother's curtain linings did the trick, but it's never worked again."

"The mythology part of Fenrir and Hyndla isn't like what we're experiencing. The paths of legend and our reality are not parallel. We have little to go on other than, as Flick has said many times, she feels she is being taught. You only have to look at the level of communication it gave us both in California way back in '84 to realise we're becoming integrated with it. How it works, and we still feel even now after all this time it's only a skeleton knowledge we possess at best, is another branch of the problem."

Eric went on to list almost everything they knew about the staff, ending with a few words about another unsolved mystery, the message of the runes and the only vision that made no sense, the strange sinking of a craft they all saw on the way back from Italy.

Alan suggested the 'newsreels' were, as Eric had first suggested, a test run to see if the communicator worked, citing the one in Italy some thirty years ago as the first simple movie they'd experienced. The tie-in with the moon was another area where they drew a blank. The concept of the communicator seemingly relying on the full moon as a media link was beyond comprehension. If there were lessons to be learned, then it was a belt and braces approach as ever since their university days the news had always been full of the subjects featured in the fishpond newsreels. All four friends were very aware of the problems the planet faced, they agreed there was precious little to learn from those lessons.

"Thinking about the moon again," Eric said, whilst accepting another glass of wine, "there have been at least four theories about our moon. I can give you a rundown if you wish, I bought my notes with me."

"It certainly won't subtract from anything we know and hey-ho, it might help," Flick commented.

Eric began his discourse; he had been doing some simple research ever since the moon connection had stamped itself into the proceedings.

"The Moon is our only natural satellite. At about one-quarter the diameter of Earth, it's the largest natural satellite in the Solar System relative to the size of a major planet, the fifth largest in the system overall, and larger than any known dwarf planet. In the 1800s, George Darwin, the son of Charles Darwin, suggested that the moon looked so similar to the Earth because at one point in Earth's history Earth might have been spinning so fast that part of our planet spun off into space but was kept tethered by Earth's gravity. Fission theorists posit that the Pacific Ocean might be the site where the would-be moon material came off of Earth. However, after moon rocks were analysed and introduced into the equation, they largely excluded this theory because the moon rock compositions differed from those in the Pacific Ocean. In short, the Pacific Ocean is deemed too young to be the source of the moon. The capture theory suggests that the moon originated elsewhere in the Milky Way, completely independent of Earth. Then, while travelling past Earth, the moon got trapped in our planet's gravity. The holes in this theory range from suggestions that the moon would have eventually broken free from Earth because our gravity would have been massively altered by catching the moon. Also, chemical components of both the Earth and the moon suggest they formed at around the same time. Co-accretion theory is next, also known as the condensation theory – this hypothesis offers that the moon and the Earth formed together while orbiting a black hole. However, this theory neglects any explanation of why the moon orbits the Earth, nor does it explain the difference in densities between the moon and Earth."

"There's a hell of a lot to think about here," Dan said. "Do go on, it's fascinating stuff."

"The reigning theory is that an object about the size of Mars impacted with a very young, still forming Earth about four and a half billion years ago. This object has been dubbed "Theia" by scientists because in Greek mythology – yes: mythology again – Theia was the mother of the moon goddess Selene. When Theia hit Earth, a portion of the planet came off and eventually hardened into the moon. This theory does a better job than others of explaining the similarities in chemical compositions of the Earth and the moon, apparently; however, it doesn't explain why the moon and the Earth are chemically identical. Scientists have suggested that, among other alternatives, Theia could have been made of ice, or Theia could have melted into Earth, leaving no separate trace of its own on the Earth or the moon; or Theia could have shared a close chemical composition to Earth. Until we can determine how large Theia was, at what angle it hit the Earth and precisely what it was made of, the giant impact hypothesis will have to remain just that – a hypothesis. A possible refinement of the giant impact hypothesis was published in Nature Geoscience in 2017. The new study adds that multiple objects, sized between the moon and Mars, struck Earth and the debris from these collisions formed disks around the Earth – think Saturn – before forming into moonlets. These moonlets eventually drifted away from Earth and merged to create the moon we know today. The study's authors contend that this multi-impact hypothesis helps to explain the chemical composition similarities. If multiple objects collided with Earth, the chemical signatures between those objects and Earth would even out more as the moon formed than if it had just been a single impact event."

Eric took a breather and turned to another section of his notes before starting on the final leg.

"So we can expand on this information, to the extent of doing some simple comparisons to see where we end up. The single or multiple impact theory goes some ways to explaining the chemical signatures of Earth and the moon being supposedly identical, but is reliant on several unknown factors. Venus is not far from the same mix, Mars is a member of the same club. Bearing in mind that everything in our corner of the solar system is roughly of the same composition, and the moon is the only off-world place we've actually set foot on. Further down the page we have, 'Theia could have shared a close chemical composition to Earth'. Before we start inventing theories, we might need a few more facts. 'The reigning theory is that a Mars-sized object impacted with a very young, still-forming Earth about four and a half billion years ago,' seems to indicate that the collision in Earth's infancy caused the chemical composition to be exact; however, the rocks in the Pacific are too young? So why is moon rock older than Pacific rock? Staying with the chemical composition theory, let us posit that if the moon and Earth have identical compositions, it seems highly likely that the moon was made from material already on Earth. This supports the Pacific Ocean being the birthplace of the moon; however, the scientists say the ocean is too young to be its origin. Round and round we go again. Does this mean then that the whole of Earth is too young to be the birthplace of the moon? If so, there might have been nothing for Theia to collide with as the Earth had not been formed yet. Consider also that our satellite has a few odd statistics that are up to now unique in the observable universe. Firstly, the size and position of its orbit. The moon is exactly the right size and exactly far enough away from Earth to make both total lunar and solar eclipses possible. Next, we have the moon's rate of rotation. This rotation is constant and in keeping with the Earth's own rotation. We never see the dark side of the moon, it's aways turning in sync with Earth to keep the one face showing at all times."

Eric stopped to take a deep drink.

"Finally, there's a theory the moon is hollow. In 1970, Michael Vasin and Alexander Shcherbakov, of what was then the Soviet Academy of Sciences, advanced a hypothesis that the Moon is a spaceship created by unknown beings. The article was entitled 'Is the Moon the Creation of Alien Intelligence?' and was published in Sputnik – think of a Soviet equivalent of Reader's Digest. Their hypothesis relies heavily on the suggestion that large lunar craters, generally thought to be formed by meteor impact, are generally too shallow and have flat or convex bottoms. They hypothesized that small meteors make cup-shaped depressions in the rocky surface of the moon, while the larger meteors can drill through any rocky layer and hit the armoured hull underneath. The authors reference earlier speculation by astrophysicist Iosif Shklovsky, who suggested that the Martian moon Phobos was an artificial satellite and hollow; this has since been shown not to be the case. Sceptical author Jason Colavito points out that all of their evidence is circumstantial, and that, in the 1960s, the Soviet Union promoted the idea in an attempt to undermine the West's faith in religion. Between 1969 and 1977, seismometers installed on the Moon by the Apollo missions recorded moonquakes. The moon was described as "ringing like a bell" during some of those quakes, specifically the shallow ones. This phrase was brought to popular attention in March 1970 in an article in Popular Science. When Apollo 12 deliberately crashed the Ascent Stage of its Lunar Module onto the moon's surface, NASA reported that the moon rang like a bell for almost an hour, leading to arguments that it must be hollow just like a bell. Lunar seismology experiments since then have shown that the lunar body has shallow moonquakes that act differently from quakes on Earth, due to differences in texture, type and density of the planetary strata, but there is no evidence of any large empty space inside the body. All this is common knowledge, and easy to find on the internet. Sadly, it doesn't advance our situation or provide any answers at all."

Alan went to the kitchen for a new bottle of wine. Dan looked over Eric's research notes and sat quietly for a while. It was Flick who opened her notebook next.

"Do you guys remember these?" she asked. "We had a mad evening solving them."

"The runes, a set of co-ordinates and a date I seem to remember," Alan said.

The four sat round the computer watching as Google Earth drove them through the town of Loving in Eddy County, New Mexico. The exact co-ordinates, according to Google anyway, was the Department of Motor Vehicles on West Cedar Street.

"No fortune in diamonds there, I guess," Dan mused. "The date was September 29th, 2029 if my memory serves."

"Correct, we've still got seven years to wait," Flick giggled.

Suddenly Dan's face wrinkled into a frown, he looked at Flick's notebook, turned it upside down and then reached for a pen and paper.

"Well after all these years. When was it? – 1975 – forty-seven years, a long time to pass before you discover a mistake, and, I think I may have a new theory as well," he said.

"What is it, Dan – what's wrong?" Flick looked at him slightly apprehensively.

"It says here we tried it as a hexadecimal number and we wrote it down as b5b5b, well it's wrong: 92929 as a reflection has '9' becoming 'd' but there's no way '2' turns into '5', it's nearer to 'Z', look." Dan wrote it again and turned the page. "Also we have to take into account what we mean by upside down. Look at it as a mirror image and '9' becomes 'p' and '2' becomes 's', therefore we have two sets that are not hexadecimal at all."

Alan recalled they had discarded that line of thinking anyway, but asked what else Dan had come up with.

"The date idea is fine, but looking at the timescale involved, fifty-four years, I think if these runes are in any way related to the staff and mythology it's too long in my book. I think we're on the wrong track. It suddenly came to me as I looked out the window across the road – when we were working we used to catch a bus by the bistro to our office, the cedex code is 92929. We need to get you to La Défense, the huge arch; it's thirty minutes from here."

The four left the house on Rue Caulaincourt, enjoying the crisp winter air as they made their way to the Place de Clichy metro station. After changing trains, they arrived at La Défense.

As they left the station Alan mentioned dinner, they discussed what they were looking for over a bowl of soup and came to the conclusion they would, or to be precise, Flick would know when she saw it. Starting at the building that housed the old offices of Lavigne and Courtney, they made their way towards the arch. For almost an hour they idly looked round, taking in the views and the architecture then, as they were on the point of saying good idea but – it happened.

Flick was to within a few feet in the middle of the arch; they were heading back to the metro station, when the wand gave her a clear single vision lasting about thirty seconds. She stood rooted to the spot, her eyes closed and a wide smile on her face. The others waited for the eyes to open, then started to eagerly question her.

"92929 has two meanings. First, it is as Dan predicted right here at the arch of La Défense, and it's a time, not as we thought, a date. We can go there any day we like, as long as we are at West Cedar Street in Loving, New Mexico at 9:29 and 29 seconds we get to find out what happens next," a very bubbly Flick told them.

"Would that be 9:29 am or pm, and is it local time some six hours behind the UK?" Eric the engineer asked. "And have you looked at your watches? It's 9.32 right now."

"Perhaps you just have to go to New Mexico and be there at any 9.29 for the next vision to roll in," Alan surmised. "But why did it cross reference it with Paris?"

"There can be only one reason – somehow you two are involved in what happens next. I cannot think of two people who are as close to us as you are. Also, part of the vision has all four of us holding a small metal box that's glowing green," Flick spoke openly.

"Do you think it would be a good idea if we all went out to New Mexico, go to Loving and see what happens next?" Dan asked.

"It would make a nice holiday, I'm all for it," Eric added.

They returned to Rue Caulaincourt in the dark, planning when they could meet up in London and fly out. After a few more days in Paris, they said their goodbyes, driving home with mid-May pencilled in on the calendar.

In early January Alan had emailed saying he and Dan would love to do Route 66, would Eric and Flick consider it. By the end of the week the plans were ready to fly to Chicago, where the Mother road started, a large motorhome had been rented and rooms at the airport booked. They just had to wait.

Flick uncoiled herself from Eric and sat up in bed. She had the distinct feeling she should hold the communicator and the wand. Without waking Eric, she quietly made her way to the kitchen, picking up the black rod which unsurprisingly was glowing violet from the jewel in the top. She held both items and saw the beginnings of a vision assembling behind her eyes and in her mind. She knew from previous experiences with their parents ten years ago this was not going to be a happy vision. Thankfully it was short and directly to the point. Dan had cancer. It was as simple as that. She felt the tears rolling down her cheeks and the sadness in her heart. Returning to the bedroom, she woke Eric gently; one look was all he needed. She told him, he wrapped her in his arms.

"Does he know, has he been keeping it from us?" he asked.

She shook her head.

"No, according to the communicator he has it in his lungs, he has no symptoms, nor is he likely to, not until the very end; the problem is he's terminal and if the number at the end is true to form, we look like losing him on August 19th."

"Then let's make this holiday the best he's ever had. We can't do anything more, can we?"

She slowly shook her head and said she would put the kettle on, three o'clock or not. As it turned out, the hardest part was keeping the information secret from their friends in Paris. When they met at Heathrow Airport in May, they seriously wondered if the vision was wrong. Dan seemed to be positively glowing with health, he looked fit and above all happy. The spring weather turned out to be hotter than normal, so the four friends enjoyed warm days and pleasant evenings. Slowly they meandered through Illinois south towards St Louis. More than once the forty-foot motorhome sparked memories of Wolfie and Jeepy. Eric and Flick took care to make sure Dan got to do all the things he wanted without making it obvious they were spoiling him a little. By the end of the first week, they were in Oklahoma, discovering the delights of the open road. There were plenty of side trips and days off to do silly things. Kansas and Texas came and went at the end of week two. When they arrived in Albuquerque, Alan was so taken with the old part of town they stopped at a campground next to the Rio Grande for a few days so they could visit all of it. Dan loved the art galleries and museums. They rounded off with a hot air balloon ride which completely made the entire holiday for him. Arizona followed New Mexico – the visit to Loving was going to be done on the return leg of the adventure – then California arrived through the huge windscreen. Thirty-three days out of Chicago, the four got a woman in a huge floppy straw hat to photograph them under the 'End of the Road' sign on Santa Monica pier striking their pose from the days of Escapade.

"I think we'll have that one as our Christmas card this year," Alan announced after looking at the shot on the camera.

Flick felt the words drill into her. For almost five weeks the secret had sunk below the radar, now it came home and a tear formed in the corner of one eye. Eric saw it and made a show of getting a spec of sand out of it. She smiled at him and squeezed his hand as a way of saying thank you. The journey to Loving was punctuated with more side trips, the main ones being the Joshua Tree National Park and the Carlsbad Caverns. On June 14th the camper was parked outside the Department of Motor Vehicles on West Cedar Street. Loving itself was a small village just off Hwy 285 and about an hour's drive from the caverns they had just visited. Eric placed the communicator on the table and Flick held the wand against her chest. Alan's mobile phone was showing the time, the seconds passing, a constant countdown to 9:29 and 29 seconds.

The interior of the camper went violet, Flick closed her eyes and reached for the communicator. Her face was expressionless for the entire ten minutes, she simply nodded randomly or shook her head. It was almost 9:45 when the light dimmed back into the jewel and she opened her eyes. She smiled.

"Gentlemen, I have a lot of explaining to do."

The motorhome was driven to the campground and for almost an hour Flick talked about the vision. Before she began, she asked them all to understand this wasn't a Flick the Naughty Elf stunt or caper. They all knew deep down it wasn't, but knowing the mischievous minx, as Alan had named her years ago, it was a good idea to recall just how involved they all were with Flick's Stick. As she understood it, everything that had happened since she had received the staff, wand and the communicator was the work of aliens. She waited for the flood of questions, but her audience knew an explanation would follow so they hung on.

"They, and I don't know precisely who 'they' are yet, have been looking for someone like me for a long time. I have what we call a physic ability or foresight. Most people have it to a certain extent – as an example we can often predict something will happen in the immediate future and aren't surprised when it does. Modern psychology suggests this is our brains using logic and reasoning, or a memory of a previous similar event and applying the same outcome. Whilst this might be true, it isn't the reason for my involvement. I am closer to a seer than most, not concerning prophesies, but seeing things that are hidden, in disguise, concealed out of sight or in another time. This is why I have been picked to help them. They want me to find an item left behind on Earth over seventy years ago. When I find it, they will come to collect it and the task is complete. The item is about four feet square and four inches thick – remember what I saw in Paris? They have given me the rough co-ordinates of where they think it should be and have asked if I will find it for them."

"Is it close to where we are now?" Alan asked.

"What is it, exactly?" Dan added.

Eric looked at his wife of forty-six years and knew there was a lot she wasn't saying. He decided it would keep until the time was right.

"It's about a hundred miles north of here, to the east of Roswell, yes, that Roswell. The device is roughly like a black box flight recorder but much more complex and it was on the UFO that crashed out in the desert. The thing is, the aliens knew they were going to crash so they jettisoned the device early, it was never picked up by the military as it's a long way from the actual crash site."

Eric had a question that wouldn't wait. "Flick, they haven't interfered with our lives in any way, have they?"

"No, love, they covered that point straight away. It seems they watched me and just monitored my development. There was no point in interfering with me, and later on in life with you, as there's nothing that can make my head any more receptive to physic channels. Either I have at a sufficient level or I don't. Later as our relationship deepened, you became integrated with it as well. The staff and communicator are to try and assist me in maximising the powers I have. It is as almost as we guessed, for me to learn rather than for it to teach. They watched and waited, that's all."

"Where do we start looking, Flick?" Dan asked.

"We have to drive to Roswell then head out to highway 70, heading towards Elida. We turn onto 330 near the bend in the road and head north to Floyd. Somewhere along that section of open scrub land is what they're looking for. It may be buried a foot deep or more but I will find it they say, if my powers, for want of a better word, are strong enough."

In the morning they set out; the countryside was indeed scrubland and fields, the road ran due north and the scenery never changed. After twenty minutes Flick closed her eyes and told Alan to take the next left turn. Five minutes later, she asked him to pull over onto the verge. Taking the communicator, she strode off into the yellow sandy field in a north easterly direction for about half a mile. Stopping seemingly at random, she bent down and dug into the bone-dry dirt, a small hole in hundreds of square miles of desert. The others helped dig out what appeared to be a dull metal box the size they had expected. It took all three men to haul it out and carry it back to the motorhome.

"It's made out of a material we don't have, that's for sure. There's nothing on Earth that size that weighs so much. Now what, love?" he enquired.

"Pass. Let's drive back to the main road and head for Floyd, we might be able to get a drink there," she answered.

For the rest of the day the wand and communicator were silent. The friends started making their way back towards Chicago as the motorhome was due back in a week. They stopped in Amarillo for the night and waited for something to happen. Eric had made a quick examination of the box; it appeared to be made out of the same material as the communicator, judging by the colour and lack of damage to its surface. The vision came just after Dan had finished serving drinks, the BBQ was cooling when the jewel lit up violet and promptly shifted through the spectrum to green. The ghoulish light lit up the little camp then Flick closed her eyes. Ten seconds later she announced with a smile she was to put the box on the ground by the side of the motorhome. Eric opened the locker and between the four of them did as she said. The green light concentrated to a pencil thin beam reaching up into the night sky. A low hum could be heard, then the light went out, only to be replaced by a wider blue light coming from a cloud directly above them. The blue beam bathed the box in a faint glow then, slowly at first, it lifted off the dirt and with increasing speed shot into the night sky, taking the cloud with it.

"That's it. It's over," Flick told them.

The rest of the evening the talk was of nothing else. In fact, all the way back to Chicago the conversation was all about the mysterious events surrounding Flick and the staff ever since the

Easter weekend in Wales many years before. The overnight flight back to London marked the end of what had been a remarkable holiday and an unexpected adventure thrown in as well. They all said it had been the trip of a lifetime and Dan in particular said he was overjoyed they'd all had such a great time. At Heathrow they said goodbye and went their separate ways once more.

Back in Cambridge, Eric and Flick began to try and understand the rest of the information the aliens had imparted to her, the part she had held back from Dan and Alan.

"We need to meet them. They want to ask us some questions and give us the opportunity to question them. They said we can help them with other things and they can help us. If we want to take the next step, we can signal them. All we have to do is point the communicator at the moon. You were right by the way, the home movies by the pond were test transmissions," she said.

They had been puzzling over the subject of what else they could do to help; as for the aliens helping them, that one drew a blank every time they tried to think of anything sensible.

"I'm baffled, love, we have nothing to lose it seems. I wonder where we're going to go to meet them – some deserted forest in the middle of nowhere if the Sci-Fi films are to be believed."

Sadly, Dan fell seriously ill in early August and was diagnosed with the cancer Flick had foreseen, or as she now realised, seen what was hidden. He died two weeks later, peacefully, with Alan by his side. Flick and Eric flew over and were with him as well. They stayed on in Paris to help Alan with the grief they knew he'd have a lot of trouble with. He said to Flick that had it not been for her friendship and support from the early days he would have collapsed emotionally in a terrible heap many years ago and that Eric had been the best friend he could have ever wished for. As it was, he managed to keep everything together and vowed to carry on. Unfortunately, the sadness didn't end there. The doctors say it's impossible to die of a broken heart, but Alan did. The vision that marked Alan's passing came ten days after Dan's death. Flick saw him lying in bed at peace with his eyes closed. She remarked to Eric it looked exactly like the image of his father when he went. Without waiting, they flew back to Paris and were surprised that Alan had not been discovered. They phoned the local police station, explaining they were friends visiting Mr Courtney and it was most strange he wasn't home to greet them nor was he answering his phone. In under an hour the body had been discovered and removed to the hospital. After the funeral, Alan's solicitor read the will: the entire estate – Alan was the sole beneficiary of Dan's estate – had been left equally to a French AIDS charity and a drugs rehabilitation clinic in London. The production company he ran with Dan was to be held in trust until the Marstones decided what to do with it.

In September they decided to communicate with the aliens.

"It's just you and me now, love," Flick said to Eric as he sat by the fishpond in the garden.

"It's a full moon tomorrow, your majesty – are we going for it?" he replied.

"I think so, I want to know more, I think you do too."

"Indeed, let us see where life takes us, it's been amazing so far."

Eric reached out and pulled her along the bench. When she was within reach, he gently placed his hand on the side of her face as he kissed her. She melted under his touch then felt a warm glow as he slid his hand down her neck inside her dress and sought out her breasts.

"You're a devil, Eric Marstone, a bloody devil."

She grinned then smiled as he laid her down on the grass, helping him remove the dress as she went. The Cambridge wolf howled a little later.

The full moon rose in the evening sky, Eric carried an old beer tray with glasses of wine on into the garden. Flick set the staff and communicator against the end of the bench with the jewel aimed at the pale orb. They waited. At 9:29 the jewel glowed violet, Flick instinctively closed her eyes, reopening them a few seconds later.

"We have to go inside Wolfie, contact will be made there," she whispered.

Once the door was closed the light inside changed from artificial white to a low warm orange; near the shower cubicle door a tall shape began to materialise. The being was too tall for the camper and had to sit on the front couch. Like the one that had appeared inside Wolfie at the Manchester Madhouse, it had arms which morphed from its flanks, each having two elbows, a wrist and hands with six digits, two being opposing thumbs. The fingers were long and devoid of nails. The skin was smooth, hairless and a metallic steel colour – at first sight it would have been possible to think of it as a robot. The face could have been taken from any popular magazine depicting the traditional 'grey', the large black angled eyes, small mouth and minimalist nostrils.

It spoke; they both heard the voice in their heads, not through their ears.

"Do not be frightened, there is nothing to fear. You can help us, and we can help you. The item you recovered for us has been returned to where it came from, it restores a balance that was wrong. Please be patient, I have to learn your language accurately. I will answer all your questions and I want you to ask as many as you can think of."

Flick looked at the gentle glowing creature and asked the first thing that came into her head: "Do you have a name? everyone calls me Flick."

A faint hum came from the being's head. "The nearest simple sound in your speech is 'Wesme', that will suffice. You have a lot of questions, would it be easier to hear everything from the beginning then you can ask questions about anything else?"

They both nodded.

"It is a long story, you may like to lie on the bed to listen."

Flick slipped her sandals off and followed Eric to the rear bedroom, Wesme moved with them and sat in the doorway.

"We have been visiting your Earth for many years, our interest in you began in Earth year 1908. We noticed a ripple in a balance on the planet and our attention was directed to your grandparents. The ripple passed to your parents – both of the females' genes were showing the pattern we had been searching for. We watched and waited, hoping the two females would find mates and breed; they did and you are the results. When you were four years old, we placed a sentinel in your life. While you were small it did close watching and was told to protect you but not to interfere with your life. Whatever you became was natural. We have never intervened, humans are cross-bred, not with us but with a similar species to you from light years away that happened before we were custodians; nothing was engineered or deliberately forced by us. As custodians think of us as watchers of the universe, think of it as a garden, each solar system as a plant pot full of soil, sand and dirt – you have a song that says 'we are star dust and we've got to get back to the garden'. Planets form in the mulch, some germinate, some die, sometimes we can save them, sometimes not, sometimes the pot is barren, sometimes too many species grow and war ensues. We are the gardeners who can only observe but occasionally we're allowed to tinker. You spent time in college, think of this as a larger 'Universe-ity'."

Wesme continued after allowing time for this to sink in.

"By the time Flick had lived to ten years, we knew the sentinel would be unable to continually observe you as age bought independence from your parents and you travelled further from home. A second sentinel was dispatched; they worked together until you were fourteen Earth Years. It was then the bonding happened. Would you like to see it? You should remember it."

On Wolfie's roof an image formed, a low angle showing a teenage boy and girl, smiling and talking whilst eating sandwiches outside a large stone building. They saw themselves outside the Science Museum as clear as if it were yesterday. Across the bed they exchanged glances and reached out for each other's hands.

"In order to watch both of you the second sentinel stayed with Eric and monitored your life, again without interference. Here is the next important event. We had hoped that something would take place to bring you together and we looked for anything that might accomplish this. It was your joint love of music that made it happen."

The roof was showing them inside the first of Eric's camper vans, sitting up in bed wrapped in sleeping bags with a steaming cup. There was an open packet of chocolate digestives on the shelf.

"It was here we first saw your psyches meld together. From that day we knew the bond was forged, it was now a matter of waiting, as it often is. The sentinels asked us to visit you when you went to Scotland. It was here we had the confirmation that your love for each other looked like it was going to be deep and long lasting. It was the beginnings of a relationship known on this planet as 'soulmates'. I visited you later to check again, your love for each other had increased, intensified and gained strength; this was when you were in Manchester. You both radiated a strong deep red – there is no higher colour; your love for each other is total and complete. From this point we knew your bond was forged as strong as any link could be. It's still as strong today – please look at yourselves as the beam shines."

From the alien's hand a device like the communicator sent out a rainbow in a straight line towards them. It bathed them in multi-coloured hues then the seven shades turned deep red, intensified to the point of it looking almost nothing like red at all.

"We have to move forward to the experience you had in Portugal. The way in which your prophesy hit you emotionally was of great concern to us; it is thanks to your bond that Eric managed to make you feel safe, he also played a vital part in the rescue. Once that event had passed, we decided to send you the runes in a series of dreams to see how you would interpret them. There was the death of your uncle, the awkward incident with the false policeman, and helping your friend Alan increase his confidence to be considered before we tried to see if your power was as we expected and hoped it would be. This power is the reason for our interest in you. As you can imagine there are many humans who like to think they have the power of what is called foresight, and as you have discovered yourselves, the ability to see what is hidden and where it is located. In reality the ones that have the ability are unaware of how deep it sits in the mind, how complex it is and are always a little emotionally disturbed; as you were, until the mind accepts what is happening. It's the fear of the unknown and the thoughts and feelings they are different from everyone else that causes the distress. We noticed you were becoming a little less worried as some of the unpleasant parts of life unfolded over the months and years. We searched for a way in which we could help you calm the emotional upheaval as it was obvious that you were going to have many different types of 'visions' as you began to call them, even with the ability of your mind being nowhere near to fully developed. We didn't want you to be scared, that would be of no use to you, or to us. The solution was found. Instead of asking your mind to accept aliens as being a part of Earth Life and running the risk of you ridiculing the whole thing, we used mythology as a stepping stone, something that had been well documented and to all intents and purposes was connected to seers, prophets and visions. The main thoughts behind this became the introduction of the staff and wand, hopefully they would anchor your ability, and by making the staff appear to be educating you it masked the fact it was actually you educating yourself. We gave you the tool to grow your strength as a seer by helping the unknown become the known. By the time you married and went to France we realised we had to add another tool to the box as Eric would say. It was in The Black Forest we felt you were ready for the device you call a communicator. That is only one of its many functions; we can discuss them later."

Flick reached for her drink, and Eric asked what happened next.

"Next we did more watching and waiting. Flick was steadily increasing her psychic strength through dogged determination, Inguz, I believe you taught her that, Eric, and by having the desire to lead a good life, helping others, being caring and kind; all these things made both your minds grow and in Flick's case she increased her unseen powers."

"So all this time we have been living a life that has what most people would call an occult facet attached to it and you have been trying to help us cope with this ability so we can lead as normal a life as possible and as a bonus help your species by using that power. I understand this and wondered what would have happened if Flick's visions would have continued as they were, unaided so to speak," Eric asked.

"She would have continued to have all the visions she has had, the emotional distress would have probably intensified over time, resulting in anything from depression to a total nervous breakdown. Psychic ability is not easy to live with, as I said at the beginning, the power matures and increases as time marches forward. Flick's power has been increasing naturally, the education has diminished the distress by revealing some understanding of that biggest fear, the unknown. We would do nothing to harm either of you."

Flick asked if the incident in northern California in 1984 had anything to do with how far they had both developed.

"The unfortunate event in the hills is a good example. You will recall how you both were able to remain calm and in control, you could see and sense each other's movements and the knowledge that you were both unharmed quelled any fear that might have been present. As you know, it was your knowledge of plant biology that gave Eric the time to reach your location, once there his actions made the whole affair end well for you. We move now to the Italian coast where you spent time with your oldest friends. This will bring us to the point where I have to ask if you will help us again, but first I will have to apologise for something I should have seen before it happened. Over the Earth Years the two sentinels have become, should we say, attached to their humans, so much so they have, as you would say, Flick, 'overdone it a bit'. They went on the holiday with you and adopted a lot of human traits. We first noticed they had been tinkering in the south of France when they spent an odd hour adjusting an old couple's sex life by using a process we have called Backtime to unwind them internally, and only in certain areas, about thirty Earth Years. The effects lasted until they died some fourteen years later."

"That would be Hans and Heidi, they were in their mid-eighties then," Eric said.

"We can only be thankful they were both well past the child creation stage and the course of history was not changed. It would seem not only do you have a Naughty Elf in your life, Mr Marstone, there are two Naughty Bears as well."

Flick sat up and watched as Eddy and Kenny walked towards them on stumpy furry legs across the bed until they were within reach.

"Oh flipping heck, you two are the sentinels, no wonder I could never remember who gave them to me, or more to the point when. Oh – just a minute – there cannot be, surely not – a planet populated by teddy bears, that's not possible, is it?" Flick said, reaching out for both bears.

Wesme explained they were the last two inhabitants of a doomed planet many light years away and had been with the custodians for a long time.

"If you saw them in their original form; they are shape-shifters, on Earth they would be classified as reptiles. The teddy bear image fitted in with the roles they played, remembering you were four when the one you call Eddy arrived. You can talk to them later but now I want to take you to the end of the Italian holiday in 1992. We have noticed you have never managed to discover any meaning behind the vision all four of you saw near Milan. There's a good reason for this. You were not supposed to see this vision at that time, there was a disturbance in a balance and it burst through the water and found you close by. You may recall there was no sound to the vision and no other information, like a dream or secondary vision. This is because the vision self-generated from its origin. We strongly suspect your developing power simply triggered it and here is the point where we need your help once more, just as you did in New Mexico. Will you help? You don't have to say anything now, rest and think about it, talk to the sentinels and let them know. To communicate with them simply hold them and think what you want to say; to contact me use the communicator as if you were holding a sentinel, it's a similar method."

With the last sentence finished, Wesme dissolved into the green glow and left Wolfie. Eddy and Kenny moved into the middle of the bed and lay between them. Sleep overtook the humans, eventually.

'I hope they aren't mad at us,' Kenny thought.

'Shouldn't think so, we better be careful if they ask us to go to normal shape though, we might look a bit weird to them.'

'We can only wait and see. Shall we rest too?'

'Good thought.'

A slightly confused pair of humans woke just before lunchtime. They went into the house and made something to eat and a drink. Eddy and Kenny walked in slowly, carefully watching the humans' reaction to seeing them move on their own. Flick took hold of

Eddy's paw.

'Do you guys need food and drink?' she thought, whilst watching them climbing up onto the spare kitchen chair.

'We tend to sort our own if that's alright with you.'

"Let me hazard a guess, Eddy, from what I learned last night about mythology, you're Fenrir, aren't you?" she asked, looking him straight in the eye.

The little bear nodded.

"Any particular reason for my dancing around in a pair of dining room curtains, I'm keen to know."

'We were told to make the mythology aspect deeper; to give you a reason for, or an anchor to, some of the unexplainable visions that might scare you, that and Eric was becoming deeply connected to your power. Also you look very beautiful when you dance, especially in a long dress – we couldn't resist, sorry.'

She smiled at them and ran a hand through Eddy's fur; he liked it when she did that. Kenny got treated to the same grooming; he told Eddy it tickled.

"We had better think about what to tell Wesme. I want to help. I also think they have made our lives better, especially mine, with the protection they have given me in being able to control my emotions. I definitely want to help. What do you feel?"

Eric sat on the end of the breakfast bar and thought about the erroneous vision.

"Definitely, we should help out, whatever it is they need us to do is obviously impossible for them to achieve alone, or with the help of the two sentinels. Just like New Mexico I think it's something they lost and have waited a long time to recover, just exactly what is a complete guess, we have nothing to go on. I wonder if Eddy or Kenny know?"

Flick took hold of both bear's paws and thought her question. It took five minutes before she spoke.

"They know something, but not everything. When we got the vision they reported it back to Wesme who told them it was the scene of an accident in Earth Year 1933. At the time in Italy there were political upheavals, the war was only a few years into the future and not a lot is known about the actual event. It concerns a UFO and we have half-solved the problem for them by being close to the source of the rogue transmission. The 'aircraft carrier with knobs on' is the UFO and it sank in water; where, they aren't sure. Not many years ago there was a surge in interest – at the time the Italians claimed they had the wreck at a military base near Milan; this is bull shit; they think Wesme wants us to find it."

After a shower and spending an hour looking through their photographs and videos of the holiday on the Amalfi coast, they scoured Google Earth for any lakes. They decided the water was a lake and not the sea. Eddy pressed his paw against Flick's hand and suggested they search the lakes near Milan, reasoning that they were near Milan when it happened, although there was a lot of them he suggested they start with the ones nearest the place Flick had the vision. This was logical, so Flick and Eddy scanned lakes on one laptop and Eric and Kenny used the other.

"It's like looking for a needle in the proverbial haystack, even if we eliminate the ones that don't have roads running alongside them we're going to be at it for ages. Let's grab something to eat and contact Wesme – they might have something more to go on," Flick said, crossing another possible off the list.

That evening they all met again in Wolfie, Wesme took the communicator and joined it to his own. From their position on the rear bed they all saw an expanded version of the original. It was a lake, of that there was no doubt, and it was larger than the ones they had covered so far. Eric estimated it to be roughly half a mile across – this cut down on the number of lakes to check on the computers. Only when they were about to return to the house did Wesme say was it correct to assume they were going to help. They nodded and watched as the alien dissolved into the clear evening sky.

Lakes Iseo, Como, Maggiore, Lugano and Garda fitted the new information, so the next morning the computers started flying over the waters. By the end of the first day a short list of ten possible places had been made; they left the bears to contact Wesme and see what was going to happen next.

The British Airways flight touched down in Milan on time, Eric pulled a suitcase off the conveyor and Flick wheeled the cabin bag. The car hire company had a white off-roader ready for them, Flick drove from the airport round to the local van hire rental firm, stopping just round the corner out of sight of the office. Once Eric was ready, she led off, following the GPS directions on her phone to the hotel. Eric tagged on behind in the Ford Transit. Inside the room they unpacked and waited. Ten minutes later a rainbow pierced the balcony doors, letting Eddy and Kenny drop onto the bed. The two laptops were set up, and over a drink from the mini bar and a packet of peanuts, the four had a meeting to go over the plan for tomorrow. The easiest way to communicate was for Flick to sit cross-legged on the bed with Eddy on her lap, his paw touching Kenny who in turn leaned against Eric. After a couple of false starts they discovered all four could be in on the same conversation.

"We know from Wesme how we're going to locate this craft," Flick said and thought at the same time. "I will take the wand and drive along one side of the lake, Eric will take the communicator in the van along the other side. If I get a vision, Eric will know anyway, we're able to reach out to one another automatically and we have you guys as well. Once I can establish the vision is the right one, I have to park up and walk along the shoreline until the signal is the strongest; perhaps the communicator will activate as well."

"I will have to drive up and down until I get a strong fix on Flick. Probably I will have to walk the beach or road until we get that strong signal, only we're not exactly sure how it will present itself at the moment. The van is on hand if we have to haul anything away. We start off tomorrow with Lago d'Iseo. Are you ready to eat, love?"

The restaurant was on a terrace below their room. It was a strange sensation, dining by a shimmering blue lake with two bears wearing sunglasses and baseball caps looking down on you from the balcony above.

"They're definitely becoming 'humanised'," Flick said, looking up.

"I do hope we haven't embarrassed them over the years, we've had a lot of sex in front of them and all been in the same bed a fair few times as well," Eric mused.

"We'll find out tonight, won't we, I'm sure they'll mention it at some point," she replied with one of her mischievous smirks as she brushed her bare leg against him.

Eddy sat on the passenger seat of the van, holding on to the communicator and making sure the laptop didn't slide off. Eric turned out from the hotel, Flick followed with Kenny up front holding the atlas and the other laptop. She followed the shoreline road west then north; he headed east then north. They met at the top with no results of any kind. At a coffee bar they looked at the atlas and started out towards Garda. Lunch was in Bergamo then they moved off to Como. Back in the hotel they had a late dinner and sat out on the balcony.

"Lugano and Maggiore left, three possibles on the list," Eric said, looking up from the atlas. Eddy offered a paw and said he'd been looking at the terrain view on Google and he'd come to the conclusion that the vision looked more like Maggiore than Lugano. They agreed to drive the extra miles and see if the theory worked.

In the morning they checked out and drove the ninety miles to Sesto Calende, close to the southern tip of Maggiore. As usual Flick took the west road, Eric drove the east. The signal came to Flick as she drove past Belgirate; she parked on the right, got out of the car and walked up to the ornate wall next to the water's edge. With the wand round her neck and Kenny on her back, she easily visualised Eric who had just come to a stop in Arolo. By driving towards the waterfront and walking the last few yards to a boat dock, he heard Flick tell him the signal was white hot. The communicator was humming and vibrating as well. He took several photographs and marked the spot on the map in his phone. Flick sent another message saying they would rendezvous at the southern end and find a hotel. She found a nice place by the water at Arona. Eric pulled in thirty minutes after her.

"So, part one complete, what happens next I wonder," Flick pondered as the two bears communicated in hums and beams of orange light. Kenny wandered over, flopping onto the chair by the desk, offering a paw. Eric discovered they were going to meet up with Wesme, but not here – they had to talk to others like him and it might take a while.

Eddy came over and offered Flick his paw, telling her they were to stay here until they returned and amuse themselves; also, would she be kind enough to look after her bra herself for a few days, he added with a wink. Both bears stood by the window and dissolved into a violet strand of rainbow light.

They took a walk round the town and window shopped the late afternoon away. Dinner was a romantic affair by the water's edge, then bed called and they drifted off to sleep with Flick in her usual spot, curled inside Eric's arm.

Next morning they used the car to revisit both places where the signal was the strongest. At Belgirate the communicator had hummed then three rapid short flashes of indigo light fanned out across the lake; nobody seemed to notice. Eric discreetly wound a length of red electrical insulation tape round the steel tubular top rail of the fence. On the other side the communicator had vibrated, increasing in frequency until it seemed to be in two places at the same time, disappearing than re-appearing in her hand as she moved up and down the boat dock Eric had marked. The vibrations diminished or increased until she was in one particular spot. There was a brief indigo flash from the jewel then everything went back to normal, or switched off if you prefer. Eric marked the second spot with red tape.

"It must be like triangulation but at the moment without the third point – in this case it's going to be below the water. All we have at the moment is a straight line across joining two points," he commented.

"We'll know more when our furry sentinels get back; they don't seem rushed about reverting back to their original shape, do they?" she answered.

Eric nodded agreement. "Perhaps they like being bears?"

"Or do they think their original form might horrify us, something like arachnid syndrome?"

They left the question unanswered.

It rained for most of the next day, black clouds rolled along the mountain tops, the weather in early October had been cool and up to now dry. Dawn broke to the sound of thunder rattling round the sky with lightning illuminating the room momentarily. After breakfast they had sat for a while looking out over an increasingly darker stretch of grey water and decided there was more fun to be had back in bed.

They must have dropped off to sleep mid-afternoon as they were quite unprepared for the sentinels' arrival close to six o'clock. Kenny landed gracefully on the couch, Eddy managed to hit the edge of the bed, bounced and ended up face down on Flick's head, nose to nose.

"Just dropped in, I take it," she said with a mouthful of fur. "Your take off's fine, Eddy, the landing really needs work."

Eddy made it upright and sat on the couch with Kenny, ready to have a four-way as they called it.

The storm was excellent cover for what Wesme had in mind. They were to go to the two lakeside points at three in the morning, the time when there should be the fewest witnesses. Once they were in position, Flick was to point the wand at Eric who would point the communicator at her. The wand would send the signal vision she detected, getting stronger as the communicator aligned. On Eric's side the jewel would glow brighter until a beam shot out across the water and joined the wand. No matter what happened afterwards they were to hold the alignment until the end of what was now going to be a rescue operation.

There was nothing to do other than wait. After dozing from late evening to early morning they let themselves out of the hotel in the rain, split up, and went to the two points by the lakeside.

Flick looked at her watch; at three exactly she held the wand out level in her hand pointing out across the lake to where she estimated he was, the vibration signal was almost instantaneous. On Eric's side of the lake the communicator pulsed an indigo pencil-thin beam across the water, Eddy peered out from inside Eric's waterproof jacket, telling him to angle the beam five degrees south. As the beam turned it connected and locked on. Flick saw the violet light penetrate the wand and make the end glow. Like Eric she held on tight and stood with Kenny, also sheltering inside her waterproof jacket.

The rumble began about three minutes later, the sky, already pitch black and full of dark clouds, suddenly split open, forming an oval ring of green light. The ring flickered at the edges. Flick looked up and saw the centre spot concentrate, like twisting the head of a flashlight into focus, then a shaft of green pointed down to the water, locking onto the violet ray emanating from the communicator in Eric's hand. It danced along the violet ribbon, making its way towards the centre of the lake, illuminating the water below until it stopped at a point slightly closer to Eric than Flick. The width of the oval increased and a humming sound filled the air alongside the rumble which had now moved out of the bass register in pitch and intensity. After what seemed an age, a huge dark shape broke the surface and continued rising, clumps of weed, old tree branches and other debris fell back into the water as it rose. Eric looked out across the surging water to the green, glowing UFO as it ascended and estimated it was over nine hundred feet long and a hundred deep. It was the same 'aircraft carrier with knobs on' shape at one end, the vision had only shown the final few seconds of it slipping under the surface; it must have sunk nose first, Eric realised as he looked at what was now identifiable as the stern.

Flick stared in amazement as the dripping black mass rose from the lakebed, water torrenting from it as its speed increased until finally it was lost in the clouds. The green light went out at the same time as the indigo beam; it was eerily silent, only the gentle lapping of the lake and the patter of rain drops could be heard. Eric's voice appeared in her head.

"You've got company, love, look north up the road, possibly a police car."

"I see it, you make your way back, I can bluff my way out of this one if I need to."

Eric drove back to the hotel and was surprised to see the off-roader already back in the car park.

"What happened?" he asked.

"I hid behind a tree, they drove straight past and carried on down the road, I waited a few minutes then started driving slowly south to the hotel; when I went through Meina they were parked near the jetty shining their headlights out across the water. They didn't notice me pass," she shrugged. "Did Eddy go with them, by the way? Kenny did."

"Yes, he said we were to go home when we felt ready."

"I thought one of them would say something. Let's get to bed, I could do with a couple of hours."

Brunch happened around midday. By this time the TV reports of strange sightings over Lake Maggiore had calmed down. There were several interviews with people claiming to have witnessed a huge UFO flying low over the lake. The descriptions varied from conventional 'flying saucers' to a rough portrayal of the Millennium Falcon from Star Wars. After watching until the newsreel repeated itself, they agreed not one of the so-called eyewitnesses had seen anything or had incredibly poor powers of description. In the afternoon they returned the Ford van and had two more days wandering round the lakes sightseeing before getting a flight back home.

"What happens next I wonder," Eric pondered.

"We seem to be asking that question rather a lot these days, love," Flick answered from the kitchen.

TV reports stated the Italian air force had tracked the UFO to the aircraft's ceiling then lost contact. Ground tracking followed as it accelerated to an unheard-of impossible speed then promptly vanished off their instruments. Other sky watching sources reported the same scenario, the last contact estimated the craft to be travelling directly away from Earth and placed it past Pluto within two hours.

Two days passed before Eddy and Kenny arrived back, landing in the spare bedroom. Wesme wanted to see them to explain the remainder of the alien involvement and also to offer them an opportunity that would greatly benefit them. Flick and Eric agreed to meet in Wolfie that night.

"What are they going to offer us? I can't begin to think," Eric asked.

"I would like to know more about the UFO they recovered, but like you I have only my wildest imagination dreams as to what they intend. One thing I am sure of now though, these aliens are entirely benign, there doesn't appear to be angry bone in them," she replied.

"You're right there, any species that can travel this distance and do what they have done have no intention of dominating the planet – if they wanted Earth they would have wiped us out before they even landed the first ship."

The ceiling of the camper van lit up light green as Flick and Eric lay on their backs with Eddy and Kenny wedged between them. Wesme explained the UFO had been returned to the world it came from, the occupants had been resuscitated from the survival pods and were all 'functioning normally', another imbalance had been restored. Flick asked if there was anything else on Earth that needed recovering and with a smile she was told no, nothing of any significance. It was now time to explain more about their lives from the point where they had left off to carry out the recovery plan.

"The years afterwards were hard on you both. The loss of your parents and finally your two greatest friends. We noticed how you were able to cope with the biggest emotional upheaval when your parents' lives ended and then how you still managed to make a friend's final year a wonderful experience. If you want to receive it, we can give you both a wonderful experience; however, we need to look closely at this planet you call Earth first."

"I'm going to guess you're not altogether happy about how things are turning out," Eric enquired.

Wesme looked at both of them and nodded agreement.

"This planet has been heading for extinction for a while now and we cannot do anything to stop the process. It resembles the home world of the two sentinels here with you now. I will explain what is going wrong; however, I think you already know."

The roof of Wolfie dissolved into the newsreel movies they had first seen projected onto the fishpond two years before. Wesme provided the soundtrack. The whole of the planet had been fighting and arguing since the dawn of time; peace was rare. Religion had started as an attempt to bring peace by showing humans how to live in harmony, the controllers and power hungry had corrupted the original concept for their own ends and profit. From this thirst and greed for power, control, and later, money, the planet had reshaped itself into separate segments roughly divided into the 'have or the have-nots' as they had heard it called. The balance of power shifted as new challengers rose to claw a slice of the status and profits and usually, although not entirely, this was achieved by violence on many different levels, ranging from a gang of thugs roaming the city streets to huge numbers of military personnel fighting each other with weapons of increasing sophistication. The movie changed to the subject of race riots and the results of famine in third world countries. The commentary outlined the flaw in humans that made it difficult for them to be friendly with people who had a different colour skin, regardless of religion; also, the countries that needed the most help with food production had been raped of their valuable resources by the powerful who failed to help them or pretended to help and in doing so made even more money. The next movie was about industrialisation and the way in which the planet's energy was being used. Instead of using technology and brain power to find new ways to produce new alternative energy, the powerful were making sure that nothing was done until the very last drop of money had been extracted from what they owned. Crude oil, methane gas and atomic energy, renewable power, all of these resources were so tightly controlled there was no time left to find a replacement infastructure, the panic had already started.

The well-reported problems with population control were being played out above their heads next. Wesme explained that if things carried on as they were it would not be long before the planet would be incapable of producing enough food and fresh water for the ever-swelling population, famine would become the norm in many countries, including some that had not been expected to suffer. The second problem, directly connected to the first, would be how the people paid for their food – there was a limit to how many 'jobs' were available. Even now governments had manufactured work; known as 'non-jobs' by the sarcastic, and allowed people to work less hours and share their work. Soon these same people would be protesting they couldn't earn enough to feed their families, especially those with a lot of children. In short, the aliens reckoned a global war would break out over the production, processing and control of food and water in the near future. Healthcare would be stretched to breaking point, there would be a vast housing shortage, crime would increase as normally honest people resorted to theft to survive.

"I can show you two things now you might like to check for yourselves; the powerful label them conspiracy theories, some are, but a lot aren't," Wesme added.

The first was a device known as The Buzzer. It was in Russia and transmitted a meaningless signal on the short-wave radio band. There were several interpretations of its usage but the most concerning one was the 'dead hand' concept. This was a signal which if interrupted by a nuclear attack would trigger the computers to launch missiles against the rest of the word in retaliation. The ultimate way of saying if I lose, you all lose.

The second was the various 'manufactured' viruses that had been allowed to break out of so-called research laboratories over the last hundred years. The influenza epidemic of 1922, SARS, and finally COVID 19 were, among others, in the aliens' opinion, methods of population control that the governments figured they could not be blamed for, even going as far as making it impossible to take legal action against them if a person died of the virus and doing nothing about bringing the originators of the virus to answer in a court of law. When humans managed to resist the virus, other scaremongering tactics were deployed. Global warming was given centre stage, to pave the way for food shortages, the population were discouraged to eat meat and only go for the so-called healthy vegetable options, many of which were heavily genetically modified and contained synthetic proteins. Since modified food had been allowed, the number of new and often strange allergies had increased dramatically. The aliens also had a suspicion that population control drugs and behaviour modifiers where also being introduced through the water supply.

"Now we come to the opportunity we can offer you. As with everything we are not expecting you to make a decision right now. The offer is open-ended, you may take it up at any time. You are in many ways similar to the two sentinels, they too have a lot of love in their hearts, they reflect the same dark red you do; however, their planet suffered a fate that Earth might yet have to endure, the scenario you saw earlier was the long term possibility – their world went for a faster route to oblivion. The war escalated beyond any hope of control or peaceful ending. Within two hours of your time, every living thing was obliterated; as a biologist you can see what this means. We offered the sentinels the same opportunity we offer you. They took it. Afterwards do talk to them and ask as many questions as you need to."

Flick held on to Eddy's paw and reached out to Kenny, they both looked a little dejected.

"I'm so sorry you lost your home," she whispered.

"You can of course carry on living out the rest of your life here on Earth. We will leave you in peace and the staff and wand, although they have come to the end of their usefulness, can remain with you along with the communicator. At any time you can summon me and take the opportunity. So we come to the time where you both have to think long and hard about what you wish to do. If you agree, we will take you from Earth and give you a home on what you call a space station; we would embrace all the skills you both have. Not only your psychic ability, which is extremely valuable, we would also welcome your talents as a biologist and an engineer. There is much to do in the universe. What makes a vast difference if you take the opportunity is the deep and unswerving love and devotion you have for each other and the living proof you have endured in each other's company for most of your lives; this will be very important in the time to come."

"We don't have too many years left, Wesme; if we stay fit and healthy we might both see another twenty," Eric offered.

"The life you have left is relative," Wesme began. "You have discovered we are capable of many things as yet unknown to humans and also there are things we cannot achieve alone. We can do something for you that will greatly affect your lives; however, I must make you fully aware of the implications before you proceed. Speaking in simple terms, we can reverse your ageing process and rejuvenate your bodies. We realise this has been a subject extensively covered by the science fiction authors of the world for many years, it is possible and we can make it happen to you, science fiction has become science fact. It's a more comprehensive process than the minor adjustments the sentinels performed on your Austrian friends. What you need to be aware of, however, before you commit is that after the Backtime process is complete, not only will you remain at your body's optimum age, you will live for all time, barring certain accidents. Backtime cannot reverse death or major injuries such as the loss of a limb. You have therefore to think about spending the rest of time with each other, and of course off Earth. This is why we had to be sure about your love and relationship before we made the opportunity available. If you accept you will need to make sure you vanish from the administrative systems of Earth and realise all your wealth, although you will need neither food or money, or anything else afterwards, so think of a way of disposing of it without causing anyone to be suspicious. Go and ponder, ask questions and decide what you wish to do. There is only one other requirement: two must stay on earth or two must go."

The four began talking at length until well into the early morning. Once sleep had been caught up with, the questions and reasoning began again. By the end of the third day a plan had been made, they had both agreed openly and wholeheartedly they were going to take the opportunity and live in the larger universe. They both told Eddy and Kenny:

"We don't want to live alone, it is highly likely one of us will die before the other. The possibility of living for eternity in our prime is incredible and we both want to help as we have been helped. It might sound old fashioned, but we want to do good."

In Paris the offices of Lavigne and Courtney were still at La Défense, a young lawyer had read and approved the documents Flick and Eric had brought with them, saying she would begin carrying out their instructions on the first day of December. In Cambridge their personal possessions were boxed and stacked in the spare bedroom. Both cars were sold on the internet and they emptied their personal savings account by converting it into tax-free ISAs. In every case they told the professional people involved they were planning to travel the world.

Eddy was busy uplifting the stack of boxes and Kenny was making sure Wolfie and Jeepy were ready to follow.

'Don't leave anything behind or we're in for it,' Kenny advised his slapdash friend.

At Heathrow airport Flick sealed a large brown envelope with a Paris address on the front and pushed it into the slot.

"How long till we get a gate?" she asked.

"It's just come up, shall we amble over?"

Once in San Francisco they picked up a hire car and drove to a hotel for the night. The next day saw them take a pleasant wander towards the Yosemite National Park and find a quiet corner in a partially wooded clearing away from the regular tracks. As dusk approached, they pointed the communicator at the moon. Eddy and Kenny arrived bathed in a faint rainbow. The hire car was left locked under a tree, as if to keep it in the shade, with the park pass prominently displayed on the windscreen, several hiking and trail head maps were on the back seat along with a supply of dry foods, water bottles and an open journal detailing three hikes they intended to take. A hotel booking for the forthcoming night was left as a bookmark. After making sure there wasn't anyone around, the two humans and two small bears dissolved in a light orange glow.

Three days later an Air France flight with Chantel Becquerel the French lawyer on board touched down at Manchester airport. A taxi took her to a children's home in the Cheetwood area where she was expected. Stephanie Harris welcomed her and introduced her husband Nicholas, followed by their parents, Colin, Wendy, Kevin and Alice. In the dining room they sat and listened to the lawyer's perfect English informing them of the details of the substantial donation that had been made to their small charity.

"The donation has been made in such a manner that the best legal tax advantages can be utilised; also part of the donation is the free use of the services of my company for one year starting on the first of January 2024."

"We're all so excited and mystified at the same time, we cannot think who would have donated – as you say – a substantial sum to a poor little organisation such as ours," Stephanie said.

"All will become clear, I assure you. To business. On signature of the relevant documents this charity will become the Ultimate Beneficial Owner of Cambridge Property Holdings Limited, a private limited company registered in the jurisdiction of Gibraltar. The assets of the company consist of thirty-seven residential properties in and around the Cambridge area valued in June of this year at £21,375,000 approximately. Four and a quarter million pounds sterling in the company bank account in Switzerland, and forty-three thousand pounds in an international account in Jersey. The company turnover for last year was–" here Chantel flipped over to the last page, "£873,268 with a net profit of 38.43%. The company has no debtors, liens or loans."

"Bloody hell!" exclaimed Nicholas with his eyes popping.

"To continue, there is the matter of the second company, Societé Escapade Productions, registered in Paris, France, and has for a number of years held retained profits of eighty-seven pounds and thirty one pence, twenty-eight thousand, seven hundred and three Euros, eleven cents as French Savings Certificates, and twenty-one thousand and fifty-six pounds sterling in English ISAs. I have the stock transfer forms here for the Trustees of your charity to sign for both companies, I will witness them and the business is complete. Oh, one last thing. I have a portable hard drive which I have been asked to give you, it can be accessed by any computer or a TV so equipped."

Chantel presented the papers and witnessed them adding the company seal. She bid them farewell after informing them their copies of all the documents would be sent by courier, her company would attend to all the legal side of things including the filings and contacting of the banks. After reminding Stephanie she should work out what they wanted to do and contact her so they could use the tax advantages available to ensure they maximised every aspect of their donation, she gave a discreet wave as the taxi pulled away.

"I can't take it all in, can you?" Stephanie asked the rest.

"Who are these people, has anyone any ideas? I don't have a clue." Nicholas scratched his head and looked at the rough valuation list the lawyer had left them.

Colin looked at Wendy and shrugged, his face a questioning blank. Alice had been staring out the window and thinking hard. Something was knocking to come in through the back door of her memory. Kevin picked up the hard drive.

"Shall we see if this throws any light on the problem?" he ventured, looking round the back of the TV in the corner.

The remote control danced over the menu options and located the hard drive as a media server. A few clicks later a single mp4 file icon showed up on the screen. Nicholas opened it and the screen went black for a second then a very low-resolution image appeared.

"I know that face, who the heck – I don't believe it, that's Eric, what was his name, got it – Marstone, from Leeds, he's in his twenties there, the black guy on Fender bass, he was French I think, that's Dan Lavigne, just a minute, the bass drum – look at the bass drum, this is Escapade, the college band!" Kevin exclaimed.

"So that has to be Alan Courtney on the keyboards and Flick Bowden, as she was then, is the drummer," Colin added.

"Didn't they split it up a couple of years after our weddings, they were living miles away, the last I remember was they were down south somewhere, working for a hi-tech American company, Dan and Alan went into business in Leeds and then I think they moved to France. I'm not entirely sure, mind, it's a long while ago," Alice volunteered. "Got to be coming up for forty – no, more like fifty years back."

"This is all starting to make a bit of sense now, didn't Chantel mention one of the companies was Escapade Productions or something?" Stephanie asked, looking for confirmation on the papers the lawyer had left.

The video quality had improved a little and the sound was considerably clearer, the band were now at the front of the stage taking a bow, then an unseen member of the audience yelled out, 'Do Toad, Do Toad'. The video broke up for a few seconds then the camera pointed at Alan with a beer in his hand; Eric and Dan were stood either side of the drum kit and Flick was pounding out the old Cream number on her own.

"That was me yelling," Kevin beamed as he spoke, "this has to be the Crown and Compass near Stockport; it was a huge venue back in the mid-seventies."

"And I was the one doing the filming," confirmed Wendy.

Toad finished and the picture broke up before showing a high-quality modern clip of a couch in a pleasant-looking lounge. Two figures walked round and sat down facing the camera.

"Hi guys, I guess you've worked out who's behind the little Christmas present you've just received. Eric and I have been retired now for a few years and we had this idea to donate most of our, for want of a better word, wealth, to your deserving cause."

"We were thinking about the gig you just watched, sorry the quality wasn't so good in the seventies, and we were thinking about the Hadrian's Wall walk and the charity gigs we did together," Eric continued after holding up a large picture of them at the Wallsend monument. "We know your kids, Nick and Steph, are carrying on with the good work and as we have no children of our own this is what we came up with."

"It's me again." Flick was holding up a company registration certificate to the camera. "We're Cambridge Holdings and Dan and Alan ran Escapade Productions, we sadly lost Dan to cancer a while back and Alan followed him ten days later. He wanted us to present the company to a worthy cause, so that's how it came to you."

"Make sure you call the lawyer in France, she's inherited Dan and Alan's company, they left her the stock because she's good and honest," Eric added. "We're going to spend the next few years travelling, there's still a lot of places we've not seen yet and hopefully before we kick the bucket we can knock a few places off the list. We'll drop you a postcard from time to time, have a great Christmas, bye."

They both waved at the camera until the screen went black.

"Bloody hell!" Nicholas said again. "Nearly fifty years ago, bloody hell."

The car hire company reported their vehicle as stolen two days after the return date passed. The actual car was discovered by hikers two weeks after that, by which time Flick and Eric had been gone for forty-two days. A search of the surrounding area turned up Eric's wallet with his credit cards, driver's licence and ninety-five soggy dollars in cash still inside. Hanging from it on a ring were the car keys. Police examined the car and its contents, the findings were presented to the court of enquiry a month later. They had come to the conclusion from the circumstantial evidence that Mr and Mrs Marstone had set off on one of several hikes in the park and had somehow become lost in the wilderness. The car contained enough evidence to support the theory that foul play was not a part of the scene. The court returned an open verdict of missing.

Back in the UK the police in Cambridge visited their home address, the neighbours and later their friends all told the same story – they were selling up and travelling the world, seeing all the places on their 'bucket list'. The first stop was going to be America. Further questions led to the undivided opinion the Marstones had a rock-solid marital relationship and they were always on the go doing something, laughing and joking, enjoying life to the full.

Eventually the French law firm were asked to provide details of the donation that had been carried out just before they left England for what was now looking more like the final time. The process was entirely legal, a video of the interview in Paris was used to show there was no pressure or force used. The fact of the second company being donated added weight as other people, albeit dead, were involved and the majority shareholders had been the original owners of the law firm controlling the transfers. Further evidence was processed when Nicholas and Stephanie played the video on the hard drive to the investigating officers.

By October Mr and Mrs Marstone were declared a missing persons cold case, with special circumstances. The authorities had agreed there was nobody with a motive to kill them, their wills and testament amounted to approximately £87,000 in a single bank account, which had been operated normally right up to the day they left for California, they had two private pensions that would have given them an excellent standard of living without depleting their account. Furthermore, the value of their estate would have raised a kidnapping or ransom scenario; however, the donation of the majority of their wealth had ruled this out. The overwhelming evidence of their solid mental and marital stability added to the issue and finally the fact that although they were both over seventy years of age they were fit, experienced hikers, that according to the evidence were starting a road-trip of a lifetime. Privately the investigating officers held the belief they had fallen into an icy stretch of water and died of hypothermia, or it was down to a wild animal attack.

Over the course of the year Nicholas and Stephanie made several trips to Paris. Chantel had devised the best way of liquidising enough of the donation to build what they in mind and at the same time endow it for the foreseeable future. Property to the value of £12,500,000 was sold and a large old manor house had been purchased; this one had a considerable acreage of grassland attached to it, unlike the one Stephanie's parents had been asked to stage a charity show at in 1975, which is where the six of them had got the idea from. The inside was fitted out to make it suitable for children with special needs, the idea being to give their long-suffering parents a much-needed break for a few weeks. Respite care normally didn't run to allowing enough time for the parents to mend the problems in their relationship with each other and hopefully save it. This establishment was going to change all that. The grassland was carefully turned into a scientifically-designed adventure playground divided into areas that reflected not only the ages of the children but their wildly differing capabilities as well. Most of the activities were not only fun but carefully designed to deliver special treatments or be rich in social interactions, all in fresh new ways. It took most of the year to convert and build. Nicholas worked closely with the various contractors whilst Stephanie started hitting the media to get coverage of what was happening and at the same time discovering they were receiving a lot more donations from the public than ever before. The opening ceremony was held in March, the Mayor pulling the cord to open the curtains across the plaque in the main entrance.

"It is my great pleasure to declare this wonderful enterprise well and truly open; welcome, boys and girls of all ages, to the Escapade Hotel," he announced with a wide smile.

Underneath the main sign were the names and pictures of the four musicians and two slogans, carved into the wood in a flowing script, 'The Show Must Go On' came first, below was 'Where There's a Will There's a Way', and right at the bottom, carved in capitals, INGUZ and the double X's.

Seven years later the 'Escapade' as it was shortened to had become the best respite care facility in the country, Eric and Flick were also declared legally dead in America and England. No clothing, equipment, bodies or body parts were ever found other than the wallet wedged half in the mud near a stream. Chantel opened a large brown envelope and read the will. She informed Nicholas the charity was the sole recipient of the remainder of the Marstones' estate.

Eric held Flick's hand and squeezed it as they stared in awe through the huge floor to ceiling window in what Eddy had told them was their new home. The view was one Eric had yearned to see ever since the Apollo mission had landed on the moon in 1969.

"Look, you can see Britain now, and there's Spain," he told Flick excitedly.

"This is amazing, I'm going to have to pinch myself to see if I'm dreaming." She smiled.

They were led along well-lit passages and made several vertical trips in large elevators. Kenny stopped outside a tall pair of doors, roughly the size of a set of double doors on Earth but twice as high. He reached out for a hand.

'Take a picture of the sign on the door, until you learn the language it will help you find your home.'

He waved a paw at a yellow circle in the middle and the doors parted. What was inside made Flick open her mouth and gape in astonishment. Eric too stood just inside the threshold with no words coming from the space between his teeth. Once through the huge doors they had stepped into the hall of their Cambridge house; beyond it was the dining room, the lounge and all their furniture. Flick headed for the kitchen, Eric mounted the stairs. They met in the garden where everything they remembered was in its proper place including Jeepy by the pond and Wolfie under the tree. Looking up, they saw a blue cloudless sky high above them. They sat down on one of the benches and spent a while just looking at everything there was to see, wordlessly, but with increasingly larger smiles.

Eddy jumped up onto Flick's lap.

'Do you both like it? We tried to get it as close as possible,' he thought direct into their heads.

"It's absolutely perfect, we love it. Thank you both so much," Flick thought and spoke at the same time for both of them.

'Go upstairs and rest now, the first time you travel in what you might like to call an atomiser is a bit unsettling, worse than ten continuous rollercoaster rides over a ploughed field.'

Eric sat up in bed and spent a while trying to take it all in.

"Makes Star Trek seem tame," he said just before his eyes shut.

Flick undressed, found her hairbrush exactly where it should have been and looked round the bathroom door. Finding the toothpaste wasn't hard either; she came out and made to hang her bra across Eddy's head.

"You still OK with this little job?" She grinned at him then wormed her way into Eric's arm.

She swore to Eric in the morning Eddy had puffed his chest out, perhaps it was pride, she proffered as a reason.

The time had come for them to be taken to the Backtime machine. Kenny had explained to them how it would be a more complicated and longer operation than he and Eddy had performed on Hans and Heidi. Their Backtime process was going to cover every single cell, every atom and one of the most important things was how skin was treated differently to everything else. He went on to explain skin had to be immersed in a fluid that allowed it to be at the correct tension and flexibility across the Backtimed body. The process would take four Earth hours and they would be asked to enter the pool of fluid and swim around in it, making sure they completely submerged themselves by diving down to the bottom and coming back up to the top every ten minutes or so. This way the skin would be exactly the right size and shape over the entire surface of their bodies. The only thing that would not Backtime was their hair – this was due to it being dead when it left the skin – however, the replacement hair that grew after the process would be the colour and texture relative to the age they now were.

Eddy asked if they had any questions. Many years ago Eric had undergone a vasectomy as it was what they both wanted and the simplest procedure of the two sterilisation options. Flick had passed childbearing age some thirty years ago. The question was simply a matter of what would they have to do after the Backtime process to avoid Flick becoming pregnant. Eddy replied by saying Eric's procedure would not be reversed and Flick would not have to consider ovulation or menstruation; adjustments could be made if they agreed. They did.

The first part of the process was to expose them to the beam emanating from the ceiling, the pool they were floating in unaided took care of their skin. They undressed, Flick unhooked the silver chain to place her wand next to the other jewellery and slid into the buoyant clear liquid with Eric. Eddy collected their belongings and left, closing the door behind him.

It took almost fifteen minutes before they began to notice the first differences – the veins in their hands were less prominent, wrinkles began to smooth out and the tops of their arms looked a little less thin. After the first hour had elapsed eyesight was improving and muscle growth could be felt and then seen. Strength in all limbs increased, it took less effort to dive to the bottom of the pool. The effects in the second and third hours were felt more than observed as the process reached the internal organs; they both laughed as the fluid bubbled when trapped wind was released. The final hour concentrated on the brain, then making the last few external changes. They swam around and floated, idly looking at the bodies they remembered when they were twenty-five or so and could only until now see in old photographs.

Eddy opened the door and brought them a long clear cup of bright pink liquid.

"Drink this, it will refresh you, you might like to call it lunch."

"Wow! I can hear you. Without having to touch you," Flick gasped in amazement.

"This is going to make things so much easier," Eric added. "I was wondering how we were going to communicate if we're apart."

Eddy smiled and collected the empty glasses from them.

"You might like to try thinking to each other, that still works, you have said many times in the past, Flick, that Eric has taken the words right out of your mouth."

She thought about the words, 'Love you to the moon and back' and received 'Love you to the end of time' in return.

"That's still amazing, and here we are on the moon!" She grinned.

"Just the end of time to do then," he joked.

Back in their garden Kenny showed them what else the communicator was capable of. Apart from what they'd already discovered and that it was a small limited use Backtime device, they were fascinated to learn it could provide them with air to breathe for a short time, transport them over short distances, although long by Earth standards, by effectively reducing and redirecting gravity. It held a small non-perishable supply of food and drink and a lot of other extremely handy and practical tools Eric found totally incredible. Kenny gave Eric another communicator, identical to the one Flick had but coloured dark brown. He asked if this one was any different. He learned they were identical, it was just a different colour so they could tell them apart.

They spent a while trying out their newly acquired knowledge. Flick found she could float above the pond just by thinking, by putting it into her mouth could breathe easily underwater. The next experiment gave her a deep warm feeling of achievement. By pointing the jewel at a wilting plant the flower opened and the plant stood up when she thought the word 'heal' – Eddy said she had sent the plant Backtime two Earth months. Eric repeatedly watched with total wonder as the device became a wrench, a saw, a screwdriver, in fact after an hour he only had to look at something and the device would become the right tool for the job. He too attempted to hover above the pond, it took him three attempts and a pair of wet feet before he got it right.

Eddy came in and asked them to come across to the corner of the garden behind Jeepy where there was another door they hadn't noticed before. It was covered in climbing plants but the foliage moved with the door when it opened. On the other side was a laboratory complete with a workshop and a space with desks, and above them every book and manual they had ever owned. The last piece of equipment was so incredible they had to sit down the impact was so great. Built into the wall was a monitor screen of huge dimensions, it was controlled by touch, voice or thought, the screen could divide into many smaller screens either overlapping or mitred together. It could accept inputs and give outputs to both of them simultaneously, and incorporated the most advanced, huge, 3D printer they had ever seen. Eddy asked Flick to think the word 'clothes', the screen responded by showing a picture book of her entire Earth wardrobe; each item had a yellow circle underneath the image. Her told her to press the button. A small drawer opened below the screen, inside was the dress she had selected.

"When it's dirty, place it in here and the next time you select it you'll get a clean one," Kenny explained. "If you want something new or things start to wear out, you can duplicate it using the printer, watch," Kenny said, picking up one of the towels from the Backtime room. He tossed it in the printer drawer and pressed another yellow button. In under ten seconds the drawer reopened and revealed two identical towels. One damp, one dry and new.

"Feel free to play with it, any mistakes can be re-cycled in this drawer here," Eddy pointed to the larger grey-fronted drawer on the extreme right.

"Over here in this corner are the blue drawers, this is where you find food and drink. The principle is the same, think 'food', select what you want, collect it from these drawers, trash goes in the green bin," Kenny said. "Any questions?"

The next part of their familiarisation was to help them learn the written language. They were both given what could only be described as a very large but impossibly light pair of headphones, they were to wear them whenever they felt the need to rest or sleep. As their minds cleared and brains wound down, the headphones would impart the written word into their memories. It would take two rests, Kenny said.

Eddy thought it was a good time to tell them about the concept of 'night and day'.

"You've been living for over seventy Earth years, going to bed when it's dark and getting up when it's light. Night and day don't mean much up here, or anywhere else in the universe when compared to Earth. I guess you've experienced jet lag many times, this lifestyle can generate similar effects. We think until you become acclimatised to living in this environment you should try and keep to Earth time. Up to now you have been going to bed when you see the artificial sky getting darker; this has been programmed to keep a sense of night and day for you to be stable in. As time passes, you will accept there is no real night and day, but you can adjust the sky yourself to compensate for how you're feeling. It takes a while and you may get a little disorientated, but time is something we all have a lot of, don't rush it."

It was Flick who used her communicator and thought the word 'night' and the light in their rooms would dim, the sky in the garden would turn black and they could look up at the stars. They lay in bed looking at themselves and touching each other. The impact of the events over the last few hours had not completely sunk in yet.

"You look so beautiful, Flick, exactly as I remember you, it's only your hair that's still as it was, like mine I guess, everything else seems to be back in 1977," Eric whispered.

"I totally agree, my love, it's incredible," she answered, wearing her mischievous face and winking just before she climbed on top of him. "I'm just testing, a little experiment, that's all."

"Of all the women on that planet below us I somehow managed to find the most beautiful, utterly wonderful, cleverest, wanton girl that ever drew breath, fall hopelessly in love with her and now it looks as if I'm stuck with her for eternity." He just managed to finish the words before his mouth found itself pressed between two large familiar breasts.

"Enough talking, your Highness, actions speak louder than words. Do your husbandly duty, Mr Marstone, I'll settle for page thirteen, a twenty-four and a thirty-one if you're not too tired."

"No rest for the wicked it seems."

"You're a devil, Eric Marstone, a bloody devil."

Some time later a wolf howled.

The next few weeks were spent learning new skills and finding their way round the huge spaceship that sat inside the moon. The moon was indeed hollow, inside were three other ships similar to the one they were now calling home. Eric become amazed by the moon. He told Flick it was made of a material that can morph into anything they want it to, Wesme explained it's somewhat more than a material, he and Flick would be given the opportunity to examine it.

"It's possibly the perfect combination of biology and engineering so it will interest both of you."

They came to the conclusion it was a living cross between metal, ore and stone, ultimate bioengineering except it had happened naturally.

Jeepy had a drum kit and a guitar inside as well as the garden chairs. Wolfie had all the photographs from before the digital age and every journal and notebook they had ever written. The artificial evenings were spent watching the movies of their adventures, reading old diaries and experimenting with the foods Flick found on the monitor. Eric had eventually managed to combine three liquids that tasted more or less like wine, only the colour was wrong – Chablis wasn't bright orange. One 'evening', they had programmed the blue sky to fade to black over the course of four Earth hours, Eddy and Kenny, who dropped in often, asked if they could live with them. Eddy explained they had enjoyed their time at the Manchester Madhouse and Cambridge, and they really missed them. They moved in the next 'day', occupying the larger of the two spare bedrooms. It was then revealed they were, like them, lovers.

As time passed they narrated their story of how Wesme and the others had offered them the same opportunity they had taken. They were the last two survivors of a horrendous war that destroyed, as Wesme had said, everything on their world. Eric asked what had made the aliens offer them the opportunity to Backtime. First Kenny told them that not only were they were a couple with a deep love for each other, Eddy was actually female. She had the rare quality of being a shape shifter with an extra skill which was useful to Wesme and the aliens.

Here he had to fill them in with some background.

"Our kind can all shape shift, but if we choose to copy another living being, then all other shape shifters know which is the copy. This means any criminal activity where duplication might be useful is not possible as any duplicate might as well have a label on saying 'FAKE'. Eddy's special skill was to be able to duplicate another being without any other shape shifters being aware. Right until the destruction of our world she was monitoring what was happening in the corridors of power on both sides of the war without being detected by using her ability and reporting back to Wesme as things unfolded."

This was why Wesme had removed both of them before their world destroyed itself. The question of what they looked like in reality was never actually asked. Eric and Flick didn't want to push them as they had never offered to morph into what shape could be called 'native'. Slowly though there were changes. The two bears altered in subtle ways: Kenny lost his straps and openable section, Eddy's belly no longer had a zipper, they both formed knees, just the one pair of elbows and if you looked hard their paws had fingers and a well concealed opposing thumb. Eric asked why they had become bears in the first place.

"I looked around Letchworth a lot when Flick was small, I had guessed at a Teddy Bear when I arrived. It seemed to me a bear never looked out of place anywhere, so I never saw any reason to change. They were seen all over in many different places, most children seemed to have one, but they blended into the bigger picture," Eddy replied, "Later when Kenny arrived permanently we used the same shape. Over the years we still saw no reason to change. Looking back we became just another accepted thing in the everyday world of humans."

Wesme arrived soon after the sun had illuminated west Africa. He wanted the four of them to come to what he called the bridge, saying this was the nearest English word to describe it.

Several other aliens were floating just above the deck as they entered the main area. Eric was amazed as he'd expected to see huge rows of screens and flashing lights along with banks of controls to operate the millions of functions that a ship this size must need. Instead he looked across to two aliens sending rainbows and single colour beams out of communicators to a single matt black panel.

"This makes anything we've got look like an abacus," Flick said.

"It's all about light waves, I started to read about it when Einstein's theory was starting to be expanded, Quantum Physics, String Theory and so on as you know."

Flick nodded as Wesme approached. Communication was so much easier now. Wesme had learned English and they had managed to master the aliens' humming. It made more sense if you thought the sound rather than listened to it. Nobody needed to say anything as telepathy took over.

They were being asked to retrieve another object; however, this time it was going to be a lot harder. The object was part of a ship similar to the one they were on. Some time ago it had been near a planet in a distant galaxy when it had been affected by a pulsing wave that effectively caused it to crash land on the planet below. This was the final information the ship sent. As with the ship in the Italian lake, the crew had taken to the survival pods and sent out a distress call. The signal was so weak it had barely been detectable, the same pulse had all but disabled it. As the briefing unfolded, the ship was tracking the source and had locked onto a vague point of origin based on the ship's previous transmissions. This was where Flick was needed – her ability to locate the pod accurately among the pulse interference was vital to the rescue. All four looked at the screen showing a blue green planet that appeared to be covered in a tidal slush. The surface was best described as a flexible skin of strong sand. The green areas being harder and thicker than the blue, which were thin and unstable. Silicon-based life forms were detected living on the surface and another species that lived under the skin of the planet in what to be for the present was surmised to be a sea of molten glass. The screen went black.

"That is the end of their last report," Wesme told them.

The rescue mission was to begin immediately and would comprise a three-stage journey after which more accurate information would be gathered. They intended to park in an orbit outside of any pulse fields they could detect in order not to suffer the same fate as the previous ship. The first stage of the journey was a light speed jump to the nearest wormhole. Stage two would be the wormhole transfer, then the final stage to the planet in question. The whole journey time would be eleven Earth months, there would be another briefing when they arrived, Wesme informed them as they were shown off the bridge.

"I wonder when we start," Eric thought out loud, a practice he was becoming used to adopting.

"We've started," replied Kenny, "two weeks to the worm hole; unfortunately it's not just past Pluto," he added.

"How long in the wormhole, Kenny?" Flick asked.

"Only a matter of minutes, the long part is the ten months to the planet at the other end, to say it's a bit remote is an understatement," he answered.

"Time for a beaker of blue tea and a yellow sticky bun with pink blobs on in the garden then, I think I'll jog back and get some exercise."

36

During the months that passed the ship drew closer to its target. Flick and Eric spent their time discovering and learning as much about the spacecraft as they could hope to understand. They found out most of the ship was actually given over to the propulsion system, survival machinery, general storage areas and other specialised equipment. They once tried making love in zero gravity, giving in after neither could stop laughing. Another alien with an English name sounding like 'Korra' had taught them the ship's layout and showed them how to use their communicators as a map and a means of transport.

"That explains the wand's GPS and traffic bulletins." Eric smiled.

"Clever, the way they reflected the communicator's power to the wand, Eddy hadn't delivered it when we found that French butcher shop." Flick grinned.

"Same goes for traffic jams on the way to Stephanie's christening," Eric added

Wesme took them to one of the holds at the front of the ship and showed them a Shuttle Pod.

"When we arrive, the first stage will be for you to try and narrow the search field. In order for you to survive on this planet you will have to work within the confines of this pod, it will protect you against anything that world can throw against you, we just need to teach you how to use it."

An intense training course followed; by the time the ship was within a month of the target planet, Flick and Eric were good enough at working the many built-in tools and instruments and manoeuvring their pods inside the ship's hangars to be considered ready. It had taken a while to adapt, just thinking the action you wanted was enough rather than pulling on levers or pressing buttons.

They entered orbit. On the bridge considerable progress had been made. The pulse had weakened considerably and was visible in the orange ray shooting out from the front of the ship. The briefing had some new information to reveal.

The crust or surface of the planet was occupied by amphibians who managed to live on small creatures with hexagonal-shaped bodies which they farmed from the glass sea. They were aware of the much larger creatures that seemed to be feeding on the same food source but in greater numbers. When the larger creatures arrived at a place where food was being gathered, the smaller amphibians hooted and howled, becoming agitated and angry. This was creating an imbalance and Wesme announced it was the start of a familiar pattern. The other aliens hummed their agreement.

The ship continued to orbit the blue green world, the pulse although weak was still managing to jam or scramble the supposed signal from the survival pod. The new problem was the nature of the signal itself. Kenny explained they were now tracking two signals, neither one was accurate or exactly in the format they were expecting. No sooner had a lock been established than it vanished, only to start again somewhere else, not once but twice.

"I wonder if one is a mirror or ghost signal," Eric asked, looking at the display.

"We thought the same; however, they have two separate signatures and one is far more erratic than the other, when we can hang onto them for long enough that is," Kenny replied.

Two Shuttle Pods were landing; Wesme was in one, the other pilot coupled the pod up to the black control panel with a yellow ray. Information from the pod flashed across the wall, the signal had been strongest near the south pole and the second erratic signal had been found to be at its most stable roughly two miles under the surface, but appeared randomly all across the planet. More details of the two species were uploading, the amphibians were spending most of their time on the hard crust near the pole whilst the larger 'sea' dwellers were excited about the second signal and had begun to converge on it only to change course when its erratic nature shifted location. It seemed they could sense the signal and it attracted them. Wesme told them the problem in locking onto the signal was continuing – they had tried three times at close range and the same thing happened, the signal stopped transmitting.

"This has prevented us from making a simple rescue; it is now becoming complex," he telepathed.

Flick and Eric climbed into the Shuttle Pods and followed the programmed course to the planet's surface, coming to rest side by side a hundred feet above the crust. Eddy and Kenny were in a third pod a little way off near to where the glass sea began. Flick started the detection cycle and confirmed the crust was a high-density silicon with another element fused into it.

"The other material is not in the database," Eric reported.

The sea turned out to be molten silicon or liquid glass. Whatever the unknown material was, it effectively stopped the molten sand claiming the crust. It was managing to effectively block the change of state that should have happened.

They began the search, the pole signal was detected and followed; as the pods grew nearer the signal weakened. By the time they were hovering over the calculated point of origin there wasn't anything to register other than static.

"I'm feeling we should separate and see if I can have a vision; you move off and hold on to your communicator," Flick said.

Eric put two miles or so between them, Eddy and Kenny followed. Ten minutes later she reported there had been no activity.

"Shall we try the other more erratic signal or have you got another idea?" Eric asked.

"There's nothing to lose," came the reply.

The pods moved over the spectacularly-coloured sea towards the second signal point. Roughly halfway over, Flick had a vision and her device jewel lit up. She called out to the others, and stopped the pod. Slowly she flew backwards on the same course, then stopped when the jewel lit up and began to hum. Moments passed as she swung her pod up and down the flight path, then at right angles until the point where the strongest hum was located.

"I have a contact point, Eric, fly in a circle using my pod as a centre, move out a few miles when you complete the first lap; Eddy, Kenny, do the same but two miles higher, let's see if we can triangulate and lock on."

On the screen back at the ship, three red dots glowed and fired out a thin blue beam which met on the surface of the sea. Above them Korra moved the ship into position and sent its green ray down to the connection point and drove deep into the molten glass.

Eric said afterwards as soon as the surface of the sea broke open, he recognised part of the object being raised as similar to the object recovered in the New Mexico desert. It looked as if it had been attacked. Kenny was of the same mind, there were deep gouges in the top. After the object was safe in the main hangar, they discovered their prediction was right: the larger lifeforms had tried to eat it, the gouges matched the oval hole at one end of their bodies. Wesme arrived from the bridge.

"This is what we feared when the two signals appeared. We have recovered the ship's recorder, it is embedded in this section of the remains. We have not recovered the survival pod, this is part of the general wreckage."

The recorder was interrogated and more information placed in the ship's computer. Sadly there wasn't anything helpful about where the survival pod might have ended up.

Korra spoke to the four of them in the garden.

"We have to re-think our strategy; there are several possible outcomes. The pod may still be on this planet but unable to send a signal. If the ship exploded before dropping into the planet below, the pod may have been blown out into space or it could have crashed into the satellite we can see from the window. Lastly, the pod may have been totally destroyed, in which case there is nothing to recover. We are discussing the next course of action; rest now and we will meet again later."

On the bridge, activity on the screen was unfolding faster than humans could take in. Wesme told them there had been no new signals detected from the planet or its satellite. A decision had yet to be made on the next course of action; here, Flick asked if she could make a suggestion, and her wish was granted.

Several other aliens joined Wesme and Korra whilst Flick explained her idea.

"I'm Flick, the human with psychic powers," she said to introduce herself to the others, a little unnecessarily but she had not managed to rely totally on telepathy yet. "I think if I can take a pod down to the planet it will take me a while, but I can fly over the whole of the surface searching for weak signals or another vision. If I take one of the sentinels with me, we can both fit in one pod, they can communicate directly to you. If I find anything, then my husband Eric and the other sentinel can join us and triangulate the points needed. If this fails, then we do the same to the satellite. If that fails, then it would appear the pod might be lost. But we don't want to give up; where there's a will there's a way, Eric and I always say."

Wesme and the others hummed between themselves, the word 'Inguz' came out at the end. Korra turned to them and telepathed:

"We are agreed, your idea is a practical one and we support it. Go and begin your search; we have alerted the pod bay."

Flick and Eddy flew over the planet from pole to pole without finding a single signal or receiving any visions. Kenny and Eric had constantly watched the screen on the bridge, both holding their communicators tight. Hope diminished after they landed in the pod bay to take their ninth rest period. When the tenth period was roughly two-thirds over, they ran out of planet to search. Flick was still adamant she wanted to do the same to the satellite.

"I can't give in, Eric, I feel it's out there, I know it, I told Korra. Eddy senses something as well."

"I understand, I'm hopeful too and think we must follow this to the end, for better or worse we have to eliminate everything possible."

Eric held her close to his chest, she smiled and kissed his cheek. He looked down and saw two closed eyes, sleep had taken her. He thought 'dark' and the lights went out.

Whilst they rested, the ship had moved to place itself in orbit round the satellite. Roughly a quarter of the size of the planet, it was the last hope of finding the survival pod.

Flick eased herself into the flight seat, Eddy hopped onto her lap. Since this search operation began, she'd started wearing one of Flick's old bras, suitably adapted, as a flying helmet just as she had in the past. Nobody commented on this, not even Wesme.

It was almost at the end of the third search period the vision hit. Flick let Eddy connect the wand and communicator to the ship whilst she put the pod in a static hold. The screen on the bridge lit up like a fairground ride and Kenny grabbed hold of Eric. Two more pods joined the first and soon all were locked onto the joint wand and communicator signal. Both were glowing blue and pulsing. Back on the ship Korra moved them into position. Wesme and two others were humming about why the wand was acting as it was, they decided it was Flick's power that had activated it.

Once again a large lump of battered material was lifted out of a pit full of dusty gravel and rock-strewn debris that had been its grave for some time. By the time the pods were back in the hangar the survivors had been transferred. Seventeen more aliens climbed out of their resuscitation chambers, none the worse for their ordeal. Wesme asked them to come to the bridge, here they met the survivors and were thanked individually.

As the years passed Eric and Flick became accustomed to their new life and although they worked hard at anything they were asked to do, they never managed to forget their old home, the Earth. Once Eric had dimmed the sky over their garden and he and Flick were looking up at another new galaxy sat on the old bench with their arms round each other when Kenny pointed up and told them the star in the middle of a cluster of sixteen was their old home. Eddy looked up and told them they had asked to go and see if it was still barren; it was, he said, with a sad edge to his thoughts.

Eric wondered how Earth was faring, Flick's rough calculation estimated it to be 2480. The four spent some time recalling their travels together, an enjoyable slice of nostalgia. Every once in a while the drum kit and guitar came out of Jeepy for a jam session in the simulated evening. Flick put the dining room curtains on and Eddy turned into Fenrir just so they could see her dancing in the garden. Kenny went over to Jeepy and disappeared into the supplies room behind the old 'Toad'. A few minutes later he emerged with his paws behind his back. He told Flick to close her eyes and open her hands, then he placed a packet of chocolate digestives across her palms.

"It took a bit of programming, but you guys always said where there's a will there's a way."

Time passed and the garden became a sort of memory lane for all of them. It was when the ship was near to Alpha Centauri that Wesme came to speak to them about Earth. The information he had for them wasn't good, no matter which way you looked at it. Life on Earth was almost at a critical level, spiralling towards extinction or destruction. They listened and asked if there was anything they could do. Wesme said it was probably too late; however, there was one chance, if they could plant the seeds of a new idea into just a few minds it might be possible to make a new start. Everything would be in vain if the powers that held the machinery of destruction unleashed it.

"Paradoxically, we need their greed for money to outweigh their passion for violence this time," Wesme commented to them.

The ship entered the moon and from there Flick and Eric made a series of visits to the most likely-looking individual the computers and sensors could detect. Oddly enough he lived to within two miles of where Dan and Alan's house used to stand. It would be January, 2788 when they arrived.

37

You will recall I was asked if I had ventured outside my door and to try and understand everything they had told me to record. I am unsure about how they manage to appear in my room. They say they are living and working with aliens, I cannot make any sense of this, but they are real enough, to see and to touch.

My first task then was to try and make sense of what I have been told through the tale. It was a lot more difficult than I could have ever imagined. My friends from the past are called Marstones. Their world, their life, was completely different to my own small world. I could not comprehend how they could mix and mingle with so many other people. I haven't seen anyone 'in the flesh', as they call it, for many years. So long ago I cannot put a date on it. In my world we live a segregated life, eating, sleeping, working without ever leaving our residence.

The viewscreen allows me to work and communicate with fellow workers, friends and anyone from government who needs to. People never meet in person, I have no family. The concept is beyond me. I don't need to leave the residence structure, all my food arrives by drone, one has landed today – it has enough to last me for the next period, the friends from the past called it a month. Water for drinking arrives in the same manner four times per period.

I am alarmed about sex. The Marstones have told me they actually enjoyed the feelings and sensations so much they had sex as many times as they could. I needed to understand the words lust and love, they told me. I will ask if they had robots for sex in their time.

I turned my attention to the book of maps, an atlas they said. I became fascinated with Scotland: the viewscreen said it was a place *near farm AF3419. The history files informed me it contained forests, mountains and fishing rivers. The fishing rivers had been dammed to make fishing farms, the forests were cut down and all the animals were harvested. There were no pictures of Scotland in the computer library but there were on the iPad. I did see a picture of a fishing lake once, I couldn't imagine anyone wanting to travel over such a huge mass of water, either on it, under it, or above it. Now I am quite interested.*

My absorption in the atlas grew and before long I felt the urge to go outside and discover what there was to see. It was difficult, to say the least. For a long while I wandered inside my own residence structure trying to find the way out. After almost getting lost I copied the idea of the atlas and made my own map of the residence. I had looked from my window to try and calculate how many levels I would need to descend to the ground. I chose a cloudy day and could only count the nine levels below me before the clouds interfered. Either by good fortune or wisdom I managed to find the level of the ground. I felt strange, I didn't belong here, it was almost alien to me. There wasn't a single person down on the ground, I wondered if I was breaking the Code and a Police droid would arrest me. Only service bots and drones going about their tasks could be heard no matter how hard I strained my ears. There wasn't any sign of humans at all. There's nowhere to walk. The ground is full of trenches and rubbish. Rain sits in oily puddles. The sky is yellow, the sun looks blood red with a pale edge. I cannot find the moon, even down here. Across from my structure is another identical edifice. They stand in a long line all the way to the horizon in every direction. The horizon is not as distant as it should be, the yellow mist stops me seeing too far. Outside is quiet, eerily so, only the passing of a robot or drone, from which I hide, shatters the silence. I am shaking, I don't know why, there's so much I don't know yet, but I feel I want to know, even need to know. I returned to my structure and spent time looking over the atlas in detail; as it went dark outside I climbed into my sleep unit and continued to read the tale and look at the atlas. I wondered what it felt like to have another human lying here beside me. I wondered what it would feel like to touch another person. I wondered where in the atlas I was.

After sleep I woke, thinking about Portugal – like Scotland it featured in the tale and there were lots of pictures on the iPad. I asked the viewscreen, it had little to no information about Portugal. It was now incorporated into Spain, and that was known as farms AP 9921 to AR 5629. There was a whole section on cereal production and the coastal regions had a lot of fish farms. The main area of human population residences and work structures was at the Lisbon Commercial Centre. I started running down the Portugal entries, the viewscreen scrolling upwards as it made its way to the top of the list. I overshot and ended up in the next folder; it was named Paris. I don't know why but Paris seemed strangely familiar to me. In the afternoon I left my residence and began walking down a long wide gap in the residence blocks. In the ruins were old piles of stones and heaps of metal. Near a river I found an odd structure – it looked like a giant metal table on four legs which formed large metal arches. The top had long since vanished, if it ever had a top. I found a stairway leading up each of the legs but after fifty steps the way was barred with twisted metal and a chain running through the girders. Back in my residence I found a picture on the iPad of the whole structure; it is inconsistent because the female Marstone is in the picture, she obviously cannot be that old, thirty at most, yet it was a tower apparently built hundreds of years ago by Eiffel, an old time construction company no doubt. This seems to be proof that I am in Paris, I have to wait now until the Marstones return to confirm my theory about my location and what period of history they come from. I will continue to venture out into the city each day after I have completed my work schedule.

I have made another map of my own detailing the paths I have used. I can wander further away from my residence now I am sure of my way. The river is nearby, I can get there easily as I can walk further each day without getting tired. Some of my clothes are too big around the waist. I have made a strap from four package belts, my trousers don't fall down now.

I have discovered a whole system of tunnels under the city. They have large vehicles mounted on two metal rails that run in the tunnels, I think it is an old way of moving food across the city. It was here that I found her. She was hiding behind an old wooden box. I don't know who was more scared, her or me. I sat down and opened up a packet of sweet-food, placing one or two lozenges on the bench seat then walked away. She stepped forward and took them, looking at me as she did so. When the realisation dawned on her I was not going to attack, she smiled slowly and sat on the edge of the box. After a while she got up and walked slowly away into the tunnel. I think she wanted me to follow her, so I did so, also slowly and at a distance to avoid alarming her. At each turn she waited for me, then pointed down a side tunnel. By the time I had peered into the gloomy shaft she had gone but on the floor was a wooden plank with a strange item on it. The thing was as bright orange as the sun, about the size of the palm of my hand and soft to the touch. Instinct told me to pull it open, inside was wet and sticky. I sampled it. Never before had I tasted anything like this, the soft inner sections were also sweet and sticky. I ate it all but the orange skin.

The next day I went back to the tunnel and placed an assortment of foods from my supplies on the wood box. I did not have long to wait. She took the cartons and smiled at me, this time she allowed me to get closer before she moved off down the tunnel. At the split in the rails, she pointed as before, but this time she didn't vanish into the darkness. As I pulled another orange ball apart she came up behind me and held out a thin branch with black oval balls attached by stems. She pulled one off and pushed it towards my mouth. Over the next days we explored the underground passages together. She showed me where the food was coming from. At the end of one tunnel a whole storehouse full of plastic boxes was being stacked by robots and drones. When the robots were at the other end of the cavern, she opened a crate at random and took some of what was inside, replacing the lid afterwards. This was how she had survived. She lived in the tunnels and stole her food and water as it came through the store. I have found out she can talk. Now we can make real progress.

The Marstones came back today, they found us near the river. I told them I was in Paris, I babbled a lot about the things I'd found out. I told them about the city and asked how it had come to end up this way. They said it was all down to greed and war. I asked if it was only Paris, or were all the places in the atlas the same. They looked at each other, they seemed to communicate without speaking, the one with the red hair, the female, said if I wanted to they would show us some of the places in the atlas, we had to trust her and her friend. I told her I didn't know what trust was. The male Marstone told us.

We found ourselves stood between them, they had taken one of our hands each. The female held a small black rod with a violet jewel inset into the top in her right hand, a rainbow emanated from it when she closed her eyes. The male held a similar device. The walls seemed to dissolve and I found myself unbelievably floating in thin air above the city. Near the ruined steel table by the bend in the river we landed next to a what looked like a large sanitation droid. The Marstones beckoned us forward to the door that had opened up in the side. We sat down as the door closed, and the vehicle, for that is what it was, lifted off into the dusty city air. The speed increased, we were flashing over hundreds if not thousands of structures identical to the residence I lived in, the river was a grey-blue ribbon snaking below us. Suddenly the structures stopped, only to be replaced by countless fields of yellow and green. The never-ending squares finally did end, next to the biggest expanse of water I have ever seen; the speed increased, but it was almost meaningless now as I had nothing to refer to. A cliff rose out of the water then more land full of yellow and green fields continued towards the horizon, all growing identical plants and some bushes or trees.

We stopped near the edge of another cliff, the plants here were similar to the previous bushes, completely covered in the orange balls, with others bearing yellow coloured ovals. I wanted to try a yellow ball but the male Marstone advised against it. He was right, it doesn't taste good. We stood on the cliff top and looked at the water below, behind us droids were removing the orange and yellow balls from the trees and placing them in containers they pulled behind them. I didn't see another living person. The female said there were fish that lived in the water, we ate the fish, as we ate the plants from the fields, but I didn't recognise them as all my food comes as powders or lozenges. The male Marstone told us this was once called Portugal. We returned to the vehicle and rose into the air again, all that day we visited other places. I went to Rome, Moscow, Delhi, Beijing, Canberra and New York. Everywhere looked the same. At one point I asked if there was anywhere that resembles how it appeared in their time. They looked at each other and took us to a strange place with nothing in it at all. I asked where we were, they said this was deep into the Sahara Desert, a land covered in nothing but sand for as far as the eye could see. Not all the desert was empty, however; a lot of the vast stretches of sand had electrical generation panels lined up in their tens of thousands across the dunes, but no humans, just more droids. We returned to Paris. I told them about how I had discovered the female in the tunnels, they seemed happy about it. We went to the tunnels so she could show the Marstones all the things I had seen; she asked why had the world turned from their day to this broken landscape.

They told us about the wars. Fought by governments backed by huge corporations. The politicians that made vast fortunes as the continuous battles for control of the energy and food supply raged. Multi-national industrialists monopolised production of robotic droids along with residential construction projects, population control drugs along with overly expensive healthcare. This was just some of the financial pies grubby fingers were pushed into.

It was a long time ago when the population of the earth had begun to spiral out of control. Despite all the human efforts to save it the planet could not harvest enough food to feed the billions of *people who were living on it. Government had started trying to find new ways of growing food. The foods we could grow were genetically modified to make each plant grow twice as big and therefore feed more people, and of course make twice the profit. This worked better with crops than animals but still the population grew, even though in some parts of the planet it was against the code to have children. Over the years another problem arose that was almost as bad as the food problem.*

The vast numbers of people who were being born grew up and needed work; this would allow them to earn money and buy the food they needed and pay for somewhere to live. It soon became apparent that there wasn't enough work for the people to do. Some people managed to earn enough to survive by sharing their work with a friend, later the government made it compulsory, limiting the number of working hours per person to twenty-five in a seven-day cycle. That figure dropped to fifteen very soon afterwards. Then people complained they couldn't earn enough to eat. The government begrudgingly lowered the rent for a residence. Soon they introduced free transportation to work. Later everyone worked from their residence. Even then the greed started to increase to unheard-of levels. Governments would buy up whole crops only to misjudge the amount they needed and watch as the food went bad in the stores. Supply ships were taken over at sea by other countries in acts of piracy. Idiotically, crops were being burnt in the fields and farm animals slaughtered by neighbouring countries' soldiers and airforces in a ludicrous attempt to starve their so-called enemy into submission or face death. Soon wars were breaking out. Armies were fighting each other to protect the food supply.

During this time the mandatory birth control laws were passed, these failed and even closer controls were bought in. In the end all females were sterilised at birth, men were required to provide the health service with two semen samples to be frozen. Slowly the world moved to a situation where the entire population either worked in food or energy production, there were no other industries other than robotics, computer technology, construction and healthcare. The population shrank to a number that was almost sustainable, but it was to no avail. Eventually one large war managed to bring everything to a head. Although there were no major atomic explosions, the battle took over a year to run its course and afterwards the remaining counties agreed the only way they could survive in the aftermath was to make peace and try and feed everyone.

It seems hard to understand that I have no freedom compared to the Marstones. If I fail to do my work quota each day, my food and residence will be terminated. My healthcare will likewise cease to exist, I will cease to exist. I am worried. It seems even the peace that followed is not without the powerful few controlling the population. They promoted secular living, discouraging physical social contact by making people so scared of catching a virus or communicable disease they became paranoid and isolated. Sexual contact was discouraged then stamped out with the free issue of sexbots. Behaviour modification drugs were introduced into the water supply to dispense with anger and promote calm and peace. Personal transportation was eliminated, first by making fuel prices so high most people could not afford to buy even enough to go to work, secondly by permitting only public transport to be used; however, it did not take the politicians long to realise the public transport idea was contradictory to the virus scaremongering, so they virtually locked the whole planet down and used drones and robots to deliver anything the population needed and if possible reduced the number of options of items available to buy. In under a hundred years, everyone was living in identical apartments, wearing identical clothes, eating identical food, watching the same TV programmes, using the one and only government-controlled social media network and thinking identical thoughts. In a strange way, a lot of people felt safer and happier with all their thinking done for them and their obsession with trivia leapt to an unimaginable new high. Yet the female in the tunnel has survived. The male Marstone is talking to her.

It seems there is only her. She used to live and work in a food processing plant. One day she became unhappy with watching food being chopped, squeezed or sliced, so she waited to the end of her work period and vanished into the tunnels, not realising the computers would automatically delete her from the records if she failed to pass the security checking program. The Marstones are talking silently to each other. They are looking at the two of us and pointing to the atlas.

If we want to go, they will take us to Vancouver Island. It is the last refuge left on earth where we can live out our lives as close to theirs as possible. There is a good chance we will both live longer once we stop eating the government-supplied food which contains additives to restrict our life duration – one of my friends has long suspected this, sadly he died last year aged thirty.

The island seems deserted, there are some animals left and the land is good enough to grow some of our food. The big companies have ignored it due to a lot of the island being volcanic and will not grow the highly modified crops they need. As far as it's possible to determine, the governments of the world have forgotten about this place.

We went to have a look at the island. It is a beautiful place; neither of us have ever seen anything so wonderful. There are animals in the forests called elk and bears. We have found an old house made of logs and sheets of metal. The wood will need to be replaced but it will suffice for the present, it has six rooms and a freshwater stream running from the mountains behind. A bigger water fed by a river is close by, fish are jumping up the waterfalls. The Marstones have shown us how to chop wood, fish, make fire and provided tools to work the land. There are trees with nuts and fruit we can eat, and we can catch fish now we know how. Until we can grow cereals and vegetables to supplement these basics, we will have to survive. We are staying on the island.

Last night I had a strange dream, I thought I saw the Marstones standing over us radiating a violet light as we slept. My body began to feel warmer and it started to tingle. I woke lying in her arms, she said she had been dreaming too. Something had been inside her, she said. It had altered a part of her, she was rubbing her belly and looking thoughtful, but she didn't know what had happened. The male Marston has given me three names, I am Daniel John Robert. The female has named my friend Alana Helen Avril. They call us Dan and Al.

The Marstones have left us now. They have taught us many other things, including how to sail the boat we found in the bay. We have several more books; one is a list of foods that can be made into better foods – this is a recipe book. Another book is full of pictures of how the world used to look. The last one is full of pictures of two humans. It is called the Kama Sutra or the book of love. We face the future together, unafraid.

We didn't know at first the tale was a story of how things could be for us, now: it came to us both when we were sat by the campfire one evening. This is why we have to let you read it as it was dictated, then you may wish to join us on the outsides living in freedom. There are eight more couples who have joined us on the island; they have children, all born here. The earth is good enough to grow corn, barley, and potatoes as well as many vegetables. Looking back at where I am today, thousands of miles from where I once lived, surrounded by mountains and forests with a female for company and love, friends I can touch and animals to care for. I thought this life was impossible. Actually I was unaware it could even exist, I could not imagine it. We are now both forty-two cycles old, and we have children too, unbelievable.

38

With the seed set they crossed their fingers and hoped for the best. Wesme says they will observe and report on progress from Vancouver Island.

Time passed, the four friends were asked to help many times for varied and different reasons. The ship set off to visit both new and old worlds, task after task is completed and another balance and harmony is restored. More time passes. They arrive in a familiar corner of space, a cluster galaxy with one larger planet in the centre. Eddy looks out and wonders if anything new has happened on his home world. Kenny asks a similar question of Wesme, who investigates for them. He returns and says the surface may be safely visited, there is simple vegetation and primitive life forming; the excitement in his thoughts is noticeable.

Following a briefing on the bridge where the aliens expressed interest in monitoring the sentinels' old world, the four of them are asked if they will stay and observe the developing planet but not interfere in the course of events.

Soon after they agree to be observers, the mother ship spawns a miniature version of itself, it has all the four will need until it returns. This smaller ship has been placed in orbit, there's no reason to disguise it. For a while they monitor the state of the bear's old planet from their home and workshops, and study what's happening to the lifeforms below. Flick and Eric used their joint knowledge to learn about these survivors thriving in the aftermath of a destruction which had once eradicated everything. Eddy and Kenny are showing them the geology and geography which thankfully did not get wiped out. A lot of the central area is land, rocks and sand, while the polar regions are water. Back in their day it would have been called a 'Goldilocks' planet, neither too hot nor too cold. The atmosphere was close enough to Earth's to allow them to dispense with breathing apparatus, the oxygen content is a little lower, but trees are in very short supply at this moment in time.

One planet-day, corresponding to thirteen and a quarter Earth days, as Eric had calculated, a new type of life was detected on the planet below. The sensors left on the surface and floating on the water announced it on the ships screen.

Kenny is excited, he thinks it is very similar to one of the very first more complex beings to have existed on the surface; it had muscles. Eddy is looking through the files and finds a picture, once her chocolate digestive crumbs have been cleaned off; the creature is comparable to a jellyfish from Earth.

"Shall we go and take a look, your highness?" Eric shouts up to the bathroom.

"Why not, there might be something else interesting down there as well – I've done it again, I can't find my bloody bra!"